C R DEMPSEY

Bad Blood

Book One of Exiles

CRMPD Media
Limited

For Mena and Maya

Contents

Acknowledgement

Thank you to all my family and friends and all of those who helped to create this book.

Special thanks to Mena (endless patience and support), Eoin (advice and inspiration), Richard Burnham (feedback and support).

Thank you also to the professional support of:

Book cover: Dominic Forbes
  Editing: Dominic Wakeford
  Both these individuals can be found on www.Reedsey.com

1

1571

The barley bowed beneath the rough hands of the stranger as he bobbed their heads to test their health. The harvest melted into the landscape as it stretched to the shore of the lake where it extended its beige tentacles beneath the water and beached itself on some of the adjacent islands.

The stranger broke off a spike of barley and separated a swollen grain, which he split between his teeth.

"This is good land," he said as he spat the husk out.

He looked up at his companion, sat upon a horse-driven cart.

"The Lord Deputy will be pleased if we can help bring these lands into the fold," he continued.

"I don't know why we bother to bribe these savages," came the scornful reply. "Their allegiances flutter in the wind so often it's not worth wasting good wheat seed. We should wait for them to kill themselves off in some bitter feud about who owns the best bog and clear the survivors off the land. Only when these lands are truly English, will they know the Queen's peace."

The stranger's eyes returned to the landscape, and he sucked in the beauty of the rolling hills, the woodlands and how the land slipped into the lake and protruded in the knees and elbows of islands of a contented bather. His mind shredded the beautiful landscape and cast it upon weighing scales, as he quantified the value of everything in cattle and coin. He turned to his friend.

"Bury your opinions deep under your weighty commission for each chieftain swearing loyalty to the crown. Nobody wants to know what you think. Now let us go and fill our pockets so we may return to England with a head full of tales to embellish to impress young ladies and if that fails, pockets full of coin by which to dazzle them long enough to blind them from your ugliness."

The stranger held up the remains of the head of barley and saluted his companion.

"For the crown, for the Lord Deputy, for your fat belly!"

The ugly man patted his stomach, a well-rounded collection of covetousness. They laughed, and the stranger jumped up onto the cart, and with a lash of the whip, they continued towards the village.

* * *

The village lay before the strangers, neatly tucked into a gap between the luscious forests and the gentle lapping of the lake waves upon the shore. Fields of barley were hemmed in at every available opening, as a protective barrier against starvation. The cows roamed freely, grazing on the delicious grass with a profusion of young calves to support the healthy herd. Pigs poked around the periphery of the village, searching the nooks and crannies of the village palisade and the gnarled and knotted roots of the trees on the shore of the lake for any morsels of food they could find. The village had thrived under several years of peace. However the scars of raiding scratched the surface of the prosperous façade, as testified further up the lake shore by the blackened soil of burnt crops. The stranger smiled. He had his leverage.

The two men and their cart entered the boundaries of the village. Their English accents betrayed them as the villagers approached and conversed. The villagers cleared a path for the strangers and gave directions towards the shoreline and the chieftain's house. A boy ran ahead to warn of the approaching visitors.

The boy ran to his chieftain who was warming himself by a fire at the lakeside. The chieftain made jokes with men from the village who sat with him. The boy stopped, for his leader looked jovial and at peace. But the chief had noticed him.

"What do you want boy? Release your tongue!"

"Sir, sir! Strangers are here! Englishmen with a cart full of grain!"

The chieftain scowled.

"Send them here and be quick about it, boy! I suggest the rest of you come back when I have seen these visitors off!"

The men of the village got up and walked away. Two of them went and escorted the Englishmen into the chieftain's presence. The strangers bowed; the men stayed in case they had invited in assassins.

"My name is Peter Squire of Leicester, and this is my friend, John Brodie of Liverpool. We bring you greetings from Queen Elizabeth and her Lord Deputy in Dublin," said the husk-eating stranger.

"I am Cathal O'Keenan Maguire, the chieftain of this village and the surrounding countryside. Sit my friends, eat, drink but be quick about your business. It is harvest time, and I am expecting the men from the Maguire to collect their dues any day now. If they catch you here, it'll mean your deaths. Your deaths will mean my lands full of Galloglass until I can fill the Maguire's pockets with enough reassurance of coin that I am loyal. If that fails I'll have to send him the first male born of the finest men of the village to persuade him of my loyalty. As time is short, excuse my bluntness, but why are you here and what have you got to offer me?"

"The protection of the crown and an army far more powerful than all the Gaelic lords can put together!" replied Peter Squire.

"As much as I yearn to be free of the yoke of the Maguire, or any lord I must pay duties to, he is my kin. Connor Roe Maguire has offered me better terms for my loyalty, and he is the lord of the closer branch of the Maguire clan. But as soon as I make a move against Cuchonnacht, my rival for control of the village, Michael O'Flanagan, will be straight to the Maguire to usurp me!"

"We come with the offer of lands and titles supported by the crown. Your son can inherit your title and your lands. You can pay a nominal rent to the crown and owe no loyalty, duty or warriors to a chieftain who imprisons your children and forces them to go and fight to extend their power. You can have the protection of Connor Roe and live a life of peace."

"I want peace but fear it will not come in the way you suggest. You want to side with one Maguire against another. I will be the pips squeezed and squashed on the floor when the winner grips his prize."

"There will be no prize and no squeezing when the crown gets its way. There will be no clan wars, no retributions. You will all be landed gentry, not interfering with one another, everyone minding their own business, all under the protection of the crown."

"The crown is weak in this part of the country. Cuchonnacht Maguire keeps the peace through his political skill while the old lords of Ulster slog it out for supremacy. That is why we have peace, not because of the crown."

"The crown is coming to assert herself on her lands of Ireland once more. Look at the O'Reillys to the south. Have they not been quiet since they ceded their lands to the south? Hasn't the raiding stopped? Surely it is best to be on the winning side?"

"I'll be long dead before your Queen does any winning."

"I'm sorry you have so little faith in the crown. However, we have brought you a gift of wheat seed as a declaration of goodwill from the Queen. You have no wheat, but it is merely the first down payment from your mutually beneficial relationship with the crown."

"And how does the crown assert herself in Fermanagh exactly?"

"Through Connor Roe Maguire and your support for him."

"I cannot support Connor Roe now. He is weak, and Cuchonnacht Maguire is strong and supported by the O'Neill clan. Now leave, before you get me in trouble and Cuchonnacht replaces me with a more pliant chieftain."

"Thank you for hearing us out and please have the grain seed as a gift from the crown, as a reward for being a loyal subject."

"Leave the grain and come back when Cuchonnacht is old and frail, which I fear will not be too long."

"So we have your support if Connor Roe was ever to put himself forward to become the Maguire?"

"If those circumstances were ever to arise, then Connor Roe would be my favoured candidate."

"Then we bid you farewell."

Cathal called his men and instructed them to unload the wheat seed, and the strangers departed with an empty cart.

* * *

Several days later, Cuchonnacht Maguire's men rode past freshly hoed fields filled with the precious wheat seed as they made their way to see the chieftain. They came with empty carts to fill with their dues in barley. But behind them another wagon rattled along the dirt road, filled with prisoners. The men set their carts down in the centre of the village and waited for Cathal O'Keenan Maguire. Cathal's men went to the stores to fetch the sacks of barley they had set aside from the harvest. Once the bags were on the carts, Cathal came to speak to the Galloglass constable, the leader of Cuchonnacht's party.

"Not travelling via boat this summer?" said Cathal pointing to the lake.

"Some of the chieftains are paying with cattle, and we have to drive them overland. A much longer and arduous trip for me this year."

"I trust all is in order and you have received twenty percent of our crop as agreed?"

"I have looked in your stores, and I will take your word, for what it's worth, that you have paid in full."

"What do you mean 'for what it's worth'? You are addressing a Maguire chieftain, not some mercenary lackey you can throw a couple of coins at for his obedience!"

"And you, sir, are addressing Donal MacCabe, the recently promoted Galloglass constable and enforcer for Cuchonnacht Maguire in these parts. Let me reassure you, I know who I am addressing. While we collect dues, we are also searching for disloyal chieftains, ones who take a fancy to the English coin, seed or presents of Connor Roe's cattle.

"We noticed on our way in you had planted a new crop, straight after harvesting the other one. Now I said to my men, I can't remember you planting so many crops when I was here six months ago, or a year ago! How did dear Cathal come into such good fortune to be able to plant a second crop? Was it all the protection the MacCabes gave him to save him from being raided by the O'Reillys? Well, yes, and that is partly why the Maguire gets his twenty percent, thank you very much. But if Cathal O'Keenan Maguire is doing so well, surely he should contribute more? Since I have recently gotten promoted, surely I should try and impress the Maguire and increase his yield from this area, and we'll all get rich together? Wouldn't that be nice? But the Maguire wouldn't like me taxing loyal subjects too much, so I thought twenty percent is just fine for everyone. That is, until I discovered this!"

Donal clicked his fingers, and his men threw Peter Squire and John Brodie off the back of the prisoners' cart and onto the ground. "These two confessed to giving you the Queen's wheat. Now we like to know where everybody stands. It keeps everything nice and simple. These people support the clan and the Maguire. These people should piss off back to the Pale and the English where they belong. Now, these two, where do they belong? I'd say in the middle of a dark wood with their throats slit by robbers trying to steal their wheat seed. But you? I don't know where you stand. Do you support the Maguire? Will you sell him out if the price is right? But in your favour, you have an abundance of crops, more than enough for you and your villagers. The Maguire needs loyal servants in this area and to protect his interests from Connor Roe and his English masters. So it may be in everyone's interests that the Maguire looks upon you favourably, exercise a bit of forgiveness, to take you back into the fold. The best way for you to show loyalty and to repay the Maguire's generous offer is to extend coin and keep to a troop of Maguire Galloglass. What do you say to that?"

"No! Er, I mean we have only had one good crop and are surely too far away from the county borders for the Maguire to base some Galloglass here! The O'Reilly raids have died down! We would be more than willing to make a greater contribution to the Maguire if that should meet his needs?"

"Here is a perfectly fine place for my master's Galloglass. Please make preparations for them to make them feel welcome. Maybe they could replace the children that your disloyalty made us take? Nevertheless, they will be with you in due course."

Cathal gasped for breath as he felt his control slipping away, as his disgruntled villagers filed back to their homes.

2

1585

Eunan looked on as his father, Cathal O'Keenan Maguire, gripped his mother's hand as she screamed. The room was dark except for a single candle illuminating his mother's bed. The place was haunted with his mother's screams as the furniture, ornaments and candle smoke absorbed them and echoed them back in an endless loop. He wanted to help, but he was brushed aside by adults rushing around, for he was in the way as usual. His mother seemed unusually bright and cheerful during the pregnancy, and both herself and his father cradled the womb as if were laden with gold and the answer to all their problems. But once it came down to it, the actual act of giving birth, nothing seemed to go right.

He wondered why they wanted another child because, for all of his thirteen years, it never seemed like they wanted him. He baulked when watching his mother in agony, for every expression of pain penetrated the thick wall surrounding his heart, but his father made him stay to "see what you put your mother through." Eunan would much rather have taken out his frustration by throwing his axes at the wooden target at the back of his house, beside the wood, but his father insisted he shared his mother's bounty of pain. Her generosity seemed endless.

His childhood was a patchwork of pain sewed together with intermittent periods of pleasantness, mainly when his parents left him to do what he wanted. But not now, for his mother's suffering suffused his very sinews. The birth hours dragged, and her screams got worse. Father and the physician were both worried that the birth had been going on for so long. His father became so anxious that Eunan was banished outside. He went out by himself and threw axes at the stump, waiting for news.

The axes thudded with monotonous repetition, not that anyone noticed. Those adults that were kind enough to speak to him said that one day would become a great warrior and fight in many great battles far away from here. But when he called his father to see him throw his axes, he said that he was good at it due to his bad blood and that his parents wished they had a better son that was not polluted like him.

Eunan kept throwing his axes until he heard one final howl, and the screaming stopped. He ran inside. His father was crying, covered in blood holding the new baby. But only his father howled. Cathal saw his son looking expectantly at him.

"You're cursed," he hissed. "Look at my beautiful daughter," he sobbed. "Barely out of the womb and unable to take a breath!" he said, holding the baby forward so that Eunan could see her. A blue baby, with eyes that never opened, a neck that never grew the strength to support the head, lungs that never took in air to cry for her mother's help. But Eunan's lungs could fill with air; he could scream for help. He did, but once again it fell onto deaf ears.

Cathal sank to his knees wrapped up in his pain.

"She is dead! Yet you live!" his father cried.

Eunan burst into tears and ran over to his mother to seek solace. But she lay on the bench, her head turned as if she were asleep. The doctor battled to stem the flow of blood from between her legs.

"Get out of my way, boy! I have to stop your mother from dying!"

The tears became a stream upon which solace floated away. Some of the women from the village came in and tried to help the doctor. The kindly neighbour Mary took Eunan by the hand and led him outside.

"I know your parents can be mean, but one day you will realise why and hopefully forgive them."

"I know why," Eunan fumed. "It's because of my bad blood. They tell me all the time. I wish I could cut my arm open and watch all the bad blood float away into the lake. Then my parents would love me."

"Don't say such dreadful things. You're just a boy. If you ever need any help, just come around to my house."

Eunan sat on the ground and cried into his hands.

The sunken faces of the women of the village emerged from Eunan's house.

"The baby is dead. Something went dreadfully wrong. I don't think the mother will ever walk again. I think the boy has brought a curse on their house," said one.

"Don't be stupid. He's just a lad. And shush, he'll hear you." Mary turned around and Eunan was gone.

She started to panic. "We must find him! We must find him before they come back!"

"What! The boy is gone! Organise a search party! We must find him! We must find the boy!"

The villagers came out of their houses and organised search parties and began to search the surrounding woods.

* * *

Deep in the woods, Eunan sat on a stump and stabbed himself in the arm. Blood began to trickle slowly from the puncture wounds. He sucked his blood out and spat it on the ground. Someone heard his angry mutterings. A giant stood before him, his beard a blaze of red, in chain mail and a metal helmet, with a giant axe that reached as far as the man's shoulder and had an enormous curved blade the size of his face.

"What are you doing, boy? You'll hurt yourself!"

"I just killed a baby, and I'm trying to get rid of this bad blood!"

The warrior put down his axe, sat beside the boy and took his arm. He squeezed the splinters from Eunan's forearm with a tenderness the boy seldom felt.

"How did a boy like you kill this baby? I don't believe it. Is someone playing a cruel joke on you? If they are, they'll have me to answer to!"

Eunan's eyes brightened up.

"Will you protect me?"

"I can show you how to protect yourself, how to be a great warrior if you like? But first, wrap this cloth around your arms to stop all that bleeding."

Eunan nodded and smiled, and hope came back into the veins of the boy.

"What's that on your belt?" asked the warrior.

"It's my axe. I throw it. Do you want to see?"

"Show me, boy!"

"See that branch over on that tree?"

"Yes?"

"Watch me snap it!"

Eunan threw his axe, and it whizzed through the air. But it only grazed the branch. Eunan frowned with disappointment.

"Don't be angry, boy. That was good for someone your age."

Eunan flopped down on the ground. He looked up at the soldier again.

"Can I come with you?"

"You're far too young for where I am going."

The boy's disappointment softened the soldier's heart.

"But one day you can, if you train properly. But you'd have to train every day."

"I will. I will!" Eunan cried.

"Now show me where you live?"

"Do I have to go home?"

"Your parents will miss you."

"They won't!"

"Come on!" the warrior said, picking Eunan up by the arm.

Eunan trudged towards the edge of the forest.

"Are you Galloglass?"

"I am. How did you know?"

"I can tell by your axe. Can I be a big, strong warrior like you someday?"

"Yes, but as I said, you have to train every day!"

They came to the edge of the woods and ran into one of the search parties. The neighbour grabbed the boy and shielded him from the warrior.

"We have nothing to give you for the boy. We are poor, and you have no use for him."

The Galloglass pointed his axe at the villagers.

"Why is this boy running around the forest trying to hurt himself? Are you his mother?"

"No. The boy's mother is sick."

"The boy still needs looking after. If I find the boy in the forest again, or see any more self-inflicted injuries, I will do more than point my axe at you!"

"Be away with you and don't threaten us! The village warriors will be here soon! Go before they find you!"

"Mark my words and look after the boy!" the Galloglass said as he disappeared into the woods.

The villagers huddled around the boy and turned for home.

"Do you think he sent him?"

"Maybe. Let's just bring the boy home."

* * *

Eunan returned home, and the villagers told the tale of the Galloglass finding the boy. Upon the mention of Galloglass in the forest, Cathal was civil to the boy, though his world was collapsing around him. His wife had seldom left the bed since the stillbirth cast her down into a pit of illness and depression. Her dark moods led her to banish Eunan from the house, and she forbade him from visiting her. Eunan took up lodgings in the outhouse. There he stayed and did his chores and practised with his axes, and kin and villager alike left him be.

The physician attended Fiona regularly because she was the chieftain's wife, but he could do little to help her except assess what was wrong and attempt to ease her mind from worry. As a consequence of her complications during childbirth, she would never walk again. The local carpenter made her a barrow within which she could sit. Cushions and blankets from her neighbours made it comfortable. Her husband would sometimes wheel her into the garden, and Eunan would sneak a peek at her through the neighbour's window. Her face was a storm of anger, and Eunan still did not go home for no invitation was extended. Eunan was somewhat pleased, for Mary the neighbour was kind and fed him, and he was left in peace to throw his axes. He vowed to run away and become a Galloglass. That hope helped him persevere.

3

1585 - Return of the MacCabe

H arvest time came again to Cathal and the villagers. They gathered the crops, filled the stores and planted the seed for the next season. But all manner of beasts gathered who also lived off the harvest. The villagers chased the rats from the stores and the crows from the freshly hoed fields. But the biggest monsters had yet to make themselves known.

One morning the call came.

"Ships on the lake! Ships on the lake!"

Ships on the lake were a common sight since they were the primary mode of transport, but everyone knew what the call meant.

The village went into a frenzy. Villagers started to empty the store and hide grain where they could. There was no time to transport it to their best hiding places on the islands of the lake. They hid their valuables and their children. But Eunan was not treated so. No, he was invited back into the house and dressed in his best clothes. Cathal was even pleasant to him.

"Ships to shore! Ships to shore!"

Cathal went down to the shoreline. Out on the lake were three large riverboats of the Maguire. Harvest time meant the Maguire had come to collect his share of the grain and store it in his Crannogs in the northern part of Upper Lough Erne. These man-made fortified islands were almost impossible to capture or rob, which meant the Maguire could hide out on the islands of the lakes of Erne indefinitely.

From behind the large boats came smaller boats filled with soldiers and tribute collectors, which rowed towards Cathal and other villages on the south-west side of the lake. Cathal saw no point in hiding, for if he hid the Maguire's men would take whatever they wanted. So he sat and waited as three boats rowed ever nearer.

Once the boats reached the shallow waters, Cathal's men grabbed the ropes cast from the vessels and moored them to the shore. Donal MacCabe leapt from the lead boat and strode ashore, straight to Cathal.

"Hello, Cathal, I hope the harvest went well. The Maguire needs the help of all his loyal chieftains, and I assume you will prove to be one?"

"Come this way and see what I can contribute to the Maguire!" said Cathal, pointing in the direction of the stores.

The village had their own, much smaller, Crannogs in which they stored their grain. Two swordsmen guarded the only entrance via a footbridge. Donal counted the sacks the villagers had stockpiled on the shore for the Maguire and sent two of his men to count what bags remained in the Crannogs to tally the harvest yield.

After a while, the men came back and whispered in Donal's ear. Donal laughed to himself.

"The harvest's a bit down this year, isn't it? Now, I can only judge your honesty by what I can count, and you have given me twenty percent of that. Previously we've found grains you've hidden, so I hope you've done a better job of hiding them this year. But I'm afraid I have some bad news for you. The Maguire has had to pay the coin and keep of the English troops imposed upon Fermanagh soil. The cost is in turn, passed on to you. That means the tribute is now thirty percent!"

"What! I can't afford that! My people will starve!" exclaimed Cathal.

"No, they won't! They'll just have to eat all the grain you've hidden from us. I'd be careful now, between you and me, and don't get the blame for the supplementary tribute, for it was treacherous chieftains like you that undermined the Maguire and led to the English being on our lands."

"I am a perfectly loyal chieftain to the Maguire! How dare you insinuate that I am anything but!"

"It's a long fall from your high horse! I've been coming here for years, and I know you! That's why we need to sort out who's who and who should be the chieftain in particular districts, for things are always happening to chieftains and then someone more Maguire-friendly takes over.

"The Maguire needs you to swear loyalty to the clan. We've been hearing rumours that you have received emissaries from Connor Roe and also the English, yet again. The Maguire needs to know that you are with him."

"Do I not pay the Maguire his dues at every harvest, send my men to fight for him when he calls? Are these not true showings of my loyalty to him? Why is it strange that I should have contact with the most powerful Maguire in my region? Is that not the clan hierarchy? Why don't you ask Connor Roe about his contacts with the English? Whatever the Maguire decides to do about it, when he comes to call, I will answer as I always do."

"We are glad to hear you state your loyalty so forcefully. However, the Maguire hears you have a son not far from coming of age. The Maguire would like to extend an invitation to him to enjoy an education that only the Maguire can provide."

"Thank you for your offer, but my son needs to grow up protecting his people. There's many a raider out there today, and we need all the men of fighting age we can get."

"The Maguire would view it as disrespectful for such a generous offer to be refused!"

"Please don't take my boy," Cathal protested.

"The Maguire will take a boy and return a man. He will take several boys and return several men. Gather the sons of the prominent men of the village and deliver them to us by sunset. Then we will return to the Maguire with your loyalty pledge."

Cathal saw it was useless to protest.

"I will see you at the centre of the village at sunset," replied Cathal.

"I trust you will order your men to stand aside while we take our additional ten percent?"

"I am a loyal servant of the Maguire."

Donal MacCabe ordered his men to enter the stores.

* * *

Cathal made sure that Eunan remained within his sight for the rest of the day. He took Eunan by the hand at the appointed time and led him to the centre of the village. Cathal promised Eunan that he would meet some warriors who would give him some training, so he was happy to follow. The light turned to shadow, and grim-faced men stood in the village circle with their first-born young sons. They glared at Cathal when he arrived with his smiling boy.

"What have you told him?" asked one.

"I thought you'd be the one smiling when you got rid of him!" muttered another. Cathal glared at the mass of faces but could not identify who was making the comments.

The Galloglass stood at the edge of the circle nearest the road to Enniskillen. Ten of them stood with one of their hands pressed to their axe shaft. Cathal crossed the ring to speak to Donal MacCabe.

17

"How many of our children does the Maguire wish to take?"

"Enough to ensure your loyalty. Your children will be well taken care of in Enniskillen. I'm sure you've schooled them in the duties of noble boys towards their clan?"

"They're just that, still boys. How many do you want?"

"Five, including yours."

"Here, take him and be off with you."

Cathal let go Eunan's hand and turned his back and walked back towards the villagers. The other fathers knelt and hugged their boys goodbye and praised them for their bravery, while Eunan looked at the line of Galloglass and cried. They led them across the circle to the Galloglass.

"Cathal?" called Donal MacCabe.

Cathal walked across the circle again.

"Take him back. We want your boy, not some impostor."

"He is my boy!" Cathal fumed, and he stormed over to Donal.

The Galloglass raised their axes.

"We came for the chieftain's son, and we are not leaving without him," said Donal.

"He is there, standing in front of you!" protested Cathal.

Cathal pointed at the boy, who started to cry again.

"You would have us believe a chieftain would give up his son without so much as a tear or a goodbye and walk away from him?"

"We said our goodbyes in the house."

"This boy is an impostor! Hand over the real boy and we'll not mention this deception to the Maguire."

"He is the real boy!"

"He doesn't look like you. We don't want any bastards!"

"He is born of my wife, resembles his disabled mother, and is my son! What more do you want of me?"

"Why did you give him up so easily? No father I have seen has given his boy up so easily as you?"

"He is brave and doesn't want his father to embarrass him."

"So he does that himself by balling his eyes out crying? No, hand over the real boy, or we'll return and take him."

"Enough of this nonsense. Take your prisoners and go. I will discuss this with the Maguire the next time I am in Enniskillen!"

"Is the real boy a prisoner of Connor Roe?"

"Take the boy and leave!"

The Galloglass leader stared at Cathal, and Cathal turned his back and walked off.

"Leave the impostor, take the rest. Let's go," said Donal.

The Galloglass took the other four boys and walked towards the road. The other fathers started to shout, "Take the boy! Take the boy!" They turned to Cathal and demanded that he make them take the boy. Cathal ran and grabbed the boy's hand, and they caught up with Donal MacCabe.

"Take the boy! He's mine! I wish to pledge my loyalty to the Maguire! Take him as a sign of my loyalty! All the other fathers can vouch that he's mine!"

The constable stopped and looked to the other fathers who had also come after them.

"The boy is his?" he asked.

"He may not seem it, but he is the boy's father!" replied one.

"Take him!" said Donal as he pointed to the boy. "But I would pray, Cathal, that when the boy turns of age he does not come back and repay you for this night!"

The Galloglass took the crying Eunan by the hand and disappeared into the descending darkness on the road to Enniskillen.

4

1585 - The Prisoner

The boys tripped over themselves as they were bundled into the boats waiting for them by the shoreline. The Galloglass were still loading the grain onto the other vessels, but Donal MacCabe could not wait for them to finish. They had to leave now in case the boys' parents changed their minds.

Eunan sat up towards the front of his boat, and the other four boys were in the middle. The craft set off in silence. They rowed for a considerable time until they saw the lights of the Crannogs bouncing on the gentle waves that lapped around the boat.

"Where are we going?" asked Eunan.

"Be quiet!" snapped the Galloglass. "Do as you're told, and you may yet live!"

Eunan sank back into his seat.

There were a set of four Crannogs in the lake, each of varying size. The boat made for the largest of these, which was about one hundred meters from the shore. They moored on the pier on the north side of the Crannog.

"Everybody off!" cried the Galloglass guard and the boys were only too willing to obey.

The man-made island was protected by a wicker wall and on it were several large buildings, all used as store rooms, and several smaller ones, used as barracks for the Maguire's soldiers. There were several more small piers where other boats of varying sizes landed and dispatched their cargoes of smaller livestock and grain. The Maguire did not build these islands. They had been there for as long as anyone could remember; hundreds, maybe thousands, of years old. The Maguire merely adapted them for his purposes.

"This must be where the Maguire stores his tribute before it gets transported up to Enniskillen!" said Senan, one of the boys from the village. "My father told me about this."

"Where are all the cattle? I thought that the Maguire liked to get paid in cattle?" asked Eunan.

"They go overland. More dangerous, but you'd never fit the cattle on the boats," replied Senan.

"Enough talking and follow me!" barked one of the guards.

The guards led Eunan and the other boys to one of the smaller houses where they were fed a thin gruel and given straw to sleep on and blankets to wrap themselves in. The five boys settled in as best they could, cold and hungry. As they shivered, other groups of boys arrived later in the night and found Eunan and his friends had taken all the blankets.

The night grew cold and as Eunan and his comrades slept, the other boys armed themselves with sticks. The boys came upon Senan, unravelled him from his blanket and beat him when he tried to resist. Senan's yelps awoke comrade and guard alike. Eunan leapt up and punched the nearest boy to him full in the chin. Eunan grabbed an end of Senan's ex-blanket. The other boys attacked him and forced him to let go. Eunan fell to the ground, and the hand that broke his fall felt some stones. Eunan picked these up, and his arm remembered the hours of practice with the throwing axes. By the time the guards

21

came in and broke up the fight, Eunan had recovered the blanket, and the faces of his assailants were a mess of blood and bruises. Eunan's prize was Donal MacCabe was informed of his fighting skills, and Eunan kept all the blankets.

Nobody got much sleep that night, since the air of distrust had only grown as the night got colder. Senan and the other boys huddled behind Eunan. When dawn broke, the guards came and bundled them on to another boat destined for Enniskillen. This was a larger riverboat, and it was able to take the boys and a sizeable cargo of grain. There were not many Galloglass on the vessel but there were several cargo boats in convoy and several smaller boats full of soldiers escorting them.

The boat ride was relatively pleasant, for it was much more reassuring to travel during the day to somewhere you knew you were going to. Most of the time Eunan just lay back in the boat and enjoyed the view as the guards left the boys alone. To alleviate the boredom, Eunan also took pleasure in pissing over the side of the vessel when he knew the boys from the previous night were downwind and could do nothing about it. The guards just laughed as long as he did not piss on them.

By nightfall, they could see the lights of Enniskillen and the boys crowded to the front of the boat to get the best view.

Enniskillen Castle was the seat of the Maguire. The Maguires had chosen an almost perfect defensive position upon which to build the castle. It was built on an island, surrounded by the River Erne, which acted as a defensive barrier to keep out all but the most determined of enemies. The castle had large walls and a singular bridge that protruded like a tongue to lap up any visitors and swallow them inside. A sister island held the castle island protectively to her breast, which contained most of the bustling town. Mooring posts and jetties spiked into the river at any available opportunity and the River Erne was flush with small boats either fishing or carrying produce up or down the river from other parts of Fermanagh, to be sold at the busy markets of Enniskillen.

The boat moored in the town of Enniskillen and the cargo unloaded. The guards escorted the boys through the town, over the drawbridge and into the castle. Most of the boys were in awe, for they had never left their villages and only heard of such citadels and the Maguire in stories.

The guards lined up the boys in the courtyard of the castle. A roll call was held based on the notes Donal MacCabe's men made. Rank in the clan hierarchy parted boys from their village fraternity. Rank also meant privilege and the important boys joined families that made up the inner Maguire clan or associated families. Eunan was one of those more important boys, as he was the son of a chieftain.

Eunan had impressed Donal MacCabe with his fighting skills in the Crannog, so he was given to Desmond MacCabe, an old Galloglass warrior, who had faithfully served the Maguire clan throughout his career. Donal told the boys they were here for several years and promised them a good education. The MacCabes would teach them fighting skills if they showed loyalty to the Maguire, and the sons of chieftains could become the Maguire's favoured heir for their clans. Eunan liked the sound of that, but was mainly glad he was a chieftain's son, for he did not have to clean up the boats like the lesser boys.

Eunan waited to be claimed by his new family in an enclosure guarded by Galloglass. Desmond MacCabe sent his servant to collect Eunan. The servant made himself known to the Galloglass and claimed Eunan. Eunan stayed with the Galloglass while the servant fetched the horses. The servant was nervous, for Eunan was a strong young man who could easily overpower him. Eunan assured the man that he would not ride away and escape and that he was looking forward to meeting his new master, of whom Donal MacCabe had said many good things. The servant eyed Eunan suspiciously but reverted to loyalty to his master. They rode out of the castle together. The servant was tall and skinny and quivered like a frightened rabbit and Eunan considered following him, far more exciting than going home.

They rode for a couple of hours through forest and field until they arrived at a large house planted amongst a grove of trees on the banks of Upper Lough Erne. It reminded Eunan of home: the rolling fields, the lake dotted with small islands, the fields of barley. He began to cry.

"Please don't do that when the master comes," said the servant. "He doesn't tolerate any crying. You'll find yourself a stable boy, and that would be very demeaning for the son of a chieftain."

Eunan nodded and dried his eyes. He straightened his clothes and wiped his face, for he wanted to look impressive.

The servant inspected Eunan, and upon being satisfied he was presentable, opened the door of the house.

"Master, I have returned with the boy from Enniskillen. He is anxious to meet you!" the servant announced to an empty room.

Eunan was anxious, but not in the manner the servant meant. Eunan heard some noise from upstairs. Then came a roar.

"Bring him to the kitchen. I will meet him there!"

The servant turned to Eunan.

"The master is coming."

Eunan did not reply.

The servant brought Eunan to the kitchen and invited him to sit on the bench. Eunan sat and waited while fidgeting with his hands.

"Don't do that either. The master doesn't like it!"

"He sounds just like my father," muttered Eunan.

"Don't do …"

"I know. He doesn't like that either."

The kitchen shook with the pounding of the stairs. A large hand hooked around the door, and a rounded body bounded into the kitchen and sat himself down. Eunan's new master was a once-muscular man whose body had succumbed to the good life, like a retired bear with an endless pot of honey. He sat and grinned. But at the servant.

"Arthur, is it time to eat?"

"Soon, master."

Desmond MacCabe eyed the boy.

"Is this him? He's a bit small and scrawny."

"He's had a long journey, master. The conditions would not be of the manner you are used to."

"Humph! I hope he hasn't come here with expectations in the sky of being a little lord! What can you do, boy?"

"Nothing."

"Pardon? Speak up, boy!"

"What do you mean 'what can I do'?"

"Tend the horses, cook, fight? Eh, read, write! Whatever young boys are supposed to do these days?"

"I can help around the house. I used to help my mother!"

Desmond turned away with annoyance.

"Arthur, I think this piece of babysitting is going to be rather tedious. Give him my weapons to clean and show him the stables. What a way to earn the pennies of pension from the Maguire!"

Arthur produced a bowl of stew, gave it to his master and Eunan was forgotten, both in mind and stew distribution.

Arthur led the hungry and disappointed Eunan out of the house and to the shore of the lake. Arthur directed Eunan to "sit" on a couple of tree stumps that looked contemplatively out onto the lake. Eunan sat upon one. He looked out, and every lap of the waves whispered to him of home. Dark clouds blurred the reflections on the lake.

White horses energised the waves. Meanwhile, Arthur had fetched an eclectic collection of weapons.

"He likes to be able to see his face in the blade when you're finished. Oh, and if you want to gain favour with him, stand up and present the weapons as if you were a warrior saluting his lord."

Arthur left Eunan sitting amongst a pile of dirty weapons. He sat alone, by the lake. Anti-climax hung heavy on his shoulders. Time passed slowly, and Arthur was not coming back, so he decided to clean the weapons.

Several polished weapons later, the sun began to sink over the lake. The oranges and purples glistening on the shimmering lake made his eyes moist again. Desmond emerged from the house and strolled over to where Eunan sat. Desmond joined him, but on the nearby stump. It was the first time Eunan noticed his limp. There were two piles of weapons, those loosely acquainted with Eunan's cleaning cloths, and those that were not. Desmond picked one from the smaller collection and inspected it. The curl of his lip told Eunan that Desmond was not impressed.

"Is this supposed to be clean?" he asked.

"Yes, sir."

"I don't know if this is laziness, inexperience or both. Either way, it won't do," and Desmond dropped the sword.

The weapon clanged as it clashed with the other supposedly clean weapons and Eunan's heart dropped with it. Desmond got up and turned towards the house.

"Arthur!"

Arthur came running out of the house.

"What is it, master?"

"Get the boy to clean out the stables. He's terrible at cleaning weapons."

"Yes, master. Come here, boy!"

Eunan obeyed, and Arthur led Eunan to the stables.

"I tried to tell you, I tried to give you a chance. Now you are a stable boy and will have to do well at this to dig yourself out of that!"

Arthur brought him inside the stables and Eunan baulked at the smell.

"That's your first job, get rid of the smell. We haven't had a stable boy in a while. Get to know the horses, so that when the master comes down to take them out, they will be well behaved. Then he may let you clean his weapons again!"

Eunan fumed at his new role.

"I am a chieftain's son! My father is a great man in the Maguire court!"

"Don't speak like that in front of the master! You wouldn't be here if your father were such a great man! Be quiet, follow my advice, and all will be well. The shovel is over there, and there is plenty of water in the lake. I will return before sundown to inspect your work. I would advise you to deal with the smell first, or else it will be difficult for you to sleep out here."

"What! I should sleep in the house like a chieftain's son and not out in the yard like a dog!"

"You will find it way more comfortable if you first deal with the smell. I would get on with it as you have until sundown."

Arthur went back to the house.

Eunan picked up his shovel once he realised that Arthur meant what he said that he was sleeping out here. All the stables had been cleaned out by the time Arthur returned. Eunan had created a pile of manure, downwind from them. Arthur was mildly impressed.

"Half a job well done," was the limit of his praise.

"Half a job?!"

"You've got to spread the manure evenly over the fields, not shove it into a pile. But we can leave that until tomorrow."

Eunan cursed Arthur and thought of more vicious curses for Desmond. He sat in the stable and stared at the house until he realised that they were serious about not letting him in. He went to prepare his bed but had to take straw from the horses, for there was nothing else for him make his bed. He settled down for an awful night's sleep.

* * *

Eunan spent the next couple of weeks cleaning the stables, distributing the manure across the fields and waiting for Desmond to treat him like a chieftain's son. Desmond ignored him, and Eunan kept shovelling. Finally, after being asked every day for two weeks, Arthur invited Eunan back into the house.

Eunan entered and forgave the mess of the house, for the stables had considerably lowered his standards. But his mood was immediately lifted by the fire warming his bones. Desmond stomped down the stairs; Arthur had learned long ago to be punctual with dinner.

Arthur went to the stove and ladled out three bowls of broth. Desmond got the biggest bowl and Eunan the smallest.

"You're a better shit-shoveller than weapons cleaner. We may make a horse boy of you yet," said Desmond as he shovelled another spoonful of broth into his mouth.

Eunan exploded from his chair.

"Horse boy? Horse boy! I am the son of a chieftain! Yet you tie me to your stables to tend to your horses. I should be treated with the respect I deserve!"

"You are. Your head would be split in two by now, with a temper like that on the battlefield. You have to earn respect, and shovelling shit only deserves a modicum of it. You can come and stay in the house when you earn it and are more useful to me."

"When will that be? What can I do?"

28

"You will find out when you are ready. Anyway, I called you in for I need to go to Enniskillen to consult with the Maguire. Instead of leaving you here, I thought that you could come with me. Then we can see if this 'chieftain's son' has any uses."

"I would like that," and Eunan calmed down, sat down, and began to eat his broth.

"Good. We will set forth after this meal. But first, a surprise inspection of the stables."

* * *

They strode down to the stables, making accommodation for Desmond's leg. Eunan was nervous, for he wanted the inspection and prospective trip to lead to better things, like being a resident in the house, getting better chores, going h... No. Even life with Desmond and living in a stable was better than that.

Desmond held his inspection. He patted the horses and looked for signs of mistreatment. Eunan was lucky he had fed the horses and cleaned the sheds just before he was called to the house, so the horses were content and had little time to make a mess.

"You are getting better, boy. You always need to look after the horses, for you have no better friend in a fight."

Eunan nodded and absorbed his praise without exchanging it for emotion. Desmond turned to him.

"My usual horse please, and gather the weapons. There are still bandits in this county, despite my best efforts."

Arthur had instructed Eunan thoroughly about Desmond's likes and dislikes about horses and weapons. Eunan had memorised his instructions, for sometimes there was little to do between horse defecations.

Desmond looked rather pleased with Eunan as he mounted his horse and tied his scabbarded sword around his waist. Eunan mounted a far less impressive horse, and they set off for Enniskillen.

Before they got very far, Desmond turned to Eunan.

"Do you know who I am, boy?"

"I assume you mean in the past, for I know what you do now."

"I can still muster days with shades of my past glories."

"No, I don't know who you are, but can smell a tale or two from someone with such a prestigious standing in Enniskillen."

"Good answer. I knew you'd be ok once you settled in. I am one of the Maguire's main advisors on military and political matters."

Eunan looked somewhat confused. How could this old, rounded man with a limp have such knowledge in military matters and other such complicated worldly things?

"I know I may not look it now, but I used to be the head of the MacCabe clan, the main Galloglass family of the Maguire clan. That is, until I got wounded and was no longer able to fight."

Eunan looked behind to Arthur for reassurance, and Arthur nodded with such enthusiasm that he decided to believe him. Eunan recognised his opportunity.

"Can you teach me to be a Galloglass?"

"I can train you if you show yourself worthy of my time. Then you can do with your skills as you wish. Become a Galloglass, remain a chieftain's son, fight for the Maguire, follow your father. All choices."

"I would like that. May we start training when we return?"

"Let's see how we get on together on our trip first, shall we?"

They made considerable progress on their journey before Desmond wished to converse again.

"So why do you want to become a Galloglass? Why not become a chieftain like your father, or is being a Galloglass part of the plan to become chieftain?" asked Desmond.

"I want to get as far away from my father and his village as possible," replied Eunan.

"I see," said Desmond as he looked a little grim. "There are chieftains, and then there are chieftains. You're here because the Maguire considers your father to be disloyal. Too quick to turn his head for the English shilling. Every Maguire has a duty to his clan, to the clan leader and the Gaelic ways of life. But some clan leaders need to take the boys of wayward chieftains as hostages to remind them where their loyalties should lie, all for the good of the clan, of course!"

"I know where my loyalties lie. I want to be part of the Maguire Galloglass!"

"How much do you know about the Galloglass?"

"They are heroic warriors once from the isles of Scotland that came to Ireland many centuries ago. They found themselves in the employment of kings, clan chiefs and chieftains and they fight for them and ensure the freedom of the people."

"I should employ you as my balladeer and get you to write some ditties about my exploits!" said Desmond, roaring with laughter. "It won't take long for those illusions to be shattered, boy, given that the north is almost in a perpetual state of war. You'll soon change your mind once you experience real war. I'm going to Enniskillen because there is a power struggle in the O'Neill clan, and, just as your village is subservient to the Maguire, the Maguire is subservient to the O'Neill. That is, once we are sure which O'Neill it is we are subservient to! Then there is the question of the English garrison in Enniskillen. When all of these issues seek their resolution in blood, then you will see who the Galloglass are!"

"But you led the Galloglass?!"

"So I should know, shouldn't I? Anyway, I have no intention of shattering all your illusions in one afternoon. I still want you to do some work and not mope around with an air of despondence. Just watch and learn and receive the education worthy of a chieftain's son!"

They arrived at the bridge to Enniskillen town beyond which the castle lay. The town and castle were smaller than Eunan remembered but were impressive nonetheless. Desmond led him through the town and straight to the castle. Imposing stone walls protected a large central tower, which was the home of the Maguire. There was no grand reception for the arrival of Desmond that Eunan imagined the ex-head of the Galloglass would receive. Desmond dismounted, handed Eunan the reins and pointed in the direction of the stables. Desmond walked towards the tower. Arthur discouraged Eunan from following him.

There had been a general summoning of the Maguire nobility. Most had brought the hostages they hosted on behalf of the Maguire. Eunan tied the horses in the stables and went to find the boys from his village. They were glad to see him. They had been treated well and exchanged many tales, but the dynamic had changed. They now went to him to seek protection.

They soon found themselves in the fields surrounding the town, were given weapons, and trained with the other boys who also found themselves to be reluctant guests of the Maguire. Eunan was delighted since Donal MacCabe himself was giving the lessons. Arthur kept a close eye on Eunan, for he knew his master would summon him once he was needed.

Eunan spent a week in Enniskillen, mainly undertaking military training with the other boys in the fields and sleeping under the stars. He did not see Desmond even once. Finally, Arthur came to fetch him.

"Come now, it is time to go home," said Arthur.

"But I don't want to go back to my father, anything rather than that!"

"Lucky for you that's not the home I meant. Hurry along now. Desmond is waiting for us in the castle."

Arthur didn't recognise Eunan as he sported such a broad smile.

"Can I continue on my training?"

"If you have earned yourself enough of the master's time you can. Now come on!"

They rode to the castle to wait for Desmond, who soon emerged. Desmond was silent most of the way home, and Arthur told Eunan to hang back. Eunan had never seen Desmond look so troubled. Desmond was so distracted, he even allowed Eunan to sleep in the house.

* * *

The next day Eunan was up early and played along the lakeside, exploring all the beached boats and counting the islands. Some men arrived to wake Desmond and Arthur. Eunan could hear in the distance that they were the young men from the village. Indeed, they were only a couple of years older than him. Then he realised why they were there.

"If he's going to train them, then he can train me!" he said, rushing over to join the group before Desmond could separate him. Too late!

"Eunan! Stand over there. These boys are going to be horse boys, and I need to train them so. It's no role for you. Arthur will give you some jobs to do!"

"You promised me training, so when is my training to begin?"

"This is no time to argue! Oh, just get in there!"

Eunan's training began. He excelled over the other boys, for he seemed to have a natural skill for fighting. He still stood apart from them for he was a chieftain's son, and they were common boys from the local village. But they all felt war was coming, and they would need every man and boy they could get.

Desmond admired Eunan's aptitude for fighting. Eunan and Desmond become firm friends, and Desmond began to place much reliance upon him. Eunan started to escort him to Enniskillen regularly, for the Maguire was in much need of counsel. Since Desmond was there so often, the suggestion arose that Desmond move back to Enniskillen. However, he politely declined as he thought himself too old for all the court politics and his lakeside residence gave him a clear head and perspective, which truly made him useful for the Maguire.

While Desmond was in court, Eunan was given private tuition in reading and writing, amongst the many things his father had neglected to do. After Eunan had made some progress, Desmond allowed him to carry his papers for him to and from the court. For now, Eunan could recognise words and could tell what was valuable and what was not. But nothing was more complex than the workings of the court itself.

The court of the Maguire was a mass of factions since the O'Neills up north were at war with each other, and the Maguire owed allegiance to the incumbent O'Neill, Turlough Luineach O'Neill, through various traditions and treaties. The Maguires had two main factions, one supporting Turlough Luineach O'Neill, and the other, led by Cuchonnacht's son Hugh, who backed Hugh O'Neill, the main rival for the title of O'Neill. There was minor support for a rival faction of the O'Neills, the MacShanes. Connor Roe led another influential group, that of the pro-English side of the clan.

Eunan was confused.

"You'd better get used to it, boy!" said Desmond. "That's Irish politics for you. If you aren't fighting your rival clan or the English, you've got to watch your back for all of your local rivals looking to stab and rob you. That's why Cuchonnacht has done so well to stay in power for so long. He's managed to balance the O'Neill war of succession, the English, the bordering Irish clans that keep raiding and Connor Roe Maguire, and yet stayed in power for so long. Imagine if you were getting your balls squeezed every day and your only escape was to die!"

"Why would anyone want to become the Maguire?"

"Why indeed. I'd much rather be enjoying my old age beside such a beautiful lake."

"Are we going to train again?"

"Yes, but I would be negligent to only train your body and not your brain. You are, after all, a chieftain's son."

"Even after what you told me, I'd rather be a warrior!"

"Warriors are just pawns, especially Galloglass. Wouldn't you rather be moving pawns about then being sent to your death and not know the reason?"

"I don't want to use people."

"We shall make a great funeral pyre for your naiveties when you become a Galloglass and a man. You are either giving orders or taking orders, and everybody undertakes a variance of both. You want to be more giving orders with a bit of flexibility so that you can make a choice."

"Surely if you become the Maguire you can do as you wish?"

"You can't turn in an Irish court without someone trying to plant an axe in your head."

"So how come you lasted so long?"

"Luck and ensuring I had enough allies to protect me. Failing that, I always made sure I had enough cattle and coin to pay off my rivals if nothing else would suffice."

"And what did you do for the Maguire?"

"I was head of the Galloglass in my time. The enforcers for the Maguire, those that do the dirty work. The head of a clan can only manoeuvre in the space he has in the hierarchy of lords. In the north, the Maguires merely stand and wait."

"So why didn't you go and work for a more powerful lord, like the

O'Neill?"

"He has many Galloglass and many Scottish mercenaries. The Maguire paid well, and there was a vacuum at the top. My family filled the void and have served the Maguire well for many generations."

"So what would you advise me to do?"

"Shut up, do your training, keep your eyes and ears open and your mouth shut!"

"Ok!"

"See! You ignored my advice already!"

5

1585 - Enniskillen

I t was not long before Desmond was summoned to Enniskillen once again. Eunan was sent to the lakeside to prepare the boat. Critical documents engrossed Desmond, which a rider from Cuchonnacht had delivered – he therefore needed to study them on the journey.

Eunan had to ready the vessel for three passengers as Arthur also accompanied Desmond on all his long trips. They took their places in the boat with Arthur upfront to guide, Eunan in the middle to row and Desmond on the most comfortable seat on the back doing important work for the Maguire.

Desmond groaned as he read his papers.

"Things are moving so fast boy, my heart is awash with fear for the Maguire, as well as myself, of course," was all he said before returning to his papers.

Eunan dipped his oars gently in the river, for he knew his master did not want to be interrupted.

Eunan was instructed, upon sight of Enniskillen, to row to one of the small piers on the side of the castle, for Desmond wanted as few people as possible see him arrive. The English soldiers, who had a garrison in Enniskillen, had spies everywhere.

Eunan tied up the boat and knocked on the gate. They entered the castle via a side passage. This time Eunan escorted Desmond into the main building as Eunan now had the role of carrying his papers. Two Maguire soldiers led them across the courtyard and into the main building. They climbed two flights of stairs and were shown to the main hall. At one end was the clan's table which was the head table at feasts and also the meeting place for the Maguire and his advisors. Desmond pointed to his position at the table and Eunan lay his papers out just as Arthur instructed him. Several other men were already there having hushed conversations in corners.

"Who is this boy?" hissed a tall man who, upon sight of Eunan, strode over to Desmond.

"He's my assistant, Donnacha, so leave him be!" said Desmond. "A chieftain's son is he, one upon whom you will soon place great reliance if we are to survive these turbulent times!"

"What we need is a miracle, or the King of Spain, to deliver us to freedom, not a boy! Let this be a test of his courtly manners, and if he fails there are plenty of stables that need cleaning," replied Donnacha O'Cassidy Maguire.

"You never lost the ability to warm up a room with all your hot air! Once we get down to serious business, you'll have forgotten he's here!"

"The boy is your responsibility, and it will be your neck in the noose if he turns out to be a traitor or a spy!"

"You just make sure the English stay out of earshot for our meeting. If we get betrayed, I'll hold you responsible."

"I serve the Maguire faithfully, and if he gets betrayed, I'll see those bastards who did it hang for it!"

"Don't use up all your rope at once, because you won't run out of necks to wrap it around if things turn out the way we think they will."

"Humph! The Maguire should be here soon. I need to go and arrange his escort," and with that, Donnacha was gone.

* * *

Once his chores were done, the awe of the great hall absorbed Eunan's attentions. Huge tapestries adorned the walls, depicting the great myths and battles of the Maguire clan. The battle standards, the flags and emblems of the Maguire and the different septs that comprised the clan Maguire told of their greatness and long history. The exaltation was perpetuated by the stories and tales of those who inherited their legacy. Such emblems left Eunan cold. The men of his village would gather fireside and tell tales of old times. The exploits of the Maguire. Glorious battles. St Colmcille. However Eunan would be in the periphery, for his father made him look after his mother, and he could only overhear.

The room began to fill with the important men of the Maguire clan. A mixture of landed gentry and hardened warriors alike embraced Desmond warmly. Such reverence surprised Eunan, for Desmond's hobbies seemed to him to be eating stew and complaining. The men caught up with each other and discussed the happenings in the world, but something would not allow their enthusiasm to go beyond a simmer. Finally, Cuchonnacht and Hugh Maguire arrived, and they took the two seats at the head of the table.

Cuchonnacht was old and frail, but his mind was as sharp as ever. The reverence that surrounded him rivalled that of the tapestries as he held the Maguire clan together. The greatest Maguire in living memory kept the Maguires relevant in an ever-turbulent world. The Maguire nobility secretly feared that soon Cuchonnacht and the tapestries would be as one and the greatness of the Maguires squandered by youth.

Hugh Maguire was several years older than Eunan but was being groomed by his father to be his replacement. Kind words said about Hugh Maguire were that he was a warrior, had a considerable level of skill and showed good aptitude on the battlefield. However, many of the nobles had a different assessment of the aspiring leader. Hugh Maguire lacked his father's diplomatic skills and was arrogant. They thought his recklessness likely to extinguish the Maguire flame in search of glory, when defeat was the only certainty. The youth of Eunan yearned for glory and recognition and did not want his ambitions doused by frightened old men, so he reserved his judgment.

Cuchonnacht also had a younger son, named after himself, who was around Eunan's age. Cuchonnacht the younger also occupied the shadows alongside Eunan and learned his court skills by assisting the head of the Maguire court, Donnacha O'Cassidy Maguire.

The various factions previously mentioned by Desmond were not visibly noticeable to the inexperienced eyes of Eunan. But the absence of the most obvious dissenter, Connor Roe Maguire, was noticed by everyone else. Another sphere of influence gravitated around Edmund Magauran: a senior member of the clergy, personal friend of the Maguire and the primary Maguire contact with the Spanish throne from his contacts built in his training in the religious colleges of Spain.

The arrival of the Maguire was to silence, and beneath the silence, tension grew. Desmond fiddled with his belt in preparation for an awkward meeting. Eunan stood at the edge of the room in the shadows, waiting if Desmond needed him.

Cuchonnacht lifted himself out of his seat with an intake of breath.

"Welcome esteemed leaders and warriors of the Maguire clan. It is to my regret that I need to discuss with you such serious matters. But we need to speak in hushed tones, for we find our lands occupied by the forces of the crown. The lords of the north had previously agreed to English troops on their lands with each lord, 'to replace our reliance upon Scottish mercenaries.'"

The room rumbled with discontent.

"As I tried to explain to Hugh O'Neill, the Scottish may be a burden, but they do our bidding and return home to Scotland for the winter months, thus ending our expense. These English soldiers are a year-round burden. They expect payment and food, but they also raid our lands for their enrichment. Our people have to suffer the coin and keep of having to feed and pay these English soldiers both specifically where they are based, while the greater Maguire clan has to suffer increased tribute to 'subsidise' the new expense."

"We know the people are suffering! They suffer twice, with the English soldiers and the blight of famine. However, neither the Maguire nor the English is willing to bare the reduction alongside the people!" said one chieftain.

"What is the Maguire going to do about it?" interjected another.

"I can only campaign through the O'Neill in the Irish Council, and Hugh O'Neill is the only effective representative for us in that forum. However, the war for the O'Neill succession continues. The latest news I have is that Turlough Luineach O'Neill and Hugh O'Neill have reached an agreement!"

Rumblings ruminated around the hall. The O'Neills' civil war had a direct effect on the Maguires as they were the subordinate clan. Therefore, no matter what Cuchonnacht had advised them to do, the Maguire court had split into factions.

"Turlough Luineach has ceded control of central Tyrone to Hugh O'Neill for a term of three years!"

"What happens to us?"

"Has drink finally gotten the better of Turlough's brain?" said a chieftain, exacerbating the well-known rumour that Turlough Luineach was an alcoholic.

"We still owe our allegiance to Turlough Luineach O'Neill but still have a large border with Hugh O'Neill, and as he is so active with the Irish Council it would be to our severe detriment to make him our enemy. Therefore our policy remains the same. We co-operate with and pay our dues to Turlough Luineach, while being friendly to Hugh. We do not send men or mercenaries to aid either. Anyone caught breaking these rules will have their lands torched and their cattle confiscated."

Mutterings reverberated around the hall.

"The same goes for cooperating with the English. Anyone rumoured to be considering surrendering their lands to the English, to be regranted them back with an English title, without first consulting me will receive the same treatment."

Rumours rippled across the hall about Connor Roe Maguire.

"As for Connor Roe, I will deal with him. Please sent more men to Enniskillen to be trained to fight. I fear there is a war coming that could threaten the very existence of the Maguire clan. The MacMahons, our neighbours, have recently been shired and the expectation is that it will soon be subject to surrender and regrant.

"We are now at the front line. All the proud clans that surround us to the east, west and south have fallen. The situation is dire, but the Maguire are a proud people with a long history and strong allies. The northern lords and the King of Spain can deliver us. But we must be vigilant and not get drawn out to fight before we are ready, for this battle must not be our last. That is all."

Cuchonnacht sat down.

Desmond stood up.

"All hail the Maguire!"

"Hail!"

"As the Maguire said, we are short of men, and the price of Galloglass keeps rising due to the amount of work about and the shortage of

Scottish mercenaries. Send me all your able-bodied men not required on the land so I may train them. God speed your journeys back to your lands."

The chieftains of the Maguire disbursed and spilled out into the courtyard. Eunan's hands shook after Cuchonnacht's speech, but he gathered up Desmond's papers and waited for the transcript of the meeting to be completed by the scribe. He ran down the stairs and into the courtyard to catch up with Desmond. Desmond was engaged in a heated debate with some of the chieftains.

"Just send the men and don't make us enforce the Maguire's rights. I've got to go. The boy is here. We've got to stick together or surely we'll all perish! Goodbye."

"Fetch the horses!" Desmond barked at Eunan.

Desmond said very little on the ride home, his head still stuck in Enniskillen. Eunan fiddled with his dagger that hung from his belt. When would duty call for him to fight for the Maguire?

* * *

After the first trip, Eunan and Desmond travelled to Enniskillen regularly to hear blow for blow about the struggle for power in the O'Neill clan between Hugh and Turlough Luineach and another faction, the MacShane brothers. Desmond always eulogised about what an excellent job Cuchonnacht did to keep the Maguires from taking sides, and the more Eunan heard about the complications of Irish politics, the more impressed he got.

The north was in turmoil, but the only thing that concerned Eunan was that he could not fight. Desmond would train him at home by the lake, but when they were in Enniskillen, he would not let him out of his sight.

Soon, Eunan and Desmond were on the road back to Enniskillen once again.

"Why don't you just live there?" asked Eunan

"I told you before, I like the lake!"

"It would be so much easier!"

"You are my paper carrier boy, not my wife! I bet you didn't speak to your father like this or is that why he was so eager to give you away?"

Eunan went silent.

"I'm sorry boy. But you can't be that easy to hurt, or you'll never survive as a chieftain's son!"

"They'll never know about my father when I'm on the battlefield, but I'll use his memory to smash through their skulls!" replied Eunan who rode ahead of Desmond and out of earshot.

Desmond had noticed how little the boy spoke of his home and his parents; in those brief moments when he did, it was always in a negative manner. He sometimes wondered why but never pressed the matter too hard, for he was pleased with Eunan and liked him, so did not want to hurt his feelings.

They arrived back in Enniskillen, and panic hung thick in the air. Desmond's mood darkened having received the reports from the MacCabe Galloglass constables. He rushed upstairs to the main hall, where Cuchonnacht was waiting for him.

"Go lay out my papers," said Desmond.

He directed Eunan to the end of the high table that dominated the top of the room.

The swiftness and precision of Eunan's setting of the papers would have pleased Desmond were he not too engrossed in stern whispering with Cuchonnacht. As more of the chieftains arrived, Desmond retired from conversation to prepare for the meeting.

When the chieftains were assembled, Cuchonnacht hauled himself to his feet.

"Fellow Maguires, I bring you grave news. Some of you may have heard rumours, but all I can say now is that the rumours are true. Connacht has fallen!"

Murmurs circulated across the room.

"What do you mean sire?" asked one of the chieftains.

"The clans of the province of Connacht have accepted the offer of the crown of surrender and regrant. They have sold their Gaelic tradition for English titles, hereditary inheritance and taxes paid solely to the crown and her instruments."

"They'll be after us next! English soldiers were just the start!" said one chieftain.

"My news is not finished. The crown has made Connor Roe Maguire a knight of the realm!"

Cries of "no!" and "traitor!" filled the room.

"We should march to Lisnaskea and hang him!" exclaimed one.

"There will be no hangings nor marching anywhere. By ourselves, we are weak and have too many potential enemies. The internal war still rages in the O'Neills. The O'Donnell is weak and further weakened by the surrender of the clans of Connacht. We must consolidate Fermanagh. The Galloglass will collect dues and obtain pledges of allegiance from those that may waver. Remember your pledges of men and materials to the Maguire, for I may call upon them soon. May God speed you back to your peoples."

Cuchonnacht fell back into his chair for he could stand no more.

"But the burden on the people grows worse!" said another chieftain. "The weather this year has been terrible and has decimated our crop yields! Yet the demands of the Maguire does not fall in tandem! I fear the people will starve and turn to our enemies if the Maguire cannot protect them from the English demands!"

"I hear what you are saying and am speaking to Hugh O'Neill to press the Irish Council to remove the troops from the north. If the people starve, the Maguire will open up his stores and feed the people himself! On that, you have my word!" replied Cuchonnacht.

Desmond got up and raised his goblet.

"All hail the Maguire!"

"The Maguire!"

But the hail was not as enthusiastic as it once was.

The room emptied, except for Desmond and Eunan.

"The Galloglass will be returning to your village. Do you wish to leave and help your father?"

"No, I'd rather stay here with you."

"As you wish, but you will have to return home someday!"

"In the meantime, shall we go home?" Eunan smiled.

6

1586 - Enniskillen

The winter of 1585/86 was a burden to man and beast. The Crannogs and store houses, both legal and illegal in the eyes of the Maguire, were only half full in August but rapidly dwindled. The people went hungry and brought their gripes to the Maguire, who in turn bought them to Hugh O'Neill, who in turn brought them to the Irish Council. The whole of Ulster suffered, and the threat of rebellion and Spanish invasion resounded through the fields, forests and mountains of Ulster. Therefore Hugh O'Neill had leverage. The Irish Council agreed to a reduction of troops to five hundred and fifty, but that did not mean that the crown had given up on its plans to crush the Irish lords of Ulster.

Much pressure was exerted on the Maguire by the crown. Cattle raids became the norm, and the Irish Privy Council tried to get him to submit to surrender and regrant. Hugh O'Neill attempted to defend them and divert attention elsewhere but Turlough, the O'Neill the Maguire were subservient to, said nothing. He was trying to get royal support in his war with Hugh O'Neill or, at the very least, get the council not to favour Hugh O'Neill.

* * *

Desmond set out for Enniskillen with Eunan, but he plodded along as if it were a funeral march. It was as if something had died in Desmond's brain. Ever since he heard the news, his age rapidly caught up with him, and he needed far more help from Eunan and Arthur. Desmond instructed Eunan to ready the boat, for he had much work to complete on the way to Enniskillen. They had not gotten far before Eunan grew concerned.

"Sir, what ails you?" he asked.

"What ails me? The world I dedicated my life to defend is dying before my eyes. I fear I have no place in the next, on earth nor heaven. It is time to pay for my sins, for this frail body cannot carry the weight of them no more."

"Why such despair? Your frail body still managed to lap up his breakfast this morning! Truly the Maguires will still exist after this day?"

"It is the beginning of the end. I fear nothing can save the Maguire or the northern lords now. The English have too many shiny shillings and fattened cows for our greedy chieftains to resist!"

"We will fight for the Maguire!" exclaimed Eunan as he held up an oar and splashed Arthur in the process.

"Speak for yourself!" said Arthur as he dusted off the wet.

"Admirable resolution, but only a united north with the aid of Spain would stand any chance."

"Then that is what we will do!" said Eunan as he placed his oars back in their stirrups and rowed as fast as he could, before quickly tiring.

"Save your energy boy. You'll need it!" said Desmond.

When they arrived in Enniskillen Castle, it was like going to a funeral. English soldiers stood in pride of place in the castle yard.

"The usual mercenary scum from the Pale," muttered Desmond as he walked to the main building.

A grey-faced Donnacha O'Cassidy Maguire was waiting for them by the entrance.

"Hello, Desmond. 'Tis a sad day. The Maguire wishes to see his main chieftains and advisors before we go and meet the English delegation."

"Well, I knew I wasn't coming to a party!"

He turned to Eunan to take out a fraction of his frustration.

"Be quick with you, boy!" he said, as Eunan hurried along behind with the bags.

"I assume Cuchonnacht is going to explain how all of this came about?" asked Desmond.

"Cuchonnacht will say what he has to say!"

"So I'm in for a cryptic day of nods, winks and interpretations. Should suit you perfectly! I hope I don't get my throat slit for getting one of the hand signals wrong!"

"You always find a way to come out on top Desmond! This way!"

The Maguire had arranged the main hall for the entertainment of the English officers, so Desmond climbed the stairs to the next level.

The guard opened the door for Desmond, and the Maguire stood before him in his private reception room with his two sons and a few of his most important supporters from the clan. Desmond was shown to a seat as the Maguire paced the room.

"We all knew this day would come!" said Cuchonnacht. "They were rolling up the clans as they made their way northwards, and we knew we'd be next!"

"We all knew we were doomed when they imposed English soldiers upon us and we could not hire Scottish mercenaries. At least you knew what you got with a Scottish mercenary, and they'd go back home after the summer. But this lot just want to bleed us dry, bury the carcass and sell our land to English settlers!" said Desmond.

"If you knew, why didn't you do something about it!?" said one of the chieftains.

"For all of Cuchonnacht's tactful steering, the waves of pressure were always going to overwhelm us eventually."

"Don't be so morose old man!" cried Hugh Maguire. "We have many warriors, and Spain will come to our aid. Edmund Magauran and a delegation from the bishops are putting our case to him right now. The great Catholic war against the English heretics will finally come to Ireland!"

"We haven't seen much of them yet, and all help will come with a heavy price. Be sure you'll be willing to pay it. All minnows look tasty to a bigger fish, albeit they are steeped in the brine of Catholic sauce!" replied Desmond.

"Your homespun wisdom veers towards blasphemy at times!" said Donnacha.

"At least it will save me from the priest hunters when they come to string us up for hiding Catholic priests! Besides, if we don't give frank understandable views, then we are of no service to the Maguire. Save your linguistic trickery for the English downstairs!"

"I'll have no more said against the Pope!" exclaimed Hugh Maguire. "He sent arms and troops not even six years ago to help the rebellion in Munster!"

"And look what happened to them!" said Desmond. "All my efforts are to persuade you to use your guile and restraint and not to get hunted down and killed by the English, as if the Maguires were a pack of stray dogs!"

"Well, I've got a room full of English officers downstairs who want the Queen's papers signed and a yard full of English soldiers to make sure I do it. As much as your breath warms the room, I have to save most of my people while I still have options. Hugh O'Neill swears the papers are meaningless and I should sign then to buy us time. I'll sign those papers as it still keeps the Maguires together and alive. I hope you'll join me in some prayers later, so the good Lord will send us a saviour," said Cuchonnacht.

"Amen to that!" said Donnacha. "Let me assist you along with Desmond, and we will stand beside you in your hour of need and make sure you are still the Maguire tomorrow!"

Desmond waived at Eunan and Eunan gathered the papers and ran after him.

The English officers smiled as they presented the agreement. Cuchonnacht baulked at the seven hundred cow fine to remove the troops and the equal amount for annual rent. After some initial reluctance and reassurances from Donnacha, Cuchonnacht signed the papers. The English officers were jubilant, rolled up the documents, shook everyone's hand and left. The Maguires had swapped tanistry for English titles. The crown had won.

7

1587 - Enniskillen

Eunan felt the warmth of his mother's arms then the smothering of her breast.

"Come with me!" she said.

"Mother, you can walk!" exclaimed Eunan.

"I could always walk, boy. Now hurry! They are after us!"

Eunan started to run. He reached his mother's hips as she ran, his head bobbing alongside her belt. His father appeared in front of them from behind a tree. By his flank was a blood-drenched axe.

"The boy will hold us back! It's him they want not us!"

"He is our boy, no matter what happened!"

"Give him here, give him here!"

His father reached out to grab Eunan, but his mother held him near.

"We can't give him to them. We can't!"

"Give him here!" and his father's blood-soaked hand reached out for him.

Eunan reached for his weapon but managed to knock over everything in his way.

"You're going to have to give up those dreams or explain them to me! Either way, you're keeping me awake!"

"I just tripped Desmond. I'm sorry, go back to sleep!"

But Eunan could only perch awake at the end of his bed.

"Those dreams hold no truth. My mother never held me like that!"

* * *

1587 arrived, but the burden on the people did not diminish. The soldiers may have left but the rents demanded by the Maguire to pay the fine and the crown's rent had decimated his resources. The O'Neill civil war raged onwards but Cuchonnacht, with considerable skill, avoided both getting embroiled or allowing his clan to disintegrate into warring factions. The news from up north remained grim, and the previous settlement between Hugh O'Neill and Turlough Luineach O'Neill solidified, and Fermanagh remained under Turlough.

The first part of the year was relatively stable for Desmond and Eunan, for they managed to stay beside the lake for long periods. Eunan's training was progressing well, and he could now beat all the local boys in all forms of combat. But Eunan's achievements were not rewarded by displays of emotion from Desmond. This coldness led Eunan to recall his father, someone he had banished from his mind, certainly during the day. Eunan had not heard from his father, nor sought news of him. This puzzled Desmond but Eunan fended off any such inquiries by changing the subject to one of more perceived interest to Desmond, such as food or Eunan's failures. Desmond was happy with his new companion so decided to leave it be. However, harvest came, and the peace ruined when Desmond once more received an urgent summons to go to Enniskillen.

When they arrived in the main hall, Cuchonnacht was already deep in conversation with his son Hugh. Eunan laid out the papers and Desmond made small talk with some of the chieftains as they arrived in dribs and drabs.

Donnacha O'Cassidy Maguire banged on the table to summon everyone's attention. Cuchonnacht rose in the silence.

"Fellow Maguires, I have nothing but grim news for you, and I don't know where to start. We are under grave threat. But this time it is not the war of the O'Neills, but the English!"

The room went quiet, for Fermanagh had been awash with rumours, and refugees had taken to wandering into its forests, often leading to violence. Many a wandering band of Galloglass had heard of the growing tension and entered Fermanagh, to offer their services to find the coffers of the Maguire empty.

"The MacMahons of Monaghan and O'Hanlons of Orior, have both been shired. They renounced tanistry for hereditary titles due to the pressures exerted by the crown."

There were only low-level murmurs in the hall, for most already knew.

"Does the O'Neill know of this?" said one of the chieftains.

"MacMahon and O'Hanlon owed their allegiance to Hugh O'Neill, and O'Neill has brought his protests to the Irish Council and the English Privy Council. He is demanding compensation and the reinstatement of his traditional rights."

"But does it matter? We had 'surrender and regrant' a year ago, and nothing happened!" cried one chieftain.

"I'm glad you view the diminishment and impoverishment of the Maguire clan as being nothing! The crown means to divide up the clans into their rival parties, thereby destroying the clan structure and their strength. Thus, nothing truly does become nothing!

"Hugh O'Neill's fight in the Irish Council and the English Privy Council is like attaching a giant leech to clan Maguire. To get anything done, you need to bribe everyone with cattle and coin, and they do not come cheap! Everything Hugh O'Neill achieves comes at a price to us. We also have to pay Turlough Luineach while he plays the opposite game and tries to win favour with the English as the block to Hugh O'Neill becoming the master of Ulster!

"But the English are more serious about Monaghan than they were last year with us. The MacMahons would not accept a sheriff, so Bagenal, the English lieutenant of Tyrone, invaded and imposed one upon them. That, my fellow Maguires is the fate that awaits us!"

The room was silent.

"Where is Connor Roe? Why is he not here?" said one chieftain.

"I may be old and frail, but I can still hold the Maguires together. My best Galloglass are upon his lands, ensuring his loyalty and guarding the borders against incursions from the MacMahons."

"This indeed is tragic news," said another chieftain.

"Tragic though it may be, it is not the worst of my news."

Desmond bowed his head, for he knew what was coming.

"Hugh Roe O'Donnell has been kidnapped by the English!"

There were audible groans around the halls.

"The O'Donnells are now preparing for a war of succession. The Maguire will stay neutral, just as we have done while the O'Neills fight it out!"

"Have we ever been in such a precarious position? Our allies disintegrate before our eyes, and the English surround us and destroy our brethren one by one!" cried one chieftain.

"The Maguires are still here, have our lands and can fight. Therefore we have been in worse positions. We need to stick together and bide our time."

"Half the O'Donnells have sided with Turlough and half with Hugh O'Neill all to gain the upper hand!" said another.

"Bide our time for what? We are going to get swallowed up by someone. We may as well pick sides and go down fighting!" cried a third chieftain.

"That is only a good strategy if you can pick the winner. Otherwise, we'll just be one of the casualties on the roadside the winner steps over," said Desmond.

The room started to break into factions where most picked one of O'Neill septs, and others sided with the O'Donnells. They argued furiously while the Maguire sat and caught his breath. The arguing soon got too much for him, and he rose again to rebuke his followers.

"We will remain united, or you will suffer my Galloglass! Now get out, all of you!"

Cuchonnacht collapsed into his chair, the meeting having visibly drained him.

The MacCabe Galloglass moved in and cleared the room. Desmond lingered in the shadows until it was safe to approach Cuchonnacht.

"I fear the worst. I feel we may perish soon."

"Indeed, destiny will have us die, but the Maguire must live on through my son Hugh. A little rash and quick-tempered he may be, but he is a good warrior and can lead. If Connor Roe becomes the Maguire, then we are doomed."

"If we are to be doomed, would it not be better to surrender now and spare the lives of our people?"

"There is some hope. Edmund Magauran, a good friend of the Maguires, has been made Archbishop of Armagh by the Pope. That gives us better standing with the King of Spain, a man of the true faith. Edmund can persuade him of the righteousness of our cause, and the King will send aid."

"I hope you are right sire. I hope you are right!"

8

1588 - Enniskillen

The pressure in Fermanagh in 1588 crushed the minds of the old and weak but fuelled those who thought they could not die. The new year opened like a chasm to Desmond, who could only foresee the demise of the Maguire. In his blackest moods, he took to his bed, and it took considerable effort on Eunan's part to get Desmond out to the lakeside and continue the training. With an axe in his hand, confidence seared through Eunan's veins. He was a year older, had a year's more practice, was nearly at fighting age and had not missed any of action, for Cuchonnacht had managed to steer them towards peace. A miracle, considering the two leading powers of the north were still embroiled in their civil wars.

In the cold and rainy days of February, Desmond returned to Enniskillen. Eunan's energy got Desmond up and carried Desmond back to the Maguire. This time, when Desmond entered the room, there was only Cuchonnacht, Hugh Maguire, Donnacha, his assistant young Cuchonnacht, Edmund Magauran and a handful of trusted allies waiting for him.

"Things must be serious," said Desmond, as Eunan behind him did his well-practised role of laying out the papers.

Desmond turned to his companions and Donnacha's scathing looks.

"The boy is not a spy, he will be a loyal Maguire chieftain soon," Desmond reassured him.

"We'll need as many of them as we can get!" interjected Hugh Maguire.

"What's happened that you need to summon me in such a clandestine manner?" asked Desmond.

"Hugh O'Neill has regained control over the MacMahons. Now we are under pressure from the both of them and on the other side of Fermanagh to side with Hugh O'Neill, and from Donnell O'Donnell to side with Turlough Luineach," replied Cuchonnacht.

"You have always steered us out of trouble before. What's changed?"

"Now, age has me in its claws and won't let go. I don't have the energy or will to resist much longer."

"Then it is almost time for young Hugh to succeed you!" said Donnacha.

"I fear that the forces pulling Fermanagh may be too strong for such a young man to hold together. Sorry Hugh, but it is nothing I have not said to your face in private," replied Cuchonnacht.

"It is either me to become the Maguire or Connor Roe, and I don't have to ask as to whom you'd prefer. But the Maguires, for all your ability to avoid war, never stand alone. If we wait forever we will be scattered in the wind like all the other Gaelic lords the English have subdued. Soon will come the time to pick sides!" said Hugh.

"Have you not picked sides already, Hugh?" asked Cuchonnacht.

"I travelled north to help Turlough's son, Art O'Neill, in good faith against some rogue Scottish invaders. Then he tried to double cross me. Art O'Neill is nothing. As soon as his father dies, he will just be another nothing chieftain Hugh O'Neill subjugates. Hugh O'Neill is the only one to help us, and he is on the winning side."

"I thought the plan was not to get engaged in any fighting?" said

Desmond.

"Know your place MacCabe," said Donnacha, "or that place will be permanently fishing by the lake."

"At least I would feed the people, which would be better than your efforts!" replied Desmond.

"Gentlemen, the last thing I need is for my advisors to fight, especially in a time of axes, not words," said Cuchonnacht. "Whatever Hugh has done is done and is in the past. He will be the Maguire when I am gone, so he has to get used to decision-making and the consequences of those decisions. So advisors, time to advise. Like it or not, young Hugh has chosen war, so who should we side with?"

"The obvious choice is Hugh O'Neill. But first, he must gain the upper hand in their civil war and secure his alliance with the O'Donnells. The north is doomed unless the O'Neills and O'Donnells unite," said Desmond.

"We still have the King of Spain. If he came to our aid, we could throw the English into the sea and restore the one true faith!" said Edmund Magauran.

"England and Spain are almost in permanent war. Are your priests still agitating for support in the Spanish capital?" asked Cuchonnacht.

"The Lord in heaven will provide."

"He is certainly taking a circuitous route," said Desmond.

"You cannot question the ways of the Lord," said the Archbishop.

"And we only know the ways of the Lord through you?"

"Forgive him please Archbishop," said Cuchonnacht. "He is wary of death and tales of the afterlife remind him of all the battles in which he has fought. He prays as hard as any when he is not distracted by such memories."

"We need defenders of the faith who have such experience."

The bishop returned to his previous subject.

"We still have many priests coming from the Catholic colleges of

Spain and Rome, so we still have many and growing connections. My senior priests never miss an opportunity to promote our cause to King or Pope."

"All-out war grows nearer every day between Spain and England. Surely the Spanish know they would have much support here?" said Desmond.

"The plans of the King are fickle. His hatred for the heretic Elizabeth is an obsession with him due to her piracy of the high seas. But my agents tell me that he plans something big for this year. We have work to do! We have to present the King with a united front of support. We need to give him a reason to come. Also, if we are strong, it means we'll have a greater chance of more power for us when the King liberates us from the heretic queen."

"This gives us hope and more reason to hang on and survive for a few more years and remain neutral. But we need to survive to be liberated!" replied Cuchonnacht.

"Hugh O'Neill has also tried to contact the King for support," said Hugh

"If he succeeds, he will have our support," replied Donnacha.

"I agree with you, gentlemen, in all of what you have said. So we must prepare for the future and given the Maguires the best possible chance," said Cuchonnacht. "Therefore, I have arranged for Hugh to marry Hugh O'Neill's daughter in secret and seal our alliance with Hugh O'Neill."

"I hope this is wise!" said Desmond.

"Now is not the time for old men. It is time for us to retire and leave the fighting to the young men and let them make their ways in the world. Time is calling for us, my old friend."

9

The Marriage of Hugh Maguire

News began to spread throughout the north.

"The Spanish are coming!" cried the messenger as he ran through the castle yard.

"Shut him up!" cried Desmond from one of the tower windows, "or we'll have a riot on our hands!"

The guards ran to silence him, and the messenger was directed to the great hall to give the Maguire the message.

"I beg your pardon, Lord," said the messenger as he knelt and coughed up his lungs.

"Settle yourself down, boy, then speak!" said Cuchonnacht.

"Thank you, Lord."

Cuchonnacht and his advisors gathered around the messenger.

"The Spanish king has sent the greatest fleet ever assembled against England and her heretic Queen! They sail for England and will meet with the Spanish army in the Netherlands. They say the Queen is doomed and refuses to leave her castle because she is so afraid!"

"Is there an army sailing to Ireland?" asked Desmond.

"Not that I have heard. However, rumour has it the King promises the lords of Ireland arms and ammunition. Muskets, pikes! All the latest weapons used in Europe!"

"Archbishop, does this correspond with what you have heard from your agents?" said Cuchonnacht.

"It does, Lord. They also say that the King wishes to send us assistance, but the Armada has swallowed up all his resources."

"But if the Armada succeeds we won't need Spanish help, for the head of the snake will have been cut from her body!" exclaimed Hugh Maguire.

"Don't get too excited just yet," warned Desmond. "It won't all be sweetness and light just because we're under a Catholic king. The stronger and more united the lords of the north are, the better the outcome for us when it all comes to a head."

"So what do we do, oh Maguire?" said the Archbishop.

"The same as we did today and the day before. We sit and wait."

* * *

The Maguire sat and waited. But fate did not allow him to wait for long. Hugh O'Neill, who appeared to be getting the upper hand in the north, was surprisingly defeated by Turlough Luineach at Carricklea in April 1588. However, this was not a decisive victory, and Hugh O'Neill decided to turn his attentions to stripping away the less loyal elements of Turlough Luineach's support. He marched into Fermanagh and raided the villages and levelled the lands of Connor Roe and his supporters. These acts elevated his support in Fermanagh as he advanced towards Enniskillen. When the army of Hugh O'Neill appeared on the horizon, Cuchonnacht did not even summon his men. He threw open the town and castle gates to the invader.

Hugh O'Neill took up residence in Enniskillen at the invitation of Cuchonnacht, and the local lords came and paid homage and pledged allegiance. Hugh O'Neill was keen to cement the new alliance with the

Maguires and had brought his daughter for the pre-arranged marriage to Hugh Maguire. Cuchonnacht and Desmond were reluctant to outwardly side with Hugh O'Neill due to the ongoing strength of both Turlough Luineach and the MacShanes. However, Hugh Maguire had committed himself to Hugh O'Neill's cause ever since he turned on Art O'Neill, and, with the support of Donnacha O'Cassidy Maguire, jumped at the chance.

The Maguires made preparations for the impending wedding. They invited Hugh O'Neill's closest clan allies and the leading O'Donnells that were allied or at least sympathetic to him to cement old and new alliances. The only outstanding arrangements were the terms of the wedding and the secret partnership. Both sides sat down in the great hall of the Maguires and Cuchonnacht: Hugh Maguire, Desmond and Donnacha represented the Maguires, and Hugh O'Neill and Cormac MacBaron the O'Neills, while Edmund Magauran, the Archbishop of Armagh, mediated.

"There is a long struggle ahead, Cuchonnacht. Age is turning against me as it is against you, but it isn't a time for old men. The vibrancy and foolhardiness of youth are what is needed to carry the fight to the English," said Hugh O'Neill. "We overthink," and he pressed his index finger into his right temple.

"I know my time is nearly up. But it is my duty as the Maguire to his clan to steer them on a path that they will both survive and prosper on. You have many enemies and fewer guns, pikes, axes and swords than them. Why should I commit the fate of my people to you, to perish with you on the fields of Tyrone and have them suffer the wrath of the victor?"

"Our fates are intertwined whether we like it or not," said Hugh O'Neill, crossing his middle finger over his index finger. "We are fighting for no less than the survival of our Gaelic culture and the one true church. The English are coming for you and are likely to string you and all your family up so they can make Connor Roe the Maguire. If we lose this war, both our clans will be scattered apart and divided at the behest of the English. Do you think I offer you a choice? It's simple. Live and fight for your freedom or watch from the side, while your future generations – as they toil as English tenant farmers – wonder why you didn't fight for them!"

"I acknowledge the graveness of the situation that you have so admirably painted with your words, and the Maguires will fight to the last for our freedom. However, my main gripe is with the English. I have no desire to fall to the sword of Turlough Luineach or the MacShanes if they win and take revenge on your allies!"

"You will only know the victor when it is too late! I have stood up for the northern lords in both the Irish and Privy Councils. I have solidified the houses of O'Neill and O'Donnell with the marriage of my daughter to Red Hugh O'Donnell, the favoured successor to the O'Donnell clan. God help him in that English jail. Now I offer the same alliance to the Maguires. What has Turlough or the MacShanes done to unite the north?"

Hugh Maguire butted in.

"He is right, father. If there is any hope, it is with him!"

"Just as much as it is my duty as the Maguire to protect the clan, it is also my duty as your father to stop you from getting your head blown off!"

"I'd rather my head was blown off and lying in a ditch than to rot in an English prison!"

"At least you'd still be alive!"

"Which brings me back to my first point, father," said Hugh Maguire. "What we, what the Maguires, what the north need are headstrong young men who can lead their clans into battle. I remember the stories of your bravery under Shane O'Neill, a headstrong young man just like your son. Now I think it is time for your son to take over!"

Cuchonnacht and Desmond looked at each other until Cuchonnacht spoke.

"When you truly are the O'Neill, and you have united with the O'Donnells and the lords of the north, we will gladly follow you with my son as the Maguire!"

The room was silent. Hugh Maguire was delighted, but Hugh O'Neill was silent.

"I trust your word Cuchonnacht, and your pledge is good enough for me," said Hugh O'Neill finally. He raised his glass. "To the Maguire and the rebels of the north!"

"The Maguire and the rebels of the north!" The room echoed back.

"Let's get this wedding done!" cried Donnacha, and he made another salute.

The room turned to the celebration, and Hugh O'Neill turned to Cuchonnacht and Hugh Maguire.

"I know you can't openly support me, but I'll take my future son-in-law under my wing and ensure he's a fine soldier and leader for when the war comes. There's no point for anyone if he has to learn when it's too late!" he patted Cuchonnacht on the knee. "You know it makes sense!"

Cuchonnacht smiled, the smile of a man who destiny left behind. Hugh Maguire followed his future father in law to discuss his prospects. Donnacha grinned at Desmond for he knew Desmond's days in Enniskillen were over.

Eunan began to pack up the papers and Desmond hung back from the crowd of well-wishers to Cuchonnacht.

"Does that mean we won't be coming to Enniskillen anymore?" asked Eunan.

"We will if Hugh Maguire has any sense!"

10

1588 - Spanish Armada

Over the following months Hugh Maguire, with the assistance of Hugh O'Neill, gradually took over the running of the army of the Maguire and the secret hiring of Scottish mercenaries. Hugh Maguire, active help from Donnacha, progressively side-lined his father. All of this was kept secret from the other lords of Ulster for fear of reprisals from Turlough Luineach.

The lords of Ulster listened to the news of the ongoing saga of the Spanish Armada first with elation and then with a dreadful disappointment. The news came that Spanish ships had been seen off the coast of Scotland and would be making their way past Ireland. The fleet was decimated, by defeat in battle, and terrible storms off the shores of England and Scotland. The Irish lords heard rumours that the ships were full of soldiers and modern weapons such as guns and pikes and were eager to retrieve as many men and materials as possible. The lords posted men along the shores of Northern Ireland to look for ships that may have run aground.

The lands of the Maguires were landlocked, but Hugh Maguire did not want to miss out on any potential weapons bounty or Spanish soldiers he could get his hands on. He could not turn north for the

O'Neills, and the O'Donnells were being pressurised by the English to show their loyalty by executing or handing over any Spanish sailors that came ashore, and also by handing over any weapons. Hugh Maguire turned west to the O'Rourkes, the Sligo O'Connors and the Burkes of Mayo, for he was trying to forge alliances with lesser clans so he would not be so reliant on the O'Neills and O'Donnells. These clans were in a similar position, fighting for survival against the steady encroachment of the English. Hugh Maguire sent Donnacha to negotiate, and all the clans readily agreed.

* * *

Eunan and Desmond settled back into life by the lake. They would train first, then maybe indulge in some fishing, or rowing out onto the lake to visit various islands, followed by dinner prepared by Arthur. If Eunan was lucky, the day would be topped off by tales from Desmond's past, which Eunan had to guess if they were tall or true. Desmond still trained the local boys, mainly because Eunan wanted him to, but with much less enthusiasm than before. Desmond said he should aim higher and that he would learn nothing by constantly beating boys he had repeatedly beaten.

Desmond embraced a life of semi-retirement, until one day he received a messenger from Hugh Maguire. He read the message and cursed. "What does he want?"

"Does it not say?" asked Eunan.

"No, it's just a cryptic message saying how urgently he needs me. Maybe he realises just how useless Donnacha is!"

"I will gather your things and prepare the boat!" said Eunan, and before Desmond could object, he was gone.

Eunan was now becoming a young man, with a growing muscular stature and a shock of red hair. His skill with axe and sword proceeded him, and he was a devout follower of Hugh Maguire. He looked nothing like his father, a fact he revelled in telling Desmond whenever the subject came up. He leapt at the chance to return to Enniskillen and be near the action once again.

When they arrived in Enniskillen, only Hugh Maguire and Donnacha O'Cassidy Maguire were waiting for them.

"Welcome my old friend!" Hugh Maguire embraced Desmond when he entered the room.

Desmond's suspicion suppressed the thought of reciprocating any warmth.

"We have a mission for you that fits your unique expertise," said Hugh Maguire.

"What expertise is that? I've been enjoying fishing at the lake because that's all I thought you wanted from me."

"You served overseas as a mercenary?"

"And got paid good money for it, and then from your father. But you know all this. Why are you asking?"

"Because we have a special mission for you if you wish to do a great service for the Maguires."

"I have continuously given great service and my health and youth to the Maguires, so why stop now that I am old and crippled?"

"Good. Donnacha will tell you all about it!"

* * *

Desmond and Eunan found themselves on the way to the lands of the O'Rourkes, a clan just down the road and pecking order from the Maguires. One-time rivals, now useful allies.

Desmond served with many of the older generations of O'Rourkes, both in Ireland and overseas. He had acquired a knowledge of Spanish weapons and tactics in his mercenary days spent in the Netherlands.

Desmond realised why the Maguire gave him this mission. He needed him to train the MacCabes in the new fighting techniques from the continent.

Hugh Maguire warned Desmond that the Lord Deputy of Ireland knew the Spanish fleet was coming. The Lord Deputy had decreed that severe punishment would be bestowed on any lord found harbouring Spanish fugitives. English troops were dispatched from Dublin to enforce the decree. But Desmond knew that any mission Donnacha had volunteered him for would be dangerous.

Upon his arrival at the village where they met their guides, Desmond found himself amongst old friends, and they exchanged stories from the past and updated themselves on their failing health. The guides led them to a sympathetic village in Sligo O'Connor territory, and Desmond and Eunan took up lodgings in a village on top of a cliff overlooking Sligo bay.

"You'd better make yourself comfortable boy. The way the remains of the Armada is circling Scotland, the O'Neills and the O'Donnells will get the first pick of the carcasses, and we'll get the dregs. The more Spanish and weapons we can save, the better the chances the Spanish King will send an army to help us!" said Desmond.

"With the destruction of the Armanda, surely King Phillip will suffer the same fate?" replied Eunan.

"King Phillip is the richest, most powerful King in the world. He has a power way beyond what the northern lords or you and I could ever dream. Even I have respect for him! He is a devout Catholic and hates the heretic queen with almost as much passion. I'm surprised we've had to make so much effort to persuade him to invade!"

"So what do we do while we wait?" asked Eunan.

"Make allies of the O'Rourkes and the O'Connors and train their men so they can fight alongside the Maguire."

So they did just that. They waited. They heard the news of great storms and the rumours that the remains of the fleet sunk off the islands of Scotland. They were despondent, but Hugh Maguire told them to stay where they were, for there were still some stragglers limping back to Spain.

They remained in the village until one morning they heard a shout. "Ship ahoy! Ship ahoy!"

Eunan ran to the top of the cliff and Desmond hobbled after him.

"Master, look yonder! We prayed, and God has provided!" Eunan announced to the world.

Desmond reached Eunan, leant over and caught his breath and looked out onto the bay. On the jagged rocks was a Spanish galleon, jack-knifed in two. Out of its belly spewed men, ropes, barrels and shattered wood. The men washed ashore, and the locals wasted no time to go down and rob them, killing anyone who resisted.

"And what he giveth with one hand, he taketh away with the other! Go and summon the O'Rourkes!" ordered Desmond. "We must stop this slaughter before they kill all the useful ones!"

Eunan ran as fast as he could. Desmond made his way down to the beach. The O'Rourke warriors drove off the locals. They started to gather all the boxes and barrels that had washed up on the beach into one place. Desmond took command.

"Gather any weapons or supplies together and don't touch them until I inspect them. Don't kill any more Spanish! Gather the survivors all together so I may speak to them. This is very important. Any disobedience will be dealt with by the O'Rourke," he barked.

The men of the O'Rourke grunted their obedience. They gathered together the injured and dishevelled Spanish sailors along with their equipment. They dutifully rowed out to the bay and fished out what men and equipment they could.

Desmond's face was grim as he inspected the beach.

"What's the matter?" asked Eunan.

"This is shite!" said Desmond, and he went over to speak to the Spanish survivors.

"Who's your leader? Can any of you speak English?"

They all looked away.

"I'm a friend, the best hope you have of getting off this beach alive! Now can any of you speak English?"

A man got up, of indiscernible rank, his uniform having disintegrated into rags.

"I can. I can speak for the crew. The ship's captain is dead, and many of the surviving crew are ill. I am Captain Arlo Ruiz."

Desmond waved him over and then walked with him out of earshot of the O'Rourkes. They sat down, and Desmond took some bread out from his bag and offered it to Arlo. He wolfed it down. After a quick burp he looked ready to talk.

"What was your ship carrying, may I ask?" asked Desmond.

"Soldiers, weapons and bibles for the English infidels."

"So if you didn't shoot them, convert them?!"

"Why do you speak of the Lord so?" Arlo snarled.

"I am an old man who has seen many battles, including serving with the Spanish army of the Netherlands. I have seen many more deaths than conversions. The barrel of a gun does not win many hearts and minds!"

"You served with the mercenaries?"

"I spent many of my best years earning the Spanish King's coin, drinking his wine, fornicating with the local prostitutes and all I had to do for him was kill who he told me to! A bargain at half the price! Are there any more ships with you?"

"We got blown off course in a storm in the middle of the ocean two days ago. We saw some ships wrecked off the coast to the north of here. There may be some ships behind us, but for now, we are alone."

"Are there any more galleons out there or just smaller pataches?"

"The other ships have survived your horrific weather much better than our cursed ship. Only the minnows and the weak perish on your rocks."

"Try and redeem yourself and earn your life, little minnow. There are a lot of greedy war chieftains to satisfy, and yours is the only shipwreck with any guns. Are you a captain in the navy or infantry?"

"Most of the survivors, including myself, are land infantry."

"Ah, you wriggle off the dinner plate, little minnow! You are most welcome here, Arlo," said Desmond as he slapped him on the knee. "We have plenty of work for you to do here until we can arrange safe passage home. Now I must go and see what my men have salvaged, and you return to yours, and we'll arrange for accommodation for you all!"

Desmond got up and walked over to inspect the haul of treasure that had spewed forth from the ship. Arlo followed him over after he had consulted with his comrades regarding their welfare. When the shipwreck had been picked clean, they managed to assemble one hundred and forty working guns and over two hundred pikes.

"That's a decent haul for a single galleon," said Desmond. He turned to Arlo. "Can you train us how to use these?"

"I could, but the guns aren't very reliable. You could learn to use them in a couple of weeks, but you wouldn't know how many guns would survive the training."

"You do the training and let me worry about that," replied Desmond. "Now let's load all of this up and bring it to the village and make it look like we were never here. The English will soon hear of this shipwreck!"

The one hundred survivors of the shipwreck were brought to the village, fed and re-clothed. Fintan O'Rourke arrived, having been sent by his father to supervise splitting the spoils with the Maguires.

Desmond walked around with Arlo and spoke to the survivors

individually and established their rank and skill levels. Once completed, Desmond dismissed Arlo and went into a house with Fintan. The chieftain's hut in the O'Connor village was a sombre place to be. Desmond and Fintan were worried. They had gotten a limited amount of weapons, a hundred new mouths to feed, and the English army coming for them.

"It is time for us to leave," said Desmond. "It's only a wee galleon, poor picking for all our labours. Why don't I take the survivors and their baggage back to Fermanagh for safekeeping? Your messengers have said that the English are bearing down hard to get here!"

"The O'Rourkes are not taking all the risks and none of the rewards!" Fintan responded.

"And those rewards will get you hung before you have the chance to use them. They are better off in Maguire country and out of the reach of English sheriffs. Once the heat has died down, the Maguire will share the rewards with you."

Fintan circled the room and returned to the table.

"My father will kill me for this, but you're right. Take the most skilled and the better weapons back to Fermanagh. Give me a token to give to my father, and I will make sure the English do not pursue you."

Fintan left. Desmond gave his men the order to go.

* * *

There were no horses for Arlo and the other Spanish soldiers Desmond selected, so they were forced to walk to the River Erne. The spare horses were given to the carts to transport the newly acquired weapons. Arlo came to speak to Desmond as he could stand the wind and rain of the bogs of Ireland no more.

"What will happen to my comrades? Your chieftains have made so many approaches to my King looking for help, and here we now are! I assume you are going to treat his subjects well?"

"We have to split you up to ensure your safety from the English. Then we can smuggle you back in groups to Spain. You need to be patient as we wait for the heat to die down."

Arlo was sceptical but knew he would not get a better answer from Desmond. He went back to his men and lied to them about the answer Desmond gave them. They smiled all the way to the River Erne.

The English arrived in the O'Rourkes' village the next day looking for survivors from the shipwreck. They were greeted by the bodies of the O'Rourkes' Spanish sailors swinging from the trees.

* * *

Once they arrived at the River Erne, the Maguires had assembled several boats to transport them up the river. Most of the Spanish were dropped off at various islands in lower Lough Erne so they could go into hiding. Arlo was brought to Enniskillen to meet Hugh Maguire so that Hugh could assess Arlo's usefulness. Hugh Maguire insisted that Desmond stay with Arlo and help him train the Maguire Galloglass. Desmond and Eunan were given lodgings in the tower, and the additional responsibility to ensure that Arlo was content and did not try and escape. They had to convince him he was not a prisoner.

As for the training, unfortunately, the Maguires suffered from a severe lack of guns, for the guns they had retrieved from the shipwreck had suffered water damage, as Arlo had predicted, and therefore jammed or otherwise broke quickly. The Maguire metalsmiths could not replicate nor repair the guns. Guns were otherwise hard to get hold of since the English restricted the distribution of firearms to their forces only, and most illegal gun importing was controlled by Hugh

O'Neill or by northern lords with Scottish connections. The pikes, on the other hand, could be more easily replicated and the Maguire's craftsmen set about producing as many as possible.

Arlo was very uneasy about his new situation, irrespective that the Maguire had tried to make him feel as comfortable as possible. However, Desmond dismissed any inquiries into the fate of his comrades or how he was supposed to get home.

Arlo did, however, cooperate fully in training the men and kept his frustrations with the quality of the soldiers to himself until he was alone with Desmond. Desmond reassured him they had plenty of warriors at the same level as Eunan, but they needed the necessary attention to expedite their learning. Desmond warned Arlo that if he failed to produce good warriors, he would be diminished in the eyes of the Maguire to his old 'minnow' status and thrown back in the sea.

Hugh Maguire, under the influence of Cuchonnacht, tried to keep his support for Hugh O'Neill as quiet as possible in order not to offend any of the other northern lords, as Hugh O'Neill had not yet decisively established his supremacy. Hugh Maguire concerned himself with gaining the support of the chieftains of the Maguire clan for the inevitable election of a new Maguire as Connor Roe had already started to do the same in the south of the county.

11

Captain William Mostian

Eunan was overjoyed to live in Enniskillen, being at the centre of what he thought were preparations for war. Armed men came to the gates nearly every day to offer their services to fight for the Maguire, only for the majority to be turned away by Desmond. Desmond declined Eunan's daily requests to join the MacCabes Galloglass. Desmond told him he should have loftier ambitions.

Desmond could see that the boy was starting to mature and should soon be returned to his father, for Cathal O'Keenan Maguire had not breached his oaths to the Maguire and therefore should receive his son back. Desmond began to mention to Eunan that it may soon be time to go home. Eunan would turn away and secretly curse his mentor, for he wanted to join the army of Hugh Maguire and fight for the survival of the clan.

However, further north, Turlough Luineach O'Neill was far from beaten. He started to hire English mercenaries, and one such mercenary, Captain William Mostian, ex-sheriff of Tirconnell and now mercenary for hire, was sent south to deal with the rebellious Maguires. The Maguire scouts spotted him on the borders with

Tirconnell and word was quickly sent to Enniskillen.

Hugh Maguire wanted to resist and show his support for Hugh O'Neill, but Desmond advised against it, and Cuchonnacht overruled Hugh. When Captain Mostian arrived outside the gates of Enniskillen, the gates were thrown open again, and no resistance was forthcoming.

Captain Mostian quickly made himself at home. He took over Enniskillen Castle, and Cuchonnacht and his entourage retreated to the islands of lower Lough Erne. Hugh Maguire took to the countryside to raise soldiers. Captain Mostian had few troops and was limited to holding Enniskillen and conducting raids across the county. Desmond took Eunan and Arthur and joined Cuchonnacht on Devenish Island.

Devenish Island had a small church and fort as it was the main island hideout of the Maguire and the traditional family burial ground. The island was impossible to attack without resorting to amphibious assault, and the defenders could see for miles across the lake. Captain Mostian had neither the manpower, will power nor experience to mount an attack of that kind, so Cuchonnacht and most of the royal household were free to move around the islands as they wished. The Crannogs of the lower Lough were well-stocked and the forts on the lake well-defended. They just had to wait until Captain Mostian got bored, got recalled or Hugh O'Neill came to the rescue.

Hugh Maguire sent word to Hugh O'Neill and waited for a response. Captain Mostian sat in Enniskillen and tried to send the tribute of the Maguire to Turlough Luineach. But while the Maguire Galloglass still collected from the chieftains of the county, the tribute never left the Crannogs as Captain Mostian could not enforce it. Soon Hugh O'Neill and Cormac MacBaron re-invaded Fermanagh, Hugh Maguire became active again, and Captain Mostian fled. Cuchonnacht came back to Enniskillen from Devenish Island, and the Maguires were back in control once more.

In the meantime, the house of O'Donnell was also having their own war of succession. Donnell O'Donnell, son of Sir Hugh O'Donnell, elder half-brother of Red Hugh O'Donnell, sheriff of Tirconnell and a supporter of Turlough Luineach, had by now gained the ascendancy and was also the nearest O'Donnell power base to the Maguires. The Maguires had owed their allegiance to the O'Donnells before owing it to the O'Neills, and Donnell O'Donnell was keen to resurrect this. He came to Hugh Maguire with an offer he thought he could not refuse.

12

1589 - Enniskillen

1589 was a dark time for the Maguires. While in the previous years they had survived the ebbs and flows of the northern lords' succession wars, this year was different. Cuchonnacht grew frailer by the day. His energy and influence waned. Young men eager for war took up prominent positions in the clan. Hugh Maguire was desperate to become the Maguire and build up his forces, so readily accepted Donnell O'Donnell's offer of patronage. Weapons and Scottish mercenaries began to cross the border.

The potential rebels were encouraged by the news that the English Counter Armada, which had hoped to sow the seeds of rebellion in Portugal and to finish off Spanish sea power, had been a dismal failure and that the Spanish fleet was recovering from the disaster of the 1588 Armada. The promise of a Spanish army was not dead.

As Cuchonnacht faded, Desmond also became a periphery figure. He spent less and less time in Enniskillen, Donnacha O'Cassidy Maguire having taken over the role of the main adviser to the Maguire. The lack of functioning guns hampered the retraining of the MacCabe Galloglass. Donnacha ensured that the blame was laid firmly at Desmond's feet and he was relieved of his position to be replaced by Arlo, who had now befriended Donnacha. As much as Arlo did not trust Donnacha, at least it was not rumoured that he ordered the execution of the remainder of Arlo's comrades in the O'Connor Sligo village.

Desmond concentrated on training Eunan and the local young men in the art of warfare and for recreation would sit by the lake, and when his fishing was disturbed, admire Eunan's axe-throwing abilities without ever letting on what he thought of Eunan's skills. The boy's head inflated too quickly.

One day a sullen messenger arrived for Desmond. Desmond thought nothing of it upon first sight, for messengers seldom brought good news.

"I'm sorry," said the messenger.

Desmond took the letter, and the messenger left. Desmond's heart dropped before he read halfway.

"I must find the boy."

The last of Eunan's hand axes thudded on the centre of the target. Eunan smiled to himself as he was starting to produce the precision and consistency sought. Desmond looked on, his heart a storm for what came next.

"Come over here and sit on the stump beside me, I wish to speak to you," said Desmond as he tried not to appear too serious.

Eunan obeyed, for it was rare that Desmond spoke to him in such a formal manner, except when they were in Enniskillen.

"I know I'm a grumpy old man and can be hard to put up with at the best of times. But I think we've formed a bond and become friends, having overcome the obstacles of my, your, our, personalities!"

"I agree!" Eunan laughed and fiddled with his axes.

"I thought you might! I have a present for you," and Desmond turned and reached behind himself and his hands returned with a large, heavy leather satchel.

Eunan's eyes lit up with delight as he placed the package on his lap and heard the dull thump of leather-wrapped metal.

"Well, open it then!"

Eunan untied the leather straps and unfurled the leather bag. Inside four small pockets were handcrafted throwing axes, decorated with beautiful Celtic designs surrounding the symbol of the Maguire.

"Did you get these made for me?" said Eunan, visibly touched.

"They are specially weighted to make them fly better. When you throw them at someone's head, please try and retrieve them! I went to much trouble to get them made.

"Now you have come of age, a heavy burden will weigh upon your shoulders. I'm afraid I have terrible news for you. Cuchonnacht is dead! You have to fight for Hugh to become the Maguire to ensure the survival of the clan. It is time for you to go home and ensure your father backs Hugh Maguire, and raise some soldiers and fight. The time for old men is over and our time together, unfortunately, is done."

"But I don't want to leave!" said Eunan as he fought back the tears.

"Don't be like that now! You have to be tough! You have a lot of hardship in front of you if you live long enough. Arthur! Bring the boat!"

"Where are you going?"

"To the islands. It is safer there. I fear there is going to be a civil war between Hugh and Connor Roe, or worse, we fall to the English! You must go home and do your duty. Stop Connor Roe, save the Maguire. Arthur has left you a fine steed to bring you home. You are a warrior now. You can beat anyone, be they English, Irish or Galloglass. Goodbye, but if you ever need my help, come to look for me on the islands."

Eunan started to well up, but Desmond was gone. He was already on the lake. Eunan's horse awaited.

13

Return of the Prodigal Son

Eunan was not expecting much, so he got nothing. Not the sun nor wind on his back, the chirping of the spring birds nor firm ground for his horse underfoot greeted his journey. The callous day of his return was frosty, as if even nature was telling Eunan not to return. He rode his horse into the village, as yet untroubled by his presence, and received no warm embrace from family, friend nor neighbour.

His weary head spun, so he decided to see if he could rest in an abandoned house on the outskirts. It was better than going home. He had outgrown the outhouse.

The village looked different, backward compared to cosmopolitan Enniskillen, as if the years had not been kind to it in his absence. Or maybe the village was showing its displeasure of Eunan's return. The burned fields and houses told that the raiding had returned, but the scars did not reveal the perpetrators.

"Hey! Who goes there?" came a voice from the shadows.

Someone had discovered him. The sounds of his horse gave him away.

"Eunan O'Keenan Maguire has returned!" he proudly announced.

"I would've stayed away if I was you! Who wants you here?"

The shadow emerged. It was his uncle Fergus. Eunan never knew why Fergus disliked him so much, but with his newfound experience, he put it down to family rivalry.

"No matter your opinion uncle, I have returned. Is there somewhere I can shelter, as I don't want to disturb my parents?"

"I wouldn't disturb your parents at all. I can give you my outhouse, the pigs might still like you, and you'd do no better with your father. I'll feed you then show you the road. It will be all the O'Keenan Maguire hospitality you'll get!"

"Well, thank you, uncle, for this evening's hospitality nonetheless. We shall judge tomorrow morning when its light shines upon us."

"This way!"

His uncle led him to his house and pointed towards the outhouse.

"Everyone would forgive you if you left before morning!" his uncle said, leaving him. "I wouldn't even disturb your parents by telling them you were ever here!"

"Thank you again, uncle. I will see you again when the sun does shine."

"Heed my warning! Things have gotten a lot worse around here. Food had become scarcer now that the MacMahons have been driven from their lands in Monaghan by the Queen's sheriff. Many of them have come here to Fermanagh. The people are in no mood to be reminded by the likes of you of Galloglass and coin and keep. Trouble follows you here as it has always done. Do us all a favour and be gone at first light. I don't want to see you again!"

Eunan just looked at him.

"As I said before, uncle, thanks for the hospitality nonetheless!"

* * *

83

Eunan awoke and felt for his throwing axes. Today was a day he thought he would be glad of them. They were still beside him. He lay on the straw and tried to plan what he would say to his father, but he got up when words failed him. He dusted himself off and walked into the morning sunshine outside. Nature's beauty had not diminished in his absence, but it all felt hollow to Eunan. He could not wait to leave, to get back to Enniskillen, but he was here to do his duty.

He left the village and made his way up a nearby hill to Senan Leonard Maguire's house. Eunan had heard he had gone home before him.

Upon seeing Eunan, Senan ran out and warmly embraced him.

"Why did you ever come back?" Senan asked. "You were far better off on Enniskillen!"

"I came back to do my duty for Hugh Maguire. I expect you to do the same. Are you ready?"

"Well, yes. But the village is more of a nest of vipers than the court in Enniskillen!"

"Are all the boys here?"

"Yes, they're all back and waiting."

"Well, there's no time like the present!" Eunan marched out towards the village. Senan paused.

"Are you sure?"

"Is anyone? Come on then!" cried Eunan.

* * *

The village had bloomed into life when they returned. Everyone rushed around to prepare for the planting season or to fetch food for their families. No one seemed to recognise or pay much attention to Eunan. He knew where his father would be. Senan went to get the Enniskillen boys.

His father sat fireside, lakeside. It was just as Eunan remembered him, deep in conversation with some of the important men of the village. He had aged considerably; the lines in his face were more pronounced, his belly more rounded and his hair nearly white and his beard not far behind. He looked jaded but could still muster the energy to impose his will on dissenting voices from the village. Eunan did not recognise many of the men around him. There was no sign of Michael O'Flanagan Maguire, who was his father's rival when he left for Enniskillen, or anyone of Michael's ilk.

Eunan stepped forward and stood on the other side of the fire.

"Hello, Father, I have returned!" he boldly announced.

Cathal looked up and recognised him.

"You should have stayed in Enniskillen. You'd have a far better life there."

It was the kindest thing Eunan remembered his father saying.

"Come here, boy and let me bring you to your mother. Then you can leave and go off and lead another life."

Cathal came across to Eunan and started to walk towards the house.

"Father, I am here on a mission. I am here to gain a pledge of loyalty to Hugh Maguire and to raise soldiers in his name!"

"If you did that, you'd probably be dead and me along with you before you got to the road to Enniskillen. This is a frontier village. It is almost too much for me to stop the rival factions from killing each other. As soon as war breaks, this will be the front line."

"The very survival of the Maguires is at stake!"

"My very survival is at stake every day. Cuchonnacht was never a good friend to us. His Galloglass always took too much, stole some of the Maguire's share and then blamed me. The next time the Galloglass came, they would ask for more, so on and so forth. Hugh Maguire is cut from the same cloth, except he wants to start a suicidal war with the English! At best it will be back braking taxes, at worst we all get wiped out.

"Connor Roe is just across the lake and has powerful English allies. If I side with Hugh Maguire, the destruction of the village is my reward at the outbreak of hostilities. If I side with Connor Roe, Hugh will concentrate his attack on the other side of the lake and will be sick of war by the time he turns on us, and will readily accept our surrender. Therefore, while the two leading contenders for the Maguire slog it out, we survive."

"Father, there comes a time to fight and not be a coward. Don't stand in my way when I declare the village for Hugh Maguire!"

"Eunan, go live your life somewhere else and don't sacrifice it for somewhere you've always hated and has always hated you. Now come see your mother, say your goodbyes and then leave!"

They reached the doorway of the house, and Cathal invited him in. His mother was there, sitting in her barrow, her broken spindly legs either side of the wheel. There lay before Eunan a bitter grey old woman, but she still remembered her son.

"What are you doing here? I thought we'd gotten rid of you for good!"

"No, Mother. I have been to the big town and have returned older and wiser. It is now time we all fight for the glory of the Maguires!"

"You just don't get it, do you!? I don't want to explain. I want you to have a happy life so no one will tell you. Your father had protected you from the truth, but if you do this, he may not be able to anymore. Go before you destroy everything!"

"I don't know why you both hate me so, but I'll leave now and won't be back!"

"Leave this place and don't return, but good luck!" his father yelled after him.

Eunan left the house, his heart broken in two. Not even the pebbles would collide for him when he kicked them. He walked towards the centre of the village, only to be disturbed by some jovial voices. He looked up.

Senan had gathered the other boys who had been to Enniskillen. They all smiled at Eunan and showed him their hidden weapons. "We are here now!"

"My father is a coward!" said Eunan. "He still sides with Connor Roe. It is time to stand up for Hugh Maguire against all his enemies. Let's take this village for Hugh Maguire!" exclaimed Eunan as he lifted his axe aloft.

"Let's take this village for Hugh Maguire!" the boys chanted back.

They laughed and made merry as they walked. However, as they walked the men of the village hurried past them.

"Cathal Maguire is about to speak. Raiders are coming!"

"Quick, let's hide until we see who they declare for!" said Eunan.

Eunan grabbed Senan and dragged him behind a house.

"I will go into the crowd and see what my father says. You hide with the boys and jump out at the right time."

"How will I know…"

"You will know."

Eunan left to hide amongst the houses nearest the centre circle.

14

Death and Banishment

An eerie sun illuminated the fog floating on the lake. Gossip flowed through the village that Cathal O'Keenan Maguire had something important to say. The men came from the fields or across the lake to gather in the village. Women and children peered over their shoulders on the periphery.

Cathal marched from his house surrounded by some burly men, most of whom Eunan recognised. Michael O'Flanagan Maguire gathered at the edge of the circle with several men, half of whom Eunan did not remember. Eunan reckoned they were displaced MacMahons from Monaghan or renegade O'Reillys from down south, both fleeing surrender and regrant. The crowd felt very uneasy. Cathal and his scrum of men forced their way into the centre of the circle, and his men carved out space from which Cathal could address the crowd.

Senan and the other Enniskillen boys hid on the outskirts of the circle. However, they had a sudden bout of nerves.

"If we're going to do this, I need a drink. Old man O'Keenan Maguire isn't known for his short speeches!" said one.

The other boys nodded in agreement, and they went off to find some ale.

Eunan crouched behind some baskets at the side of a house. He made sure he was within axe-throwing distance of his father. He concealed his hand from prying eyes as he reached to his belt for his throwing axes. The remaining villagers started to rush to the circle as Cathal began to speak.

"Villagers, you may have heard that Cuchonnacht is dead and the succession for the Maguire has begun! We have always tried to steer clear of getting involved in inter-clan warfare, but some young usurpers have come into our midst to declare the village for Hugh Maguire..."

Michael O'Flanagan Maguire and his men began to force their way through the crowd.

"This village will not change who we support in clan Maguire..."

Eunan reached into his leather pouch and carefully selected his most trusted axe from Desmond's gift set. The blade was beautifully polished, the haft as smooth as silk, and she flew as straight as an arrow – any error would be the fault of the thrower. He trusted this axe with his life to swiftly end the lives of others. The axe quivered in his hand as he contemplated his next move.

"...while I'm still alive!" continued Cathal.

Eunan kissed the face of the axe.

"Fly straight and true!" he whispered to her.

Eunan stood on a block of wood he had gotten to give him sufficient height to get the axe over the crowd. He flung the axe and crouched down behind the basket again. A tear fell from his eye.

Michael O'Flanagan Maguire stuck his hand beneath his coat and pulled out his axe. He leapt towards Cathal Maguire, axe flailing. Cathal Maguire froze and was covered in the spray of blood, brains and bone as the head of Michael O'Flanagan Maguire disintegrated beneath a beautifully polished axe of the Maguire. Michael fell onto Cathal's feet, staining Cathal's clothes with blood. Michael's supporters fled. Cathal's supporters ran to see if he was okay. Eunan looked up over the basket and saw the huddled crowd and the shrieks of mourning. He could not see his friends leaping to seize the moment. He went to look for them.

A man ran through the village with a heavy burden on his breath.

"They're coming! They're coming!" he cried to whomever he came across.

Nobody stayed to ask who. Eunan put down his axe and looked south. Horsemen rode straight for the centre circle of the village and made for Cathal. Cathal had not time to pull his weapon nor the axe from Michael O'Flanagan's head.

Cathal stood in the circle. A handful of his supporters stood behind him. An English mercenary, who they recognised as a former sheriff, sat on his horse before them and spat on the ground. His horsemen gathered behind him.

"Are you a Mac or an Oe?" snarled the English captain.

"Maguires are neither Macs nor Oes!"

"Who's your dead friend? Are you Irish having a bit of a tiff? Can't decide which Maguire to support?"

"State your business or leave! My men will be here soon!"

"You and your couple of friends are audacious thinking we're not going to shoot you where you stand. We're here on behalf of the Queen and her supporter, Connor Roe. Who's that you've just killed?"

"I've killed no one!" exclaimed Cathal.

"Oh, the brave liar. You stand before me covered in blood with a man with an axe in his head at your feet. I presume you're Cathal Maguire?"

"The very same."

The foot soldiers of the English mercenary started to enter the village.

"Now we always had you down as a Connor Roe man. Is that correct?"

"I've always supported Connor Roe in any clan dealings where I was required to choose."

"Very good. Now how did this man come to die?"

Before Cathal had a chance to reply, a chant came towards the centre circle from the village.

"We're going to take this town for Hugh Maguire! Hail Hugh Maguire!"

Eunan's friends had found their courage in alcohol.

"So that's how he died?" exclaimed the English Captain.

"No! No! No! You've got it all wrong! I'm a loyal supporter of Connor Roe! Come on, look at the blood! It's all over me because he died beside me! Someone threw the axe, probably to defend me from him!"

The shouts for Hugh Maguire grew ever closer and louder. A glint on the axe caught the eye of the English Captain. He turned to one of his foot soldiers who had started to gather behind him.

"Bring me that axe and be quick about it!"

The man ran over and pulled the axe from Michael's head.

"It's got the symbol of the Maguire on the axe, sir. Looks a pretty fancy axe to me!"

"Show me!"

The Captain took one look at the symbol on the axe, before drawing his gun and shooting Cathal in the face. Cathal flew backwards, his face disintegrating into a mass of burnt flesh and lead.

Eunan almost threw up in his hiding place.

The English Captain rode into the centre of the circle. His entourage of ten Irish horsemen stood behind him while he unrolled his papers.

"By order of the Queen, we represent the sheriff of Monaghan. We are here to take all cattle we believe stolen from the sheriff for use by her majesty's army for how they see fit. The Maguire also owes the Queen money, and we're here to collect. We will crush any resistance with brute force. Fetch the cattle and kill anyone who resists. Also, go find who's singing that stupid song about Hugh Maguire and kill them."

Some soldiers ran down the road towards Eunan's friends, and the rest of them started to raid the village, systematically searching every house for any valuables they could steal and rounding up all the livestock. They killed anyone that got in their way. Eunan ran to warn his friends.

Senan and his friend marched down the street towards the circle, laughing and chanting as they went. They dismissed the villagers fleeing from the circle as 'cowards' and started to sing the praises of Eunan O'Keenan Maguire and how he should lead the village instead of his treacherous father.

In the meantime, several boat loads of Galloglass rowed across the lake to the village. They drew their swords and axes, leapt into the shallow water and waded ashore. They ran and grabbed the nearest woman they could.

"Where's the boy?"

"What boy?!"

"Don't make me kill you!"

"Oh. Oh! He hasn't lived here for years!"

"Where's Cathal Maguire?"

"In the village square. That way!"

The Galloglass threw her aside and marched towards the village square.

The English soldiers made their way towards the shouts for Hugh Maguire. Senan and his friends stopped. The English soldiers were in front of them, blocking their way. They looked at each other and then at the English soldiers.

"This is it, boys!" said Senan. "Come on, boys! Charge for Hugh Maguire!"

"HUGH MAGUIRE!"

The English soldiers lifted their muskets and in a puff of smoke, where once stood Eunan's friends now lay a tangle of bodies, as their lives drained into the soil.

Eunan bit his lip. A line of blood rolled down his chin. His hands formed fists, and his nails dug into the palm of his hands so hard they also drew blood. He cursed himself for his cowardice in the face of his friends' bravery. But what now? His father was dead. His friends were killed, and the place was crawling with English soldiers. He grabbed a battle-axe from a fallen village soldier. What to do next? Save his mother! Eunan ran towards his father's house. But between himself and the house were English soldiers ransacking the village.

A hand hooked his elbow from behind. His raised his axe to release himself from the grip, but it was his uncle Fergus.

"Don't be a fool all your life! Get on your horse and tell Hugh Maguire. It'll do your mother no good to have a dead son and a dead husband on the same day. Go! I'll take care of her. Return swiftly!"

Eunan bade his uncle farewell. He changed direction ran towards the lake shore, for he knew he could find a horse there. The sheriff and his men were going berserk by now, running down villagers and shooting them in the back. Those who could were running towards the sanctuary of the woods. None of them got there. Eunan made his way around the backs of the houses attempting to evade the sheriff and his men.

Suddenly his neighbour ran in front of him from between two houses. She tripped on an overturned basket and fell to the ground. Behind her came the bulk of a horse, belonging to the sheriff's men. With a tug of the reins, the horse's hooves came down upon the woman. Eunan was incensed. With a flash of his axe blade, the horse was felled.

But the axe was trapped under the body. Eunan grabbed for one his throwing axes, and the sheriff's man staggered up from under his horse's saddle and drew his gun. Eunan hesitated. What if he missed? The man's finger hit the trigger. From behind the man, an axe fell and swiped his arm straight off.

"I told you to run!" cried Eunan's uncle as he stood over the man to finish him off.

Eunan ran. He turned when he heard a gunshot and saw his uncle fall as another of the sheriff's men shot him from behind. He ran down to the shoreline and sure enough, near his father's house were some horses tied to a post. Eunan noticed the Galloglass down by the shore but was too busy freeing the horse to see whose side they were on. He jumped on top of the horse and dug his heels into his horse's side, fighting back tears.

He rode through the centre of the village, for that was the most direct way. He thought of Desmond and what he would do. He rode through to the centre circle and saw his throwing axe on the ground. He pulled up his horse and got down to retrieve the axe.

"What are you doing, you Mac scum!" came a voice.

Eunan instinctively reached to his belt and turned and threw the axe towards the sound of the voice. It was the first time he killed a man up close. He retrieved both his axes, remounted his horse and fled.

15

The MacSheehys

Eunan rode as far away from his village as he could, until both he and his horse were exhausted. He stopped, dismounted and gave her a rest, while he looked back through the hills. A plume of smoke dissolved into the sky. Then to the right, he saw another plume of smoke, and to the right of that again, another. He didn't know what happened in his village, but the burden of being their last hope lay heavy upon his shoulders. All he knew was he must ride to Enniskillen and get the Maguire. His village, his family were relying upon him.

It was a day's ride, and there were many stragglers along the route searching out the sanctuary of Enniskillen or venturing further north to seek the protection of the O'Donnells. They were mainly women and children with some lightly armed men who would be no match for the English mercenaries. Eunan did not stop for anyone. He kept on riding, only pausing to rest and water his horse.

The road eventually went through a forest. The horse slowed to a trot for the path was stony, and the last thing Eunan needed was a lame horse. Eunan rounded a corner, and before him, a felled tree blocked his path. A man, bareheaded but dressed in the chain mail of a Galloglass, stood in his way with his axe drawn across his shoulder, ready to strike.

"Where did you get that axe boy?" he demanded.

Eunan reached for one of his throwing axes.

"I wouldn't do that if I were you," came a voice.

Eunan looked around, and three archers had their arrows pointed at his bare head.

"Throw your axe to the ground and get off your horse slowly," the voice commanded.

Eunan obeyed. Once off his horse with his hands raised, the men removed the back axe from its holster and his belt laden with throwing axes.

"I need them, keep them safe," Eunan barked at the thought of being parted from his axes.

"Oh, we will," said the man with a smirk, as he shoved Eunan in the back to get him moving.

"I have little money, but you can have it. I'm a local lad, and someone will miss me. If you give me back my possessions and let me on my way, we'll say no more about this."

"Quiet lad! There's someone we'd like you to meet."

The men brought him to a campsite in a little clearing some distance from the road. There were more men there, all in various states of dress and battle readiness. They had the chain mail, helmets and axes of the Galloglass but they appeared to have fallen on hard times. Beyond the men was another camp with women and children. There were some animals there, the odd cow, but both human and animal looked skinny and not well kept. The men brought Eunan to the tent of their constable, the leader of their Galloglass sept.

Eunan stood in front of the constable, doing his best not to appear afraid. The constable was older than the rest, dressed in his chain mail with his worn, grey beard. He seemed to be jaded, as if kindness had abandoned his soul many years before.

"So what have we got here then?" the man asked.

"We found him wandering in the woods," one of the captors replied.

"I wasn't wandering, I was…"

"You were what? Are you an English spy?"

Eunan spat on the ground.

"If you are the sheriff's men, just kill me now just like you killed my family."

"We're not the sheriff's men, but if all your family are dead, you're of little use to us. There's no ransom money for orphans. Give us a reason not to kill you," replied the leader.

"You don't look like bandits," replied Eunan. "You wear the battle dress of Galloglass."

"Who's to say we're not bandits and we just killed the Galloglass and stole their armour?"

"Bandits couldn't do that. What clan are you? Who are your masters?"

"We have no masters, and you talk a lot like an English spy. I'll ask you one last time, why should we not rip out your tongue and roast your body over our fire?"

"You are here because you think war is coming?"

"War always seeks the Galloglass out. Death or glory, or if we're lucky we get paid before we have to make that choice!"

"I can get you permanent employment with the Maguire!"

"And who are you to have such a brag?"

"I am the son of Cathal O'Keenan Maguire!"

The constable flinched.

"Never heard of him! Anyone ever heard of him? You told us your family were dead, so I assume you're lying. Take out his tongue."

The men began to drag him away.

"No, no! Wait! I am the son of Cathal Maguire. If you come to our village, he will pay you. We need protection from the English sheriff. Hugh Maguire is his cousin. War is coming, and there is plenty of land to pillage and steal!"

"Why should I believe you?"

"Have you got a better offer? If you did, you wouldn't be hiding in the forests!"

"We're not hiding!"

"Well, you're certainly not gainfully employed."

The leader considered Eunan's offer.

"We'll go to your village, and if we don't get paid, we'll kill you instead. How does that sound?"

"My ears will ring with your gratitude when you are handsomely employed. Are you going to release me now, your talisman of good fortune?"

"You talk yourself up so much I don't know which I'd prefer: to kill you or to take all the riches you say you have on offer! Release him! What is your name, boy, so I can get all your promises written down for my amusement! Get the priest! Get the priest! I have a contract to make! Bard! Bard! Strum a song that laments me as a hero, one here to free this green, fair land from your oppressive English overlords while I strike a bargain with this young man so that he may win his freedom! Sit, sit by the fire and let us make this contract."

Eunan sat by the fire. Someone gave him some food and ale. He nodded his head in appreciation before tucking into his meal, for he was famished. The leader sat beside him.

"Priest, priest, come and sit down. We have a bargain to make. Now it is between, Eunan Maguire if I remember correctly?"

"You do."

"And me Seamus MacSheehy."

"I've heard of you."

"Good. My reputation precedes me. Then you will know that I am expensive!"

Eunan smiled in response. The priest scribbled.

"Now, how many heads of cattle does your village have?"

"About twenty."

"So your plan for your village is to swap oppression by the English for famine? How do I know your father will keep such a bargain?"

"How many warriors do you have?"

"I have to pay each of my men a cow. They're risking their lives you know!"

"The Maguire will pay you handsomely for protecting his subjects."

"Are we back to ripping out your tongue so soon? Have you so little to bargain with?"

"If my father cannot pay you the Maguire will. He is an honourable man!"

"Which one of these men is the honourable one? I have buried so many of my kinsmen fighting for 'honourable men'! Look at me now! You say I am in the forest waiting for gainful employment. I am here because of non-payment by so-called 'honourable men'. All my wealth is my men. If I throw their lives away fighting for 'honourable men' with nothing to show for it, their wives and children starve. It looks like all we have to exchange with each other is whose group of siblings dies of starvation. And there we are, back to ripping out your tongue again!"

Eunan blurted out the first thing that came into his mind.

"If my father doesn't pay you, then I will go into your service."

"But you would already be in my service; I would be entertained by watching you getting your tongue ripped out."

"I would provide you with far better service as a warrior!"

"So, I suppose you can start entertaining me now. If you can beat one of my warriors in single combat, then I will take you up on your offer. Finn, would you do the honours please?"

A young warrior, who looked slightly older but smaller than Eunan, stepped forward.

"Try not to kill him," said Seamus. "I'm talking to him, not you Eunan."

"What are the weapons?" asked Eunan.

"Axes, of course! We are Galloglass!"

Another of the Galloglass stepped forward and offered each of them an axe.

"Can I have my own?" Eunan asked.

Seamus nodded his approval.

"Fight!"

The Galloglass formed a circle around the combatants and cheered Finn on. Finn circled Eunan, trying to corner him, jabbing with his axe. Finn unleashed a semi-circular swing. Eunan dodged out of the way.

"Try and leave him in one piece, Finn. We may get a couple of cows for him yet!" said Seamus.

Finn jabbed some more and his comrades stepped back to form a funnel Finn could trap Eunan in. Finn swung his axe from right to left. Eunan kicked him in the knee and hit him in the cheek with the butt of his axe handle. Finn went down like a sack of potatoes. He pleaded for mercy with Eunan's axe blade on his neck. The circle of comrades parted and Seamus stepped in.

"You've done this before. As much as I hate to see my men beaten, spare him, for I only have twenty. Finn can be a scout until he earns his place back."

"I won, so why don't I become the Galloglass, and he the horse boy?"

"You're so sure of yourself! I'll tell you what. We'll take you as an apprentice Galloglass, and Finn can be an apprentice Galloglass horse boy."

Finn's face was a mask of fury.

"However, Finn gets the opportunity to challenge you once a month. If he wins, he becomes a Galloglass again."

"And what happens to him?" growled Finn, who had by now gotten to his feet

"That depends on how many cattle and how much land he can get for us. Now, firstly Father Padraig will finish writing our agreement, then let us all get some sleep, for tomorrow we head for Eunan's village."

16

Return to the Village

The next day fifteen Galloglass set out for Eunan's village with five left behind to guard the women and children. They rode two by two with Eunan and Seamus at the front, with Finn demoted to scout. Finn pointed to the numerous plumes of smoke on the horizon before them.

"It looks like the sheriff has been busy," said Seamus to Eunan.

Eunan bowed his head and dug his heels into his horse's side.

They met various stragglers along the road who told tales of the English pillaging and destruction. Eunan became even more downhearted.

"I've seen this all before, the same old pattern," said Seamus.

"How so?" replied Eunan.

"We are veterans of the Desmond rebellions in the 1570s and 1580s. Put down by the usual band of English, their mercenaries and Irish traitors like the O'Neills. We fought for the Desmonds. We were the pride of his Galloglass. Only to be defeated with help from Irish traitors. I'll never forget that, and neither should you. A friend is a friend as long as you have enough cows and land to pay him with."

"You must know the O'Neills are the power around here. Only the

O'Donnells can challenge them. But you've come to the right place if you are looking to get hired for war. It never ends, but it's hard to remember who's on whose side."

"Well, we heard about the MacMahons getting cleared out of Monaghan, and we reckoned the Maguires were next," said Seamus.

"Why fight for a losing cause? Everyone else you have fought for has lost?"

"The English have always been our sworn enemies, right back to our Scottish forefathers. Some have succumbed to the English shilling, but we've always remained faithful to the Galloglass code."

"Albeit for whichever Irish lord paid the most."

"Don't get too cheeky lad. Your father still has to come up with the cattle you promised us. We were on retainer with the Desmonds, their best men! Technically mercenaries but name me a soldier who isn't?!"

"Me!"

Seamus laughed.

"It's great you can retain your sense of humour with the bleak days ahead! Your village should be coming up soon, shouldn't it?"

Eunan just looked at him.

"It's just beyond the next hill, beside the lake."

* * *

They rounded the hill, and the devastation of the village hit them in the face. The houses were smouldering ruins, the dead people and animals littered the ground, and all the boats were either taken or destroyed.

"Not a cow in sight," sighed Seamus, but he was silent when he saw the reaction on Eunan's face.

He wasn't quite that cold-hearted; not when he still had hope of being paid. Eunan leapt from his horse and ran into the village. He went straight to his mother's house. Seamus gave Finn the nod to follow him.

The burnt embers of Eunan's former home lay at his feet. He searched through the rubble, and the charred remains surrounding it. He found what he assumed to be his uncle's blackened body and the horse of the mercenary's man he had taken down. He searched around the back of his house and found the wooden stump he used to chop wood. There was no sign of his mother. He found carbonised wood that resembled her chair. A piece of her blanket. But not a body. He went to the centre of the village to find his father's corpse.

The centre of the village was full of bodies, some intact and some burned. He could not identify any particular one to be that of his father. Finn caught up with Eunan and offered to help him look. Eventually, they found someone who was still alive. It was Padraig O'Dwyer Maguire, a man who had lived on the outskirts of the village. He often used to combine with Eunan's father and uncle to trade with other villages or make the weekly or monthly trade trip to Enniskillen, depending upon the season. Padraig raised his head and croaked for water.

"Where are my mother and father?" asked Eunan.

"The well, look down the well…" And with that, Padraig was gone. Eunan lay his head gently on the ground.

"Goodbye my sweet friend," he said before running off to the well with Finn.

The well was outside the village, bedside the forest. The hut beside the well was still intact. There were no outward signs of violence. Eunan and Finn crept towards the well, wary of who might be lurking at the edge of the forest. Finn kept watch as Eunan looked down the well. It was deep and dark and sucked Eunan down into an emotional swirl. Finn picked up some stones.

"Here, throw these down and listen for the splash of water."

Eunan obeyed. No splash met the falling stone.

"I think the old man was right," said Finn, putting his hand on his friend's shoulder.

Eunan broke down and cried until his bitter tears seeped into the ground.

"Come on, we've got to go."

Finn started to walk away. But all Eunan could think of was all the pain and heartache he had put his parents through in his life, and when they needed him the most, he was not there to defend them.

Finn ran back and grabbed him by the arm.

"Come on, let's go! The English will be here soon with their lackeys. Come on!"

They returned to the entrance to the village where Seamus and the other Galloglass were waiting for them.

"Poor pickings here today, boy!" said Seamus and Eunan just ignored him. "So how are we going to get paid? I haven't seen any cows today. As handy as you are with an axe, it isn't going to feed my men. So what is your suggestion before we start to live off the land?"

Eunan bit his lip. Then he remembered something his father told him, the cause of all his strife.

"The new Maguire is getting inaugurated near Lisnaskea. If we leave now, we may be able to make it there on time. All his chiefs and allies should be there. If we are going to get gainfully employed anywhere, it will be there. But we need to set off now."

"That's music to my ears. Shall we depart?"

17

The Feast

Eunan and the MacSheehy Galloglass set off for Lisnaskea and the traditional inauguration site of the Maguires. Wind nor rain nor bog underfoot could not slow them down, for Seamus smelt money. Eunan, as the provider of the opportunities for wealth, was never allowed to wander out of Seamus' sight. A plot had hatched in Seamus' mind, an inauguration born and a contract signed. Eunan was now the O'Keenan Maguire.

The pressure of being the O'Keenan Maguire weighted heavily on his shoulders. An O'Keenan Maguire with no O'Keenan Maguires. His new mentor may have an answer, or at least provide some solace.

"What am I to tell the future Maguire of who I am? I have no battle honours to brag about, no people who follow and look up to me, no cattle to feed my people. I am nothing, nothing but saddle sore."

"In that you are wrong. One thing that buys you respect, especially when war is in the air, is muscle. You have us, your Galloglass. There will be chieftains at Lisnaskea with fields full of cows, villages full of people but they will have no Galloglass, and the Maguire will turn his nose up at them. But when you show up there, you will have your name and your Galloglass, and nobody will care about cattle or peasants. They'll be too busy thinking about the war and what they can gain, or how long they will stay alive for, or who could potentially want to kill them."

Eunan was perplexed.

"How come you know so much?"

"I have served many, many chieftains, good and bad, lofty lords and low-down landowners, and seen much death and many, many wars."

Seamus smiled at Eunan, and Eunan gazed out to the road ahead and tried to picture his destiny, be it good or bad; a lofty lord, or dead in a ditch. But Eunan's bout of nerves would not end. Seamus was tired of the boy's melancholy as he knew the boy would have to act big to gain the respect of the upper echelons of the Maguires. They passed through a forest, and at a suitable knoll, Seamus leapt from his horse and ordered the column to stop.

"Go stand up on that rock, boy!"

Seamus searched around for a suitable stick and a smooth stone. The Galloglass got down from their horses and gathered beneath the rock. Seamus climbed up behind Eunan.

"Take these!" Seamus placed the stick in one hand and the rock in the other.

"On this rock, I now anoint you...Oh, I need some water!"

Finn threw up his water container. Seamus opened it and threw the contents at Eunan.

"I now anoint you the O'Keenan Maguire!" he gestured to his Galloglass.

"Hurray!"

"As per our previously signed contract, you agree to pay us for our support, and you delegate all decision-making, military or otherwise to me. In turn, you become the O'Keenan Maguire."

"But I have no people to lead?"

"What do you call them?" Seamus pointed down to the Galloglass who laughed below. "Don't insult your followers as your first act of becoming chieftain! Oh, yes, I forgot something."

Seamus grabbed Eunan by the shoulders and spun him around.

"Don't forget who you are! Don't forget who you are!"

Eunan was so dizzy he fell to the ground.

"Don't lose your rock! Put it in your pocket. That is the lucky rock of the O'Keenan Maguire!"

The Galloglass laughed, and Seamus climbed down and got back on his horse.

"In your own time chieftain! We've got the main event inauguration to go to!"

* * *

They travelled for two days, over bogs, through forests and, if they were lucky, roads in the right direction, until they came to the Enniskillen / Lisnaskea road. They were slowed down mainly by the lack of discipline of the Galloglass who slipped off to steal food or cause mischief at the first sign of temptation. Seamus did not try and stop them, for he knew his men were hungry and needed to be at their best for what was ahead.

They followed Eunan since he knew the path well; his father had brought him to Lisnaskea on several occasions in his youth when gatherings of the Maguires were called, or sometimes to the regional markets. Eunan had wanted to take a boat across the lake. However, Seamus had insisted on travelling overland as he considered that they needed to bring all of their equipment to look impressive for the upper echelons of clan Maguire, and also to protect themselves if they got attacked.

There were many war parties on the road to Lisnaskea who eyed each other nervously, for they could not tell who was in the pay of the crown or which Maguire. All chiefs and warriors were battle-ready, all fearing an ambush – especially those who were loyal to Hugh Maguire.

Eunan and his band of warriors had the market town of Lisnaskea in their sights, and Seamus stopped his men in the forest before the town so that they could clean and refresh themselves, in order to look their best before parading into town. However, Eunan doubted whether such efforts were worthwhile as the town was probably already full of soldiers and mercenaries and nobody would pay them much attention. Seamus ignored him as he most often did if he did not need him, and ordered his men to ride into town two-by-two, led by himself and Eunan.

Lisnaskea town, the traditional home of the Lisnaskea Maguires, was dwarfed by the backdrop of Castle Skea, the home of Connor Roe Maguire. The Lisnaskea Maguires were from the traditional senior branch of the family and the Enniskillen Maguires the junior branch. While Connor Roe nestled comfortably in the pocket of the English, the fact that outside Lisnaskea was the traditional inauguration ground of the Maguire meant that the inauguration had to happen there. If the Maguire were not inaugurated there, the inevitable challenges to the new Maguire's legitimacy would inevitably follow, so it was worth the risk to hold the ceremony there.

The town was full of makeshift ale houses and market stalls run by local opportunistic farmers trying to cash in on the influx of visitors keen to show their generosity and wealth. Once Seamus saw all the alehouses, he rode at the back of his entourage to keep their attention on the task at hand, while also inflating the importance of Eunan O'Keenan Maguire.

Connor Roe Maguire's Galloglass stopped them when they approached the castle. Seamus and his men had reached the point beyond which only the Maguire clan chiefs, their important guests and select bodyguards were allowed to go. Seamus recognised that the Galloglass were MacCabes, the traditional elite troops of the Maguires. The Lisnaskea Maguires employed a specific branch of the MacCabe family and the MacCabes had been granted lands in the region for their services. The MacSheehy Galloglass were invited to camp on the outskirts of the town while Eunan was allowed to take Seamus as his bodyguard when he returned to enter the castle.

Villages of tents surrounded Lisnaskea. A small cluster for each of the Maguire nobility and their followers and soldiers. The cluster size depended on the person's importance. The most significant clusters were those of dignitaries invited from other clans. It was a time to make alliances both in the county Maguire and the counties beyond. Eunan and his entourage of Galloglass pitched their tents at the edge of the southern tent village. The Galloglass were left behind under strict instructions to behave themselves. Temptation lay not too far away. The favourite for the title of the Maguire had brought a herd of cattle and set them to graze nearby in anticipation of the alliances he had to pay for, and the debts he had to pay off, to fulfil his ambition, not to mention the abundance of alehouses.

The centre of the village had been cleared of citizens and surrounded by a ring of MacCabe Galloglass with their beautiful chain mail and polished hooked axes – evidence that they worked for the regional power. Everyone who entered the inner circle was disarmed and allowed only one unarmed bodyguard.

The MacCabes and the MacSheehys had a long-running feud; so long-running that no one could remember how it started. They usually did not stop and pause to remember before swords were drawn. They had been, like all Scottish houses of Galloglass, on different sides in the many conflicts of Ireland but also sometimes the same side.

Eunan and Seamus approached the guards.

"Only Maguire kin with voting rights or invited dignitaries allowed past here. There're no bearing arms. State who you are and declare your intentions!"

Eunan stepped forward and began to remove his throwing axes from his belt.

"Eunan O'Keenan Maguire, son of the deceased Cathal O'Keenan Maguire of the Knockinny Maguires. Claiming voting rights for the O'Keenan Maguire sept."

"Go to that house over there and see the priest." The Galloglass pointed to a large hut, and looked Seamus squarely in the eye.

"And who may you be?"

Seamus embraced the merest sniff of a fight.

"I'm the chief's bodyguard, and where he goes, I go."

Another MacCabe came and stood between them.

"Not with that, you're not. Leave the sword here, and you can collect it when you leave."

Seamus spitefully undid his sword and his belt with scabbard attached fell to the ground.

"I think I know you," said the first Galloglass.

"That's 'cos I'm pretty, just like all the proper Scottish Galloglass!"

The other Galloglass stood between them again.

"Follow your master, and we'll try not to piss on your sword."

"That sword is as good for scooping oysters as it is for chopping the balls off gutless, so-called Galloglass. It'll be perfect for chopping your little balls off if you put your cocks anywhere near my sword."

"Follow your master there and hold your tongue, or else he'll be looking for a new bodyguard!"

After a swift rude gesture, Seamus caught up with Eunan.

"You've got to stand up to these pretend warriors or they get too cocky. And if they get too cocky, their master will ask for compensation when he finds two corpses!"

Eunan ignored him.

"I'm worried, Seamus. What if they find out I'm a fraud and all the villagers are dead, and that it was my fault!"

"As I have told you before, it's a war, you have twenty Galloglass, and that's worth a lot."

"But how do I pay you?"

"You don't worry about that. You get me in, and I'll get plenty of payment enough."

They entered the hut and here sat a priest bent over some papers with a quill. He raised his head.

"What brings you here? I heard that Cathal O'Keenan Maguire was dead," said the priest.

"He is, I am his son, and I inherited his title," replied Eunan.

"Was elected into his title!" interjected Seamus. "My men and I all voted for him."

The priest ignored Seamus.

"My condolences to you, I hope your father has a swift journey to heaven."

The priest looked down and examined his papers.

"So you are lucky enough to have inherited your title just before another war. Long may you enjoy the fruits of your father's labour. But now it is time to defend your clan. What can you contribute to the efforts of the Maguire?"

"I bring twenty Galloglass."

"The harvests over by the Cladagh River must be good, for my records have your lands as being bogs and forest and sparsely populated, and you don't look like a man of means," said the priest.

"He is a great warrior, a master of the axe and the best cattle rustler I've ever known," said Seamus. "Hugh Maguire himself would be proud to have such a warrior ride along with him."

Eunan signalled to him to be quiet. Seamus didn't take it well.

"He also volunteers to help the Maguire consolidate his power, if you know what I mean. If the Maguire doesn't get voted in unanimously."

The priest glanced at Seamus.

"I have noted your request and will pass it on. There is a great call for a person of your skills at this time."

Seamus smiled at Eunan's scowl.

"The feast will begin at sundown, and the voting will be after that. Your fellow chiefs are in the great hall, should you wish to converse with them before voting commences. I suggest you speak to Hugh Maguire and court his favours. You should be able to obtain much gainful employment."

"I think we will, won't we Eunan? Where is this hall you speak of, and when is the ale served?"

"The guards will show you, and you will have as much ale as you desire. However, I would keep your wits about you and watch your backs."

"This just gets better and better. Ale, a fight and plenty of profit. Good luck, priest. I'm sure you will be very busy crossing off the names of the dead from your book while we bear arms to protect you!"

"Look after yourself, Eunan," replied the priest ignoring Seamus again.

The guards pointed them in the direction of the castle and the Great Hall, but the destination was obvious.

The MacCabe Galloglass lined the streets on the way to the great hall. Interlopers approached from both sides of the street and engaged in probing conversation to find the person of influence and an indication of which way they were likely to vote.

"And who may you be?" said a nobleman dressed in a red cape to Eunan.

"Who are you?" grunted Seamus as he stood in front of his master.

"Please, I am addressing the Lord."

113

The nobleman turned to Eunan. Eunan immediately recognised him but said nothing for fear of being outed as an impostor. Donnacha did not recognise him.

"I am a representative of Hugh Maguire. You may have heard of his exploits fighting the English?"

"I have."

"Well, he wants your vote, wants you to join him and also to know what you can bring to the fight. What part of the family are you from?"

"O'Keenan Maguire, and I've got twenty Galloglass."

"Oh, really? Wait, do I..." and Donnacha put his arm around Eunan's shoulder.

"Really," replied Seamus, who parted the two men. "And his Galloglass need something to do and get paid. Who around here do we need to talk to in order to strike a bargain?"

"You can talk to me. Once you have voted for Hugh Maguire, we can talk about serving the Maguire's cause."

"My own cause is a bit more pressing. Now, how about you make us an offer before we look around and talk to the other candidates?"

"The Maguire will have created a few enemies along the way to getting elected. But he will still need their support for the upcoming war. He will need some loyal, trustworthy men to visit some of his clan for him."

"For a fixed rate that we can negotiate, and for whatever extra payments that may come our way depending on what level of persuasions we need to employ, you may have a deal."

"As long as your master votes for Hugh Maguire there will be plenty of work for men with your special talents. Come and ask for me, Donnacha O'Cassidy Maguire."

Seamus slapped Eunan on both shoulders.

"Do you hear that? You have sorted us out already. All you have to do is vote for Hugh Maguire, my men and I get paid, you get trained as a Galloglass, and we get to kill Hugh Maguire's enemies for fun! You can even throw your little axes at them!"

"How do I know I want to vote for Hugh Maguire? Should I not talk to the other candidates first?"

Seamus gave him a friendly pat on the face.

"One of the things I like about you is your sense of humour! You wouldn't want to stand in between your Galloglass and a good payday, would you?"

Seamus turned to Hugh Maguire's emissary.

"What's your name again so we can meet up afterwards?"

"Donnacha O'Cassidy Maguire. Don't worry. I will come and find you after the vote."

They waved goodbye to Donnacha as he rushed off to another newly arrived chief who had been intercepted by a rival fixer.

Eunan and Seamus reached the entrance to the castle. Its rounded towers which loomed overhead impressed Eunan. Seamus, by force of habit, made a note of how many arrows were trained on them from the towers and castle walls and how they could make their escape if need be. Two Galloglass standing in the entrance parted their axes, and they entered. Eunan was surprised Seamus did not try to insult them.

"They're the good ones. They guard the lord. I may have a big mouth, but I'm not stupid."

The courtyard was surrounded by soldiers and filled with the gossiping nobility of the Maguire. It was not long until they were all invited to join Connor Roe and the other influential guests in the main hall. Seamus hooked Eunan by the elbow, for he did not want to lose him in the crowd.

They made their way into the Great Hall, but both Seamus and Eunan had been in greater. A throng of people created a din harsh on the ears of a country boy from a small village. Seamus and Eunan slipped down the sides of the room until they could find a sufficient observation point. Seamus watched the men and Eunan stood back and observed the walls of the hall.

The colourful war banners of the various septs of the Maguire clan draped from the ceilings. It was impressive, but nothing like Enniskillen. Three long tables parallel to each other dominated the hall, and an overarching raised head table at the top overlooked the others.

Hugh Maguire stood at the top table and puffed his chest out to make himself look important. Eunan remembered him as an arrogant boy, but everyone made mistakes when they were boys. It looked like he had not learned from his. He had made an effort for today's vote, looking every inch the future Maguire; richly dressed but still a warrior, his arrogant smile deployed to charm lesser chieftains votes whose peoples were squeezed between himself and Connor Roe.

It was also the first time that Eunan laid eyes on Connor Roe, the man who had played the devil in the background for most of his life. The man he held responsible for his father's death. Connor Roe had undoubtedly made an effort, decked out in the most elegant imported clothes from England. Eunan could smell his pitch from where he stood, prosperity, the English coin. It worked on some, for there was a queue of chieftains waiting to speak to him.

Seamus did his own assessment of the candidates for the Maguire, nodded to Eunan, and they tried to make their way through the crowd to the top table. They were accosted en route.

"Hey, where are you from? I haven't seen you before?" said a well-dressed man who stood in their way.

"Unless you've got a good offer, get out of our way. We're voting for Hugh Maguire," replied Seamus.

"The Lisnaskea Maguires can offer you cattle!"

"How many?" said Seamus, grabbing Eunan and stopping to listen.

"How many warriors do you have?"

"Twenty Galloglass."

"Forty cattle!"

"I can steal them off you when Hugh Maguire kills of his enemies! Get out of my way!"

"Eighty cattle!"

"Eighty cattle is good for one vote!" exclaimed Eunan. "That would replace the lost village herd."

"It's an insult! I could steal eighty cattle in a day and still come back and fight for the Maguire the next. Enjoy being hunted down when you lose!" Seamus cut the conversation off.

He pushed past the Lisnaskea Maguires, going to where he considered the real power to be.

Hugh Maguire showed his bejewelled wife off to the room, never forgetting to remind anyone within earshot that she was Hugh O'Neill's daughter and that he had her father's full support in any endeavour he would undertake if he became the Maguire. Hugh Maguire then stood beside emissaries of Hugh O'Neill and Donnell O'Donnell. His puffed-up pride and less-than-subtle hints said he had the support of the O'Donnells and the O'Neills, and he dished out enough promises of land and cattle to win the election by a landslide. The finest young men of Fermanagh swarmed around Hugh Maguire as he seemed to be the rising star and possessed an aura of a man destined for greatness. Connor Roe Maguire did not have a chance.

The northern clergy also gathered around Hugh Maguire, and they let it be known to anyone who would listen that he was the favoured candidate of both the Pope and the King of Spain. The sound of Spanish came from men lurking in the shadows of the hall, from men who looked Irish in their dress and appearance but had the etiquette of being from a far away and more sophisticated land. The sound of fresh Scottish accents was also to be heard, not like Seamus who had been subsumed by the local dialect. No such interest surrounded Connor Roe Maguire, but the stench of English money did have its attractions for some.

Seamus walked towards Hugh Maguire, but two Galloglass stepped forward and barred his way. Seamus spoke over the edges of their blades.

"I'm pleased to make your acquaintance, sir. I have here my master, Eunan O'Keenan Maguire, a fresh victim of the English. He lost his family and village to the English sheriff and is here with his twenty Galloglass, which he has paid for with the last of his village's cattle, to plead his allegiance to you to help you rid Maguire Country of the English pestilence! He would love to meet you."

The two Galloglass looked over their shoulders for their master's reaction.

With his ego fanned and recognising a familiar name, Hugh Maguire waved them through. He was young, ambitious and impatient. He also liked a dramatic gesture and to appear benevolent. He itched to get this election over with so he could get back on his horse and fight again. But he could always do with more warriors.

A red-faced Eunan froze, so he gripped his lucky stone in his pocket and approached. Seamus prodded Eunan and Eunan bent the knee and his head.

"Eunan O'Keenan Maguire and his Galloglass at your service, Lord."

"Please rise, I am not the Maguire yet!" came the reply. "Eunan! It is so good to see you again! I hope you enjoyed your time in Enniskillen?"

Seamus beamed like he had found his pot of gold.

"Indeed, I did! Is Desmond with you?" replied Eunan.

"Alas, he is retired. He has not been seen in Enniskillen for many a moon. But now the Maguires need warriors. I assume you can ride a horse with the skill of a warrior?"

"As good as any man in my village," said Eunan as he rose and found himself taller than Hugh Maguire, even though Hugh stood on an elevated platform.

"You should come and ride with the Maguire noblemen. The Maguire horsemen are the envy of all the north, as well you know!"

Seamus could feel the Maguire's coin slipping into his pocket but did not wish to lose his money maker.

"He has twenty MacSheehy Galloglass, all veterans of the Munster wars, who silently vanquished the Earl of Desmond's disloyal kinsmen and are expert cattle rustlers. Not to mention his Lordship's skills with throwing axes. He's an accomplished assassin."

Hugh Maguire was impressed. He slapped Eunan on the shoulder.

"There's always a great demand for men of your skills. Come and see me tomorrow after the sun goes down. I will have plenty of work for you before this day is done."

"We will sir, we will." Seamus grinned from ear to ear.

He grabbed Eunan by the elbow, and they bowed as Hugh Maguire went to speak to his next kinsman. Seamus and Eunan slipped back into the crowd.

A few moments later, Connor Roe Maguire's chief steward slammed his staff into the floor.

"Gentlemen, please take your seats and let the feasting begin!"

Both Maguire candidates sat up on the top table, along with the representatives from the O'Donnells, O'Neills, the clergy and other dignitaries from other minor clans. Stewards showed Eunan his allotted seat. He had a good view of the top table, while Seamus stood in the wings and watched his master.

The stewards served food, and Eunan was treated to endless meat, bread and wine while Seamus watched from the side and tried to guess who he would be asked to kill when Hugh got elected. Seamus noted that Eunan had difficulty fitting in, for Eunan still felt unworthy. He was quieter than the rowdy old chiefs who ate as if it were their last meal. The hall became rowdier and rowdier as the bards came out and the ale was drunk. The inevitable songs of heroes, battles and glory began. There were endless salutes to the various Maguire heroes of the past, and how the chosen Maguire would emulate and better them. Eunan started to feel the effects of the ale, and his tongue became looser. Seamus thought he might have to intervene until the steward slammed his staff in the ground again.

"Gentlemen, the time has come to elect the new Maguire! Please take your seats!"

The singing stopped, and the drunken chiefs slowly returned to their allotted places. The steward stood before the three benches.

"Clansmen of the Maguire! This is a momentous evening where we elect the new Maguire. We face a grave threat to our existence, for we only have to look across the border to what happened to the MacMahons – our fate could be the same as theirs!"

"It is not the time for grandstanding. We must see things in perspective!" shouted Connor Roe Maguire as he rose from his seat.

"You will each get your turn!" replied the steward. "We have for you two candidates, both from different branches of the family, and both with very differing views as to which direction the clan should go. And of course, for you all, many gifts as they share the wealth of the Maguire clan!"

The roar of the chieftains almost lifted the roof off the castle.

"But first of all, we have Connor Roe Maguire, of whose generosity and the generosity of the Lisnaskea Maguires we are indebted to for this evening!"

The chieftains again roared their appreciation. As Connor Roe Maguire rose to speak, Seamus signalled to Eunan to come and talk with him.

"He's in the pocket of the English," said Seamus as Connor Roe Maguire gave a speech stating the MacMahons had brought their fall upon themselves and how cattle rustling had decreased since the MacMahons were displaced.

"Watch who votes for him and how many soldiers they have, as they're probably our first jobs for Hugh Maguire."

Seamus sat down as the hall rang out with the roars of appreciation of the chieftains to the promises of the lavish gifts Connor Roe Maguire would give them on his confirmation as the Maguire. Connor Roe made constant affirmations that he was the representative of the senior branch of the clan and how he would bring peace. He sat down, and Hugh Maguire rose.

"Now must I tell you the tales of my dearly departed father Cuchonnacht Maguire, who brought peace to Fermanagh? Peace with the O'Neills, peace with the O'Donnells..."

"And sold us out to the English!"

Hugh Maguire froze and then recovered his composure.

"My father also secured peace with the English. He had a simple choice. Become subject to the crown or be removed by the crown. But how does this tarnish the greatness of the Maguires? Did the O'Neills and the O'Donnells not submit to the English crown on similar terms forty years ago? And where are they now? They sit amongst us as the lords of Ulster, sovereign in their own lands, leading the resistance against the crown! Does this deal diminish them? I say no, and if you say different, have a look at the evidence you see before you today!

"As much as it pains me to say it, but the forces of England were too strong for us at the time. The lords of Ulster were divided. But who brought them together? Who gave us the time to gather their strength? Who got back Fermanagh for the Maguires in perpetuity? My father, Cuchonnacht Maguire!"

There was a huge roar from the hall.

"But now it is different. We have allies. Some are here with us tonight from the great clans of the O'Neills and the O'Donnells. Some remain in the shadows but will come to our aid should the need arise. But we, the great clan Maguire, will throw off the oppressive yoke of the English and rise once again!"

The chieftains roared and banged their goblets on the table.

"Do I need to recite to you the stories of how I have vanquished our enemies and brought glory to our clan, or should I just serve ale and let the bards sing you the songs!"

There was an immense roar from the chieftains.

"The generosity of the Enniskillen Maguires is equally as legendary but as yet, not yet put to a tune!"

"Hurray!"

"But it is not my exploits or my generosity that I am here to win you over with tonight, even though they will help…"

"Hurray!"

"It is with these!" said Hugh Maguire with a flourish, as he stepped back. The main doors of the hall were flung open and in marched a hundred Redshanks, Scottish mercenaries armed with muskets, a gift from the O'Donnells to their preferred candidate. The Redshanks lined the walls of the hall.

"And I also brought these!" Hugh Maguire's men carried in large wooden crates and placed them on the platform upon which the top table rested. Hugh Maguire picked up an axe and smashed a box open. He pulled out a musket.

"I have enough muskets to arm ourselves and defeat any of our rivals, and any force the English may throw against us!"

The hall erupted in cheers.

"Now who wants to vote against me?"

The chieftains mobbed Hugh Maguire.

Connor Roe Maguire slipped away in the commotion.

18

Inauguration of the Maguire

Bodies of the Maguire chieftains littered the hall. Seamus returned to pick his way through. He found Eunan beneath one of the benches in a pool of ale, food and vomit. Seamus had been the guest at many a feast where usually he was once of the more enthusiastic participants, but the previous evening he was not allowed to join in. It was evident to him that this was Eunan's first feast. It was now daylight, and the preparations for the inauguration had begun. Both Hugh Maguire's Redshanks and Connor Roe Maguire's Galloglass had assembled in the courtyard of the castle to escort the dignitaries to the traditional Maguire inauguration mound, Sciath Ghabhra. Seamus needed to invest in a bucket of cold water and fresh clothes to ensure the Maguires would accept his master.

The bucket of cold water was applied much to his master's consternation.

"What the hell are you doing!" cried Eunan as he spat water from his mouth.

"Get up and get dressed," growled Seamus. "You've got work to do."

The hall was being cleaned and cleared while Eunan got changed.

"I feel like I've been beaten over the head with a hammer! What happened last night?"

"You set yourself on the path to becoming a Maguire, and now you've got to complete the task."

"Did Hugh Maguire get elected?"

"You really can't remember, can you?"

Seamus led Eunan out into the courtyard and stood him near the Hugh Maguire Redshanks for safekeeping. Eunan was surprisingly one of the first of the dignitaries to arrive and not the most dishevelled. After what seemed an age of standing, Seamus had to prop Eunan up.

"Here drink this," and Seamus gave Eunan a flask of liquid.

It seemed to do the trick as Eunan was almost immediately revived.

"Here, give me that! I may need it if walking to the inauguration is necessary."

Eunan put the flask in his pocket and liberally drank from it whenever he felt he started to fade.

"Watch how much you drink! We want you to remember today! It's the day we start working for the Maguire!"

Hugh Maguire finally arrived, surrounded by his Galloglass, the most important clergy in Fermanagh, the O'Neills and O'Donnells and also the closest of his supporters. No one, armed or unarmed, could get near him. Standing aside from him, surrounded by MacSweeney Galloglass, was Donnell O'Donnell, currently the leading power in Tirconnell.

"The big boys are here!" Seamus rubbed his rough hands in glee.

Hugh Maguire's aides accounted for all the nobles, and then the short procession to Sciath Ghabhra began.

The procession was met by cheering crowds as they left the protection of the castle walls. The crowds chanted Hugh Maguire's name and hailed him as the new Maguire. Eunan and Seamus were somewhere near the back of the procession, and Seamus had them nestled in amongst the Redshanks for no one would be foolhardy enough to attack the Scottish mercenaries.

The procession left the town behind them and started to walk towards the sacred mound they could see before them. The Redshank peeled off and created a defensive circle around the hill to protect the dignitaries from ambush. The dignitaries then surrounded the mound and only Hugh Maguire and his right-hand men, Donnell O'Donnell and the clergy climbed the mound. Seamus was allowed to stand beside Eunan and watch the ceremony. Eunan needed Seamus, for the ceremony was long, and he was still unsteady on his feet.

The priests draped Hugh Maguire in the ceremonial robes of the Maguire. He stood before the stone chair of state that protruded from the mound. The Brehon stood before him and read him the laws applicable to the Maguire and how he should rule the clan. Hugh Maguire recited the oath of the Maguire, and the clergy blessed the ceremony. Donnell O'Donnell then presented Hugh with the long white rod of sovereignty. Hugh bowed in reverence, acknowledging the O'Donnell power to nominate the Maguire. Hugh Maguire presented himself to his clansmen while his attendants recited his lineage back to the first-remembered Maguires. Donnell O'Donnell then spun Hugh three times to the left and three times to the right, to survey the lands of the Maguire, while Hugh repeated the Latin chanted by the clergy.

The priest gave his blessing and pointed towards the stone seat carved from a large rock. The bards and harpists played a celebratory song, and the crowd roared as Hugh sat down.

The lesser chieftains were then invited on to the mound, to file past their new leader. Eunan was towards the back of the line. Seamus stood back and watched the ceremony. Eunan was by now feeling physically better but had become overwhelmed with nerves, being a country boy in such illustrious company. He reached Hugh Maguire. Eunan took his hand and kissed it and said, "The Maguire." He nodded in subservience to Donnell O'Donnell who stood beside Hugh Maguire.

Eunan took his place with the other chieftains.

Hugh Maguire rose from his chair, and the crowd hailed him as "The Maguire."

They all paraded back to the castle to continue the feast.

Eunan had by now sobered up and took his place on the benches once more. The formality of the event had loosened somewhat, and Seamus was allowed to sit beside Eunan. Seamus found himself much more comfortable in the present company than Eunan, and he was soon mouthing along with all the Maguire war songs even though he had not heard most of them before.

Seamus saw Hugh Maguire argue in the corridor with Connor Roe Maguire and Connor Roe swiftly exited again. Seamus was curious and went to see what was going on. He walked straight into Donnacha O'Cassidy Maguire.

"It is time to make our bargain," said Donnacha.

"Well, my master has an empty village and empty fields which is nothing when compared to my empty purse."

"Nothing fills a field like a Maguire cattle raid. I foresee your master's fortunes changing soon."

"Just as I see your master's fortunes changing too. However, every good chieftain needs a united clan. I believe I can be that unifying force."

"The Maguire can be very generous in his gratitude to those who help him. First, we feast, then we raid, while throughout it all, noting those that waiver. Stick by me tonight while your master gets to know his clan better."

"Lead the way fine sir!"

Seamus and Donnacha left to spend their evening in the shadows.

* * *

The next day Eunan awoke to find himself in his tent with Seamus shouting at him through the tent flap.

"Get up you lazy eejit! We've got work to do!"

Eunan crawled out of the tent to find that Seamus and all twenty Galloglass were fully armed and armoured with horses at the ready.

"I wouldn't advise you to go like that. A little cow might stick her little horn in you, and you'd be no good to nobody!" Seamus and the Galloglass laughed.

Eunan crawled back into his tent and got ready for battle as quickly as he could.

"And don't forget to pack all your little axes! We may find you someone to throw them at!"

Eunan climbed back out and stood before the Galloglass. Finn ran forward and helped to adjust his chain mail.

"At least you look a little respectable now in front of the Galloglass," scowled Seamus. "Come on, we haven't finished yet! Time to collect the first payment for your vote!"

They marched around Lisnaskea, and there they were met by the other chieftains and their men, but with a few notable exceptions.

Hugh Maguire rode to the front. "Come on men! It is time to fill the coffers of the Maguires with plunder from the English!"

He pointed forward, and everyone cheered.

It did not take long for Eunan to realise that they were heading to the new plantation of Monaghan and the old MacMahon lands. Sir Ross MacMahon had died, and now Monaghan was breaking down into a war of succession. The English were attempting to break up the county, but Brian MacHugh Og had established himself as the MacMahon as per the Irish custom. Hugh Maguire was keen to support him by diminishing his rivals.

Eunan saw the delight on Seamus' face as at last, he saw some action. Eunan was nervous, for now he had to prove himself in battle to all the Maguire clan.

"Send the Kern forward," ordered Hugh Maguire and the lightly armed troops led the way into Monaghan.

The Maguire had a definitive route once he got to Monaghan and the cattle were plentiful and the opposition sparse. But Seamus had another plan. Some of the east Fermanagh chiefs had sided with Connor Roe Maguire but still went on the cattle raid under the assumption that Hugh Maguire wanted to heal the rift. He did, but not in the way they thought.

Donnacha O'Cassidy Maguire directed the raiding parties and sent Seamus out with Shane Og Maguire, one of Connor Roe Maguire's main allies. They arrived in a wood on a hill above a village. Fifty cattle grazed the land before them, with few villagers in attendance.

"Lead the way, Lord. I am but a mercenary and servant."

Shane Og sneered at him as his horsemen gathered at the top of the hill. Seamus and his men lined up behind them.

"Lord?"

"What do you want, Galloglass?"

"Prepare to meet thy maker!"

The Galloglass swung their axes into men or horse and whomever the blade penetrated fell. The Galloglass finished off the bodyguards and left a wounded Shane Og to grasp the remains half of his right leg and crawl away.

"Politics isn't good for your health," said Seamus, and he lobbed Shane Og's head clean off.

Seamus kicked the head into a bag and slung it over his back.

"If you want paying, you always need to keep a receipt," he said to a shocked Eunan.

They returned to the main force of the Maguire after herding some more cattle along the way. Seamus explained to the chieftains that Shane Og had gone off by himself after a herd of cattle he had been spying on, and did not return. Seamus said his first duty was to mind his young master and not Shane Og. The Maguire gave his blessing to the story and would hear no more grumblings.

The Maguire sent out more raiding parties, and he paired Eunan and Seamus with Art O'Byrne MacMahon. It was not long before the head of Art O'Byrne MacMahon found itself in Seamus' bag. Before the raid was out Seamus had three bags full of heads, two of the newly settled English farmers of Monaghan and one of the enemies of Hugh Maguire.

After several days of raiding, the Maguire considered it a suitable success and gave the order to turn back to Castle Skea and distribute the loot. The whole party were in a jubilant mood with few casualties, but with a few notable absences that were assumed to have defected to the English. Connor Roe Maguire had stayed with the party, but that was considered to have been under duress. They reached Castle Skea where a hastily assembled court convened in the courtyard. The Maguire took his seat, surrounded by his Redshank. The stolen cattle awaited distribution according to the instruction of the Maguire.

The whole event became a celebration of the cattle raid and everything and everyone that was robbed, murdered, or both, for the glory of Hugh Maguire. Eunan's turn came, and Seamus handed him one of the sacks. They dragged them across the yard, a trail of blood marking their route back. Seamus upturned his bag first. The heads bounced off the ground and then settled in a bloody, muddy pool. Seamus rolled the foreheads with his foot and gave a running commentary about why he had removed a particular head.

"...and this one is a local English farmer from whom we liberated one hundred cattle. No, it's not him. Where is he? Sorry, Lord. Eunan, can you empty your bag?"

Then there was a mound of heads.

"Ah, there he is," and Seamus kicked the head like a ball towards the Maguire.

Hugh Maguire smiled as the head came to a stop before him.

"Donnacha! Give this man the one hundred cattle he liberated and also the gratitude of the Maguire! I believe I will see you later before you go?"

"At your earliest convenience, my Lord," said Seamus as he bowed.

Eunan looked at Seamus, copied his bow and hurried back to their place amongst the chieftains.

"Can we go home now?" asked Eunan.

"We have not finished our business, yet the village will be more prosperous than ever when we return, and this from only one raid!"

The assembly broke up, and Eunan and Seamus went to collect their cattle from the stolen herd. Seamus directed his men to take the cattle to their encampment outside Lisnaskea.

"Eunan, come on, I have arranged for us to meet Donnacha. Pick up the bag and let's go."

Eunan dragged the bag after Seamus as if he was the lord.

* * *

Donnacha and Hugh Maguire met them in the twilight outside the castle walls. Seamus took the bag from Eunan's hand and walked up to the Maguire and dumped the heads at his feet. One of the heads bounced off Hugh's shin.

"Here are your enemies, Lord. If there are any hesitation marks on the neck, they were the work of the boy," said Seamus with a touch of pride. "We offer our further services to enable you to consolidate your power." Seamus bowed.

"That is excellent work! How fortunate am I to find such skilled

Galloglass with a shortage of work and empty pockets. If you can fill your sacks with the heads of my enemies, I can fill your pockets with their money, and your fields with their cows. Are you ready for more work?"

"My axe is sharp and clean and eager to hack your enemies out of Fermanagh and beyond."

"I thank you both for your service from the bottom of my heart. Go and help yourself to a further one hundred further cows with my permission. Return to your lands, and I will call for you when I am ready. I need good warriors like the both of you!"

"Thank you!" said Eunan as they backed away. Donnacha handed some papers to Seamus, and Seamus and Eunan left to collect their additional reward.

As they left the castle grounds, the Maguire collected his hostages to ensure the loyalty of the lesser clansmen. Eunan and Seamus were exempt.

They joined up with the MacSheehy Galloglass, and Seamus dispatched two of his horse boys to ride ahead and collect their families and bring them to Eunan's village. After several days' ride, slowed by having to herd the cattle, they arrived back in Eunan's village. It was still deserted, except amongst the ashes of the old village, the Galloglass families waited for the warriors to return. Once they were back, they put the cattle to pasture and set about rebuilding the village.

19

Recruiting for the Maguire

Seamus got up the next day and summoned his men to the centre circle of the village. Seamus stood and surveyed the ruins and the surrounding lands and devised a plan.

"Bury the dead, start building shelters and a stockade, and a few boats while you're at it," ordered Seamus. "We're always going to be a frontier town."

"But that will take forever! Surely we must go and fight!?" said Eunan.

Seamus saw the impatience of youth and did his best to quell it.

"We did a good job back there. They will come looking for us when the time is right. In the meantime, you are the O'Keenan Maguire, so we need to get you something to be a chieftain of!"

They spent several months working hard, planting crops, building houses and constructing the stockade. Eunan proved himself invaluable at exploring the nearby islands on the lake so they could provide shelter and provisions for the villagers in times of danger. They even managed to attract some new residents as the word of a village of Galloglass spread across the region. Seamus put these new residents to work and also started to train new soldiers.

In the meantime, Eunan continued his Galloglass training and had made good progress. Seamus thought it would be about a year, with more actual combat experience, before Eunan could be called a Galloglass. Eunan continued to hone his skills at both making and throwing axes. However, he became increasingly sidelined when it came to running the village. Seamus had told him that a great war was coming and he needed to perfect his skills as a warrior instead of doing 'peasant work' like sowing crops or resolving the petty gripes of the villagers. Why would he need to do it, since he would be off fighting for the Maguire? Seamus said that he would take care of that as he had much experience of running his Galloglass units. The only time Eunan was needed, it seemed, was when someone with the name Maguire was required to meet some dignitaries or attend some event. On these occasions, Seamus had Eunan on a very tight leash.

It was quiet until the spring of 1590 when a rider came with a message from Donnacha O'Cassidy Maguire. He handed it to Seamus. Seamus went straight to Eunan where he was out in the fields with Finn, practising throwing his axes.

"Eunan!" Seamus called.

"One moment please!" The throwing axe scraped the top of the distant shield target and fell to the ground behind it.

"He would have lived and is now charging towards you with his sword to slice you in two. You may have to send your horse boy here out to throw his javelins at him to try and slow him down," said Seamus, pointing to Finn.

"You distracted me!"

Seamus laughed.

"There are many distractions on the battlefield. For one, your friends and neighbours dying because you didn't kill your opponent!"

"Humph. Well we're not on the battlefield now, and I've plenty of time left for training."

"No, you don't. We have more missions for the Maguire."

"What do we have to do now? Isn't Fermanagh at peace?"

"He still has enemies, I still have holes in my pocket, and you are no nearer to being a contender for the Maguire. So no, for hired assassins, there is no such thing as peace."

"Who is our next target?"

"I don't know. We'll find out when we get there. But we have to leave now. The next meeting of the Maguire is nearly two days ride away in Enniskillen."

* * *

After a hard ride, Eunan and Seamus approached Enniskillen. They stopped to admire the view. In the fields before them, they saw the MacCabe Galloglass both in training and training others. In certain areas, Galloglass taught young farm boys the art of fighting with spears, axes and swords. In other fields, squares of pikemen grappled with their pikes and learned to fight in formation to varying levels of proficiency, while a select few fired muskets and men on horseback learned tricks.

"They are preparing for war. They don't train in secret anymore, so they are expecting it to start soon," said Seamus.

"And a new type of war. Look how the Galloglass fight!" exclaimed Eunan.

"War is easy firing at a shadow in the distance. What skill and cunning is there from squeezing a trigger? You learn nothing until you smash a man's head open with an axe and feel the blood spatter on your face. They may have their weapons designed to fight from afar, but there is always a place for a warrior like me, and you someday, on the battlefield."

They saluted the men training as they rode past and the men

saluted back. Seamus recognised the language spoken by some of the instructors, which identified them as being Spanish. Some of the men from the Armada still survived. Eunan and Seamus crossed onto the larger island and then to the bridge before the castle. Their letter, signed by Donnacha O'Cassidy Maguire, got them straight through to the main castle and an audience with the Maguire. Hugh Maguire was waiting for them and remembered them well.

"Welcome! Come in my friends! You have had a long journey!"

"Thank you, sire," said Eunan. "We are here to serve!"

"And the Maguire is grateful for your service. I presume my previous gratitude has been to your satisfaction? I hear your land prospers again by the lakes?"

"Your generosity has reaped a wonderful harvest for us, sire!"

"What troubles our Prince of Fermanagh?" asked Seamus.

"I trust you have seen the men train outside?"

"Your men train with the weapons of modernity, but you still call for the Galloglass?"

"I always have a place for men with your unique skills. But I also need men to make up my armies. How many warriors have you managed to gather as you consolidated your territories?"

"We now have forty Galloglass, all nearly fully trained," replied Seamus.

"Any horse?"

"None, I'm sad to say. What nobility there was did not survive the last English raid and the axe is more my weapon, so I have dedicated myself to the Galloglass," replied Eunan.

"Forty Galloglass is a good number for your territory. I have faith you have trained them well. Now I have a problem with some of the O'Rourkes to the west. I put out a similar call to them, for them to state how many warriors they can declare. I got no response, and some alarming rumours came back to me.

"As you may know, there have been outbreaks of violence between Sir Brian O'Rourke of West Breifne and the Governor of Connacht for the past couple of years as part of the general resistance to English rule in the province. However, Sir Brian has finally been defeated and has fled for Scotland and Bingham, and his men have occupied his land and are preparing to settle it with English farmers. Sir Brian's son, Brian Og, has fled to Fermanagh, and I have offered him your services to help persuade some of the O'Rourke chieftains located on the borders of Fermanagh to declare for us. One such chieftain is Shea Og O'Rourke, and if we can convince him, I think others will follow.

"So meet with Brian Og, solicit a respectable pledge of warriors from Shea Og O'Rourke, or if not find someone else in his clan who can pledge the warriors, taking, of course, your fee for your troubles. Donnacha will supply you with some men, for I wish to see your command ability. We'll need some commanders in the days and years to come."

"The MacCabes and the MacSheehys don't exactly see eye to eye," replied Seamus, dubious of the standard of men he would lead.

"War is a fickle business, and to be a chieftain requires flexibility as to who is your enemy and who is your friend. You understand that Eunan, don't you?" said Hugh Maguire, turning to address the master.

"Yes, sire."

Seamus was suitably humiliated and swore revenge beneath his breath.

"And if you complete this mission and yourselves and the MacCabes don't kill each other, and I get my pledge, I may consider you for a more important mission. One that, if you complete it, could solve your money issues forever!"

"Consider the MacCabes to be closer to me than my brother!" said Seamus, cheered by the talk of a handsome fee.

"Your dead brother?" asked Donnacha, who had done his research.

"The pre-death closeness I felt for my brother! And if I avenge the MacCabes half as well as I avenged my brother, they would be lucky to have such a friend as me!"

* * *

Eunan, Seamus and the ten MacCabe Galloglass slowly rode up the narrow roads in the hilly, barren terrain. Their meeting with Brian Og along the way had been brief, but he had at least given them a local scout to help them circumvent the worst of the bogs. Their journey was made doubly difficult by the lack of forest cover, which meant their party could be spotted some distance away. After a tricky trip, the party rode into the main village of Shea Og. Seamus was not impressed.

"This is a bit shabby-looking to me," he moaned.

"What do you expect in this land of hills and bogs?" replied Eunan.

"I expect to get paid! My sword may judder as I withdraw it from Shea Og in bitterness for his life being sacrificed for so little. No, I'll be more sadistic. I'll let you kill him. Let him feel the shame of being a poor chieftain by having a cheap, inexperienced assassin take his life!"

Eunan glared at Seamus.

They reached the village but in truth had been followed in the bogs for miles by Shea Og's men. There was no protective wall, so they rode straight into the centre of the village where a hefty, greying warrior with one hand firmly on the haft of his axe stood.

"To what do I owe the pleasure of twelve armed soldiers riding into the centre of my village?" bellowed Shea Og.

"You owe the pleasure to your lord, the Maguire. He protects your lands with the lives of his soldiers like us," replied Seamus. "While you may admire our weapons, we are here to count yours and see what

137

you can pledge to the Maguire and his cause."

Seamus dismounted fingering his scabbard and stood before Shea Og. Shea Og eyed him suspiciously.

"Why didn't you say you were emissaries from the Maguire? Please, come in and join us." Shea Og pointed towards his hut whose entrance was surrounded by his burly sons.

"Wait here!" Seamus ordered the MacCabes.

Seamus signalled to Eunan, and they edged their way towards the hut.

"Please, leave your weapons there," said Shea Og, pointing to the ground in front of his waiting sons.

Seamus stopped and felt for his scabbard again.

"If I kill you and all these Galloglass, how will my village ever repay the Maguire, if not with our lives, when he comes seeking compensation?"

Seamus shrugged his shoulders in response.

"Then, why disarm us?" asked Eunan.

"How can we enjoy our meal with swords pointing at each other?"

Seamus smiled as if he had been in this situation before. Eunan froze for he had not, and did not know what to do, except follow Seamus' lead. They laid their weapons on the ground. When Shea Og's sons made a move to retrieve them, the Maguire Galloglass went for their weapons. The sons backed off. The area around the arms became no man's land.

Both parties, now disarmed, entered the hut and sat down, followed by Shea Og's sons. Shea Og invited Seamus and Eunan to eat.

"After your kind sir," said Seamus. "I like to talk business on an empty stomach."

Shea Og helped himself to the meat and bread and smiled at his guests. However, Eunan could only hold back, but not disguise, his hunger. Shea Og reckoned Eunan was the softer of the two.

"All that riding must have gotten you hungry, boy!"

"I'm a Maguire chief!" said Eunan, determined to stamp his authority on the situation. Shea Og laughed.

"They get younger all the time. What is the life expectancy of a Maguire chief these days?"

"About an hour," replied Seamus as he bit into some bread.

Shea Og's sons reached for their hidden weapons.

"Now then boys, be careful who you point your little cocks at. Let the big boys have their chat before you try to tickle us to death. Shea Og, how many men can you pledge to the Maguire?"

"Who says I want to pledge to the Maguire? Brian O'Rourke has fled, the English are on my doorstep, and the Maguire is next on their list!"

Seamus laughed and took some meat.

"Ok, either tell me how many men you want to pledge, or if not, how many cattle you have so I can get paid, and be quick about it."

Shea Og rose to his feet and pulled out a dagger.

"No one comes to my house and threatens me!"

"Sit down, or you'll hurt yourself with that," said Seamus as he carried on eating. "Now, how many men do you have to pledge?"

"Who says I want to pledge for the Maguire?"

"Look, pledge, just bloody pledge or hand over the knife and I'll get someone else to pledge!"

Eunan ate on. He was nervous but did not want to let on, even though Shea Og and his sons could smell the fear emanating from him.

"No one threatens me!" Shea Og lunged at Seamus.

Seamus dodged the knife, grabbed Shea's wrist, pulled a knife from the small of his back and skewered Shea's hand to the table, and then reached for some more bread. The sons froze.

"You gentlemen have a decision to make. You can sacrifice your lives to try to save a dead man, or you can count up how many men you can pledge, and the highest pledge becomes chief. What's it to be?" said Seamus.

No one moved. Eunan ate on.

"And the pledge is?"

One of the sons made a run for the door.

"Eunan!"

Eunan whipped out a throwing axe from his belt. It whizzed through the air and struck the man in the back of the shoulder. He collapsed and tried to reach back and pull the axe out.

"Oh, for God's sake!" cried Seamus. "Just kill him!"

Eunan pulled out a small axe from his boot and threw it. It grazed the man's arm.

"Can you not kill a man in one go with your little axes?"

The other two sons looked at each other.

"Look, these two think they have a chance now! Even Shea Og is tugging at his dagger! Just kill him!"

Eunan leapt from his seat and drowned in the screams of agony as he wrenched his axe from the man's shoulder. One of the sons moved to help his father. Seamus picked up a knife from the table.

"Not if you want to live!"

Eunan dispatched the son with one blow to the back of the head. Eunan sat down to continue eating while covered in the man's blood. Shea Og knew he would not survive.

"So now we know that none of us is unarmed. What is it to be, Shea? You either pledge or whichever of your remaining sons who wants to be chieftain pledges. Either way, I'm leaving with a pledge. You can also throw in some cattle for all the inconvenience you have put me through!"

"I'll never pledge for the Maguire!"

"You just don't know when to give up, do you?"

Seamus pulled the knife from Shea Og's hand. Shea Og screamed and pulled his hand back to cradle it in his chest, as blood ran down his arm and onto his clothes.

"You forced me to do this Shea!" Seamus got up and grabbed Shea Og by the neck and dragged him towards a pot was boiling over a fire. "Watch them!" Seamus ordered Eunan.

The two sons made a move for Seamus, but Eunan produced two throwing axes, and they froze.

"Last change for a pledge!" Seamus said, dangling Shea's head over the pot.

"I'll never pledge!" cried Shea.

Seamus thrust Shea's head into the boiling water.

"I'll pledge," said one of the sons.

Seamus let go, and Shea Og dropped to the floor and held his hand, thankful his face was still intact.

* * *

Seamus and Eunan rode into Enniskillen Castle with thirty cows and a pledge of ten horsemen and forty Kern from Shea Og's son. The son had also given four young boys from his immediate family as hostages to ensure their ongoing loyalty.

Seamus' acts of cruelty left Eunan cold and disgusted. He had not joined the fight for the survival of the Maguire to intimidate some old chieftain stuck in the middle of a bog while taking his children to ensure his dubious loyalty. Was this how he had ended up in Enniskillen?

Seamus rode proudly at the head of the column, for he had gained himself the respect of the MacCabe Galloglass, as someone who could get things done. A man who knew, and could do, what was needed in times of crisis. They rode back to Enniskillen in the rain.

When they arrived, they were invited straight into the tower, given a change of clothes, and then headed to meet the Maguire.

"Welcome, my friends. I hear we will never have any trouble with Shea O'Rourke again!"

Seamus laughed.

"He did need some persuading, but he paid us handsomely for our troubles!"

"Do you have another mission for us sire, or may we guide our new cattle home?" asked Eunan, attempting to change the subject.

"I have the second, more lucrative mission for you, now that you dealt with my previous problem so well."

"Name it!"

20

1590

Seamus and Eunan found themselves with ten Galloglass, escorting a man in a cage on a cart on the road to Tyrone, in pitch darkness. Eunan was tired, for he had not gotten much rest in the busy past few days. Seamus worried about the safety of his newly acquired cattle and how safe they would be in Hugh Maguire's possession. While the Maguire was the most lavish benefactor he could find, he did not trust a man of whom he had to ask his chief minister, Donnacha O'Cassidy Maguire, whose side they were on when he got up in the morning. The man in the cart would not keep quiet.

"You know who I am, don't you? Turlough Luineach will be out there looking for me! Why don't you make yourselves rich and spare yourselves a cruel death and just set me free? We can say I escaped. What would Donnell O'Donnell, the overlord of Fermanagh, say? He'd..."

"Please shut up! You're giving me an earache! I don't care whose side you're on, whether you're on the same side as Hugh Maguire, today, tomorrow, whenever! You're getting ransomed to Hugh O'Neill, and then you can whine on to him all you want. But please, just shut up!"

cried Seamus.

"What's your name?" asked the man.

"Seamus MacSheehy. Why do you want to know?"

"Well, if we're going to be on the road together for a couple of days, I'd like to know your name."

"I would enjoy your time on the road no matter how long it is, for I think you'll enjoy it far more than where you're going. But I think you're just going to wear my name out with your whining, so I'm going to ride ahead." Seamus did just that.

It became light, and their journey was nearly at an end.

"Seamus! Seamus!" the man called.

"Shut up! I'm not going back there!" Seamus said, keeping his eyes on the road.

"Just name your price, and you shall have it!"

Seamus brought his horse to a stop.

"I'll come back there, but just to shut you up!" Seamus turned his horse around and put his face up to the cage bars.

"You must be valuable, for I was given strict instructions not to lay a hand on you!"

"So you don't know who I am! I'm Hugh Gavelach MacShane O'Neill!" He stood back proudly, waiting for the response.

Seamus did not disappoint.

"Wow! No wonder Donnacha, the sly oul fox, didn't tell me who you were! I would have charged him twice the price!"

"Whatever they're paying you, I'll double it! You said it yourself, they're underpaying! Who wants to be a cheap mercenary?"

"This young man here does!" said Seamus, as Eunan came up to ride alongside the cage.

"We're getting near the meeting point. Can you keep him quiet please?" said Eunan.

"Do you know who this is? Do you know how much he is worth?"

exclaimed Seamus.

"Less than the honour of the Maguire. Nobody is going to release him. Our men say that Hugh O'Neill himself has come to meet us!"

Eunan's chest swelled at the thought of meeting the great man. The same man's name grated on Seamus as he thought how many of his men had died at the hands of Hugh O'Neill, and now he was supposed to support him against the English when Hugh never sided with the Desmonds in their rebellion against the same foe.

"You'll find honour comes cheap and disposable. I prefer coin and cattle!" smirked Seamus.

"You'll be against all of us if you want to free him!" said Eunan. "Now let's just deliver him and return to Enniskillen."

They proceeded on for another couple of hours before they met the O'Neill scouts. They directed them into a nearby wood. Once they entered the forest, they realised O'Neill's men surrounded them.

Seamus turned to Hugh Gavelach. "No wonder you were sneaked over here! If I knew how much you were worth..."

Just then a voice called, "Who goes there?"

They entered a clearing in the wood, only to be surrounded by O'Neill horsemen. Eunan rode up to them.

"We have delivery of the prisoner Hugh Gavelach MacShane O'Neill from Hugh Maguire."

A portly man in his fifties rode up in full battle dress. He looked every inch the lord, but his grey speckled beard told of his weariness.

"Tell Hugh Maguire Hugh O'Neill thanks him. His cattle are in the fields to the south. My men will feed you and then take you to the cattle. I thank you for being so honest in your task."

Eunan smiled and nodded his head at such esteemed recognition. Hugh O'Neill turned to the man in the cage.

"Hugh Gavelach MacShane, I have you now!"

"You should have had him for a lot more!" muttered Seamus as he went to collect Hugh Maguire's reward.

* * *

Seamus and Eunan returned to Enniskillen. Hugh Maguire ordered them to stay, for he had more tasks for them. However, events from the north soon overtook them. Hugh Gavelach MacShane O'Neill was hanged, apparently by Hugh O'Neill himself. Hugh O'Neill's enemies lined up at the London Privy Council to give 'evidence' against him. Hugh O'Neill was put on trial for murder, and Hugh Maguire was accused of being entangled in the plot. Panic ensued in Enniskillen. Donnacha O'Cassidy Maguire had to regularly appear before the Irish Council on behalf of his master who feared for his safety. The alliance of the northern Irish lords appeared to have petered out before they had even come together. Hugh Maguire, as a man of action, could only sit on the sidelines, waiting for fate to reveal herself. He had to do something. He summoned Eunan and Seamus.

When they arrived, Hugh Maguire was pacing the floor.

"What is it, sire? Is it more dire news?"

"When is the news not dire? No, I have received a summons from Donnell O'Donnell calling for his subordinate chieftains to supply him with men. As Hugh O'Neill is otherwise engaged with the Privy Council of London and fighting to save his position and, indeed, his own life, Donnell O'Donnell may be our only hope. He is in alliance with Turlough Luineach so, if circumstances dictate, Donnell may be able to get us back in favour with Turlough without too much retribution. Therefore I want you two to bring one hundred men to the aid of Donnell O'Donnell and assist him in consolidating his power in Tirconnell."

"It would be an honour!" said Eunan as he bowed.

"I was hoping you would say that. The men are waiting in the fields to the north. I will wait here for news from Donnacha from his meeting with the Irish Council to see what my fate is."

"We will fight for your freedom, no matter what the English court says!" exclaimed Eunan.

"Thank you, Eunan. You serve your clan well!"

Hugh Maguire dismissed Eunan and Seamus, and in the corridor, Seamus complained in Eunan's ear that he should have fixed the price before agreeing to do the job, but Eunan just dismissed him. They retrieved their travel equipment and clothes and met up with the MacCabe Galloglass in the fields of Enniskillen. They set off for Ballyshannon Castle to unite with the forces of Donnell O'Donnell.

The once-great county of Tirconnell after years of decline had descended into chaos, and clan O'Donnell was involved in a chaotic war of succession that had first started in 1580. Hugh McManus O'Donnell, the reigning O'Donnell, had gone senile. Donnell O'Donnell, his son from his first marriage, had been declared sheriff by Lord Deputy Fitzwilliam and had the support of the crown. Donnell O'Donnell also had the support of Turlough Luineach O'Neill. Donnell O'Donnell had subjugated much of western Tirconnell, and after seeing off several rivals, was now challenging his father for the title of O'Donnell. Hugh McManus O'Donnell was protected by his wife, Finola MacDonald, better known as Ineen Dubh.

Ineen Dubh was from the powerful MacDonald clan of Scotland and had been a courtier in the Stuart court of Scotland. Her mother had married Turlough Luineach O'Neill. Both marriages had been arranged to increase the power and influence of the MacDonald clan over all of Northern Ireland and not just Antrim and Down. Both these women had powerful connections in Scotland and controlled the recruitment of Scottish mercenaries coming to Ireland. Ineen Dubh was determined to hold the title of O'Donnell for her son with Hugh McManus O'Donnell, Red Hugh O'Donnell, who at the time was imprisoned in Dublin. However, Donnell O'Donnell was wary of Ineen Dubh and her methods of warfare. Her son's previous leading rival for the title of O'Donnell, Hugh O'Gallagher, who led the forces of Turlough Luineach to victory over Hugh O'Neill at the battle of Carricklea, had gone to her castle in Mongavlin and was murdered by her Scottish mercenary bodyguard.

Donnell O'Donnell had called out to all his subservient chieftains in southern Tirconnell and surrounding districts to face Ineen Dubh, her mercenaries and the O'Donnells of north western Tirconnell. Into this cauldron marched Eunan and Seamus.

Donnell O'Donnell had cornered Ineen Dubh and her force of mercenaries in western Tirconnell. Upon coming into Donnell O'Donnell's camp, the soldiers directed Eunan and Seamus to a spot where they and their men could pitch their tents. The soldiers passed on an invitation to them to feast with the commanders of O'Donnell's army that evening, as they were going to attack Ineen Dubh the next day. They were all gathered around a central fire and seated on benches with tables. Donnell O'Donnell and the most prominent leaders were at the top and roamed around drinking ale, bragging and making speeches while the men drank, ate and cheered. As soon as Seamus realised, from the bragging of the various commanders, the strategic positioning of both forces, he nudged Eunan.

"Let's sit at the back. I don't think we're going to be here too long."

Eunan looked concerned. He was here representing the Maguire and wanted to be seen by Donnell O'Donnell and his dignitaries to be doing so. Yet he followed Seamus, and they picked their way through the tents to circle around and seek less prominent seats at the pre-battle feast.

"Put that down!" Seamus said, smashing the container of ale out of Eunan's hand. "We're going into battle tomorrow. If you have to be drunk or hungover to face the blood and killing, go home and become a farmer and fornicate fat milkmaids for the rest of your life. These fools will get themselves killed tomorrow. They talk about these Scottish mercenaries as if they were nothing, yet one of those Scottish Highlanders or Islanders would pound any of our pathetic Galloglass into the ground!"

"But listen to how he rallies the men! We have Ineen Dubh cornered!"

"They all give great speeches before they die," said Seamus. "Look at how they are armed, with axes, bows and swords to take on the might of Scotland. If you want to serve your master well, bring back his Galloglass, but leave a few bodies behind as a sacrifice to our master's honour before we depart."

"How can you talk like such a coward?" shouted Eunan.

"How can you talk like such a fool? I'm old for a Galloglass! I've seen more action than you've thrown your little axes in anger. You've only killed one or two men with those axes, haven't you? Well, that proves my point. Do you think it will be so easy to defeat Ineen Dubh and the pride of the MacDonald clan? They built their power on skilled mountain ambushes, and that is exactly what we are walking into. I'm not going to die in a bog for no more importance than a man's honour, who hadn't even the decency to fix his price before sending me off to war!"

"I will lead the Maguire Galloglass into battle tomorrow! You can either come with me or fuck off back to Fermanagh and get your people out of my village!"

Seamus smirked.

"You bark a lot for a little sparrow!"

Eunan stormed off into the night.

* * *

The next day Donnell O'Donnell drew up his battle formations and started the march up the valleys towards Doire Leathan. The MacCabes were towards the front of the column as they marched. Eunan rode out front, surveying the tops of the hills. But Seamus was not beaten yet. He rode ahead to bend the ear of the MacCabe constable, Donal MacCabe.

"Look at what a good position you have! Right in the front! You can catch all the arrows while Donnell O'Donnell steps over your bodies to get the glory!"

Donal MacCabe grinned back at him.

"Why does my earhole have to be filled with such sarcasm? Has your young friend usurped you?"

"He thinks a lot of himself for one who has achieved so little. His virtue and courage will be your graveyard."

"Save yourself if you want to flee, mercenary! We have the courage of the Maguires, and we can defeat any enemy!"

"I have met you many times on the training ground, Donal. I never took you to be a naive fool!"

"And I never took you to be a coward!"

"You lead the elite of the Maguire's forces. What is cowardly about avoiding certain defeat? If you throw your lives away today, you greatly weaken the clan you serve!"

"Who says we'll lose? Who says we'll die! Only you, the cowardly mercenary! Be gone with you before I hang you from the nearest tree!"

Seamus saw that if he persisted, Donal's resistance would soon turn to violence. He rode forward to Eunan.

"The enemy is near. You need to dismount and join the ranks."

"So you stayed and overcame your cowardice! Let us forget our conversations of last night and prepare for battle!"

"I will take the horses. You go and stand behind the first rank where

I will join you."

The army meandered along the valley floor. Donnell O'Donnell and his best men came to the front, for they had almost reached where his scouts had said Ineen Dubh had been camped. The MacCabes were behind them, and Seamus marched directly behind Donal MacCabe as if he was following him. The army walked beneath the crest of a small hill: five hundred of the finest warriors Donnell could assemble, armed with axes, swords and bows with their beards, long hair, chain mail, tunics and standards of the various assembled clans. It was a sight that would intimidate most Irish lords on sight and O'Donnell knew it. Something stirred from behind the hill.

"Arrows!"

Seamus had taken up position behind Donal MacCabe. He turned to the hill on his right to see a hail of arrows raining down from the sky. They barely had time to raise their shields if they had one.

"Eunan! Duck!"

Seamus swung his axe against Donal MacCabe's exposed calf. Donal cried out and fell backwards. Seamus grabbed his shoulders and sheltered from the shower of arrows. Eunan lay nearby under another Galloglass body.

"Stay down for the second wave!"

Arrows showered Donal MacCabe's body again, but the worst Seamus suffered was to be covered in Donal's blood. He threw his arrow-punctured lifeless body off him.

"Eunan! Run!"

The remains of Donnell O'Donnell's army broke and ran. Ineen Dubh's men charged over the top of the small hill and attacked from both sides of the valley, and the battle was over. Donnell O'Donnell was dead, and his army routed.

Seamus saw Eunan in the crowds of soldiers trying to escape the valley. He ran over and grabbed him.

"Come with me!"

They ended up in a wood and managed to gather together a few of the MacCabe stragglers.

"Donnell O'Donnell is dead!" said Eunan, trying to get his breath back.

"And so would you have been if you hadn't listened to me!" replied Seamus.

Eunan hung his head.

"I should have listened. I've been a fool. You're in charge on the battlefield."

"And the rest! Foolish ideas like loyalty and honour only get you a mass grave in some bog that wasn't worth fighting over."

"But you don't turn your eye for every pretty penny!"

Eunan surveyed the remains of the once proud MacCabe Galloglass.

"What are we going to tell Hugh Maguire?"

"You leave that to me. He'll have far worse things to think about than us. The thing is not to give him anything to dwell upon."

* * *

They made it back to Enniskillen several weeks later after gathering the remaining sixty-five of the one hundred Galloglass together again. Word had long since reached of Donnell O'Donnell's demise, and Hugh Maguire had already made peace with Ineen Dubh and agreed not to send any more warriors to those who may oppose her in Tirconnell.

Hugh Maguire summoned them once more. Hugh was stricken with worry about what was happening in Monaghan. Brian MacHugh Og had made himself the MacMahon in the traditional way with the support of Hugh O'Neill. Fitzwilliam, the lord deputy of Ireland, had supported Hugh Roe for the title and subsequently provided military assistance.   Brian McHugh defeated Hugh Roe and Fitzwilliam switched his support to Brian MacHugh after apparently being bribed by him. Hugh Roe was then imprisoned and executed. Hugh Maguire barely asked after his Galloglass and was thankful that Eunan and Seamus had returned. The trial of Hugh O'Neill continued.

Only Fermanagh now stood between the English and the O'Neills and the O'Donnells.

21

1592 - Smugglers

1591 was a relatively quiet year for Eunan and Seamus. Hugh O'Neill managed to avoid any of the murder charges sticking to him, and the trial eventually petered out. The succession war of the O'Neills continued with low scale raiding by both sides for most of the year. Ineen Dubh consolidated power in Tirconnell for both her husband and her imprisoned son without any new contender emerging. Hugh Maguire kept to himself and continued his preparations for war, while being both demoralised by the defeat at Doire Leathan and eager to refill the ranks of his lost Galloglass.

Eunan and Seamus returned to their village all the richer for their exploits. They escorted home, with the help of the MacCabes, one hundred and fifty cattle which they released in their meadows surrounding the village. The village now had a stockade, and the population had swelled to a respectable three hundred civilians. No one had survived the massacre from Cathal O'Keenan Maguire's time, so the core of the population were the families and men of the MacSheehy Galloglass. They had been joined by more stragglers: fleeing MacMahons, O'Rourkes and O'Reillys keen to escape the English and their new plantations, and displaced Maguires seeking

154

sanctuary. They had around twenty Galloglass and twenty trainee Galloglass, which was a sizable force considering the population. They had plenty of boats and an island network that, in times of trouble, could sustain several thousand people for short periods of time. Their village had become a substantial hub in the region.

Seamus returned to his wife and settled down. He led the village, supervised its construction and trained the men like any other Maguire chieftain. But Eunan would remind everyone that he was the O'Keenan Maguire, even though there were no O'Keenans left. When someone would try and contradict Eunan, Seamus and his Galloglass would interject and silence the dissent by whatever means were appropriate. The villagers began to wonder why Seamus favoured Eunan so, making him chieftain in name only, when in these times of war only might and muscle counted. But Eunan was a Maguire and as such held the key to Enniskillen, for without Eunan Seamus was simply a wandering Galloglass.

Eunan and Seamus themselves came to a sort of understanding where Seamus would train Eunan and teach him how to train others as long as Eunan did not interfere in his business. Eunan was happy with such an arrangement as long as he made progress and the village prospered.

However, such domestic bliss would only ever be short-lived since a Galloglass of Seamus' skill was always in demand. In the cold of January 1592, they were once again summoned to Enniskillen.

Hugh Maguire had visibly aged, with the weight of the survival of the Maguires resting on his shoulders. Donnacha stood beside him, and they both seemed brighter than the last time Seamus and Eunan had seen them, as if they had hatched a new plot.

"I need you to be discreet in escorting someone home!" said Hugh Maguire.

"Can you not keep your concubines in the castle?" suggested Seamus

Hugh Maguire laughed.

"More discreet than that. I need you to bring Red Hugh O'Donnell home."

Seamus gave Eunan a stare that said, 'don't dare say yes until we fix a price!'

"Do we have to break him out of jail first?" asked Seamus, not out of fear, but for a wish to cost the job correctly.

"No, he managed that himself. He has many enemies, both Irish and English, who want him dead. Hence why I need my two best warriors, most capable of exercising discretion, to sneak him back to Tirconnell."

"This sounds like a dangerous job," said Eunan.

"It is, and you are also at Hugh O'Donnell's disposal, so make what arrangements you see fit. I foresee you both coming back as prominent servants of the Maguire clan and will have suitable disposable wealth that would suit such a prestigious position."

"How suitable?" asked Seamus.

"You would be two of the wealthiest and most prominent men in southern Fermanagh!"

"And a good buffer for you, for your enemies would most likely come from the south!" said Seamus.

"I couldn't choose two better men to protect an exposed flank!"

"So when does this mission start?" asked Eunan.

"Be on your horses at midnight and set out towards Tirconnell. Your temporary master will make himself known. Now go and prepare, and tell no one of this arrangement."

They got into the hallway.

"Satisfied?" asked Eunan.

"We could be the shortest reigning lords of southern Fermanagh in history, but we could not have struck a better bargain," replied Seamus. "But getting to know Red Hugh will also gain us favour in

Tirconnell, and where there is favour with a more powerful lord, lies opportunity!"

At the stroke of midnight, they set out from the town on horseback. They had left the castle earlier and entertained themselves in the town so as not to draw attention to themselves and the fact they may be leaving. The road was empty, for the countryside at that hour of the night was full of bandits. But Seamus was not afraid. He had spent the afternoon sharpening his weapons and had encouraged Eunan to do the same.

They rode for a little while, always wary of the few other road users. There was no sign of their guest. They continued on some more until the road became surrounded by woods. They turned a corner, to be surrounded by men.

"Out of my way or feel the wrath of my axe," cried Seamus.

"The only wrath around here is mine," came a voice from the shadows.

"Show yourself!"

A dishevelled man on horseback emerged from the shadows.

"Put it down, that axe is mine!" he said.

Seamus and Eunan knew this was their man. Eunan smiled, for Red Hugh was not much older than he, yet he could feel his charisma even though Red Hugh had merely uttered two sentences. Even Seamus was impressed with his presence.

"Lead us as you desire," said Seamus as he bowed his head.

"Let us go to Tirconnell, but cross country, for many of my enemies wish to prevent me from making it home."

He turned to his previous escort.

"Go men of Maguire, and I thank you for your service. We must be discreet as we travel home this evening."

The Maguire men bade their farewell but three of Red Hugh's companions remained; Turlough O'Hagan sent by Hugh O'Neill to escort Red Hugh home from Wicklow, where he hid after his escape, and two scouts sent by Ineen Dubh. The six men set off into the dark night on the journey to Tirconnell.

They rode for hours, silent but at a steady trot, in the dark following Red Hugh's two scouts. Eunan and Seamus rode either side of him with Turlough O'Hagan at the rear. It was a cold, windy night, and the windy seemed to pick up an additional chill when they could not avoid the thick of bogs that dogged their route.

They eventually dismounted and stopped to rest. Eunan began to search for wood.

"No fires!" ordered Red Hugh, for the paranoia of prison had not yet left him.

They did not sit down as the ground was damp and cold. They paced and ate to satisfy their need for warmth and sustenance.

"We'll be at the castle in the morning," said one of the scouts.

"Loyal O'Donnells," said Red Hugh in response to Seamus' inquisitive looks.

"Loyalty is an expensive commodity these days," replied Seamus.

"And most of the time it is only temporarily for sale," replied Red Hugh.

Eunan noticed for the first time that Red Hugh had a limp.

"What troubles thy foot sire? Do you need help to get back on your horse?"

"A souvenir from my time at her majesty's pleasure."

"We have heard the stories. What happened?"

"I fell for the cunning of the English in their desperation to keep my father under control. They pulled up their ship to dock and lured me and some of the O'Neill nobility on board. The promise of drink and women was too much for naïve youth. I was kidnapped and sailed to Dublin to spend my time in jail as a result of my weakness.

"For many a year, I sat chained in squalor, with my fellow Ulster nobles and rats for company. I escaped once and got as far as Wicklow, but the cold got poor Art O'Neill and would have gotten me except, in a stroke of fortune, I was recaptured. I got my toes removed on my foot, for they could not save it from the frostbite. They threw me back in jail, but some well-placed bribes by Hugh O'Neill provided for my escape. Fiach MacHugh O'Byrne hid me in Wicklow until I could be smuggled north to Tyrone by the good grace of Hugh O'Neill. I spent several nights with him in Dungannon Castle plotting the expulsion of the English from our homelands. That leads me here, to you. On the verge of my bid to rescue the O'Donnell clan from servitude!"

"And a very commendable objective it is too!" said Seamus.

"Are you ok to travel?" asked Eunan.

"Aye, I'm fine to travel and anxious to get there. We should be in Ballyshannon Castle by morning, where we can rest and see what havoc the English have caused."

"How do you know the castle is still in loyal O'Donnell hands?"

"My mother has sent men from her bodyguard, the finest Redshanks in all of Ireland, to hold it for me. I am rested now, so help me onto my horse and let us depart and make haste!"

They rode for the rest of the night, and just as Red Hugh had said, the castle was within sight. It loomed before them, covered in shadows in the morning light. A drizzle of rain made them feel all the more uncomfortable after their long night ride.

"So what do we do now, sir?" asked Eunan.

The grim smile he offered meant Red Hugh did not know, but he hoped for the best.

"Let us venture forth and see what the response is!"

They rode up the road at a meandering pace, wary of ambush and wanting to keep out of archer range before the castle revealed itself friend or foe. It was quiet until they reached the castle gate. Seamus got off his horse and rapped the butt of his axe on the gate.

"Who goes there?"

"Red Hugh O'Donnell!"

The noise of scurrying feet was followed by the sound of the chain of the gate being pulled up. When the gate opened, there stood Eoin McToole O'Gallagher and his Galloglass constables. They looked for Hugh and Hugh took the blanket off his head.

"Hugh!" they cried, and they rushed to help him down from his horse. "You are injured!"

"I am fine! I am just grateful to be back in Tirconnell!" and he revelled in being able to grip his faithful clan members by the shoulders as he climbed off his horse.

Hugh took a few steps but could not escape his limp.

"Quick, quick get the physician, get some hot water! Get him to the fire! Send riders to his parents. Tell them that Red Hugh has come home!" cried Eoin.

"It is so good to see you!" Hugh said, collapsing into Eoin's arms.

Eunan and Seamus entered as honoured guests, and they were fed, bathed and rested before being brought before a refreshed Red Hugh.

Hugh's foot was now in bandages, and the colour had started to return to his face. He still looked gaunt and had resisted the best efforts of his hosts to feed him, as he had to gradually recondition himself for being out of prison. Delighted faces surrounded him.

"Sit, my friends," he said to Eunan and Seamus upon their arrival.

"You look better, my Lord," said Eunan as he bowed.

"I feel better mainly for being home! But the news from Tirconnell is sobering. An English Captain by the name of Willis has been made sheriff in Tirconnell. He has unleashed a reign of terror and theft upon the land. The house of O'Donnell is deeply divided, my father is old, but my mother and her Scottish mercenaries fight gallantly on. If only the O'Donnell men were as brave and crafty as her."

"What will you do sire?"

"We must rid the lands of the English, by any means. It will be a long and bloody struggle with much pain and death of friend and foe alike. However, I need some men of composure and stature to fight this war. At this moment in time, I also need some men who are unknown to both the English and less loyal O'Donnell brethren. The risks will be high, but the rewards great. You both come highly recommended by Hugh Maguire. May I borrow you from him and have the loyalty of your axes?"

Seamus looked at Eunan, but Eunan's mouth had already opened.

"I pledge my axe both to you and St Colmcille," he said, bending his knee and offering his axe to Red Hugh.

Seamus was astonished by this but only had a second to react.

"My master speaks for me," he said as he bowed his head.

They were dismissed from Red Hugh's company and left the main hall. Seamus grabbed Eunan by the throat and pushed him up against the wall.

"What the hell was all that St Colmcille shit?"

"Let go...My throat...Let...go!"

Seamus released him.

"What was that for?" said Eunan as he regained his breath. "St Colmcille is the patron saint of the O'Donnells! Do you know anything? Some priests predict that Red Hugh is the chosen one to free us from the English. Pledging to St Colmcille will endear us to Red Hugh and get us an abundance of work."

"It's not the amount of work I take issue with, but I can safely predict that St Colmcille was not a good negotiator and exchanged his deeds for heavenly, not earthly goods! No matter for who or why I get my head chopped off, I'm not going to heaven, so there's no point in trying!"

"Rest assured the work will come pouring in!"

"Tell me what your plan is before you open your mouth the next time!"

"You'll be the first to know."

Seamus slapped Eunan on the back, and they did their best to forgive each other, but they both failed.

22

Homecoming

Red Hugh sent messengers to all the O'Donnell clan chieftains loyal to his father across Tirconnell to announce his return. He promised the chieftains would be rewarded for their continued loyalty and invited them to Ballyshannon Castle to pledge their allegiance to him. The pledge was open to anyone who could guarantee a minimum of four horsemen.

Tirconnell was still in chaos, for the defeat of his half-brother Donnell O'Donnell had left a power vacuum in Tirconnell which Lord Deputy Fitzwilliam had quickly, and profitably, filled with Captain Willis and two hundred English soldiers.

Captain Willis unleashed a reign of terror across the land. He first divided the lords of Tirconnell through bribery and the promise of land and power if they supported the crown. He looted from those that refused his advances, and they were defenceless against him since there was no stout O'Donnell to protect them. He took hostages and ransomed them back to the chieftains. The primary resistance came from Ineen Dubh and her Scottish mercenaries. The lords of Tirconnell were trapped between the bribes of Willis and the strong-arm tactics of Ineen Dubh, so only those who were traditionally allied to Sir Hugh O'Donnell's branch of the family could initially be trusted.

The first to arrive at Ballyshannon Castle was Red Hugh's mother, Ineen Dubh and her extended bodyguard of Redshanks. Upon her arrival at the gate, she was directed straight to the tower where Red Hugh waited, for he did not know what reception he would receive and his followers feared his assassination.

Eunan and Seamus were sent to stay in a house in a small village within walking distance of Ballyshannon Castle. Eunan had nothing to do but reflect on how he had gotten this far. He was troubled when he saw Red Hugh reunited with his mother, for he knew his mother never felt like that for him when she was alive. He thought of his father, how he killed him for what he thought was a righteous cause; it still grieved him deeply. He thought of Desmond, the nearest person he ever had to a real father and wished he was by the lakeside with him. He thought long and hard about his complicated relationship with Seamus and how Seamus had propelled him so far. He thought of Hugh Maguire, of his scheming and his efforts to ensure the survival of the Maguire. He thought of himself and his failings as a person, and his determination to do the right thing. He thought of Red Hugh and how the priests had told him that he would deliver Ireland from the English. He was determined to do better now that he was in the employment of Red Hugh.

He walked back to the castle and then around the perimeter upon which a little village grew. He walked deep in thought until he came to a blacksmith. He reached into his leather pouch and the axes Desmond gave him. They were too precious to throw and would be a liability for him in battle for he would always wish to retrieve them, propelled by guilt. He decided he needed some proper, expendable battle axes. He walked up to the blacksmith and showed him his throwing axes.

"Can you make me better axes than these? I cannot get a clean kill with them. They may be too light or too small."

"Give them here," said the blacksmith.

Eunan handed him the throwing axes he created in his youth. The blacksmith juggled them in his hands to test the weight.

"Do you mind?"

"Go ahead."

The blacksmith threw the axe at the door on the other side of his workshop.

"Hmm, they have their uses. Who made them for you?"

"I made them myself."

The blacksmith looked impressed.

"I can make you some heavier ones which should be more suited to battle?"

"Thank you," Eunan smiled.

"Come back tomorrow, and I'll have something ready for you," said the blacksmith.

"I am a guest in the castle."

"Did you arrive here with Red Hugh?"

"I need these axes to do his service."

"Then you shall have nothing but the best. It has been my greatest honour to serve the O'Donnell, and I would give any service to aid the banishment of the English sheriff from our lands."

A St Colmcille's cross hung from the rafters that caught Eunan's eye.

"With the blessing of St Colmcille, we will be rid of them. Since I have some time before my mission, where are the Franciscan friars of St Colmcille based? I need God's blessings before setting out on this endeavour. I heard they were victims of the sheriff."

"They used to be in Donegal town, but they were cast into the mountains by the sheriff and his heathens. You would certainly earn God's blessings and the eternal gratitude of the O'Donnell and his people if you could restore them to the Monastery. The heathen

English used their building as their barracks."

"Are there no depths to which they will not sink?"

"Come back tomorrow and receive the finest weapons in all Tirconnell."

"Goodbye, my friend, until tomorrow."

Eunan left convinced that it would aid his fortunes if his endeavours were blessed. He was determined to seek the Franciscans out.

* * *

After a fruitless evening waiting to be summoned by the O'Donnells, Eunan woke up with a headache from drinking by the fire with Seamus. Seamus had spent the last day or so introducing himself to the local Galloglass and now knew some by name. Seamus had his way of ingratiating himself with the O'Donnells. Eunan dressed, ate and returned to the blacksmith.

Upon seeing his prestigious client return, the blacksmith pulled down the cowhide from the roof of his shop that signalled he was out and invited Eunan to follow him to a yard out the back of his shop.

He handed Eunan beautifully shaped two axes, each the size of his forearm with a long curved blade at the front and a spike at the rear.

"Feel the weight of them in your hands."

Eunan smiled. He could appreciate both the weight and the superb craftsmanship of each axe.

"You even managed to carve the cross of St Colmcille into the haft!"

"To bring you luck. Just as St Colmcille banished the water beast to the depths of Lough Ness, with your help, Red Hugh can banish the English from our shores. Now try throwing them. Aim for that tree trunk over there."

Eunan threw them. They flew sweetly through the air and straight on target.

"With a heavy hit like that," said the blacksmith, "you should get a first throw kill every time!"

Eunan beamed from ear to ear.

"I think the other ones were too light. They landed me in it when the intended recipient got back up and tried to kill me!"

The blacksmith looked at him and smiled.

"I have saved the best for last!"

The blacksmith took out from another bag a large axe, bigger than the other two but just about small enough to throw. The other main difference was that it had the addition of a spike coming out of the axe eye. Eunan's eyes lit up. The blacksmith handed it to him, and he threw it gently in the air and caught it again.

"She's a beauty!" cried Eunan.

"She sure is! Now throw it at that tree!"

Eunan threw it and the main blade sliced the bark and embedded itself deep within the tree.

"She's wonderful, but I'm going to have to get used to her!"

"You're going to have to practice a lot, for you will only get to use her once in battle and then have to fight to retrieve her."

Eunan threw the axe again but this time with more control.

"You'll have to make me a few of these, for no matter how beautiful and effective they are, I'm always going to lose some in battle."

"You free us from the English sheriff and restore the monastery, and then you'll have all the weapons you could ever want!"

Eunan stayed a while longer to practise throwing the axes. He thanked the blacksmith and left with his new weapons when he heard the trumpeter from the central tower of the castle.

* * *

Eunan joined the well-wishers at the main gates and witnessed the

O'Donnell chieftains start to arrive. He stood beside the gate and ran his hands along the holes and scars of the walls that told him the castle had changed hands many times and the current occupants could only expect their stay to be temporary. In between the flashes of the colours of the O'Donnell war banners, Eunan saw Seamus. He went over to stand beside him. Seamus had befriended some of the local O'Gallagher Galloglass who told them who everyone was.

"This sure beats Fermanagh, huh?" said Seamus, slapping Eunan on the back and pointed towards the parade. Eunan acknowledged Seamus' new Galloglass friend. The Galloglass continued his commentary.

"Most of these are from southern or southwestern Tirconnell who either remained loyal to Hugh McManus O'Donnell or supported Red Hugh's half-brother, Donnell O'Donnell."

"So Ineen Dubh is the forgiving type?" asked Seamus.

"A hard woman she may be, but she's also pragmatic. If she still doesn't trust someone, she can always put them in the front line. There's still plenty of fighting to be done, plenty of work for men like you!"

"Men like me do the dirty work so that men like you don't have to!" joked Seamus. "As long as she's the forgiving type, I may just have to pay her a visit," he smirked.

Hugh McManus O'Donnell arrived separately to his wife, and he brought with him the war banners of the O'Donnells being held aloft by one hundred armed men.

"Is he still with it?" asked Seamus.

"That's debatable, but he still commands the general respect of the population, of southern Tirconnell anyway. He can still raise a decent force in his name."

Seamus shrugged and shared some of his ale with the Galloglass to keep him talking. Seamus inspected the soldiers as they marched past, noting their quality, age and armament.

"I don't see any guns or pikes. I thought that Tirconnell was in a constant state of war?"

"It is, but we have also had English sheriffs dominating for years. They confiscate any guns or pikes they can find. The lords still have their Spanish trainers secretly hidden away but if the sheriff found out about them he would shoot them on sight."

Eoin McToole O'Gallagher welcomed the dignitaries at the castle gates as they arrived. He saw Eunan and Seamus in the crowd and called them in to join them.

"Sorry friend, I think this is us!" said Seamus, and he shook hands with the Galloglass. "See you on the battlefield!"

They waved their way through the cheering crowd and past the O'Gallagher Galloglass. They were ushered into the main building. Entering the main hall, they saw an enormous feast laid before them to celebrate Red Hugh's freedom and the resurgence of the O'Donnell clan. Seamus was delighted.

"Sure beats Fermanagh, huh?" he said again to Eunan who refrained from reacting.

The battle banners of the O'Gallaghers and the O'Donnells adorned the walls. The displays were small in scale because it was one of the O'Donnell frontier castles, but it impressed Seamus and Eunan nonetheless. Red Hugh, his mother and father, sat at the top table with Eoin McToole O'Gallagher acting as host and also a number of their most noteworthy constables and captains. This time both Eunan and Seamus were given places on the long bench.

The mood in the hall was exultant, with endless toasts to the returned Red Hugh and cursing of his English captors. Red Hugh gave a rousing speech cheered to the rafters by all.

Eoin McToole O'Gallagher made a careful note as to who was there, but more importantly, who was not.

Eunan let himself go at this feast, for he was a guest and the only expectation on him was for him to enjoy himself. He threw himself into it body and soul; it was such a relief to release the tensions of the previous hard weeks. He felt that, if only Red Hugh could become the O'Donnell, Red Hugh could be the glue to hold the north together. He drank another ale and joined in the chorus of yet another song praising the exploits of Red Hugh.

Many a whisper was had in the ears of Red Hugh and Eoin McToole, as the lords of Tirconnell made known what they needed and what it would take for Red Hugh to be declared the O'Donnell. He listened and promised to act.

23

Captain Willis

The next day Eunan was awoken by a bucket of cold water.

"Wake up sleepy head! It's time to earn your keep!"

"What the...Oh, it's you!"

"Nice way to greet me. You try and drink the place dry, and Uncle Seamus was getting to know all the important people at the feast to get us work and status!"

"You're not my uncle!" Eunan said, wiping his face.

"Try and cheer up before you meet Red Hugh. He can elevate us in the world!"

Eunan dressed in the cleanest clothes he could find.

"I think Red Hugh would be more impressed by grass stains rather than vomit stains!" said Seamus.

Eunan growled and changed clothes again.

They made their way to the great hall. Red Hugh awaited them with his mother, Ineen Dubh. Seamus was a little nervous that she may recognise him.

"But why would she? All she would have seen was my back?"

Red Hugh was feeling better by the day and paced up and down the floor as he laid out his plans to Eunan and Seamus and how they fitted into them. Seamus tried to hide his smile as he thought of how much they could earn, while Eunan looked solemn. This time they were offered lands in either Fermanagh or Tirconnell, whichever they choose, as long as they survived the mission. They did not have to be asked twice.

Soon Eunan and Seamus were on the road again with twenty O'Gallagher Galloglass including the couple that Seamus had befriended the night before. Seamus was thrilled with his new Galloglass because "they are of much better quality. Sure you can almost smell the Scot off them!"

Reports had reached Red Hugh that Captain Willis and his men had been raiding in south Donegal, and Red Hugh wanted to send some soldiers to deal with it who he could dismiss as 'rogue mercenaries' if it all went wrong.

Seamus narrowed down Captain Willis' location from reported sightings to a particular village and sent scouts ahead to check out the place and its surroundings. They returned and explained that Captain Willis was there with thirty men trying to expropriate cattle from the local chieftain. The chieftain did not have enough men to defend the village. His men had abandoned him at the first sign of the English.

The village was in a lush little valley, surrounded on two sides by mountains. It was a valley the O'Gallagher Galloglass knew well from the long and bitter wars of succession, so their guidance was invaluable. Seamus could hear shots from the village. He placed half his force under Eunan's command and instructed them to circle round the village and hide on the road to Donegal town, which was the obvious escape route for the English. Eunan accepted the command but was visibly nervous, for there were numerous experienced Galloglass in the soldiers he commanded that he thought could do the job better than him. But Seamus showed faith in him, alleviating some of his anxiety.

Seamus sent his men out to the nearby valleys to herd all the cattle they could find and bring them to him with instructions not to get spotted by the English. Once the herd was assembled, Seamus and his men lit torches and drove the cattle towards the village. The momentum of the herd became a stampede. Seamus and his men drove the animals before them, and the cattle drove out villagers and Englishmen alike. The English soldiers ran out of the village and straight into Seamus' trap.

Eunan waited until the fleeing English soldiers were almost upon them and then let fly with his new throwing axes. His aim was true, and the sharp reinforced blade of the axe almost ripped the targeted English soldier's head in two. Eunan selected a new target and the second axe was just as successful. Eunan and his men jumped out with their battle-axes and cut the English to pieces. Only the sheriff and a handful of men on horseback escaped.

Seamus and his men downed their fire torches and the cattle disbursed into the fields. Seamus searched the village, found no one and marched down the Donegal road. He found Eunan retrieving his axes.

"You could have left some for me!"

"You looked busy playing with all the cows. Did we kill the sheriff?"

"Unfortunately he got away. Once we have prepared, we will follow him straight to Donegal town. Fetch the horses!" Seamus ordered one of the men.

They all mounted up, and after sending a messenger to Red Hugh to ask him to meet them with additional men in Donegal town, they set out in pursuit of Captain Willis.

The English had had a substantial head start, but local knowledge from the Galloglass cut their advantage considerably. Captain Willis only arrived in Donegal town an hour ahead of them. As they approached, they saw that Captain Willis had managed to mobilise the rest of his men and were waiting for them.

"We need a bit of guile here," said Seamus to Eunan. "Hey sergeant," he said to the senior Galloglass in their company. "Send more messengers to local lords. Gather as many men as you can. We need to surround the town and then move in. You're in charge here now. Eunan and you two, come with me. We've got a captain to kill."

* * *

Eunan and Seamus sneaked into town in the dead of night. Captain Willis and his men had retreated to the Franciscan Monastery and had sent messengers to Dublin to ask for reinforcements. Little did they know that O'Donnell's men had already intercepted them. Captain Willis had his main force in the Monastery rather than the castle because he wanted the locals to see that he was here to stay, and he was not afraid of them, hiding behind some castle walls. Besides, he had confiscated so many cattle and chattels, he needed more storage space. Captain Willis had made no provision to defend the town. Eunan and Seamus were under strict orders to evict the English, killing as few of them as necessary to get them to leave without starting a war. Red Hugh did not feel strong enough yet for that.

Seamus looked around and saw random animals scurrying around the streets. That made up his mind.

"Eunan, get me some oil."

"What kind of oil?"

"Whatever you can get as long as it burns."

Red Hugh was well enough to get on a horse again, so when the messenger arrived, he set off for Donegal town with one hundred Galloglass and fifty horse. Other loyal lords had also responded to the call and warriors began to gather outside Donegal town.

Seamus had spent his time well waiting for Eunan. He had managed to find someone who was familiar with the Monastery, knew of their old escape tunnel that ran beneath the streets and would readily accept money in exchange for a little danger. Eunan came back with a pot of oil.

"What are you going to do with the pig?" he said, pointing to the young pig Seamus had on a rope.

"Watch and learn. Now follow him there." A man came out from the shadows and led them to the tunnel.

As they walked through the pig expressed its dissatisfaction of being held under Seamus' arm.

"Can you shut that thing up?" asked Eunan.

"The poor little fella is afraid of the dark. Leave him alone."

"They can't hear us. The door is sealed at the other end," said the guide.

They proceeded up the tunnel with the pig squealing most of the way, much to Eunan's annoyance.

"Sure let him enjoy himself while he can!" replied Seamus.

They came to the doorway and Eunan greased the pig under Seamus' instruction. Seamus opened the door.

"Goodbye, little fella. Serve the O'Donnell well!" Seamus bent down and set the pig alight. The pig became a ball of flame. It ran through the Monastery spreading fire and chaos wherever it went. The squeals filled the ears with madness of anybody within range. Eunan and Seamus remained hidden behind the door.

Red Hugh was now near the town. He saw that the Monastery was on fire and took that as the signal from Seamus. He rode into the town with the Galloglass following on foot. The other lords interpreted the fire in the same manner and moved in towards the town.

Captain Willis leapt out of his bed and ordered the evacuation of the Monastery. His soldiers spilled out into the street and helped the citizens try and put out the fire.

Seamus heard the chaos outside and deemed it time to make his move. The next English soldier running past the door had his shoulder blade smashed under Seamus' axe. Unfortunately, the man was dead before Seamus could question him.

"Get another one!" shouted Seamus.

Eunan grabbed the next soldier that came along and shoved him down the tunnel. He held his axe blade to the man's throat.

"Where's Captain Willis?"

"A-across the square!"

"Where?"

"In the room beside the gate."

Eunan threw him aside and ran for the room. The English soldier reached for a knife in his belt and made after Eunan. One slice and the man's arm lay on the ground in a pool of blood. The next axe blow smashed his face.

"You're not supposed to leave them alive," said Seamus. "They come back and try and take revenge!"

The pig ran across the yard, leaving a trail of flames. One of the English soldiers shot it and put it out of its misery. The English soldiers ran out of the gate to escape the fire. Unfortunately, Seamus and Eunan did not know what Captain Willis looked like. They were looking for a Captain's uniform, but the recently departed pig was so successful in his mission that the English soldiers all ran around half-dressed in panic. The courtyard was a swarm of smoke, but every time an English soldier came across them and realised they were intruders, they had to kill them. But even as most of the English soldiers had evacuated to fight the flames, the smoke began to dissipate.

"Intruders!" came the shout and Seamus and Eunan found themselves surrounded by English soldiers.

"Put down your axe," said Seamus to Eunan. "We want to speak with Captain Willis."

"And who are you to be making demands of Captain Willis?" said a man who emerged from the crowd wearing only breeches and a shirt.

"The O'Donnell has sent us!" said Eunan, his words filled with pride.

"Did he now? And which O'Donnell is that and what does he want with the Queen's servant?" said Captain Willis, squaring up to Eunan.

"Red Hugh wants to send you and your men back to England. You can leave the Irish traitors here, and we'll take care of them!"

Seamus did not know what came over Eunan to make him so bold. Captain Willis pulled his knife from his belt and stuck the pointed blade into Eunan's face until he drew blood.

"Now, you're a mouthy one, aren't you? It's a pity I don't have time to kill you properly. String them up! Hang them from the tree in the town for all to see!"

The soldiers marched them at sword-point out of the Monastery gate. However, waiting for them outside were Red Hugh O'Donnell, fifty horse and a hundred Galloglass.

"Going somewhere, Captain Willis?" Red Hugh asked.

The English soldiers dropped their weapons. Captain Willis stood in front of his men.

"I am here as a lawful servant of the Queen according to the agreement your father made with the Queen. These two renegades have set fire to my camp and killed an unknown number of my men. Let us pass and serve the Queen's justice upon them."

"I don't think you want any more justice doled out today. Release them and leave Donegal and leave all that you have stolen behind."

"I am a tax collector for the Queen. Any monies or chattels that I have collected are not mine to give back."

"I would advise you to give them back, for I may not be able to hold the townsfolk back from you any longer!"

"I'm sure you and the people of this town are aware of the punishment for murdering a servant of the Queen, carrying out the Queen's duties?"

"I am perfectly happy to discuss your antics in Tirconnell with the Queen at a future date, but now you and your men are leaving!"

"Do you grant my men and I safe passage?"

"Yes, but only you and your men. All weapons, monies and chattels are to be left behind, or else I will leave you to the townsfolk and damn the consequences!"

Captain Willis pondered the offer. He turned and walked back to the monastery.

"Release the prisoners! Gather your things. We are moving out tonight!"

The soldiers cut the ropes around Eunan and Seamus' wrists, and Red Hugh's men cheered. Red Hugh set his men to putting out the fire in the Monastery and escorting Captain Willis to the county border.

24

Inauguration of the O'Donnell

There was widespread jubilation in Tirconnell with the expulsion of the sheriff, and Red Hugh was declared their saviour. Red Hugh had quickly put out the fire in the monastery and sent messengers to the mountains to inform the Franciscan monks they could return. The people cheered, for they saw the restoration of the monks as a sign of their liberation. Ineen Dubh and Hugh McManus O'Donnell joined their son in Donegal Castle. The lords loyal to Red Hugh were called to a conference to discuss the unification of Tirconnell.

Eunan and Seamus busied themselves in helping to clean up the mess they had in large part created in the town while they waited for new instructions. At last, news came about Red Hugh.

"Red Hugh is to be inaugurated as the new O'Donnell!" a messenger said as he ran through the town.

"I guess this means war," said Eunan.

"You're getting wiser in your old age," replied Seamus.

Eunan smiled at the praise for with Seamus, it was rare.

"Where are you going to ask for lands as your reward?"

"Don't get cocky. We've got to survive long enough to ask for our reward! We're not finished here yet."

Eunan's smile vanished. It was back to business as usual.

A Galloglass constable approached them.

"Red Hugh wants to see you."

Eunan glanced at Seamus to receive a knowing nod. They were escorted to the castle tower to be met by Red Hugh and Ineen Dubh. Seamus was a little nervous they would be recognised by her Redshanks but reassured himself again they would never know the back of his head. They bowed to Red Hugh and Ineen Dubh as they entered the room.

"You two have left me in an uncomfortable position!" said Red Hugh.

"No English sheriff and favourite to be the O'Donnell looks a pretty comfortable position to me!" replied Seamus.

"You are lucky to be under the protection of one of my allies after a comment like that!" Red Hugh fumed.

"I apologise sire. You asked us to complete a mission of getting rid of the sheriff and here we are, ready to redistribute his ill-gotten gains with him beaten and gone. You took the credit for it to boot!"

"You killed too many English soldiers! We can't afford a war!"

"What we achieved nobody was able to achieve before, through peace or violence. War with the English is inevitable, sire."

"We have achieved so much," interjected Ineen Dubh. "We need every capable warrior we can get. The road ahead is always going to be difficult."

"And littered with bodies," said Seamus.

"I would hold your tongue," replied Ineen Dubh. "You are not that good a warrior as to say what he likes to the future O'Donnell!"

"Thank you for your patience, sir," said Seamus, bowing to show he would be silent.

"I know you are due payment for your previous exploits, but the house of O'Donnell still needs your help. My father is to step down as the O'Donnell, and I am to replace him."

"Congratulations sire! A very wise choice," said Eunan.

"Thank you. As you well know, there is never a better way to fall out with your family than to get declared chieftain. Some of my relatives and bondsmen need to be brought to heel, and some need to be replaced. Some of these relatives are very careful about their safety, and it would take a crafty outsider to get anywhere near them in order for them to step aside. I've promised you land and riches, but I cannot deliver these to you until I'm the undisputed O'Donnell. Therefore, I invite you to trust me to at least double your reward and do me a service again!"

"I think we may be providing you with services for many years to come if there's no peace with the English!" replied Seamus.

"We'll get the English to accept both my son and the peace," interjected Ineen Dubh. "It depends on what you will do for glory and money."

"I will double down on the money," replied Seamus. "He'll take the glory," and he pointed at Eunan.

"So be it," replied Red Hugh. "We set off for Kilmacrenan tomorrow! But first, your anonymity is a great asset to me. If I remember from your stories Eunan, you used to serve in the court of the Maguire?"

"I did, sire."

"I wish you to escort someone with a critical mission for me."

"Of course, sire."

"Please come in!"

A tall man in nondescript robes entered the room and took the hood from his head to reveal his face.

"Hello, Eunan. You have grown to be a man since the days of looking after Desmond."

Eunan did not recognise him at first. Many faces briefly passed through the court, and most had paid no attention to him. Then it came to him.

"Father Magauran!"

"It's Archbishop Magauran, but I will forgive the inattentive memory of youth. It was a full-time job to look after Desmond. I'm on a mission to the King of Spain to fulfil what we discussed on Enniskillen for so long!"

Eunan smiled and nodded.

"I need you to escort him under cover of darkness to his ship. The letter he carries must reach the King of Spain. Then make haste back here to join us on the march to Kilmacrenan!" said Red Hugh.

"The letter will arrive!" exclaimed Eunan and he went and shook the hand of Archbishop Magauran. The three of them left the hall. Seamus went to prepare for the mission while Eunan and the Archbishop got reacquainted with Eunan also asking after Desmond.

They waited until darkness fell and brought the Archbishop to a waiting ship hidden in Donegal bay. Along the way, when Seamus had ridden ahead to scout the path, Eunan told Edmund the story of his childhood and how he was a prisoner in Enniskillen when they had met.

"That's a sad story that burdens the heart of a great warrior for St Colmcille. Here, take this piece of paper and on it is the name of a priest from the Franciscan monastery in the town. He can help you. It is your reward for helping me this night. But the Lord may call on you to fight for him again!"

"Thank you, Father. I will be ready if you need to call on me again!"

* * *

The next day the messengers went to all the lords of Tirconnell and allies across Ulster. Red Hugh and the O'Gallagher Galloglass, Ineen

Dubh and her Redshanks and Seamus and Eunan set out on the trek across Tirconnell. They had but completed half their journey when Red Hugh received a messenger and immediately ordered the diversion of the party to Castle Doe, the main fortress of the MacSweeney Fannad, one of the leading Galloglass families in the county, on the north coast of Tirconnell.

"Why does Red Hugh have to go to Kilmacrenan?" asked Eunan.

"If he were not properly inaugurated, his succession to the O'Donnell would always be in dispute," replied Seamus. "I sense trouble ahead."

They marched for another two days in the rain and wind, through mountains, valleys and forests. They came across a small castle jutting out into the sea on a small peninsula. Tall, sturdy stone walls protected the tower and house of the MacSweeney. But the castle was too small to take the entirety of Red Hugh's entourage, so Eunan and Seamus had to camp outside with most of the soldiers. When Red Hugh arrived at the gates, Donnell MacSweeney welcomed him with open arms. Donnell took Red Hugh aside.

"There's trouble in the north, sire. Not all the lords are as enamoured as I am that you are going to be declared the O'Donnell. You'll have the allegiance of the MacSweeneys but not much else!"

Red Hugh embraced Donnell again.

"All I need is the MacSweeneys, and the O'Gallaghers and all the rest will come to heel soon enough."

"Aye sire. Let's eat and drink! We can spin our plots later."

They walked into the castle each with their arm over the other's shoulder.

A feast was prepared for the lords, constables and captains in the relatively small castle buildings but there was just wind, rain, bread and warm ale for their underlings. Seamus and Eunan had some difficulties acclimatising to their new-found status.

"If they're supposed to be the best Galloglass in all of Ireland, surely they'd build a bigger castle?" complained Seamus. "If that's all his best men get, a rain-soaked oyster shell of castle slap bang in the middle of nowhere, what are we going to get paid? I think he's not going to pay us until we're dead, or for simpletons like you, not going to pay us."

"Well you led me all this way, and there's no turning back, so we may as well make the most of it and try and live!"

"You're getting more sensible by the day!"

"And more soaked by the minute. Let's try and get in the castle."

They approached the group of MacSweeney Galloglass at the gate.

"No one gets in without the permission of the MacSweeney."

"We are bodyguards of Red Hugh!"

"He has plenty of bodyguards in the castle."

"Can we come in?"

"No!" The firmness made Eunan take Seamus' arm.

"Come on. We'll just have to go."

* * *

They waited outside for two rain-soaked days watching messengers go to and from the castle.

"I don't know how the O'Donnells manage to fight wars if the weather is like this all the time!" said Seamus.

"Ah, come on!" replied Eunan. "It's not that different from Fermanagh."

"And I complain about it there too!"

"I suppose it's all sunny down in Munster?"

"Yes, but unfortunately currently occupied by English soldiers and settlers!"

Red Hugh sent messengers to the other two branches of the MacSweeney clan and also the O'Boyles in central Tirconnell and waited for their response. Two days later all three hundred of the MacSweeney Galloglass were united and assembled outside Castle Doe. Tadhg Og O'Boyle arrived with one hundred warriors led by the breastplate of St Colmcille at the head of their column. Eunan took this as a sign that Red Hugh was chosen by God to liberate the Irish, just as the priests had told him. A ray of hope spread around the camp. Then further behind in the O'Boyle column, Eunan saw a cart. The soldiers camped around the castle began to flock towards the cart. At first, the O'Boyle men tried to hold them back, but Tadhg Og waved to his men to stand down. The other soldiers brought the cart to a halt as they crowded around it to touch the stone.

Seamus and Eunan were stood back at the castle gates.

"What's going on?" asked Seamus of one of the MacSweeney Galloglass still guarding the gate.

"It's the Stone of St Colmcille."

"What did St Colmcille do with that?" asked Seamus.

The Galloglass was almost insulted.

"He was born on it! An angel visited his mother and told her to give birth on a stone the angels raised from Gartan Lough. If you pray to it, you get the protection of St Colmcille, and it'll cure your ailments!"

Another Galloglass wandered up, rosy checked from overindulgence.

"I heard that it's a magic rock to give you the gift of chastity! Anyone who stands on it becomes sterile!"

"It's a pity your mother didn't stand on it!" said Seamus.

"Hey!" said the insulted Galloglass, reaching for his axe.

"Did ya drown your sense of humour in all the free ale?" Seamus asked. "Put that away. I wouldn't want a poor English soldier to be deprived of the only kill of his military career!"

The Galloglass guard laughed and shook Seamus' hand.

"I'm going to go over there," said Eunan.

"Get some good luck for me while you're at it!" said Seamus ignoring Eunan's scowl.

Eunan returned looking happy having made his acquaintance with the rock. Seamus was seated exchanging jokes with the MacSweeney Galloglass when Eunan returned.

A messenger ran amongst the men camped around the castle.

"Attention! Attention! We leave for Kilmacrenan today! Be prepared! Be prepared!"

Seamus, the Galloglass and Eunan ignored him and carried on talking.

"So why the big fuss about St Colmcille? Why pick a monk to be your mascot?" asked Seamus.

"St Colmcille was a fighter!" said Eunan.

"Is this one of those tales of Eunan the fat who slew twenty English by firing axes out of his arse?"

The Galloglass roared laughing.

"No, as I said, he is a fighter. Once St Colmcille was called by a chieftain to slay Suileach, the many-eyed dreadful beast that terrorised the countryside. He set out with the local chieftain to find the beast. When the beast leapt out from his cave, the chieftain fled, leaving St Colmcille to face the beast alone."

Eunan leapt from his seat to act out the story.

"Colmcille fought the beast and managed to cut it in half. Head, tail," said Eunan, making rough measurements with his hands of the two imaginary parts of the beast.

"I get it," said Seamus, hoping it was the end of the story. "Is that it?"

"Then the tail came back to life! It wrapped itself around the saint while the head crept towards him! How could Colmcille survive!? He broke free and stabbed the beast in the head. With the beast now dead St Colmcille was furious that the chieftain had abandoned him and went to kill him. The chieftain cowered before St Colmcille, for he knew he could not beat him in single combat. He pleaded that the saint washed the blade before slaying him as he didn't want his blood mixed with that of the beast. St Colmcille went to a nearby stream and washed the blade but as the blood entered the stream, the saint's anger dissipated and he spared the chieftain."

Eunan dramatically collapsed on the ground to signify his story was over.

"That's a 'firing axes out of your arse' story. I bet St Colmcille was stuck in some dreary monastery copying Bible stories, dreaming of tall stories about his imaginary life he could tell ejits like you! But whatever gets your mob out on the battlefield, I suppose," said Seamus.

"I've got a better one!" said the Galloglass. "St Colmcille told this prophecy. St Patrick gathers all the Irish people together, saints and sinners alike, and leads them to heaven. He sent a message ahead to tell Jesus of their imminent arrival. Jesus said to leave all the evil doers behind. But St Patrick said, 'what kind of host are you to turn people away?' Jesus and St Patrick exchanged messages until finally, St Patrick said that during Jesus' previous divine visitations he had given St Patrick the right to pass judgment on the Irish people. Jesus relented, and St Patrick and the Irish people march towards heaven…"

Eunan was on the edge of his seat, and Seamus was poking the fire.

"Then what happened?" asked Eunan.

"They hear a bell."

"What!? The bells of heaven?"

"No, the lunch bell. It's time for St Colmcille's lunch!"

Seamus roared with laughed and Eunan howled with disappointment.

"Attention! All men to prepare to march to Kilmacrenan!"

"Well, that's our lunchtime bell! See you on the battlefield, my friend!" Seamus embraced the Galloglass goodbye.

At midday, the order came that they were moving out. All

the MacSweeney Galloglass lined up first and led the march to Kilmacrenan. It was more like an army marching to war than a celebratory inauguration procession. Word came that Niall Garbh O'Donnell had sent an army to oppose them, so everyone was on alert. A counter rumour said that Ineen Dubh had given Niall Garbh such a hefty bribe of cattle that if he was not the O'Donnell, at least now he was the richest man in Tirconnell. Another such rumour was that Niall Garbh had gone to Dublin to seek help from the crown to make him the O'Donnell. The opposition army never materialised.

They arrived at Kilmacrenan and set up camp outside the village. This time Eunan and Seamus were not dignified guests but ordinary soldiers with orders not to draw attention to themselves. The Galloglass created a ring of tents with Red Hugh and the other dignitaries in the centre. Seamus and Eunan waited for instructions on the periphery. The three northern lords, Niall Garbh and Hugh Dubh O'Donnell and Sean Og Doherty, were conspicuous by their absence.

"It could have been worse, they could have shown up with their armies!" said Seamus and Eunan nodded in agreement.

The dignitaries went to the sacred ground for the inauguration ceremony. Seamus and Eunan could see nothing, for the ceremony was surrounded by the Redshank guards of Ineen Dubh. Hugh McManus abdicated in favour of Red Hugh, and Red Hugh received his titles in the traditional manner. However, none of the lords of Tirconnell got to vote as they would have in a traditional ceremony. They had to stand by as Ineen Dubh orchestrated the event, so the title of O'Donnell passed peacefully.

Red Hugh decided to solidify his new alliance with both the lords of Tirconnell and Hugh O'Neill in the traditional manner with a raid. Hugh O'Neill was still fighting Turlough Luineach O'Neill, and Turlough's base of Strabane was in striking distance of Kilmacrenan.

The armies of Tirconnell marched into Tyrone and laid waste the lands of Turlough Luineach, stealing cattle and slaughtering any opposition. Eunan was awestruck as he had only seen the much smaller, poorer quality Maguire army in action. Seamus was delighted for he saw his fortune in the destruction of north western Tyrone. The army of Tirconnell spent a week in Tyrone, for it was only a show of force and not a full-scale invasion. Red Hugh had yet to fully secure Tirconnell.

When the raid was over most of the army marched south to Donegal Castle which had been prepared for the inauguration feast, while the rest remained in the north wary of retaliation.

"Thank God he chose a decent venue," said Seamus on the ride back.

"Try not to get us killed by disrespecting the O'Donnell!" replied Eunan.

Donegal town was in a festive mood when the columns of nobles and soldiers began to stream in to join in the celebrations. Donegal Castle flung open its gates, and the revellers in the castle united as one with the common people celebrating in the streets. There was a tangible whiff in the air that Red Hugh was on the cusp of greatness, and they were all privileged to witness it. Various drunken salutes went around the town that Red Hugh was sent by God to liberate them from the English.

Seamus indulged himself with the local whores, all on the promise of payment from the riches he would receive when released from his bond with Red Hugh. Seamus hoped that the stories of his part in the glorious rise of Red Hugh would suffice as payment, the women enjoyed them so much. He wasn't going to wait around for too long after payment. Eunan left Seamus to the whores; he was nervous as he had never done it before and felt guilty and afraid, remembering back to the teachings of his mother and the priest about fornication and sin.

Eunan went to fetch Seamus, for he had heard Hugh Maguire had arrived for the festivities.

"He may be able to get us released and paid," said Seamus as they set out to find him.

They arrived in the great hall on the special invitation of Red Hugh just as Hugh Maguire embraced him and declared to all listeners what a great leader would make.

Hugh Maguire took his seat below the main table as Red Hugh greeted the new entrant Hugh O'Neill. Hugh Maguire joined them at the top table, and the chant of "all hail the three Hughs" reverberated around the walls. Anti-English chants swiftly followed, that Red Hugh did little to discourage.

Seamus made himself known to Hugh Maguire, and Hugh nodded in acknowledgement. About half an hour later Hugh Maguire signalled to Seamus to step out of the hall. Seamus left Eunan to his ale. They met in the corridor.

"Sire, we need to be released from our bond to Red Hugh so we may return to Fermanagh."

"Fermanagh needs warriors like you. But alas, you have outdone yourselves! Red Hugh is very impressed with you and your unique skills. Once he consolidates his lands, he will be strong enough to release you. It'll not be long until you are back in Fermanagh, a rich man. Then I'll need you, for I fear the English plan the absorption of our beloved county into the Pale."

"It is not for me, I plead. It's for the boy. He's a chieftain and needs to defend his people if he's to remain one!"

"The boy will be a great warrior for as long as he lives and his tales will live for long after. But it is for the greater good of Ulster that the O'Donnell and the O'Neill unite. Then we all have a chance. You do your best for the O'Donnell, and I'll do my best for the Maguires. Our paths will cross again soon enough. Now we must get back to the celebrations, or we will be missed."

They parted company and made their separate ways back to the party. Eunan smiled at Seamus when he returned and carried on the revelling. Seamus thought up some more war stories to tell the local whores.

The celebrations continued for several days until the alcohol and most of the residents were exhausted. However, Red Hugh, with the passion and energy of youth, made his plans with Hughs O'Neill and Maguire, and his loyal lords.

25

The Monastery

Red Hugh was obsessed with the O'Donnells' past glories and their place in the clan hierarchy of Ulster and Connacht. He was determined to return them to what he saw as being their rightful place. That place was to be greater than any clan in Ireland, including the O'Neills, and for himself to be more powerful and a greater warrior than any of his ancestors. One of his first actions to meet his vast ambitions was to secretly supply men and weapons to the rebellious Lower MacWilliam Burkes in Mayo. Next, he wanted to turn his attention to reuniting Tirconnell.

However, Hugh O'Neill knew that he had to get Red Hugh accepted by the Irish Council as the new O'Donnell before Red Hugh would be able to unite Tirconnell. He smoothed the way for Red Hugh's appointment by a few strategically placed large bribes, the largest to the Lord Deputy himself. Red Hugh was reluctant to go as his trust in the Council had been destroyed by his previous kidnapping and imprisonment. However, after much persuasion from Hugh O'Neill and Ineen Dubh, and the promise of safe passage from the agents of the crown, Red Hugh went to meet the Lord Deputy in Dundalk. Hugh O'Neill escorted Red Hugh, and a deal was agreed. Red Hugh submitted to Lord Deputy Fitzwilliam, and in turn, the Lord Deputy accepted Red Hugh as the O'Donnell.

* * *

Meanwhile, Seamus and Eunan were left to their own devices as they waited in Donegal town. Seamus amused himself in the taverns and brothels where his credit was still good. Eunan decided to go back and see the Franciscan friars, for he had been having nightmares; Edmund Magauran had given him the name of a priest he thought may be able to help him.

It had been several months since he had been at the monastery, but he could already see the changes. Gone was the debris once strewn everywhere, created in the wake of the screaming pig. The priests and locals had repainted the walls, and little visible scarring remained from the fires that burned when they drove out the English. He knocked on the door. A pair of eyes stared at him through the opened slit.

"Is Father Michael here?"

"Who's asking?"

"Eunan O'Keenan Maguire. Archbishop Edmund Magauran sent me."

The slit shut and Eunan waited. After a few minutes, the door opened. A priest stood before him.

"Eunan!" Father Michael exclaimed. "I'm so glad you came! I heard of your exploits to save this monastery!"

Eunan's heart lit up at such a warm welcome.

"I'm happy the monastery looks so much better than when I saw it last, but I'm a troubled man, father."

"Well, you've come to the right place. Seek solace in the Lord, my son. He is the one sanctuary on this cruel earth," said the priest, inviting him in. "Let us go to the chapel where it's quiet, then you can tell me all about it."

They passed by the monks that were still hard at work restoring the monastery after the damage done by the English.

"Even we priests get involved when war spills over into religion. The O'Donnell warriors do a fine job of defending the faith from the heathen English."

They arrived at the chapel, and Father Michael waived all the monks away so they could speak in private.

"Come and sit here, son and tell me what's troubling you."

"Thank you, Father."

Eunan sat and tried to compose himself, but all he could do was shake and cry.

"Father! Father! Help me! I think I'm possessed!"

Father Michael tried to contain his shock at such a revelation.

"What makes you think that?"

"Everywhere I go, I'm in the shadow of death and destruction. With these axes, I fear that I have become their tool!"

Eunan showed Father Michael his axes and dwelt on the glint of the blade in the sun.

"There are good wars and bad wars, son! It depends upon what you are fighting for."

"I try to fight for the righteous Father, to free my people from tyranny, to give them a good life!"

"A man who fights for that is not possessed! You don't need a priest to tell you that!"

"It only starts there, or should I say, it started in my youth." Eunan bowed his head.

"My mother always said I had bad blood!" he whispered.

The priest bent over to reply.

"Everyone has bad blood, why do you think they get sick?"

"I don't mean it like that, Father. I have bad blood like…like…like…I have some kind of evil that possesses me. Every time something bad would happen that I was responsible for or could be held responsible for, my mother said it was the bad blood."

"And where did this bad blood come from?"

"I don't know, Father. My mother said I could be a Viking. Like one of those Vikings who destroyed St Colmcille's monastery on that Scottish island and undid some of his good works. Like the ones that used to raid and destroy Ireland. Their blood swam down through the ages and possessed me. That's why I created my axes so that I could make amends for my bad blood. I can use my axes to defend St Colmcille and all he stood for. But my mother always said I had bad blood and it has tormented me ever since."

"How does this 'bad blood' influence you?"

"As I said, everywhere I go, death and destruction follow me. The worst thing is, I'm good at mayhem and destruction. First Hugh Maguire, and then Red Hugh, took me into their service."

"I still don't know how this makes you a bad man. Many in the church and Tirconnell believe that Red Hugh is the chosen one. Chosen by God to liberate the Irish people and restore the one true faith! By doing the work of Red Hugh, you are doing the work of St Colmcille and God."

"I don't feel as if I am doing the work of St Colmcille. I feel I'm evil. How come people always die when I'm doing God's work? My little sister died in my mother's womb. They pulled my sister out in a pool of gloopy, sick black blood. My mother said I was cursed, that my bad blood drowned my sister. My mother and father died, and I couldn't save them. I killed my father thinking I was doing the work of Hugh Maguire. Yet I survived. Then I met Seamus, who has been like a second father to me. But he's a vicious and cruel Galloglass, a perfect father for my bad blood. Was I drawn to him? Is he a devil? I want to be good! I want to repent and redeem myself through working for

St Colmcille, but I can't! Until I rid myself of this bad blood, I will always be the tool of darkness!"

"Rest easy son. I may have the answer for you. Come back tomorrow morning, and I'll have a solution for you. Tomorrow is a good day on the all saints calendar."

"Thank you, Father, oh, thank you. I will return at first light!"

* * *

Eunan could barely sleep that evening. There was no sign of Seamus; Eunan thought he was telling tall tales to prostitutes again.

At first light, Eunan banged on the monastery door.

"Father Michael, Father Michael I'm here as promised!"

The door slit slid open, and upon recognising Eunan, the door opened.

"Father Michael is this way."

The priest brought Eunan into a room with a bed. Father Michael was seated on it, and a solemn monk was standing at the edge of the bed. The monk stared forward as if in prayer.

"Come in Eunan," said Father Michael, pointing towards the comfortable bed.

"Lie down and rest, and we will help elevate your pain."

"Are we going to pray?" asked Eunan.

"We are here to help you physically and spiritually."

Eunan lay his axe to rest and then lay on the bed.

"Take off your trousers and your shirt."

"What kind of prayer is this?"

"Just do as I say. I said I would help."

Eunan obeyed and lay in his dirty pants.

"Get some new clothes when you get paid!" said the priest.

Eunan was about to answer, but Father Michael gestured to him to lie down. Eunan lay down and looked at the ceiling.

"This monk is a physician. He was taught in the finest houses of London and then returned home to help the people of Donegal. Your illness is a punishment for sin, but we do not know what sin and committed by whom. Therefore, let us pray."

Eunan closed his eyes and prayed to be better.

He felt a pain on his left arm, the searing cut of a blade.

"Keep your eyes shut."

He felt a pain in his stomach.

"Keep your eyes shut."

He felt a pain in his legs.

"Keep your eyes shut."

He felt a pain in his temple.

"Dear Lord, suck away this poor man's bad blood. Forgive whatever sin led to blighting this poor sinner with such an ailment. Make him an instrument of your plan on earth. Let him always be able to see what is the right thing to do for both you, and those who carry out your will on earth."

Eunan began to feel a little ill and sat up. He looked at his body. He had open wounds and was covered in leeches.

"What are you doing?" he screamed.

"You said you have bad blood that afflicts you. With Divine guidance, these leeches will suck the bad blood away. I am also praying for spiritual guidance for you, your soul and me. This is what you wanted."

"What I wanted was to be free of this affliction. If this removes the curse, I'll do it."

"You must have faith. Faith cures all. Believe in the goodness of God, and you will be free."

"If I am to be free, attach more leeches. Suck it all away."

"You must be careful. Only a practitioner must apply the leeches to get the correct balance. Human error can undo Divine guidance."

Eunan closed his eyes and prayed as hard as he could. He imagined the suckers of the leeches crawling into his veins and hanging there until they attracted some of the bad blood that flowed through him. The leech consumed the blood and grew fat on its richness. Eunan felt himself grow weaker, but as he became weaker, he prayed harder. He prayed that they would suck all of the bad blood out of him and he would wake up restored, throw his axes away and return to his village. All of the villagers would be there, even his parents. His mother would have recovered and been able to walk. His mother and father were waiting at the village gate with open arms...

"Eunan! Eunan! Wake up!" the priest said, shaking him as hard as he could. Eunan awoke. He was covered in blood. The priest and the physician applied bandages to soak up the worst of it. Eunan raised himself onto his elbows. Even that was an effort.

"Is it gone? Is all the bad blood gone?"

Father Michael held up a bowl. Fat, bloated leeches rolled around in Eunan's blood soup, many times their previous size. Such evil repulsed him, and he gagged to remove the last of the bile from his throat.

"It disgusts me, but is it all gone?" he said as he pushed the bowl away.

"We shall see, son. Pray hard and return to me in a week when you feel normal again. If you still feel you are cursed or possessed, we can see about doing it again. But for now, go in peace, and remember, Red Hugh came to free us from the English. If you serve him, you serve the Lord."

Eunan struggled to sit up straight. The physician pointed to a chair and beside it a table with ale and bread. Father Michael went over and helped Eunan up and to walk over to the chair. Eunan threw himself on to it. The physician started to clear up.

"How do you know all the bad blood is gone?" asked Eunan.

"The body contains four fluids or humours each relating to an element found on earth. Yellow bile is fire. Black bile is earth, air is blood, water is phlegm. These elements have to be in balance, or the body falls sick. I don't know which is out of balance, but if I were to guess, I would say earth, for your bad blood is likely to be black and the punishment for sins committed on earth. But we don't know, and we bless the leeches and let them do the Lord's work. If you are truly sorry, the Lord will forgive you and cure your ailments," replied the physician.

Eunan reached over with what little strength he had and grabbed the bowl of leeches. He peered down at them, swollen with blood, lolloping around in his dark blood, writhing around in his sin. Eunan held the bowl closer to his face.

"I can see blackness in the blood!"

"That's good," replied the physician. "That's the bad elements we removed."

Eunan stared some more at the leeches sucking in more blood in their greed for his sin. Eunan began to choke from the smell from the bowl. He threw his disgusting sin on the ground, and it shattered with pieces of the bowl, blood and leech flying everywhere.

"No!" cried the physician as he tried to stop Eunan. Eunan reached for his axe and bludgeoned every leech he could see until their insides melted into the floor. Eunan stopped when no more leeches were intact. He flopped back into his seat with a sigh, dropped his axe and prayed.

"Those leeches were innocent," cried the physician. "They only did the Lord's work and sucked away your sin. Yet you destroyed them!"

"You shouldn't have done that!" said Father. "You must compensate the physician! He brought his finest leeches to cure you!"

Eunan looked away and bit his tongue.

"I'm sorry. But they stank of greed and evilness. I had to destroy them like my curse tries to destroy me. Don't worry. Red Hugh owes me a lot of money for all the death and destruction I have brought on his behalf. I will appropriately reward you for your loss. When can we do it again?"

"I'm not sure I want to do it again with you!" said the physician.

"Name your price, sir. It will be a long time until Red Hugh runs out of people for me to kill."

Father Michael looked at the physician.

"The monastery is much in need of repairs, and we always welcome contributions. We also welcome sinners and hope to set them on the path to redemption. If you come looking for help from us, you will always be welcome.

"However, you must use your strength and attributes to defend the faith and to do good. The first step would be to dedicate yourself to St Colmcille and Red Hugh. That will set you on the path to redemption.

"But now you must sleep for the body needs to replenish itself after the exhausting process of the purging of evil."

"Thank you. May all my blessings be upon you." With that, Eunan was asleep.

26

Consolidation

Eunan tried to keep his mind off his sins and put his efforts into his training as he waited a whole week before returning to the monastery. Father Michael and the physician were waiting for him.

"Red Hugh has not paid me, so I have no money to give you Father. But the treatment you gave me the other week was so immensely helpful, I can do nothing but pursue it further!"

"You have something so much more powerful to give, which is our axe, your courage and your honour. When the time comes, I'm sure you'll see it is wise to pledge it to Red Hugh and St Colmcille. Come this away and let us help you again."

Eunan returned to the campsite that evening. He hid his scars and tales of his visit to the monastery from Seamus. Seamus seemed preoccupied and did not notice that Eunan looked unwell, nor bother to enquire where he had been.

In the meantime, Red Hugh and Hugh O'Neill returned from Dundalk in triumph. Another lavish celebration was had, joined again by Hugh Maguire. The people of Donegal town celebrated the new government-approved O'Donnell, while Hughs O'Donnell, O'Neill and Maguire cemented their new secret alliance.

The next day, Seamus and Eunan were confined by their hangovers to the wrecks of what were once tents. The camp outside Donegal town now resembled a battlefield with the bodies of the drunk strewn everywhere and the odd corpse stumbling around looking for somewhere to piss. A messenger from Red Hugh picked his way through the mess and delivered a bucket of water and a piece of paper. Seamus, furious at being soaked, snatched the letter thrust in front of his face.

"Aw shit!"

Eunan roused himself upright and focused his gaze.

"What's wrong?"

"Hugh Maguire has left behind twenty rookie Galloglass for us to train! He says it's to make up for the ones we lost. I bet he didn't tell Red Hugh how we lost them!"

"Is that it?"

"No, we need to be up at Donegal Castle by noon."

"We'd better get a move on then!"

They arrived to see three hundred MacSweeney Galloglass lined up in columns ready to head south to Belleek Castle. Their rookie Maguire Galloglass stood behind them paled in comparison. Seamus went and introduced himself to each one individually while Eunan went to find out what was going on.

Red Hugh arrived surrounded by Redshanks. He gave the signal to move out, and Seamus and Eunan found themselves at the rear.

"Where are we going?" asked Seamus.

"Belleek Castle."

"Who's there?"

"Rebel O'Donnells."

When they left Donegal Town, Seamus noticed men in the surrounding countryside training to use the pike with mysterious men with

Spanish accents.

"Look, Eunan. He's been swift to start the war preparations. An axe in the head is good enough for a rebel O'Donnell, so the modern fighting techniques must be for the English."

Eunan could only nod grimly in return.

* * *

Several days later they arrived outside Belleek Castle. Hugh Maguire had joined them with some of his troops. Red Hugh rode up to the front gates and dismounted.

"Why do you shut your gates before me? I am the O'Donnell, this is my land, and this is my castle!" he shouted at the walls.

"We have our orders from Hugh McHugh Dubh," came the reply.

"And if Hugh McHugh Dubh is a member of the O'Donnell clan he takes orders from me! Open the gates or suffer the consequences!"

"We take our orders from Hugh McHugh Dubh!"

"So be it!" Red Hugh got back on his horse and rode back to his men.

"Surround the castle. Make sure no one gets in or out. We'll wait for them to surrender."

Later that evening, Hugh Maguire stole into Red Hugh's tent.

"I have connections in the castle as some of their leaders know me because their lands are adjacent to mine. Let me go and speak to them to see if I can hasten their surrender."

"Tell them I will make my final offer tomorrow. If they refuse, then I attack!" said Red Hugh. "If the Maguire can save the lives of loyal O'Donnells, the O'Donnell will be very grateful."

"I will do my best, and will be gone before you arrive in the morning." With that, Hugh Maguire left.

Seamus, Eunan and their Galloglass found themselves in the fields surrounding the castle, herding all the cattle they could find. Red Hugh decided that if the defenders of the castle were not going to let him in, his men were going to strip the land of everything worth having.

The next day Red Hugh rode up to the castle gates and dismounted.

"It is I, the O'Donnell, not Hugh McHugh Dubh O'Donnell but the actual, inaugurated O'Donnell, Red Hugh O'Donnell. As the O'Donnell, this is my castle and my lands. In my lands, you are either my friends or my foes. If you open the gates, you're my friends, and I will return your property, less the costs of you inconveniencing me. If you do not open the gates, then you're my foes. I will take your property and kill you and any of your relatives I may come across on my journey to avenge myself upon Hugh Dubh. It is your choice. But make it quickly."

A voice came from behind the ramparts.

"We only take orders from Hugh McHugh Dubh O'Donnell!"

"Ok. So what do you think will happen now? I am out here with the MacSweeney Galloglass, the best soldiers in all of Tirconnell. Do you think Hugh McHugh is going to ride over the hill, beat the pride of Tirconnell and rescue you? Do you think the English will start a war to help you? Or do you think I will lay siege to you and either starve you out or assault the castle and put you all to the sword? Under how many of these choices do you think you'll live?"

The castle was silent.

"No? No opinion? How about you all put down your arms and surrender?"

Silence.

"Ok, one final offer. I will give a bag of gold to every man who helps us open the gate. But, also, to sweeten the deal, anyone who does not help will be decapitated, and we will throw your heads at the feet of Hugh McHugh Dubh's feet. My offer expires as soon as my horse takes a shit, and he hasn't been in a while."

At first, the castle was silent. Then the gates creaked open, and some of the soldiers walked out.

"Eoin MacSweeney, you give out the gold. Seamus and Eunan, you deliver the axes," Red Hugh called out to the men standing behind him.

The soldiers slowly walked up to Eoin MacSweeney. He gave them a nod, and they dropped their weapons. He handed them a bag of coins, and they burst out smiling and stood behind Hugh O'Donnell. The more reluctant soldiers looked out from over the ramparts, and their former comrades shook their bags of coin at them. The soldiers stopped coming out.

"There is more where that came from! Come out and pledge to me and receive your first payment before I send in my men to clear the place!"

The ordinary soldiers came out, and gratefully received their coin bags.

But Red Hugh noticed that the castle was not quite empty.

"Now to the rest of you, there are no bags of coin. You missed out on that for your lack of trust in the O'Donnell. The rest of you are trading with your lives. With the number of men that came out, you don't have enough to defend the castle. I could come in and hunt you all down, but I would have to clean up afterwards, and I don't want to ruin my castle. So come out, lay down your weapons and we will negotiate for your lives."

The castle was silent again, and Red Hugh was impatient. He signalled to Seamus who readied the Galloglass to move in. With this last action, the defenders had had enough. The last of the common soldiers came out, put down their weapons and surrendered.

One by one, the leaders of the rebels followed them out. They threw down their arms, fell to their knees and pledged loyalty to the

O'Donnell.

Red Hugh smiled.

"Some of your pledges I will take, for I believe them to be sincere. Some, I will not!"

Red Hugh walked along the line. He stopped at the commander of the castle.

"Fian O'Donnell, always a thorn in my father's side. Ever the rebel, but stands for nothing. Seamus, please!"

"But we made a deal with Hugh Maguire!"

"Be careful who you make a deal with!"

With a swish of Seamus' axe, Fian's head rolled around in the mud, a perfect first time cut, without a drop of blood on Red Hugh's trousers.

Red Hugh walked on.

"Ah, Hugh McHugh's cousin! I knew you'd not be far! I could smell the poison from here! Seamus!"

Another head rolled in the dirt.

Red Hugh continued his walk along the line of prisoners until sixteen headless bodies lay in the mud. Red Hugh turned to the remaining prisoners.

"I accept the pledge of loyalty from the rest of you, and you can join your comrades. But do not forget this day and tell those you meet who are disloyal to the O'Donnell what happened! Eoin, give them each a bag of coin."

Red Hugh signalled to his Galloglass to follow him, and they secured the castle.

* * *

News of the massacre travelled far and wide. Lesser lords who had not been so eloquent in their pledges now fell over themselves to pledge themselves to the O'Donnell. Red Hugh moved north with his force and onto the lands of Niall Garbh O'Donnell. Without the possibility of government support, Niall Garbh quickly submitted without a fight and pledged his loyalty. Ineen Dubh arranged that Niall Garbh married Red Hugh's sister Nuala so that he would remain close to Red Hugh's side of the family.

There was only one remaining rebel, so Red Hugh travelled to the Inishowen peninsula and the lands of Sean Og O'Doherty. This time there was no instant capitulation. Red Hugh chased Sean Og and his men around the peninsula with Sean Og refusing to engage.

Red Hugh tired of the chase and decided to burn Sean Og's lands instead. Sean Og soon agreed to meet. They met in one of Sean Og's lord's houses which were supposed to be neutral ground. Each man was only allowed to bring five escorts, be they bodyguards or advisors. Seamus and Eunan had the privilege of being selected for this job.

The two men entered at separate entrances of the house. Everyone had to disarm before entering the house. Sean Og's lord's men guarded the house and were the only ones allowed to bear arms. The two rival groups met in the drawing-room of the house.

"Welcome to the north, Red Hugh," said Sean Og as he sat smugly in his seat.

"I am the O'Donnell to you and all men of Tirconnell. You have led me a merry dance in your refusal to acknowledge this. But this all needs to end, for we have much greater foes to fight than each other."

"At least we agree on something!"

"So be a good man and surrender your forces and bend the knee and we can find more things to agree about."

"I'll never bend the knee to you! You're an impostor! You should not be the O'Donnell!"

"I thought you might say that. Men, seize him!"

Sean Og's men bristled to defend themselves.

"I'm sorry, but your lord has let you down. Arm them!"

The lord's men handed Red Hugh's men weapons and Eunan his throwing axes. In a flash, two of Sean Og's men were dead, with a flying axe in the forehead. The other three half-heartedly fought then surrendered.

Red Hugh stood over Sean Og, as Sean Og sat with a sword to his throat.

"Sorry, but I can't be having my lords openly disobey me. Put him in chains and throw him in the cage."

Once Sean Og was in the cage cart, and the lord paid, Red Hugh and his men marched back to Donegal Castle with their prize.

Red Hugh returned to Donegal Castle and threw Sean Og O'Doherty into prison until he agreed to pledge to him as the O'Donnell. Tirconnell was now united.

27

The end of Turlough O'Neill

E unan busied himself in their camp outside Donegal town
training the new Maguire Galloglass. There were several
Spanish trainers, courtesy of Red Hugh, who taught the men
the art of fighting with pikes and also fundamental gun skills. The
Spanish trainers were devoted to the improvement of Red Hugh's
armies, despite some holding resentment in their hearts due to the
rumours that Ineen Dubh exchanged some of their comrades for Red
Hugh while he was in prison, only for Lord Deputy Fitzwilliam to
renege on the deal once he received the Spanish. Eunan received a
message that he did not bother Seamus with, and he set off for the
harbour.

He arrived as an old friend stepped off a ship. Eunan ran and
embraced him as the ship's cargo of weapons and gold was unloaded
for distribution amongst the northern lords.

"The warmest welcomes to Tirconnell, Archbishop! What news
from Spain?"

"So Red Hugh has sent you to greet me?" said Edmund Magauran.
"I'm so lucky to be met with a friendly face! The news from Spain is
good! So good in fact that soon Red Hugh may be able to acknowledge

me in public without fear of the crown's priest hunters! The great King Phillip has promised that he will send troops, guns and gold by April, as long as the northern lords will come out in rebellion and support him. I must go to Red Hugh, tell him and make preparations!"

"I have my Maguire Galloglass with me to escort you."

"They will be needed for King Phillip was most generous with his gifts to his new allies. But I forget my manners! What of you? Was Father Michael able to help with that which ails you?"

"Father Michael was most useful to me and is continuing to help! I'm very grateful for your recommendation!"

"You know the way to repay me is to pledge your axe to Red Hugh and St Colmcille and give your all in the upcoming fight against the heretics! King Phillip will cleanse Ireland of these apostates and the country will be dedicated to St Patrick and St Colmcille once again!"

"They have my axe and my heart, and when the time comes to pledge, I will pledge. But now is the time to make haste and tell your good news to Red Hugh. Your horse is there," said Eunan pointing, "and your bounty from Spain will follow, escorted by my men. Mount up and let us go!"

They rode as fast as they could, leaving the carts full of gifts to trudge along behind them. Once they got to the castle, Red Hugh was delighted with the Archbishop's news. It breathed so much confidence in him that he permitted a secret conference of the Bishops of Ireland to be held in Tirconnell to discuss the impending Spanish invasion and the unification of Ireland. After the meeting, so optimistic were the Bishops that the embers of rebellion would soon burst into flames, they wrote to the King of Spain that the lords of the north would support any Spanish invasion.

Eunan became Edmund's bodyguard when he was not training his men or in service to Red Hugh or visiting Father Michael. They became bonded together like brothers in the same cause.

* * *

Tirconnell was now united, and the only person in the north-west of Ireland who stood in the way of the secret northern alliance was Turlough Luineach O'Neill. Apart from cementing the new coalition, Red Hugh had his selfish reasons for attacking Turlough. It deprived his rivals in Tirconnell of potential Irish support, as he had choked off possible government help.

Red Hugh gathered his forces in the south and marched north to meet Tadhg Og O'Boyle, the rest of the MacSweeney Galloglass not already in his retinue, and marched into the lands of Turlough Luineach. Seamus and Eunan found themselves amongst it all with their twenty raw Maguire Galloglass.

They made straight for Strabane, the capital of Turlough Luineach O'Neill. The horsemen of both sides skirmished outside the town, but Turlough Luineach made little effort to confront the main army. He retired in good order to Strabane Castle and sent messengers to Dublin hoping that the Irish Council would force Red Hugh to retire. Hugh O'Neill, in the meantime, left his lands and made his way to Strabane with his army.

Red Hugh camped outside Strabane town. Seamus and Eunan, along with the other leaders, were summoned back into Red Hugh's presence since they were outside Tirconnell and no longer had to remain inconspicuous. Red Hugh was nervous, for he felt exposed.

"We cannot stay out here for long. We have too many enemies back in Tirconnell and too few men to fight on two fronts. Hugh O'Neill is making his way here but does not have enough soldiers to finish off Turlough himself. Does anyone have a proposal they would like to share?"

"Withdraw," said one captain.

"Leave it to Hugh O'Neill," said another.

"Burn Strabane to the ground."

"What was that, Seamus?"

"You need to show him you're serious. Let him know you are here to end this. He is old. You are young. Burn the town down and wait for him to react. If he does choose to fight, Hugh O'Neill will be here before the fighting is over. It also shows your enemies back home you're serious. Burn it down."

"What about the English?"

"Make sure you steal enough cattle and money to pay them off. There is nothing they won't forgive for enough cattle and cash."

"You heard the man! Steal everything and let it burn!"

That night Strabane burned as Turlough Luineach O'Neill looked on from his castle and did nothing. Hugh O'Neill arrived, and the next day Turlough Luineach O'Neill sued for peace. The two Hughs persuaded Turlough Luineach O'Neill to retire. Now Hugh O'Neill was the O'Neill, all but in name. Red Hugh returned to Donegal Castle well paid for his troubles with Turlough Luineach's cattle. This time Seamus and Eunan were allowed into the castle as Red Hugh was the undisputed master of Tirconnell.

Red Hugh, his nobles and soldiers, feasted long into the night. The entirety of the castle was a mass of tables and benches and the floors puddles of ale and lumps of discarded food. Amongst the most popular toasts of the evening, both sober and drunk, was declaring Red Hugh the O'Donnell the master of the north. Red Hugh beamed, for he knew he had succeeded.

The next day, the MacSweeneys started their preparations for war. Ineen Dubh sent another emissary to her Scottish allies to pay for more Redshanks for the forthcoming campaigns. She also asked for more guns and pikes so that Red Hugh could continue to modernise the army. Spanish voices rang in the fields around Donegal town and the castles of the MacSweeney Galloglass.

Seamus sat with Eunan by the fire in their camp and expressed his doubts.

"I didn't come here for war. I came to get paid so I could bugger off to some obscure part of this rain-drenched island and sow my oats. It's all starting to get a bit real now. Where were they during the Desmond rebellion? Did they help? Yeah, O'Neill helped the English, that's what he did! The glory of war is for knuckleheads like you who are too young and naive to know any better. Who thinks that splitting a man's head open with an axe for someone else's bidding makes them worthy of elevation and praise? Praise is hollow. You've got to live with yourself afterwards. Normally in some dive of a hut while the order-giver lives in a fancy castle as a consequence of your murders."

"But what about freeing our lands from the English and other such noble causes?" Eunan frowned.

"What do you know about freedom from the English? You live in a pretty little village beside a lake and never meet anyone unless you go to the market. The Maguire is like a benevolent God from afar who takes your crops and money and kidnaps your youth and, if you are especially unlucky, sends a few parasitic Galloglass to come and live with you and bleed you dry. All you would do is swap the Maguire for an English lord. You want to give your life up for some lord and the promise that your villagers will think you heroic for dying in a bog with an axe in your head? I'm old because I learned how to survive. I fear you won't make it as far, for all your yearnings to be a hero!"

"Nice speech but I think we only get paid at the end, so you're here for the duration," Eunan tutted.

"We'll be so rich when we complete this job I'll be retiring. I'll get myself a lovely young wife and have loads of children when we get back to Fermanagh. I'll hire you as my babysitter. You can mind them and tell them your heroic tales, like when you couldn't kill a chief and you forced me to boil him alive, or when your little axes would bounce off the armour of your enemies and I had to kill them for you, or when you could get it together, those numerous occasions when you axed warriors in the back of the head. Then you'll get loads of hero worship!"

"And I can tell them that their father was a big fat prostitute who wouldn't poison anyone to death unless the cattle already had his name branded on it?"

"My children will have a better life for it!"

"I think your current wife will smack you round the head with a pot for that dream!"

A messenger ran through the lines of men. Seamus cursed, for he was summoned again.

* * *

Seamus and Eunan walked into the main hall where Red Hugh sat with his mother. Their jubilance radiated around the room.

"What has his Lordship in such a glorious mood this morning?" asked Seamus.

"Tirconnell and the clan has finally been reunited. The English shall soon feel the wrath of the O'Donnells and the northern lords."

"Then our work here is done?"

"You may go home and rest until recalled for your services."

"Our axes are always available for your cause," interjected Eunan.

"Thank you, Eunan. Your dedication honours me."

"I have told Hugh Maguire that you would visit Enniskillen Castle to report to him on your way home. I believe it is on the way?"

"We shall make haste to Enniskillen Castle," replied Eunan.

"Thank you, gentlemen, for your service to Tirconnell. I bid you farewell."

"There is just one more thing…"

"And what is that, Seamus?"

"We were made promises for our dedication and service?"

"Eoin McToole will see to that on your way out. Thank you."

Seamus bowed and strode towards the door.

"Eunan, why do you stay?" asked Red Hugh.

Eunan knelt on one knee, bowed his head and held his axe aloft.

"I would like to dedicate my life, my axe to St Colmcille, yourself and your cause. I will raise a battle of Galloglass that I will call the Knights of St Colmcille, dedicated to freeing the land of the English, and the people of the false religion the English impose upon them. I fight for the Pope and the freedom of Ireland!"

"What a noble speech! I am truly honoured."

"I would also like to give one-third of my reward back to you to help arm soldiers for the cause. The second third, to the Franciscan monks of Donegal. The last third will be for the welfare of my immediate clan!"

"You truly have become a mighty warrior! Eoin, please ensure the reward is distributed as Eunan has said."

Eunan bowed again.

"Thank you, your Lordship. We will meet again soon."

"Sooner than you think. Goodbye, Eunan."

Eunan left the hall. He felt elated, and the goodness seared through his body. He felt his mother would have been proud of what he just did. The leech treatment of Father Michael had freed his soul.

Eoin McToole escorted Eunan and Seamus in the courtyard. Seamus could not bring himself to look at Eunan. Eoin McToole waved them forward. They walked out of the castle, out of the town and into the fields.

"Let me show you your reward for your service to Tirconnell!"

Eoin McToole waived his arms with such grandeur Eunan's face lit up.

215

"So many cattle! That is surely enough to make the village the most prosperous south of the lake!"

Seamus' reaction was more guttural.

"Two hundred fucking cattle for all that! Two hundred fucking cattle!"

Seamus grabbed Eunan and punched him full in the nose.

"You shut yer fucking face the next time it comes to negotiations! You're an idiot! Knights of St Colmcille my arse! How are the two of us supposed to get all these cattle home! You're an idiot!"

Eunan felt his nose. The bad blood seeped down his face, onto his lip and back into his mouth. Eunan sat on the ground and thought of his father.

28

The Wedding Arrangements

Seamus and Eunan rode through south Tirconnell with their twenty Maguire Galloglass who herded the two hundred cattle towards home. Eunan rode upfront, eager to get back to Fermanagh while Seamus scouted the periphery, studying the countryside. With mountains, bogs and woods, it was treacherous country to be transporting your wealth across. He galloped down one particular hill to confer with Eunan. Eunan had not forgiven him for the punch in the mouth, while Seamus was fields away from forgiving Eunan for giving away most of their reward. However, Seamus was determined to protect what they had left.

"I think we're being followed," said Seamus.

"What makes you think that?"

"I have consistently seen men on horseback follow us since we left Donegal Castle."

"You continue to scout, and I'll alert the men," Eunan said, digging his heels into the side of the horse and riding back towards the body of cattle.

* * *

A galleon loaded its hold in the northern Spain port of Bilbao. Its cargo of guns, gun powder, gold, bibles and a small retinue of soldiers was not that unusual for the time, but the passengers certainly were. A senior priest stood quayside at the bottom of the boarding plank and blessed the passengers as they came aboard. Irish priests from the Catholic colleges of Rome and Spain solemnly accepted the blessing and boarded the ship. Irish nobles, both banished or absconders, boarded, delighted to be going home but also anxious for what fortune may bring them on their journey. Finally, the Spanish captain and the emissaries of the Spanish court climbed aboard with a small escort of Spanish troops. They were the scouts for the Spanish King's intervention. They pulled out of Bilbao port on a clear sunny day, full of the rebellious hopes of the exiles of Ireland.

* * *

Seamus and Eunan made slow progress through the valleys of south Tirconnell. Seamus was getting ever more agitated, and he caught up with Eunan again.

"I'm telling you, we're being followed. There's more and more of them following us by the day!" said Seamus as he apprehensively eyed the tops of the hills in the valley that laid before them.

"Then what shall we do?" replied Eunan. "The cattle won't move any faster."

"Send men forward to Enniskillen to the Maguire. With a bigger escort, we'll get these cattle home. He owes us for all the hassle we've been through," growled Seamus.

Eunan turned away and ordered two of the men to go forth to Enniskillen to seek assistance.

* * *

The ship sailed along the coast of France. Archbishop O'Hely, the Archbishop of Tuam, leant over the side of the deck and stared at the French coast.

"How long is it since you saw the shores of Ireland?" came a voice from behind.

"I've come and gone many a time over these past years, first back home, then to the corridors of Rome and the halls of the King of Spain, but I've never walked the fields of Ireland and seen them free. They've given tokens of help, but never enough. The lords of Ulster are strong, but not that strong. I've prayed hard, and this is the best my prayers have been answered in a long time. How about you?"

"I've been in service for the armies of the Spanish crown for many a year. But now I want to pledge my services to the new O'Donnell. My brethren say he'll revive the O'Donnell power of old. He'll need men like me!"

"Bless you, son. And may the waves carry us home all the faster!"

* * *

Seamus and Eunan entered a valley. There was no avoiding it since it was the quickest way back to Fermanagh and the most obvious route the Maguire would use to send men to help. Its sheer sides, rock-strewn river and wooded valley, forced any travellers along a narrow path.

"I don't like this," said Seamus. "It's the perfect place for an ambush!"

"Well, it's the quickest way back to Fermanagh. I'll send more men ahead to scout the route and see if reinforcements are coming from the Maguire."

"That makes us weaker in case of attack!"

"But they can see if anyone is ahead and warn us. I'm the chieftain, so I'm giving the orders!"

"Do you remember the conversation we had where you said you'd leave military matters to me?"

"That was then. It's time I took on more responsibility!"

Seamus turned a shade of red, dug his heels into the side of his horse and rode off to check out the mountains.

The men drove the cattle down the valley until they reached a choke point with the river on one side and a wood on the other. Eunan and what remained of the Galloglass started to drive the cattle towards the gap. In their way appeared three horsemen, one with a familiar face. Eunan rode up to them.

"Niall Garbh, are you here to offer us assistance on our way back to Fermanagh?"

"Of a sort. I'm here to take back what is mine and your actions will decide how many bodies I leave lying here."

"You can't kill me. Red Hugh would immediately seek revenge," barked Eunan.

"You overestimate the loyalty of Red Hugh at your peril! What's a few dead Maguires to him for all the O'Donnells he's killed to get himself to power? Now hand over those cattle, and we'll see if I'll let you live!"

Eunan went for his axe. A flurry of arrows killed most of the Maguire Galloglass behind him.

"You won't be able to lift that axe above your head before my men shoot you down. Why don't you come with us and we'll see if we can get a nice ransom for you!"

Niall Garbh's men surrounded Eunan and took him prisoner. Seamus could only watch from the hills.

* * *

Eunan and Seamus rode back into the village, not on speaking terms.

His old Galloglass warmly greeted Seamus while the people who fled from the surrounding countryside treated Eunan as a curiosity as they barely knew him, and that was only by vague reputation.

Seamus dismounted and made straight for his house. Finn was there, with Seamus' wife Dervella, waiting for him as he had been living there minding the house in Seamus' absence.

Finn was delighted to see him.

"Welcome, Lord! What tales of glory and adventure do you have upon your return?"

Seamus walked past him and went over and kissed his wife.

"I come back to you with empty pockets and a heart as barren as your womb."

"I, for one, are glad you are back. For as much as you fight the world, you do have a warm heart. How is the boy?"

"So weak-willed. Much troubled and a heart that bleeds for any that wish to tweak it. I hope he is the making of us but fear he will be our downfall."

He took off his soaking blood-stained chain mail and threw it on the ground.

"Excuse me, dear wife. We must momentarily postpone our reunion. I must speak with Finn before I can relax."

His wife left the room, and Finn sat down, and he feared the news would not be good.

"For all the toil and labour I have been through, I return to my village empty-handed!" said Seamus as he poured himself some ale.

"How come, Lord?"

"It is a long story, but my temper is short. So I will tell it to the limits of it."

Seamus sat and drank.

"No sooner had we completed our almost unending series of tasks for Red Hugh than the boy, in a fit of stupidity, decides to go off and visit a priest! That priest poured into that idiot's brain a load of nonsense about being righteous, St Colmcille, Red Hugh being the chosen one etcetera. Guess who takes all of that seriously?

"Then comes pay day. There we are, both standing before Red Hugh with me about to stick my hand out. What happens then? He pledges Red Hugh his axe. Then our money! He gives away one third to Red Hugh's war effort, a cunning name for Red Hugh's pocket, a third to the priest who made mush of his brain, the final third he kept. But how did Red Hugh choose to pay us? In cattle!

"So there we are, the two of us standing in front of only two hundred cattle. That is only when you compare our reward with what we had to do to earn it! But then you have two hundred cattle with only two of us and twenty raw Maguire Galloglass to herd them through south Tirconnell and most of Fermanagh. Most of which is hostile territory. But as soon as we got across the border, we were hit by a raiding party led by Niall Garbh of all people! The boy is captured, and all our men killed. I had to follow them and slip into the enemy camp under the dead of night, slit the throats of the guards, all to save an ungrateful boy!

"We returned to Hugh Maguire penniless and had to tell him all his men were dead. He told us to ready our men for war was coming, and we could quickly make our fortunes again."

Seamus paused to take a long drink.

"What has been happening in the village? How many men have you raised? How prepared are we for war?"

"Things have been peaceful," replied Finn. "There's good soil to feed our rapidly growing community. The stockades are up. We have a few self-sufficient islands in the lake now. We have forty men that we could hire out as Galloglass and would not disgrace us. Plenty of Kern. A half dozen horsemen. Better than when you left."

"Good. Now leave me be, and I will spend some time resting with my wife. You are in charge until I am rested. Watch Eunan. Make sure he doesn't do anything stupid. A fine warrior he may be, but he is way too easily led."

* * *

Several days passed until Seamus felt sufficiently rested to come out and join the villagers again. Eunan had shown his younger age and restless spirit and was already back in training and beating some of the older Galloglass. However, Finn had gotten word of some ideas he was trying to spread. He went straight to Seamus, who was in the middle of making his home more comfortable by adding another room. He was not pleased to see Finn.

"Why do you deem it fit to disturb me when I am here with my wife?"

"Eunan is trying to recruit some of the Galloglass into joining something called the Knights of St Colmcille."

Seamus flung down his tools and marched into the house, grabbing his battle axe. He stormed over to the training field. Eunan stood telling stories of their adventures in Tirconnell and how he was going to form a band of holy Galloglass to fight the English in the impending war. Seamus came up from behind him and shoved him into the mud. He turned to the Galloglass who formed a circle around them.

"I don't suppose he told you the part where he gave away most of what we earned, for your welfare, to Red Hugh and a bunch of priests! Then he got robbed of the rest!"

He turned to Eunan crawling on the ground.

"How can you call yourself a Galloglass? In your first battle with the English, you would try and convert them, turn your back and then they would slice you in two! We're not going on a crusade! We're trying to survive! No sooner have you made an ally in this world, he stabs you in the back and steals all your cattle. This is not a world for priests and trying to be holy! This is a cruel and vicious world to be carved out by the axe. The axe of proper Galloglass! I put my life on the line to get robbed by him and bandits. Don't let him lead you astray. He is young and foolish, and his way leads to certain death!"

Eunan had gotten up by now and charged at Seamus. Seamus stepped aside, dodged him and then tripped him up. Eunan fell face down in the mud.

"Stay down!" commanded Seamus.

This time Eunan did not get up.

"I will return in the afternoon to commence training. Continue as before but without him as your instructor."

Seamus then stood over Eunan.

"Clean yourself up and come to my house. We must sort this out now before it goes any further." With that, Seamus stomped towards his house.

Eunan picked himself up from the mud. Only the mud shielded the red hue of humiliation from his fellow Galloglass, except they had all turned their backs on him and got on with their training. Eunan did not know which was worse, being humiliated or being ignored. He picked up his axe and walked back to his house. The sucker marks left by the leeches began to itch. He would soon need another session.

* * *

Eunan knocked on Seamus' door.

"Come!"

Seamus sat eating, casually dressed in a tunic, with his wife in attendance. Eunan had never seen this domestic side of Seamus before, sitting contented at home. Eunan thought him not capable of showing any affection or sweetness, but there it was before him.

"Sit!" and Seamus thrust forward a stool with the sole of his foot. Eunan sat.

"Eat!" and Seamus thrust forward a bowl which his wife had filled. Eunan ate.

"Listen!" and Seamus wiped his face and threw the napkin on the table.

Eunan listened.

"We need to put what happened behind us and make sure it doesn't happen again."

"What exactly?"

"All of it. From all our escapades to what happened. All of it."

"Ok. What do you propose we do?"

"I take care of all negotiations. If you pull anything like you did with Red Hugh again, I'll rip out your tongue with a pair of red hot tongs."

"I will do with my money what I want! I am the Maguire here!" Eunan roared.

Seamus took a breath.

"I like you, but you have a limited amount of use to me, especially after what you did recently. Don't test those limits. I'll be fine without you."

"So where do we go from here?"

"You are going to the bed chamber. We need to maximise our exposure to the Maguire. I have sent a message to him to find you a suitable wife from noble Maguire blood. You will be married as soon as we can arrange it."

Eunan leapt from his chair.

"What if I object? What if I don't like her? You are not my father!"

"Humph! The less said about that, the better. If it makes you feel any better, you can say that it is repayment for all the monies you lost us in Tirconnell. Don't worry. You won't miss out on anything. You'll probably be away fighting most of the time, and there are plenty of prostitutes near any battlefield."

Seamus' wife slammed something hard in the other room.

"Sorry! He's young! I'm trying to sell him a good marriage!" Seamus shouted towards her.

"Anyway, we'll leave for Enniskillen as soon as something is arranged. You should get back to training. The war should start any day soon."

Eunan stood defiantly before Seamus.

"You haven't gone yet. Have you something to say?" asked Seamus.

"I am the Maguire here, and I say when I get married!"

"I'm the leader of the Galloglass here, and you'll do as you're told. If it were up to you, we'd all be in poverty, on our knees praying for salvation, waiting to be cut down by the English so we could all float off to heaven. My way gives us a fighting chance. You must do your best for your people and what is best is to make an advantageous marriage. I'm only asking you to marry someone, not love them. There is a great difference."

Crashing was again heard from the other room.

"Those last sentences have nothing to do with you!" Seamus projected towards the other room.

Eunan glared at Seamus.

"Now do your duty, and I'll be at training within the hour."

Eunan did not move.

"Go, go!" and Seamus swished him away.

Eunan walked out.

* * *

Several days later, a messenger returned. Hugh Maguire thought the marriage idea was a great one and would arrange it as soon as he found someone suitable. Eunan, Seamus and their men were ordered to come to Enniskillen Castle with all haste.

They rode straight for Enniskillen Castle with twenty of their best men. Finn stayed behind. Seamus and Eunan were brought straight to Hugh Maguire.

"Welcome gentlemen," said Hugh, who looked in a bit of a fluster. "I have good news and bad news, both of which cannot wait. I have a perfect match for young Eunan to marry. Roisin O'Doherty O'Donnell, a cousin of Red Hugh. She is supposed to be a looker, but if that did not prove to be true, the marriage would be of great benefit to the Maguire family and their alliance with the O'Donnells nonetheless. Upon your acceptance, we will proceed as other matters are pressing."

Eunan thought of Father Michael and the leeches.

"Ok," he whispered.

"What?"

"He accepts!" cried Seamus. "Now let us arrange it!"

"Now for the bad news..."

"Is it war?"

"Not quite. Captain Willis has arrived in Fermanagh with three hundred men."

"Where is he?"

"Down south."

"I'll bet Connor Roe Maguire has taken him in."

"Aye. Captain Willis works his way towards Enniskillen."

"Why is he here?"

"They say he wants to become the sheriff of Fermanagh. We agreed to a sheriff with the Lord Deputy, but our money and cattle have always been enough up to this point to defer it. My agents tell me Willis is here of his own accord."

"We must stop him!" cried Eunan.

"That is why I called for you two. I heard so many good things about your exploits in Tirconnell."

"Are we going to strike a bargain?" asked Seamus, not letting the opportunity slip.

"I think we may be striking the ultimate bargain. The freedom of Fermanagh!"

Seamus scowled as Eunan's eyes lit up.

"When do we leave?" asked Eunan.

"Firstly, to seal the marriage, my artist needs to make a quick painting of you to send northwards while you are still pretty. You may leave upon its completion."

"If we are staying briefly, please would you direct me to the nearest priest!"

"Marriage isn't going to be that bad!" replied Seamus.

It was Eunan's turn to scowl.

"There is a little monastery on one of the islands of Lower Lough Erne. I think there are several monasteries on the lakes. Take a guide and tell them what you are looking for. But let my artist do his work first, and you can find a priest while the paint dries." Hugh turned to Seamus. "Would you please choose the men you wish to take in addition to your own? You may run into some opposition if Willis has teamed up with Connor Roe."

Eunan and Seamus bowed and bid Hugh Maguire farewell.

After being perched on the side of a chair like an agitated ape posing for his picture, Eunan was soon on the lakes looking for his perfect sanctuary. He landed on a large island covered in trees. He climbed the hill to the centre of the island to a small church and several huts. A priest came out and met him. The priest could supply him with leeches and prayers to help heal him of the bad blood, just as the guide had told him. Eunan emerged several hours later, spiritually refreshed but drained of blood. His guide rowed him back to Enniskillen as he lay back wrapped in a blanket and recovered.

29

Captain Willis Strikes Again

Eunan and Seamus were soon back on their horses and riding towards south Fermanagh. Connor Roe Maguire had indeed given Captain Willis sanctuary but had not overtly come out and supported him. Captain Willis started raiding the farms and villages of south Fermanagh on the eastern side of the lake, so Eunan's lands had not yet come under threat. In the meantime, Hugh Maguire sent word to his allies that Captain Willis was attacking him.

Captain Willis' force of three hundred men was too large and well-armed for them to take on directly. However, instead of waiting for reinforcements, Seamus decided to counter Captain Willis' cattle raids by harassing him and stealing the cattle back, albeit diverting them back to Eunan's lands to make up for the cattle stolen from them. Seamus soon ran out of men, for they were sent to bring the cattle back, and the southern Maguire chieftains were very disgruntled at how Seamus was running the campaign.

Soon Captain Willis had them on the run towards Enniskillen. Eunan and Seamus received reinforcements from the Maguire but could not stem Captain Willis' advance. The best they could do was to divert them away from their lands.

However, Hugh Maguire had received reinforcements from his northern allies. Cormac MacBaron, brother of Hugh O'Neill, had arrived with one hundred foot soldiers and twenty horsemen. The foot soldiers had been trained in modern warfare and were armed with pikes and shot. In previous years, Hugh O'Neill had been allowed English trainers as part of his role as Marshall of Ulster to aid his battle against Turlough O'Neill. Hugh O'Neill was granted a certain allowance of men to have trained in modern warfare and he had trained up to that allowance and then let the men go and taken on more raw recruits to train up to the quota, let them go and so on and so forth. Donnall and Donough O'Hagan, Hugh O'Neill's foster brothers, also arrived with one hundred and twenty shot. Alexander MacDonnell Og MacSweeney sent by Red Hugh came with one hundred Galloglass. These reinforcements considerably increased the fighting capacity of Hugh Maguire. Hugh himself took to the field. He advanced, and after a couple of skirmishes had Captain Willis on the run. Hugh Maguire and his men soon had Captain Willis trapped in a church in the middle of Fermanagh.

Hugh O'Neill's men were apprehensive about the repercussions of assaulting a church containing an English sheriff and sent word back to Dungannon, the capital of Tyrone. In the meantime, Hugh Maguire settled in for a siege.

Eunan sat in the camp and scratched the dark rings the leeches left behind. Seamus sat down beside him, and Eunan expressed his displeasure.

"If you weren't so greedy we could have beaten Captain Willis like we did the last time!"

"If looking after you and your adopted clan is greedy, then I am guilty. He had too many men. Look at how many it took to overpower him now! Save your energy, for the arrival of Captain Willis is just a prelude of what is to come. Anyway, we need to secure our pay. No better way for the Maguire to get out of paying his debts, than to get all the people to whom he owes money to die for his cause in a war. Not greed, clever!" Seamus tapped on the side of his head to reinforce the point that he had a big brain.

Eunan tutted.

Messengers arrived at the camp and were directed straight to Hugh Maguire's tent. Hugh emerged, holding a piece of paper and looked very disappointed. He called for Eunan.

"You know him from Tirconnell. Go deliver this to Captain Willis and bring us back his response."

Eunan bowed and fled the tent. He almost soiled himself.

Eunan walked towards the church and held his hands up. He was armed only with the envelope Hugh Maguire gave him.

"I come in peace!" he shouted, and he started to edge his way across no man's land.

A musket shot rang out. Eunan half ducked, not knowing from where it came.

"Stop right there!" came a shout from the church. "I won't fire a warning shot next time!"

"I come in peace! I have a message from Hugh Maguire!"

"Shout the message from there! I'm sure it's not worth risking your life for!"

"I have a letter in my hand. A letter from Cormac MacBaron, brother of Hugh O'Neill!"

"What does it say?"

"I don't know."

"Open it and read it!"

"I can't read!"

"Give it back to Cormac MacBaron then!"

"I promised to give it to you!"

There was silence from the church.

"Bring it here then. Slowly!"

Eunan staggered towards the church with his hands in the air. He stood and waited until three muskets pointed at him.

"Throw it on the step and leave!"

"I have to wait for a response."

The door of the church opened slightly, and the point of a sword crept out, stabbed the corner of the letter and dragged it back in. Sweat poured down Eunan's back while he waited.

"Is this letter true?"

"Cormac MacBaron uses the name of Hugh O'Neill and Hugh O'Neill always keeps his word."

"Who will escort us out of the county and guarantee our safe passage?"

"Cormac MacBaron has been sent especially by Hugh O'Neill to ensure that you get to Monaghan safely."

"What possessions can we take?"

"You must leave all your weapons and anything you acquired in Fermanagh."

"What if we refuse and shoot you dead here?"

"You'd all be dead within the hour."

The door slammed shut. A few sweat soaked minutes that felt like a lifetime passed for Eunan. The door squeaked open again.

"We begrudgingly accept. What happens next?"

Eunan waved his arms, and Cormac MacBaron and his men marched up to the church and formed a circle around the door. Captain Willis and his men crept out not knowing if they were steeping into their deaths. When they realised they were not going to be hacked to death they threw their weapons in a pile in front of Cormac MacBaron. They were escorted away. The men of Fermanagh cheered, but Hugh Maguire knew it was a hollow victory. Donnacha O'Cassidy Maguire had by this time arrived with news from Enniskillen. A downcast Hugh Maguire despatched Donnacha again. Hugh ordered the army to leave for Enniskillen Castle.

When Eunan and Seamus arrived, a shroud of secrecy surrounded the castle. Hugh Maguire was expecting some distinguished guests. Donnell and Donough O'Hagan were in the fields surrounding the town, training the Maguire men in the arts of modern warfare and how to use pikes and muskets. Hugh informed Eunan that his bride was on her way from Inishowen and could not wait to meet him. Eunan was very much in two minds and retreated to the castle chapel for some contemplation. Finn had arrived with twenty reinforcements from the village, Galloglass whom they had trained from scratch. He went straight to Seamus.

"What is the news from south Fermanagh?" Seamus asked.

"Captain Willis has retired in good order to the Pale. Connor Roe Maguire is preparing for war, and I think he's going to side with the English."

"Think?! He is the crown choice to be the Maguire, and I think they will inaugurate him very soon. But on a brighter note, Eunan's bride should arrive soon. Hopefully, she will be vivacious enough to keep him distracted from his previous stupidity and keep him fighting!"

"How long do we need to keep Eunan around for?" asked Finn.

"What do you think I am? Some kind of monster? He will be a great warrior one day, and with the right guidance, who knows what he could become!"

"I know what kind of man you are!"

"Only you could get away with such cheek! But I do have my limits." Seamus felt the shaft of his axe.

Finn got up and left as the going was still good.

Horns blew from the top of the castle tower.

"Whoever is coming must be here," said Seamus to himself, picking up his things and heading to the main building.

Seamus and Eunan went to the main hall along with the most senior commanders of the Maguire army and Cormac MacBaron, who had returned, Donnell and Donough O'Hagan and Alexander MacDonnell Og MacSweeney. A wall of MacSweeney Galloglass marched into the hall to give way to Red Hugh and Ineen Dubh. Following behind him was Hugh O'Neill.

"There must be something big about to start now," whispered Seamus in Eunan's ear. "Bet this is the start of the war!"

"Clear the room, except for the commanders and the specially chosen McCabe Galloglass!" shouted Donnacha O'Cassidy Maguire.

There were several nervous gulps around the room. Such a room clearance when surrounded by hand-picked guards would generally be a cue for murder. However, on this occasion, several members of the northern Catholic clergy walked in.

"Lords of the north, today we sign another plea to King Phillip of Spain!"

Everyone cheered.

"To summarise, before we all sign, we are asking the King of Spain to send an army of no less than eight thousand men, but preferably ten thousand, to land here in the north."

There was another loud cheer.

"Then, with his help, we will throw out the English!"

There was an immense roar of approval.

"We have also asked for his ongoing protection and that we would swear loyalty to him."

The cheered were more muted.

"Ladies and gentlemen, that is what we agreed," exclaimed Hugh Maguire.

"Indeed it is," said Hugh O'Neill. "We are too weak to beat the English by ourselves. We need weapons, training and experienced soldiers used to fighting pitched battles to beat them. We must be united and stop all this infighting!" he raised his goblet. "To the northern lords!"

"The northern lords!" came the response as mugs met goblet and alcohol spilt over the sides and fell on the ground.

"It is time to sign!" cried Hugh Maguire.

Everyone roared again.

Hugh Maguire handed the quill to Hugh O'Neill, as the senior lord of the alliance. Hugh O'Neill scribbled his signature and symbolically gave the quill to Red Hugh. He scratched his name, held the quill aloft and handed it to Hugh Maguire to sign. He signed and rolled up the scroll. Hugh Maguire gave the letter to the bishop who made haste to a waiting boat on the river which would lead to the sea, whereupon a ship would bring him to Spain.

Hugh Maguire shouted over the cheering crowd. "The northern alliance is now sealed!"

A boisterous night of alcohol ensued where new friendships were forged, and old grievances were temporarily forgotten.

The next day Red Hugh left after inspecting the Galloglass he left behind. Hugh O'Neill stayed slightly longer, leaving behind experienced military men; both Irishmen who had served in continental armies, and Spanish survivors from the Great Armada.

He hugged Hugh Maguire before he left.

"No matter how it appears from the outside, I still support you. I'm not strong enough yet to take on the English."

"Thank you, father in law. I put my trust in you."

"And put your faith in the King of Spain. His last ship may have sunk and taken Archbishop O'Hely to the bottom of the sea, but we'll keep trying and will succeed."

"I only wish my father was here to see the day we are finally free!"

"And that day will come soon. Goodbye!"

Hugh O'Neill mounted his horse and left. Cormac Baron followed with his soldiers while the O'Hagan brothers stayed behind with their men and took up residence on the lands of Connor Roe Maguire.

30

Roisin

Eunan's bride had arrived and was neglected due to the excitement surrounding the letter. However, once all the visitors had gone, Seamus quickly recalled her arrival. He summoned Finn from Enniskillen town to look for her. Finn came back to report his success to Seamus.

"I have found her, but you may not like what you see."

"I don't have to fuck her, and I'm sure Eunan can do her from behind while polishing his throwing axes. Bring me to her."

Finn took him into the main castle building.

"Oh shit. We should have been a bit more precise in our wife criteria," said Seamus.

"At least we'd have the alliance, and there are plenty of prostitutes to keep Eunan occupied."

"You don't know him as I do. She is exactly what we don't want, a bad influence!"

Seamus and Finn peered through the chapel door at a pious young woman kneeling on the floor deep in prayer.

"Unfortunately, once I planted the idea in Hugh Maguire's mind, he became very keen on the idea," said Seamus.

"So what are we going to do?"

"I'll think of something. But let's go. We have a wedding to organise."

That evening Hugh Maguire held a wedding feast for Eunan. Eunan and Seamus sat at the top table for the first time, alongside Alexander MacDonnell Og MacSweeney and the bride's father and brothers. They ate, drank and made merry while they waited for the arrival of the bride. Donnacha O'Cassidy Maguire came up and whispered in Hugh Maguire's ear. Hugh stood up and banged his knife on his mug.

"Lords, ladies and those of you of ill repute!"

The Maguire men roared their approval.

"It gives me great pleasure to be able to strengthen further the ties to that great clan and our friends and allies, the O'Donnells."

"To the O'Donnells!" Seamus saluted.

"The O'Donnells!" the Maguire men choruses back.

"Now let me not make the groom wait any longer! He has to consummate the marriage before he leaves for war!"

"Hurray!"

"Now Eunan, let me introduce your bride, Roisin!"

Roisin was led out by her proud father. She wore a black dress with a veil over her face. She was half the size of Eunan in her black shapelessness, but the dress billowed almost equal in width. Eunan stood before her and gazed downwards in anticipation. Roisin slowly lifted her veil. The crowd gasped, and someone laughed.

"Who laughed?!" roared Seamus. "Who laughed?"

Eunan was shocked and dumbstruck. Roisin looked at him, burst into tears and ran out of the room, swiftly followed by her father.

"If I find out who was laughing, I'm going to split their head open!" shouted Seamus.

Pandemonium broke loose. Seamus went up to Hugh Maguire.

"Did you know she looked like that when you arranged this? She's spent all her time since she got here on her knees praying. Probably praying that Eunan was blind!"

"I'll sort this out. It is a great insult to the Maguire clan, but they are our allies. I will speak to the father and Alexander MacDonnell Og MacSweeney."

"Will there be a wedding?"

"A lot of that depends on Eunan."

Eunan had run out of the hall. Too many youthful bad memories stormed his brain. He needed some space to think. He remembered sitting on a stump in a whirl of laughter. They were laughing at him. The children of the village formed a circle around him held hands and skipped.

"Who are Eunan's parents? We don't know! He crippled his mother when he was born of a monster from the forest!"

"I didn't cripple my mother! It was the next baby!"

A face and finger pointed at him.

"That's because you crippled her!"

Eunan's leech scars began to itch. He began to walk towards the building exit. He saw Hugh Maguire argue with Alexander MacDonnell Og MacSweeney.

"How could one of your clan bring such an ugly woman to be the wife of one of our best up and coming warriors? It is an insult to the Maguires! Surely Red Hugh didn't sanction this? What if I go back and tell him of the insult you have perpetrated on us?"

"Sir, sir, please calm down. The O'Donnells meant no insult by this. The O'Doherty clan are one of the most unruly of the O'Donnell lands with great sympathies with the English. Red Hugh is desperate to integrate them into the O'Donnell clan before war breaks out. Unfortunately, Sean Og O'Doherty is an ugly man with ugly children. This is the more difficult end of alliance making. What if we also send a few prostitutes your gentleman can have as concubines to make his marriage a little more bearable. A great warrior such as he will be away at war most of the time and when he is at home, all he has to do is ensure she is with child and his duty will be over. The O'Donnell realises you are doing him a big favour and will repay you."

Hugh Maguire paused to think.

"We need guns and pikes and trainers for our men."

"Red Hugh will support you in all of these."

"We need trained O'Donnell troops to assist my own."

"Red Hugh is happy to reciprocate."

"Then they shall be married in the morning."

* * *

The next morning Eunan got ready for his wedding in a room in the castle Hugh Maguire had given him for the duration of his wedding day. Seamus helped him dress.

"I am so glad that you saw it as your duty to the Maguire clan to marry this woman. As long as she is with child after tonight, your duty will more or less be over. We can drop her off at the village and then come back to Enniskillen and join in the preparations for the war."

Eunan grunted.

"What if I don't want to do that?"

"Which part?"

"Drop her off."

"What? Are you going to make her a horse boy and get her to carry your axes? Don't be so silly. You've just got pre-wedding nerves. We will get the ladies to give you a potion to make sure you are extra virile tonight."

Seamus stepped back.

"There! You look like a lord on his way to the Irish Council! That lady won't believe her luck to get to marry you!"

Eunan fiddled with his clothes and scratched his leech scabs.

"Ok! Don't do that! You'll undo all my good work!" Seamus straightened everything again. "Now try not to fidget until after you are married. Once you have done that and she is with child, then and only then, can you do what you like."

Seamus brought Eunan to the main hall where a small number of dignitaries from both the Maguire and O'Donnell clans had gathered. Edmund Magauran agreed to officiate the ceremony to impress the O'Dohertys and O'Donnells as to Eunan's status.

Eunan stood before the archbishop and waited. The bride arrived, a couple of minutes later, escorted by her father. She was an opulent vision in white. She stood before Eunan and took his hand, at the invitation of the bishop. Eunan stared at her veiled face and tried to pick out her eyes from beneath the mesh. She smiled and looked at the floor. At that moment, Eunan could see a bit of him in her, just wanting to be loved but held back by something she could not control. From that moment, she was beautiful to him. He listened to the bishop but stared at Roisin. It was like an outside voice said 'I do', but it was him. He could tell by the way Roisin looked at him. The white veil revealed her face. He kissed Roisin, and everyone cheered.

Seamus looked at Finn.

"He's taking this a bit too seriously."

It was time for another feast at which Eunan was the centre of attention. Hugh Maguire looked satisfied for the O'Doherty O'Donnells seemed very pleased with themselves for having married off Roisin. The night was a whirl for Eunan, and he soon found himself a little drunk beside the marital bed. Roisin was dressed head to toe in a grey nightgown. She was on her knees, but to Eunan's disappointment, kneeled beside the marital bed saying a prayer for help and guidance on her wedding night. She got up and lay on her back on the bed. She pulled her nightgown over her waist, enough so that Eunan could gain access.

"You can get on now!" she said.

Eunan went totally red, lucky it was hidden in the darkness.

"Er, ok."

Eunan remembered back to what the Enniskillen boys had told him. He spat on his hand, shoved it down his pants and rubbed until he was ready. He perched on the end of the bed and looked at the outline of Roisin's body underneath the nightgown.

"What are you waiting for?" she said.

Eunan got on and, with some guidance from Roisin's hand, stuck it in. Roisin turned her head and prayed some more. Eunan found it off-putting but carried on as he considered it to be his husbandly duty. He continued until he was done. He pulled out and kissed Roisin on the cheek. After which she got up, cleaned herself and got into bed.

"Goodnight husband." She rolled over and went to sleep.

Eunan sat at the end of the bed. Was that it? Was his wedding night over? Was she with child? Nothing would be answered that evening as Roisin was already asleep. Eunan lay down beside her.

The next day came too soon, for Seamus was banging his fist on the door.

"Get up, lover boy! It's time to go!"

The aggression of the knocks caused Eunan to think there was something wrong, like the English had invaded or they were under siege. He dressed quickly and ran down the stairs and out into the courtyard.

Outside, the Maguire nobility were readying their horses, and inside the castle, the O'Donnell and O'Neill men were lined up outside waiting.

Seamus went over and slapped him on the back.

"Now that you have emptied your sack into her holiness, we can get back to business."

Eunan brushed his hand away.

"Don't be so tetchy! You've only known her for less than a day. You have to get used to the banter of fighting men. They need it to get rid of the images of slicing through other men's heads, which has the irritating habit of haunting them. Come on, let's do some deeds you can pretend were glorious and boast to her about them when you see her again in the village."

"Village? Am I not coming straight back here to see her then?"

"No, it is far too dangerous for her here. If the English return, the first place they are heading is Enniskillen."

"What about her family?"

"They have their own lives to lead, their own battles to fight."

"Who will bring her to the village? Can I not do it? I am her husband!"

Finn came along with five of their Galloglass.

"Finn is going to take her. He has to go back anyway to try and raise more men."

Eunan fought back the tears, for he knew they would only bring ridicule.

"Take good care of her Finn. If you don't, you'll have me to answer to!"

"I will take as good care of her as if she was my own wife."

"Don't make her your wife!" Eunan yelped.

Finn glanced at Seamus.

Hugh Maguire came out and walked up to Eunan, slapping him on the back again.

"That was a great thing you did for the family yesterday. Now come on! Let's go steal some cattle!" he said, walking off.

"Why is everyone congratulating me as if I did them a huge favour?" Eunan asked Seamus.

"They know you feel a great sense of duty and responsibility."

"I do, but it is still confusing!"

"Get on your horse. It's time to go."

"Can I not say goodbye to Roisin?"

"No time. She will be all the more delighted to see you when she hears you were so important you had to leave straight away."

"Where are we going?"

"Connacht."

31

The Raiding Life

The Governor of Connacht, Sir Richard Bingham, had aggressively driven out the local Irish chieftains from his province and stolen their wealth. Many of the chieftains and their men had joined Hugh Maguire and made Fermanagh their new home. Partly in response to this, and also to undermine the Maguire, the Governor was a frequent raider into Fermanagh. This had been a source of much agitation to Hugh Maguire, especially since the Irish Council ignored his numerous protests. Once he received the blessing of Hugh O'Neill and secretly allowed the use of his men he had left behind in Fermanagh, Hugh Maguire set about getting revenge.

He assembled his forces, and a raid consisting of 1,100 men went into Sligo. They made their way to Ballymote Castle, for their scouts had informed them the main English troops in the region were there. Hugh Maguire moved with such swiftness and stealth he caught the English totally by surprise. Hugh Maguire ordered the burning of the town and the blockade of the English garrison in the castle. Hugh Maguire divided his forces. Half the army continued the siege of the castle and half continued the raid. Seamus and Eunan went on the raid.

They marauded around Sligo, looking for things to steal or destroy. They burned seven towns and took as many cattle as they could find. They retreated to Ballymote as soon as they encountered any serious resistance. Hugh Maguire considered the raid a success, so they abandoned the siege and went back to Enniskillen.

On their return Hugh Maguire kept most of the cattle for himself as it was 'for the cause'. Eunan still seemed depressed, so Seamus sent him to the islands of Lower Lough Erne to help the Maguire project to fortify and make the islands self-sustainable. Eunan managed to slip off and visit his Monastery, which made him feel marginally better.

Hugh Maguire enjoyed counting the spoils of his raid and threw himself into planning the next one. Seamus was sent with the O'Donnell Galloglass to south Fermanagh to keep Connor Roe Maguire in check. Eunan in the meantime returned to Enniskillen Castle, with the mission completed. He asked after his wife and if anyone knew where she was. He was directed to Finn and found him wandering in Enniskillen Castle. Eunan was alarmed at the state he found Finn in.

"What happened to you? Where did you get those scars?"

Finn turned pale.

"When did you return to the castle?" Finn asked.

"A day or so ago! Why?"

"You didn't hear what happened?"

"Obviously not!"

"She is gone," whispered Finn as he looked at the ground. "I was bringing her back to the village as instructed until we were set upon by agents of Connor Roe Maguire. Our men and I managed to fight our way out, but your wife, unfortunately, was captured."

Eunan's fingernail cracked upon clawing at Finn's chain mail.

"What do you mean she was captured? You were supposed to defend her with your life! Yet you come brazenly back with barely a scratch on you! You're lucky I'm not Seamus, but maybe I should ask him what I should do!"

"We were ambushed in a forest, Lord. We got split up into groups! I tried to fight my way back, but there were too many of them! We hadn't a chance!"

Eunan threw him aside.

"Go! Get out of my sight before I change my mind. You are lucky we need all the men we can get to fight the upcoming war or else you would be going straight back to Connor Roe Maguire to retrieve her."

"Thank you for your mercy and wisdom, Lord. I would gladly lead any mission to get her back if Hugh Maguire would allow us."

"I will speak to Hugh Maguire. Do not stray far, for you owe your Lord. If I call and you don't respond, I will hunt you down and cut you in two."

"Yes, Lord!" Finn bowed and ran away.

* * *

Eunan's scars from his leechings itched as if they were the compounding punishment for all his failures. He had to save Roisin, or he was no man. The castle was busy organising another celebratory feast, so Eunan slipped away. He went to the river moorings and paid a ferryman to bring him to his island. His scars began to burn now as his bad blood bubbled beneath his skin. His eyes welled with tears, and he stared at the shore so as not to show the ferryman he was weak, even though the ferryman did not know who he was. Even at times of such despair, pride boiled in his veins. The ferryman reached the shore and Eunan jumped out and threw him his coin. Eunan went ashore, and the priests recognised him in the dying light of the day. They knew why he was here. Eunan lay upon the table. He prayed, the priests prayed. The physician priest applied the leeches and Eunan felt the bad blood drain from his body along with his memories of everyone he had disappointed.

* * *

Hugh Maguire was so overjoyed with the success of his last raid that another one swiftly followed. This time he decided to target the county of Roscommon and penetrate deeper into Connacht if the opportunity arose. Hugh Maguire assembled his men. Eunan and Seamus again were part of the raiding party. Eunan rode with Archbishop Edmund Magauran acting as his bodyguard, while Seamus was in charge of a section of Galloglass.

Hugh Maguire probed into Roscommon and did not experience serious resistance. However, Sir Richard Bingham soon heard of the new raid and swiftly moved his forces to counter.

Hugh Maguire's men concentrated around Tulsk and soon clashed with the English scouts. Bingham moved up his soldiers, but a thick fog smothered the battlefield which prevented both sides from properly engaging. However, the mist cleared, and Hugh Maguire realised he was heavily outnumbered. A couple of covering volleys from the O'Donnell musketeers and Hugh Maguire sounded the retreat.

However, the fog cut off Eunan's group of horsemen. When the fog lifted, they found themselves in front of a section of English shot.

"Retreat!" shouted Eunan, and he dug his heels into the sides of his horse.

But before they could turn the English has dispatched a volley. Eunan could only look on as the bullets lodged in Edmund Magauran's chest and he fell to the ground as Edmund rode like an Irishman, without stirrups.

"No!" Eunan cried and dismounted from his horse and ran for his friend.

The English grappled for their powder and bullets. Eunan grabbed the dying body of Edmund and slung him over the back of his horse. Eunan just had time to mount himself and dig his heels in before he was driven off the battlefield by another volley of shot.

Eunan rode to Hugh Maguire, and by the time he got there, Edmund was dead. With a heavy heart, Hugh Maguire ordered his men back to Fermanagh.

Once back in Enniskillen, Archbishop Magauran was laid out in the castle chapel and Eunan cried bitter tears for his dead friend and mentor. Hugh Maguire retired to his room, for he had to write to Red Hugh and Hugh O'Neill and tell them that their principal contact with both the King of Spain and the Pope was dead. Hugh Maguire held a funeral mass for the bishop of Armagh in the chapel in Enniskillen Castle.

* * *

In the meantime, Hugh O'Neill did not waste the distraction Hugh Maguire's exploits had provided him. Phelim MacTurlough O'Neill, the main ally of Sir Henry Bagenal, and the crown, north of Lough Neagh, was brutally murdered by the O'Hagans, the foster brothers of O'Neill. O'Neill's men also attacked lesser clans in the region and forced them to submit. This led to the wavering lords of northeast Ulster allying themselves with Hugh O'Neill. However, the Irish Council was now alarmed and summoned Hugh O'Neill.

Hugh O'Neill appeared before the Irish Council to answer a litany of allegations. These ranged from not being able to control or being in league with Hugh Maguire, the murder of Phelim MacTurlough O'Neill, being in league with the Spanish crown, plotting a rebellion against the crown and any other complaint his enemies could throw at him. All parties spent the primarily fighting season of 1593 endlessly sending letters between Maguire, O'Neill and the Irish Council.

* * *

Eunan sat in the soldier's camp on the island next to Enniskillen Castle and sharpened his axes. He managed to recruit ten of his village Galloglass into his plan to rescue Roisin, further widening the rift between himself and Seamus. Seamus' refusal to help the rescue had led their relationship almost to breaking point.

Eunan yearned to break free of Seamus' grip as he considered himself to be a chieftain in his own right now, and that Seamus was holding him back. Eunan thought that once the war came, Seamus would be distracted by greed or reassigned to lead Galloglass somewhere else, hopefully far away from Fermanagh. Then Eunan could rescue Fiona, topple Connor Roe Maguire and take south Fermanagh for himself. He just needed to free himself from Seamus. He had his ten Galloglass seated around him. His idea of the knights of Colmcille was not dead yet.

However, Eunan's idea had not gone down well with all the village Galloglass. Some had humoured him so as not to incur his wrath. But they went behind his back to Seamus to try and prevent the mission. Upon hearing the rumours, Seamus went to confront Eunan.

Seamus brought Finn with him, for he was unsure of how he would be received. He arrived where Eunan sat and stood over him. Eunan continued to sharpen his axe.

"Good afternoon Eunan. You might hurt yourself if you make the blade too sharp," said Seamus with a smirk.

Eunan just looked at him and kept sharpening.

"You're not taking the loss of your wife, who you only knew for one day, too well, are you?"

Eunan gave Seamus a pithy look.

"I'm going to rescue her and, unlike you, my men are going to help me!" The Galloglass gave Seamus a stern look.

Seamus turned to the men and shook his finger.

"You men remember who's in charge! You'll regret any disloyalty to me!"

The men shifted uncomfortably in their seats. Seamus turned to Eunan.

"There'll be no incursions into Connor Roe Maguire's territory without the explicit permission of Hugh Maguire. He doesn't want to start a war without good cause!"

"Is kidnapping the wife of a Maguire chieftain not good enough cause?" shouted Eunan.

"You knew her for less than twenty-four hours! I could get the marriage annulled for you if it wasn't consummated."

Eunan was silent and looked away. Seamus whistled.

"I never knew you had it in you! The prostitutes of Donegal town would love you if you weren't so busy praying. How about lying? I can still get it annulled if you say it wasn't consummated."

"And dishonour the woman I married before God?"

"If I knew it was going to cause this much trouble, I would never have arranged this! Anyway, she is probably dead now. How long will you leave it until you consider her dead?"

"I'll never consider her dead until I see her body with my own eyes," growled Eunan.

"You're going to see enough death in the coming times. Forget your 'wife', pick up your axe and prepare to defend Fermanagh. If you're lucky, we can get to go and pay a visit to Connor Roe Maguire, and you can greet him with your axe."

Seamus went to walk away.

"Are you coming?" he said to Eunan.

"I'm good here."

"And the rest of you?"

The ten Galloglass remained seated, and Seamus turned and stood before them. He twisted his axe shaft and pointed the blade at them.

"I trained you. You are my Galloglass. You either come, or I split your heads open here and now!"

Nobody moved.

"Is not one of you going to challenge me? Have I trained you that badly that you're all cowards?"

Eunan put his hand out to reach for his axe shaft. Seamus wagged his finger.

"I have been good to you, Eunan. Don't make me think that they were moments of weakness I have to make amends for!"

The Galloglass looked at Eunan and saw he was not going to back down.

"I will follow you, Lord," said one, and he picked up his weapon and stood behind Seamus.

"Any more to chase this fool's errand?" said Seamus, pointing at Eunan.

One by one, the men stood behind Seamus until Eunan sat alone.

"Well, are you coming? We've got a war to fight!" said Seamus, again offering a way back for Eunan.

"I'll rescue her myself."

"Let me explain your options to you. You can come with us now, and we'll forget all about this. We'll even try and rescue her when we raid south Fermanagh. Or else you can try and rescue her yourself. If you do, you won't get past the gate as nobody starts a war without the permission of the Maguire. As a Maguire chieftain, you should know that. You'll have thrown all your good work away for an arranged marriage that lasted a day. What'll it be?"

Eunan did not move.

"Don't be a fool all your life!"

Eunan stood up, picked up his axes and his personal belongings and walked towards Seamus, and then past him towards the castle. Seamus came up from behind and ruffled his hair.

"Good man! I knew you'd see sense in the end. They all said you were a thick-headed obstinate brute, but I defended you!" Seamus smiled, but it was not the friendly smile of old.

"I'm sure you did."

* * *

The allegations against Hugh O'Neill lacked sufficient evidence for a weak Irish Council to act. The fear of Hugh O'Neill striking out towards the Pale was enough for sufficient Councillors to decline to continue to prosecute.

Hugh Maguire returned from another unsuccessful negotiation with the Irish Council emboldened for he saw that they were weak. With Hugh O'Neill's and the dissatisfied MacMahons' encouragement he secretly drew up plans to raid into Monaghan. He called his chieftains and allies together and outlined his plan. Eunan was ecstatic. The opportunity to rescue, or at worst avenge, his wife had come sooner than expected.

32

Prelude to War

Finn was busy training the village Galloglass. He could feel Eunan's eyes on the back of his head. He turned to appease his master.

"Good afternoon, chieftain. Are you here to inspect the men? Are we going on another raid?"

"Indeed we are, that's why I'm here."

"Excellent, your Lordship. I have been recruiting horse boys, so we have a full complement of men. Do you wish to see the Galloglass fight? You can fight one of them yourself if you wish?"

"Now is not the time. I wish to speak with you in private."

"Of course!" Finn turned to the Galloglass and instructed them to keep training.

Eunan and Finn spoke behind one of their tents in the campsite beside the training ground. Seamus had seen Eunan approaching Finn and had kept out of sight. He crept up and sat behind another tent but within earshot.

"Tell me exactly what happened when my wife got kidnapped. Every detail is important for our next raid is into Monaghan, passing through the territory of Connor Roe Maguire," said Eunan as he edged closer to Finn who could not back away.

"I'm sure revenge boils in your blood, your Lordship."

"It does. But see this as your opportunity to atone for your mistakes."

Finn winced at the comment but nodded his head all the same.

"As I told you before, we were in a forest strung out over a narrow path..."

"Which forest?"

"A common one, above the upper Lough on the way to the village. If we were to go there on this raid, we would need to leave the raiding party temporarily."

"That can be arranged. Continue with your story."

"There was a man who lay injured beside the road. We went to help him. Then we were descended upon."

"Who were they? Bandits?"

"No. I'm sure they were a raiding party sent by Connor Roe."

"Which way did they escape?"

"They chased me away, so I've no idea."

The anger flashed onto Eunan's face.

"Prepare the men! The raid starts tomorrow! They must be ready to break off and search for Roisin!"

Seamus came out from behind the tent.

"That wouldn't be wise. I'll go with you instead."

"It would make more sense for the whole battle to break off. We have to assume we'll meet some resistance."

"They would notice too easily, and we would undo all the good work we've done previously. Trust me, the two of us will be more than adequate."

"How'll we know where to start our search?"

"Then make that three of us! Finn will show us where."

Finn grimaced but knew he could not refuse, for it was not a request. Eunan gripped Finn's shoulder and led him back to the training ground. He was not going to let Finn out of his sight.

* * *

The next day the Maguires, disaffected O'Rourkes, O'Reillys and others joined the MacSweeney Galloglass and O'Hagan brothers and assembled outside of Enniskillen. The malcontent MacMahons would join them as they entered south Fermanagh. There were more than a thousand men in the raid with three hundred more MacMahons ready to join them.

They made their way quickly through Fermanagh, but such a large force could only evade Connor Roe Maguire's scouts for so long. They combined with the MacMahons in south-central Fermanagh. Eunan and Seamus took this opportunity to break off, and Finn led them to where he was ambushed. It was a couple of hours' ride from where the main raiding party was.

They entered the forest on the road to their village. Finn knew precisely where the ambush had taken place, but there was precious little evidence left.

Eunan searched with swollen eyes the undergrowth and pathways for clues that his wife was still alive. Seamus looked at Finn and shook his head in disgust.

"So it either never happened here, or we have some very tidy bandits."

They looked a little further, and Eunan threw down the stick he used to search the bushes.

"How would you tell one piece of thievery from another without specific evidence?"

"It's time to go," said Seamus. "We cannot be absent for too long, or we'll lose track of the raid. Someone will suspect something is up!"

Eunan kept searching the bushes.

"Come on, Eunan, it's time to go!"

Eunan stood up.

"I want to follow the route they would have followed if they were taking her to Castle Skea."

"We don't have time!" replied Seamus.

"If we ride quickly we can make the time!"

Seamus could see there would be no persuading Eunan.

"Ok, but we must leave now!"

The three men jumped on their horses and rode as if Roisin's life depended on it. They skirted around the upper lake and kept an eye out for evidence of Roisin, the location of the raiding parties and Connor Roe's spies.

After riding for several hours, Eunan suddenly veered off the path and rode down to the edge of a gully. He leapt off his horse and walked to the verge. A piece of cloth fluttered in the wind, snagged on a thorn bush. He rolled it on his fingertips and sniffed it. A tear rolled down his cheek. Seamus saw something was up and got off his horse, walking over to Eunan. He looked over the edge. On the rocks below was a woman's body, broken and covered in blood, her limbs a tangled mess. Beside her was the carriage Roisin had left Enniskillen in. Seamus wanted to throttle Finn. He had not decided if he would defend him if Eunan turned upon him. However, Eunan knelt on one knee for a few minutes and then said quietly, "Come on, let's go."

"Aren't you going to try and bury her?" asked Seamus.

"There's no time," sniffed Eunan. "I could climb down and drag her up and give her a decent burial, but in the meantime, the raid goes through Connor Roe Maguire's land, and my chance for revenge evaporates."

"Very sensible," nodded Seamus.

Eunan bent down and made a little cross of twigs and twine and stuck it in the ground.

"Thank you," said Eunan to the sky as he got off his knees when his prayers finished.

Finn brought the horses. Eunan turned and took a throwing axe from his belt. He walked up to Finn and thrust the blade into the lower hairs of his beard. A red stream of blood dripped onto Finn's shirt.

"My wife is dead. I didn't know her long, but it makes no difference to me. She's dead. If I found you had anything to do with it, so will you!"

"Hey! No fighting! Finn didn't have anything to do with it!" said Seamus, moving to try and get between the two of them.

"It doesn't quite add up, does it! No sign of any struggle where you said it would be and then she was thrown down a ravine when it would have been easier to hold her for ransom!"

"Please! I tried my best to defend her!"

"Maybe she tried to escape and rather than be recaptured threw herself down the ravine. You don't know what happened!" said Seamus.

"Stick near me Finn, for if I see you are trying to escape, you may just find an axe in the back of your head!"

Seamus grabbed Eunan by the shoulders.

"Come on, let's go," Seamus turned and said. "Get on your horse, Finn."

"Mark my words, Finn," said Eunan as he pushed the shaft of his axe back in his belt.

They mounted their horses and rode for Connor Roe Maguire's lands in south Fermanagh.

* * *

They soon found the raiding party, for it had not progressed much further as small groups of MacMahons joined in fits and starts. Seamus and Eunan found their Galloglass and joined the march through south Fermanagh. They went past Connor Roe Maguire's lands, much to Eunan's disappointment, to maintain the element of surprise. The raiders spilt over the border and spoiled all the English tenanted farms they came across, destroying crops and stealing cattle. Then they went for Monaghan Town and the English garrison there. The English occupied the walled abbey in the town and had a good complement of men. Hugh Maguire assaulted the abbey but could not overcome the volleys of shot and fortifications. Seamus and Eunan led some of the assaults and lost ten of their men to the English volleys. This was a significant loss for them to bear, so they joined in the retreat. After the unsuccessful assault, Hugh Maguire blockaded the garrison, burned the town and raided the surrounding lands. The raiding parties reached as far as Louth when Maguire sounded the retreat.

Hugh Maguire retired again to Enniskillen while distributing the spoils of the raid. Much went to the MacMahons, partly to compensate them for their loss of lands and partly to ensure their future loyalty. On the retreat home, there was no major raid on Connor Roe Maguire's lands, although minor spoiling did take place. Eunan was most disappointed by the whole raid. He lost ten men, found his wife had been killed in suspicious circumstances and was not allowed to take his revenge against Connor Roe Maguire. He went to see Hugh Maguire and got permission to go back to his village until the Maguire needed him again. Everyone from the village set out on the road home.

The roads were busier than before as people moved to areas where they felt safer. All over the north acts of assassination, intimidation and spoiling took place as the lords of the north consolidated their positions and suppressed any deemed threats in their clans. Upon reaching the village, Seamus set about recruiting some replacements to the men they had just lost. He had ordered Finn and some of his men to retrieve Roisin's body and bring it back to the village. Eunan went into mourning and took out a boat, rowing on the lake to search for a suitable burial ground for Roisin. When he spotted something appropriate, he rowed towards the selected island, moored his boat and went ashore. It was deserted and covered in woods. Its diminutive size did not reflect its immense beauty, and a small tree-covered hill on top of the island was what Eunan sought. He went back to his boat and got a shovel and proceeded to dig Roisin's grave.

When he rowed back across the lake, Finn waited for him on the shoreline. Finn directed him back to his house, where on the table lay Roisin's body, all wrapped in cloth. No one was allowed to unwrap the body. The priest came and gave mass. Eunan and his men carried the body on their shoulders down to the boat on the shore. They carefully placed the body inside. Eunan climbed in by himself and rowed away. He returned the next day.

33

The English Are Coming

Hugh Maguire had a secret meeting with Hugh O'Neill straight after the Monaghan raid. As a result of this, Hugh O'Neill again petitioned Lord Deputy Fitzwilliam for a pardon for Hugh Maguire and the minor lords of the region because the attacks were in reaction to the provocations of the English provincial governors. However, a response was not forthcoming. Hugh O'Neill advised Hugh Maguire to prepare for war.

When Dublin finally responded it was to declare Hugh Maguire a traitor. Sir Henry Bagenal was given the commission on the 11th September 1593 to raise an army and to move against the Maguires. Sir Henry raised a substantial force of over a thousand men, mainly Irish soldiers, both from the Pale and those already under his service. He also had several English officers to lead the Irishmen and also a small core of English soldiers. The Irish Council gave Hugh O'Neill the commission of assisting Bagenal and Hugh promised twelve hundred men.

When Bagenal assembled his forces, he moved first against the MacMahons of Monaghan who had supported the last Maguire raid. After spoiling their lands, he moved into south Fermanagh. He spared

Connor Roe and his supporters because of Connor Roe's ongoing loyalty to the crown. Sir Henry marched across south Fermanagh taking the route north of upper Lough Erne, thus sparing Eunan's village.

Meanwhile, Enniskillen Castle was alive with messengers being dispatched all over Fermanagh and the north. Seamus readied himself for battle while Eunan sat by the fire in their camp outside Enniskillen for Hugh Maguire had recently recalled them.

"War is upon us! The English are coming!" cried a messenger as he ran through the camp.

Eunan picked up his throwing axes and began to sharpen them.

"I hope they do you some good on the battlefield with all those muskets and pikes around. You're young and can adapt. Why don't you take up a modern weapon, or even better, become a commander like me!"

"It was always my destiny to become an axeman, ever since my mother told me I had Viking blood seeping through my body."

"One of your litany of problems is that you listened to that mother of yours. All she ever did was mess with your head!"

Eunan sneered.

"Demean another woman in my life, why don't you!? Who are you to berate me so? My father?"

"You'd have been much better off if I was. You cannot be this sensitive and go into battle wielding an axe. If you don't think yourself to death, you'll continue to be scarred for the rest of your life!"

"I already am scarred for life!" Eunan scratched his leech scabs. "At least if I died a good death for a worthy cause I may get some redemption."

"All the more pity that nobody will notice your redemption, except maybe for you. It may give you some solace, just before you die!"

"All you do is sneer and put me down!" growled Eunan.

"I'm trying to teach you! Where's the glory in having a stump of an arm and living on charity for however long your neighbours can recall whatever battle you were in? And it's no good losing a limb in a battle you lost or ran away from. Scant charity you'll get then!"

"We're going to win this war, and I am going to seek revenge for my wife!"

"I'm tired of arguing with you. Just stick near me, boy, so that I can keep you alive until you get some sense!"

A messenger approached Seamus and Eunan.

"All men of rank are to be addressed by the Maguire in the castle. Come quick!"

Seamus and Eunan were directed to the great hall once they arrived at the castle. The hall was packed, standing room only, and Seamus and Eunan slipped in at the back. Hugh Maguire stood on the raised platform beside the seat of the Maguire. He paced up and down, waiting for everyone to arrive. Donnacha O'Cassidy Maguire quietened the murmurs so Hugh could speak.

"Noblemen of the Maguire clan, I have grave news to bring you. The war has started! The English have crossed the south Fermanagh border with a large army and are headed straight for Enniskillen. It is up to every one of you to defend Fermanagh to the last. I have sent messengers to our northern allies, and we will need to hold off the English until they arrive. What I do not doubt is our final victory! Once the lords of the north are united, no one can defeat them!"

The Maguire men cheered. The MacCabe Galloglass cleared the room and Seamus and Eunan went to make their preparations to move south and stop Bagenal from attacking Enniskillen.

* * *

Eunan and Seamus arrived at the camp at Liscoole the next day and immediately began to assist in the earthworks construction. In the meantime, Hugh O'Neill set off from Tyrone with his forces to join Bagenal. His first act was to spoil the lands of Connor Roe and steal the majority of his cattle. He met up with Bagenal on the north side of the River Erne. Hugh only brought six hundred men and two hundred horse, much to Sir Henry's consternation. They began to plan the campaign but could agree on little as old rivalries began to bubble over. In bygone years Hugh O'Neill had attempted to ally the Bagenals to himself through marriage, and when this was refused, had eloped with Bagenal's sister. As if relations could sink no lower, the two had been deadly rivals for the dominance of Ulster, only united as they were seemingly both agents of the crown in their appointed roles there. After much argument, Sir Henry decided to attempt to force a crossing at Liscoole ford over the River Erne.

Hugh Maguire had been well supported by his O'Donnell allies. In addition to the MacSweeney Galloglass, they had supplied him with several units of shot, which while they may not have been the most accurate, still make enough noise to put off a hesitant enemy. The Maguires dug a trench and constructed some earthworks and covered the crossing with their shot. Sir Henry abandoned attempting to cross after he made a few half-hearted efforts. He paused to consider his next move. He estimated that he would not make progress via frontal assault without having to overcome some serious resistance.

Sir Henry then went to O'Neill and their discussions about what to do next quickly descended into an argument. Bagenal wanted to assault the ford and encircle it, but O'Neill refused to divide their forces. They eventually agreed to attempt to try and outflank Maguire and go around lower Lough Erne and cross at the Belleek ford. They decamped on the 7th of October.

Hugh Maguire's spies and secret communications with Hugh O'Neill informed him that Bagenal was going to attempt to cross the river at Belleek. Hugh rushed his old style Galloglass and kern northwards.

Seamus and Eunan were glad to be on the move. Eunan was impatient for his first taste of a proper battle, but Seamus was happy to wait. They marched for a day and found themselves once more on the south side of the River Erne digging earthworks. Eunan threw himself into it, leading his men in felling trees and carving spikes. They created their fortifications in a bend on the river that jutted out into the Belleek ford.

The Maguires received further reinforcements from the O'Donnell under the leadership of Niall Garbh O'Donnell in the form of sixty horsemen, sixty swordsmen and one hundred Galloglass. The O'Donnell positioned the rest of his forces in southern Tirconnell poised if needed.

Seamus took Eunan aside when he saw Niall Garbh O'Donnell arrive.

"Why would the O'Donnell send him to any battle if he didn't want him to come back dead? I think we're digging our own graves here!"

"How can you say such a thing? The Maguire is defending the homeland! He would never do such a thing!"

"Oh yeah? Where's all the shot? There's only a few of them in the trench. Where are all the pikemen? Where are all the Maguire men apart from us lot from south Fermanagh? It's all old school Galloglass, Redshanks and men they don't want to make it off the battlefield!"

Eunan looked around, and his heart sank.

"Don't despair," said Seamus. "Just make sure you have somewhere to run!"

"Galloglass don't turn their backs! You taught me that!"

"As soon as the English touch the south side of the river, this army will break. Galloglass need to live to fight another day. Whatever song your soul becomes part of, if you die at this battle you will soon be forgotten. The dead this day are expendable!"

"I, for one, will be making a stand."

"If you die here, today, the village dies with you. You'll not avenge Roisin."

Eunan scowled at the mention of her and returned to his men and continued to toil on the earthworks. Seamus surveyed the locality, mainly for escape routes.

Bagenal made camp a mile north of the ford. Hugh O'Neill arrived shortly after and set up another camp nearby. Bagenal sent a messenger to O'Neill to come to his camp so they could discuss battle plans. Pessimism followed O'Neill to the meeting.

"They look well dug in on the other side. We'll lose many a good man if we try a direct assault."

Bagenal scowled as such negativity. He called for his subordinates. Two English officers entered the tent and saluted.

"Hugh, this is Captain Lee and Captain Dowdall who have the honour of leading the infantry on this expedition. The time for dithering and delay is over. They will be leading the frontal assault today. Please, Captain Dowdall, tell us your plan."

Captain Dowdall leaned over a hastily drawn map of the Irish defences around the ford.

"The ford is quite deep but perfectly crossable. It depends on what kind of missiles the rebels fire at us."

"I hear they have muskets," said O'Neill.

"I hear they are cowards and run at the first sign of trouble," replied Bagenal.

"May I continue, sirs," said Captain Dowdall.

Bagenal nodded.

"We need to advance along a narrow front, the same width as the ford and force our way over. As I said earlier, our men would initially be vulnerable to missiles as they cross the river, but there is an advantage in the terrain for us that the rebels may not have spotted!"

"Which is?" asked Bagenal.

"We can concentrate our musket fire from both sides at the section of their defences directly opposite us and pin them down, limiting the number of missiles that can fire at us. If we get enough men across the river as quickly as possible, then the line should break."

Bagenal turned to O'Neill and smirked.

"Do you have any objections to this plan?"

"We could incur a lot of casualties if it goes wrong. I don't want O'Neill men leading the charge."

Bagenal waved away his objections.

"Duly noted in our victory dispatch to the Queen. Are you going to do anything for this battle?"

"Let me supply the cavalry."

"And may they do their duty to crown and country."

Hugh O'Neill went back to his camp and sent half his men home.

34

Battle of Belleek

Abreeze blew through a cold morning, and the sheets of rain eventually stopped which allowed the few Irish musket men some respite to dry off their weapons. Eunan and Seamus took their position behind the earthworks, opposite the ford. Beside them were the Galloglass and swordsmen of Niall Garbh O'Donnell.

"I hope that fucker brought our cattle!" growled Seamus.

"Shut up! You'll get us killed!" replied Eunan.

Seamus' silence was only temporary.

"Look at the weapons they have! Even I think they belong in a curiosity collection, and I'm old!" said Seamus.

"As long as they fight, we have the advantage," said Eunan as he patted an enormous wooden spike protruding out of the ground.

"I've been to many battles, boy! The Irish hate fighting out in the open. They can't wait to fuck off. They like jumping out from behind trees! This army is made to break! Those spikes will only get in your way when you are 'retreating'!"

"Don't be so cynical. We're going to stand, fight and win!"

Seamus sighed.

"You're not some ancient warrior-hero your Mammy would tell

you about, who'd pull his axe out of his ass, kill everyone and then all the priests and girls would love him!"

Eunan glared at Seamus.

"Ok, sorry. Stories you overheard other Mammies telling their boys."

Eunan lifted his axe and pointed the blade at Seamus.

"Be careful with that! Don't hurt yourself before the big battle starts!"

* * *

Captains Dowdall and Lee drew up their men on the other side of the River Erne from

Belleek Castle. The pikemen drew up in their squares and readied themselves for battle. The English musket men cleaned their weapons and split into two groups. One group positioned themselves opposite the spur of land where the Irish had their earthworks with Belleek Castle to their left. The other group went around the spur and hid in the woods on the other side of the spur. Once the musket men were in position, Captain Dowdall drew up his men to cross the ford.

* * *

Hugh Maguire surveyed the battlefield from the rear. O'Donnell shot, Galloglass and Redshanks massed behind the earthworks with most of the Maguires spread out on the wings. Sean Og Maguire, one of his commanders, was beside him to receive instructions, for he was the commander of the earthworks.

"Have you received word from Hugh O'Neill?" asked Sean Og.

"His parting words to me were 'live to fight another day'. Adhere to that, please."

"As few Maguires will fall today as possible."

Sean Og bowed and rode off to take up his battle position.

* * *

Captain Dowdall signalled the advance. The musket men on both sides of the spur volleyed into the Irish earthworks. The Irish returned fire. But their inferior weapons meant that any effective volley disintegrated at one hundred yards. The superior weapons of the English, however, meant that their volleys laid down effective covering fire. There was some protection provided by the earthworks for the Irish defenders, but hiding behind the earthworks meant that they could not lay down missile fire over the ford. The Irish shot had lost the first stage of the battle.

Captain Dowdall's men marched forward in good order with only the odd musket ball or arrow whizzing over their heads. They entered the water. The river was swift and deep but thankfully narrow at the chosen point of crossing. The men were soon up to their armpits in water and held their weapons over their heads. Their musket men still did them a good service and the Irish were unable to provide a meaningful missile deterrent. Captain Dowdall's men marched up the south bank of the River Erne but were completely soaked. They drew up their formation again, lowered their pikes and marched towards the Irish defences. Captain Lee's men then entered the ford. O'Neill's cavalry followed Captain Lee's men and crossed the ford. The few Irish musket men let off a volley, but it had little effect on the oncoming English pikemen. First, Lee's men and then O'Neill's cavalry came onshore. Dowdall's column almost reached the Irish line, and the Irish line broke. As the Irish retreated, the English musket men fired volleys into their flanks which created chaos.

* * *

Eunan braced for the impending assault, hiding beneath the earthworks to avoid the musket shot. Musket balls fizzed off the top of the wooden walls. Seamus looked over the wall and turned to him.

"I have no ambition to die for the Maguire, especially not today. I'll be back!"

"Where are you going?" cried Eunan, but Seamus was already gone.

The English volleys crashed into the Irish lines with ever increasing frequency. Eunan looked through the cracks in the wooden wall and saw the English soldiers wading through the river almost unopposed. Eunan looked for the commander, Sean Og but could not see him anywhere. He wondered if the plan was to spring up as soon as the English set foot on this side of the river. However, once the English soldiers drew up formation, the cavalry made their way upon the shore. Then Niall Garbh O'Donnell's men fled. Once they left, the rest of the line broke. Eunan pulled out his axe.

"Let's get these bastards!" Eunan shouted as he raised his head, but even his own men started to run.

The front of the English column crashed into the earthworks, crushing the wooden wall. Eunan swung his axe, but it made little impression on a wall of pikes. A hand landed on his shoulder and dragged him away. The Irish soldiers were caught in the funnel that was the spur of the land in the river. They fled, ran into each other and all coherence was lost. The only resistance that temporarily halted the English were the earthworks.

* * *

Hugh Maguire sat on his horse and watched the battle predictably unfold. He turned to his commanders.

"Have we lost many today?"

"Redshanks and Galloglass from the O'Donnell coin."

"At least some of their debts died on the field. They can be grateful to me for that. Don't engage the O'Neill cavalry. Rally the men, and we'll reassemble at the rendezvous point."

With that, Hugh Maguire turned and left with the noble horsemen of his clan.

* * *

The English pikemen marched onwards, but there was little to engage with as the Irish were far more mobile than them and were already leaving the field. The second English column of Captain Lee with Bagenal at the head started to advance towards the retreating Irish.

Eunan was on the run with Seamus leading the way.

"Follow me! We must go past Belleek Castle so we can escape into Fermanagh. The English won't follow us there."

Eunan looked behind him and saw the second column crossing the river with the general at its head.

"No! I must show some fight!"

Seamus reached out, but Eunan broke free of his grip and Seamus lost sight of him in the mass of retreating bodies. Eunan pushed his way past his fleeing comrades and towards the English general. He came upon the pursuing English soldiers, and with several blows of his axe had downed two of them. The English general was coming within range. Another English soldier lurched at him, and then another. Eunan reached for a throwing axe. His battle axe thrust down the pike, thereby trapping it to the ground, and the throwing axe plunged into the side of the man's head. The next soldier received the spike of the battle axe in his cheek. Eunan pulled the axe out. The commander was in throwing range. He threw his axe as hard as he could and ran.

* * *

Sir Henry Bagenal followed his troops forward. He trusted his Captains and would have typically left them to conduct the forward operations of the battle, but he did not trust O'Neill. The English soldiers marched forward and the Irish fled before them, just as he had predicted.

O'Neill came across the river and rode up beside him.

"Leave this to me!" said O'Neill as he rode off with his men after the Irish.

A musket backfired near Bagenal, and there was a loud bang which caused his horse to rear. An axe came flying towards him, but Bagenal changed position due to the horse rearing. He felt the thud of an axe hit his leg. He took out his pistol and fired it in the direction of the retreating Irish. One of his men came up to him.

"Are you alright sir? That looks like a nasty scrape. Do you want to see a physician?"

Bagenal surveyed the battlefield.

"The day is won, they can do without me to finish them off. Lead the way, soldier!"

* * *

Eunan saw the axe fly but not land. Too many English. Even he did not want to die on a day that would bring no glory. He ran towards Belleek Castle as Seamus had instructed. Most of the Maguire men also ran in that direction. O'Neill's cavalry did not appear to follow them. They chased to the west, where the Redshanks and Niall Garbh O'Donnell had fled.

Most of the Maguire men retreated south and reassembled in such good order, it was like it was planned. Seamus looked for his men.

Eunan looked for a way to escape, for his leech scabs burned. Seamus managed to find most of his men with only two missing. All in all, Hugh Maguire lost around three hundred soldiers; including those missing, around a third of his force. Most of these were Redshanks, or Galloglass sent by the O'Donnell, who performed poorly in battle and bore most of the brunt of the O'Neill cavalry. Niall Garbh O'Donnell had disappeared, along with most of the men sent by O'Donnell. They were believed to have retreated northwards.

Bagenal now sat in western Fermanagh, victorious. He sent messengers to Sir Richard Bingham, Governor of Connacht, proposing to invade Tirconnell and decisively defeat the retreating Scottish mercenaries. O'Neill and his men left for Tyrone as O'Neill had sustained a minor injury. Red Hugh rallied his forces in south Tirconnell to counter Bagenal. The messenger came back with a message from Bingham, who refused to cooperate with an invasion of Tirconnell. Bagenal now found himself isolated between the armies of Hugh Maguire and Red Hugh.

He had defeated the Irish and still held the field. Bagenal decided that this was enough to paint as a victory in his reports back to the crown. He set off back to Monaghan via Enniskillen. As he marched any resistance melted away before him. This reinforced his belief the Irish were well beaten.

Bagenal again stopped outside Enniskillen which again was well-defended. He decided not to attack. It was coming on to winter, and the Irish conscripts who made up a large percentage of the army wished to get back to their farms and save what remained of their harvests. No point being out campaigning while the family starved at home.

Bagenal stopped off at Liscoole where Hugh Maguire had previously prevented him from crossing the River Erne. He stopped long enough to damage the fort, just in case he had to come back and assault

Enniskillen.

Hugh Maguire followed Bagenal at a safe distance down Fermanagh.

Bagenal went to Lisnaskea to the newly appointed sheriff of Fermanagh, Connor Roe Maguire. Bagenal left Captain Dowdall and three hundred men in Castle Skea to assist the new sheriff in administering the county.

35

Flight from the Village

Hugh Maguire marched down to Enniskillen with his newly reformed army. The residents came out and greeted him like a liberator. It did not feel like a defeat to anyone as they still had what they had before the English army marauded through their lands, but now the English were gone. Their lands were spoilt, but Hugh Maguire had the foresight to send most of his cattle to Tyrone for safekeeping. But Hugh realised that this was only the beginning. He split his men in two and sent half to harass Connor Roe Maguire and Captain Dowdall, while half stayed to repair some of the damage done to the town and surrounding villages.

After a quick visit to his priest and physician on the island on Lower Lough Erne, Eunan presented himself as fit for duty. Seamus and Eunan were assigned to start a resistance against Connor Roe Maguire in south Fermanagh, so they returned to their village.

They found their former village had been burnt to the ground by Captain Dowdall and his men. They entered the destroyed perimeter walls to discover the burnt-out huts and boats, but there were no bodies.

"If there are no bodies, they should all have escaped to the islands.

We need to get some boats and search for them," said Seamus.

Seamus divided the men. Some searched for their families in the ruins, and some went to search for boats. Eunan was distraught at the destruction of the village. Tears streamed down his cheek as he berated himself for abandoning his villagers for the reward of fickle glory. His leech scabs burned, and he itched uncontrollably. Seamus saw his distress and came and put a hand upon his shoulder.

"This is what you get for supporting the Maguire! My wife was here, but if there are no bodies I'm sure she escaped to the islands. We can avenge ourselves, but I fear the traditional O'Keenan Maguire lands will offer no sanctuary in the times to come. We may have to live on the islands or go west if we are to know peace."

"I fear peace will never shine upon us again! Bagenal pushes from the east and Bingham from the south and west. I have faith in the Maguire and God, but my heart shrivels with the more people I lose. My father was the chieftain, and all the villagers died; I was the chieftain and abandoned them on a folly, and now they are all gone!"

A voice came from the distance.

"We have boats!"

Seamus took Eunan by the arm, taking into account his current sensitivities.

"Come. Let us search for our people before we fall into a pit of our despair. We must not let down those who are still living."

Eunan followed him to the boats which had their bows pulled up upon the shore.

"There are some bodies further down the lake shore," said one of the men who fetched the boat. "I didn't recognise any of them, and God only knows where they came from, floating on the lake like that."

Eunan sat and thought.

"Let's go to the most obvious places they could be hiding first, and then look at the bodies later." He turned to Seamus. "Let's split up as we'll cover the area quicker."

Seamus got in the other boat and sailed towards the islands on the right while Eunan sailed towards the left. Seamus stood at the top of the boat and called for his wife. When there was no immediate response, he called for other prominent people of the village. He saw movement to correspond with his shouts and ordered his men to sail to the islands ahead. When he neared the islands, people came out of hiding, and when they recognised Seamus, they waved at him and invited him to moor on their island. Seamus jumped into the sea when they neared shore and dragged the boat to its moorings. He was soon back in the warm embrace of his wife.

"Where were you?" she asked.

"Fighting the wrong set of English. What happened?"

"Oh, we saw them coming from far away. It was Connor Roe Maguire's men led by the English that did this."

"Did anyone die?"

"No. We all fled to the islands as planned when we saw them coming. They burned the village to the ground and stole all the cattle. We heard them say that the warriors in the village supported Hugh Maguire instead of Connor Roe and that they should all be strung up."

"How many people are on this island?"

"Twenty."

"You'll never survive here. We need to go to the mainland."

"They have packs of soldiers all over the land, burning out and evicting the supporters of Hugh Maguire."

"Then we must leave and head north so that the Maguire can protect us properly!" Seamus turned to the gathering crowd. "Take your things. We are leaving for Enniskillen tonight!"

Everyone murmured and debated the announcement.

"We have plenty of boats to bring you onshore. Once you are there, my warriors and I will escort you to Enniskillen. You will be a lot safer there than here!"

Seamus organised the boats to ferry the island dwellers to the shore. All in all, about a hundred cold and hungry villagers stood and waited for hope, with only the clothes on their backs. Eunan also returned, but he only had a handful of stragglers with him.

Seamus gathered everyone into the smouldering central square.

"Everyone, gather your belongings, and we'll set out for Enniskillen. My men will arrange carts and transport. My men and I will ensure you make it to Enniskillen securely. You will be safe there," said Seamus.

"What if we get ambushed? The woods and countryside are full of bandits and English. I don't want to die in a ditch!" said one frightened villager.

"If you stay here the best you can hope for is to live on an island, hope the war ends quickly and hope the Maguire wins it!"

"But what if he doesn't? What sanctuary then? Where are all the MacMahons now? Hiding out in the north somewhere? A skivvy for an English lord when they once owned the land? What choice are you offering us? Become a permanent refugee or take our chances on our own land?" said another.

"We will protect you!"

"When? You're never here! We're not your people. You're a MacSheehy! At least Eunan is vaguely a Maguire. But all his people are dead! You're never here, always off somewhere else fighting for the Maguire. I, for one, am going to go live on the Islands. Who is with me?"

After some initial reluctance, the villagers split in two. The original MacSheehy Galloglass and their families stuck with Seamus and everyone else went with the man who wished to remain and hide on the islands. Eunan stood in the middle.

"Well? What about you?" asked Seamus.

"It is my destiny to fight for the Maguire," said Eunan, reluctantly standing behind Seamus.

The two sides looked at each other, but no one moved towards the other. The half that was staying went back to the boats and returned to the islands. Seamus ordered his men to find carts, horses and any other type of transport that would help them on their way. It took several hours to find a couple of carts, such was the thoroughness of the destruction of the marauding soldiers of Connor Roe. The Galloglass and their families gathered what few belongings they had left and set off with most of the villagers walking behind the carts.

Crowds of people swarmed the roads, moving west to avoid the impending war. Seamus and Eunan picked up many stragglers along the way as there were few soldiers offering protection.

Eunan hung his head as he wondered whether he was a chieftain anymore. He had abandoned his homeland, half his adopted clan and was now a refugee relying on the kindness of the Maguire to feed his people. Were they his people at all or were they the families of Seamus' Galloglass, using his position to further themselves with the Maguire? He did not know anymore, but his leech scabs itched.

They passed through a forest, and Seamus squeezed the column together, so no one got isolated. It started to get dark.

"We only have a couple of miles to go before there is a clearing and we can rest for the night," said Seamus.

They huddled together and waddled towards the promised clearing. A hiss of arrows came from behind them.

"Take them onwards. I'll take care of this," cried Eunan to Seamus.

Eunan reared his horse and positioned himself at the rear with five Galloglass. Arrows whistled above their heads. Eunan stood still to create some distance between himself and the villagers.

"Do you want to know what happened?"

Eunan heard a voice, but he did not know if it was real or in his head. He saw movement in the trees. He jumped off his horse.

"Guard her with your life!" he shouted at the Galloglass and Eunan ran into the woods. Two of the Galloglass ran behind him.

Darkness surrounded him. An arrow whistled past his head.

"Do you want to know what happened?"

"Yes, I bloody do! Stand still long enough so I can kill you!"

A body moved. Eunan ran after it. He saw another body move to his right. It was close. He grabbed a throwing axe to be rewarded with the crunch of bone, swiftly followed by the squelch of brains. He ran to retrieve his axe. He heard a yelp of pain. He ran for a few moments to run into one of his Galloglass wrapped around a spear. Guts spilt out on the ground. The man yelped in pain. Eunan beheaded him to help him pass.

"Do you want to know what happened?"

Another body appeared. Eunan threw his axe. His axe-throwing skills had improved immensely, but his luck had not. He retrieved his axe from the head of his other Galloglass.

"Do you want to know what happened?"

"Yes! Tell me!"

Eunan turned to see an arrow pointing at his face.

"Move if you want to live!"

A second man came up from behind. They marched Eunan through the dark of the forest.

"If you're going to kill me, you should at least show your face and look me in the eye before you do it. That's the way a soldier would do it. The other way is cowardly. Are you a deserter?"

"Be quiet and watch your step. We're nearly there."

"I have two Galloglass waiting for me. They'll come looking for me. Release me now and run away and live!"

"They're dead. No one is coming to save you!"

They reached a clearing in the wood, and the captor forced Eunan to sit. The man with the arrow wore a hood, and the other stood behind him.

"Throw your axes over there!" ordered the man. "Now get up!"

They led Eunan at arrow point to the ravine at the bottom of which once lay the body of Roisin. Eunan felt a surge of adrenaline through his body. This is what he deserved. Everyone he ever cared about was dead because of him. He deserved to die on the rocks with Roisin. The bad blood would smash on the rock face, seep into the ground and descend to hell where it belonged. Eunan walked out to the edge of the cliff. He shut his eyes and looked to the heavens.

A warm hand was placed gently on his shoulder and pulled him back from the ravine.

"What are you doing chief? Do you want to know what happened?"

Eunan stepped back and opened his eyes.

"Sean O'Reilly!? I thought you were dead?"

His captors had taken off their masks. They were the Galloglass Seamus had trained, who he tried to recruit for the Knights of St Colmcille.

"What are you doing here?"

"Well, after we sided with you, Seamus viewed us as being untrust-worthy. So he gave us a test. Five of us were chosen with five of Seamus' men to escort Roisin to the village. As we rode down, we'd hear whispers of what the other Galloglass and Finn were talking about. They laughed and joked about how Seamus wanted to get you married to distract you from making your own way.

"We travelled on our way to the village, but before we reached the top of Upper Lough Erne, we diverted in the direction of Castle Skea. We were uneasy about it, but Finn assured us it was all part of our planned route to throw off anyone who may have followed us, and due to the numerous bandits on the road, this route was safer. We believed him but had our weapons at the ready. We came to this forest and this very clearing. We slowed down and found ourselves surrounded by Connor Roe's men. There were too many for us to fight. Finn ordered us to down our weapons. Their Galloglass constable walked up to Finn and asked, 'where is she?'

"There was only one woman with us.

"Finn pointed towards the carriage and stood back. The constable climbed into the carriage. He tried to grab Roisin, but she kicked out at him and drove him out of the carriage. He wiped his bloody mouth and spat on the ground. He climbed in determined to wrench her out."

"What did you do?" Eunan growled.

"We were surrounded by Connor Roe's men and could do little about it. Anyway, the constable grabbed at Roisin and got her by the ankle. He pulled her until she was almost out the door. With one last gasp, she kicked him in the face. He reeled back and grabbed his face, his hands covered in blood, streaming from his nose. We picked up our swords and axes and began to fight. The constable climbed into the carriage again, and in her panic, Roisin tried to scramble out the other door. She must not have realised how close the carriage was to the edge. We heard a scream as he fell to the rocks below. We fought with Connor Roe's men. We fought with Finn's men, and we lost half our number. But three of us managed to fight our way out and into the forest. We have lived as bandits ever since. We didn't know who to trust until we saw you."

"That indeed is a sad, sad tale. But why would Finn wish to give Roisin to Connor Roe Maguire?"

"I can only but suppose, but if she were a prisoner of Connor Roe, it would surely make you fight?"

"But why is Seamus so interested in me? Surely with no lands, no people he has no more interest in me?"

"Seamus is the most devious fox I have ever met. If he pays you attention, he has a reason for it that will greatly benefit himself."

Eunan wiped the tears from his face and composed himself.

"Let us get our revenge and go to Enniskillen and confront Seamus and Finn. Are you with me?"

Sean O'Reilly and his companion cheered and gathered their belongings. They set out on foot towards Enniskillen as the Galloglass who was minding Eunan's horse had already left to catch up with Seamus.

36

Siege of Enniskillen

Eunan made his way north with his two Galloglass. They acquired some horses and scoured the countryside, but could not find Seamus and Finn. Word reached them that Hugh Maguire was in mid-Fermanagh with the bulk of his forces. Eunan reckoned that was the most likely place to find Seamus.

Upon his arrival, Eunan was directed straight to Hugh Maguire's tent. Hugh was surprisingly upbeat and greeted him warmly.

"Your Lordship," said Eunan as he bent his knee.

"Get up, my faithful brother in arms and friend. We may have tasted defeat, but it is not the end."

"You still have faith sire?"

"I almost fell into the hands of the English, mistaking some of them for my own. But fate rescued me, and will rescue the Maguires and the lords of the north!"

"We are truly blessed for your survival. How would you have me do your bidding?"

"Where is Seamus? Did he survive the war down south?"

"He's like a cockroach. You can never assume he is dead unless you see his body and that his chest no longer expands. I went south with him to witness the destruction laid out by the English. But he returned north separately with his men. I assumed he came to you, but obviously not from your question."

"I have not seen Seamus since both of you went south. The English this time are well-led. Captain Dowdall is a crafty and resourceful beast. He ambushed our ships on the river and then acquired some of his own. He wreaks havoc in what once was our safe lands and controls the river and upper lake. I need you to go to Enniskillen. The castle must not fall, or he will also threaten the lower lake. I will follow you there, but I must secure our forts on the lower lake first, and then see what our northern allies wish to do. If Seamus is not already in Enniskillen, I will divert him there."

"Yes, sire. I look forward to meeting you soon in Enniskillen."

They held each other by the forearms and then embraced. Eunan departed with his Galloglass.

* * *

Enniskillen and the surrounding countryside was prepared for war. The peasants gathered what crops were available in January and filled the stores of the castle and town. Those that could not find accommodation behind the protective walls of the castle or town got in their boats and made their way to the islands of lower Lough Erne.

Eunan entered the castle and immediately made himself and his men available to Daithi

MacCabe, the commander in charge of the defence. Daithi MacCabe put them to work, expanding the moat and digging earthworks on the main island. It was hard, intensive work, especially for men exhausted after war and travel. But Eunan treated it is penance for his sins, for the bad blood coursing through his veins, for bringing death and misfortune wherever he went. His sins were many, and the moat much deeper than when initially a righteous man had taken his shovel to it. Daylight faded, and Eunan and his men went to the castle to eat, rest and warm themselves by the fire.

The castle was full of refugees from all over Fermanagh. Soldiers, women, children, priests. What food there was were rationed, for the harvest had been taken up but distributed to various storehouses around the county, mainly concentrated in the islands of Lower Lough Erne, where most of the population had fled. Eunan devoured what food he could obtain.

After searching for food he left his men, for he desired his own company to take a few moments to rest and contemplate. He sat beside a different fire with different company.

"You look troubled, son," said a voice.

"Aren't we all? War has come to Fermanagh, and I fear worse is to come. I fear the destruction of our county and the end of the Maguires," replied Eunan, not looking to see who was speaking.

"With the Lord God's help, the Maguires will endure. Maybe not as you know it now, but the Maguires will endure. God is our only true master."

Eunan looked to his right, and an old priest sat beside him. He could not see the priest's face for he wore a hood; shadows danced on the priest's face in time with the flames of the fire.

"Is the destruction of the Maguires punishment for our sins?"

"Do you think the heathen English with their made-up God sin any the less than you?"

"All I know is destruction is coming my way, for my sins, for the blood that flows through my veins. Conceived in sin, and bringer of misfortune and death for all those unlucky enough to share their lives with me. The Sodom and Gomorrah of my heart will fall, and all those around me will turn to bitter salt."

"We can all be redeemed through the Lord. Every warrior here, be they of any experience, has killed someone. If they have killed an English blasphemer or one of their lackeys, you have done it to preserve Ireland and the church. It may be a sin, but a sin committed for the right reasons, and the lord will forgive you. Trouble yourself not, for you will need all your courage in the heat of the battle. You must strike the blow without thinking or remorse, or else the lord and the Maguire will lose one of their best warriors."

"You don't understand."

"I never do, but think about it, and you will find solace."

Eunan sat in silence. But his peace was soon shattered.

"The English are coming! The English are coming!"

One last set of warriors entered the castle as the gates shut behind them. Seamus was at their head. Eunan winced at the sight of him and automatically went for his axe, but the priest grabbed his arm.

"Do you know this man?" exclaimed the priest.

Eunan regained his composure. He was confused but did not want to give away his true feelings about Seamus.

"Of course, he's my mentor, my guide. He's like a father to me."

"He's a very dangerous man," whispered the priest. "If you are who I think you are, I know of your bad blood."

"What!?!"

"Come with me!"

* * *

In the meantime, Daithi MacCabe feared the English were closing in. He ordered his archers on the ramparts fired fire arrows into the night sky in an attempt to locate the English army, but they could do little to penetrate the darkness. Anxious that they would soon be surrounded, Daithi MacCabe called an experienced scout into the empty main hall.

"Take this letter and guard it with your life. Bring it to the Maguire on Devenish Island. Tell him the English are approaching. We will hold them for as long as we can but he must come with the entire Maguire army and save us!"

Connor O'Cassidy took the letter and bowed.

"Upon my life I will return with the Maguire and save my brethren."

"Go swiftly. There is a small boat waiting for you by the river gate. Make haste for we eagerly await your return!"

Connor O'Cassidy bowed again and was gone.

* * *

The priest and Eunan searched the castle and its buildings for somewhere quiet to talk, but the castle was crowded and chaotic, and the priest trusted no one. After dawn, when the English army had not appeared, and the residents went to get some sleep, Eunan and the priest found a secluded spot.

"Tell me about your youth, son," said the priest, putting his hand on Eunan's shoulder.

Eunan sat and bowed his head. The priest sat beside him.

"It was hard. I think my parents hated me. They said I had bad blood. Something inside me made me evil. I asked priests before to help me, but they couldn't."

Eunan showed the priest the leech scabs on his arms.

"I just want to be normal. Why can't I just be like any other young chieftain? Why do I have to feel like this all the time?"

"Why do you think your parents hated you?" inquired the priest.

He thought he knew who Eunan was, but had to probe a little more to make sure. If he was not considerate, he feared Eunan might erupt.

"My mother was not shy about telling me. She was a cripple. She had a child who died in childbirth when I was young, something went

289

wrong. She couldn't walk after it and always blamed me. She said I cursed her womb, so it lay fallow, and no other child could lay in there and live. My mother said my curse was so strong that she was crippled when she tried to have another child."

"Why didn't you try and run away? A strong young lad like yourself could have joined the Galloglass at a much earlier age?"

"My father made me stay and then the guilt spawned by my mother compelled me to look after her. Then, when she needed me the most, I was not there."

"How did she die?"

"She was thrown down a well by the English when they raided our village."

The priest went white.

"Rest your axe on the ground son and brace yourself. I have a story to tell you that may give you some peace. I am old now, but in my younger years, I used to roam around Fermanagh, as a priest, saying mass and doing priestly duties for some of the more remote villages. One such village I used to tend was that of the O'Keenan Maguires. I used to speak to the chief there, Cathal O'Keenan Maguire, who I believe is your father. Well, I used to visit him and take his confession and also the confessions of the villagers, who I believe now are dead. I know that what I have pieced together may violate the confessional, but if I tell you, then maybe their souls and yours will rest a little easier, no matter where they be."

37

Bad Blood

Eunan braced himself for he thought he would hear as near to the truth as he ever would know. The priest blessed himself, and looked to the heavens and asked for forgiveness. Eunan was confused as for what, and to whom, he was asking forgiveness. But he did not pursue it for he felt the answer would be in the story. Father Patrick took a drink and began his tale.

"War came to the peaceful climes of Fermanagh as the MacMahons fled west to escape from the invading forces of the crown. The Maguires of Lisnaskea were under pressure, so Cuchonnacht Maguire, the Prince of Fermanagh, sent his elite Scottish mercenary axe men, the Galloglass, into the county to protect his lands. One such battle of Galloglass arrived in the village of Cathal O'Keenan Maguire, and as chief of the village, he was expected to make them feel welcome and supply them with 'coin and keep' for as long as they remained there. Cathal thought he had to demonstrate that he shared the burden, so he invited one such Galloglass into his own home.

"The Galloglass was as unwelcome a guest as a leech upon a cow's udder. This monster took every morsel of food, every drink of ale, every piece of cheese, drop of milk, every coin from the market. Time

291

wore on, and war did not come. But famine did; no matter what the villagers could produce, the Galloglass took it. Cathal appealed to the Maguire, but they told him his sept had to do their duty to protect the county of Maguire. So the Galloglass stayed.

"Winter came and campaigning season was a long way off. Cathal and his fellow village men had to resort to hunting rabbits to feed everyone. Every evening, the men of the village would go off to hunt and leave most of the Galloglass behind, for they wanted to stay and drink. One evening Fiona, Cathal's wife, brought the Galloglass some ale, purchased with the last of their money. The Galloglass ordered his knave to play his pipes, and the Galloglass began to drink and dance. Fiona looked worried but encouraged her husband to leave. Cathal looked back, and his wife meekly smiled back at him. He closed the door.

"He was gone for several hours. It was quite a successful evening, and he had caught three rabbits which would make a decent meal for himself and his wife if the Galloglass had drunk himself to sleep. The knave may be awake, but he would have to wait until morning to make his complaints if he did not want to be subjected to his master's wrath if he woke him up.

"As Cathal approached the house, he noticed something odd. There was a small fire outside and silence inside. At this hour, the Galloglass would normally still be up making merry and his poor wife would either be hiding or attempting to repair the destruction left in his wake. But there was silence. He opened the door. The house was a wreck. The stools were upturned, the kitchenware all over the floor, the fire smouldered neglected. The Galloglass lay slumped in a drunken heap beside the fire. He grunted and snored like the greedy devil he was. Cathal despised the Galloglass. It was the only time he thought that life might be better going over to the English than living under the oppression of the beast.

"The Galloglass' knave then appeared, grinning as per usual. Cathal often imagined drowning this devil child in the lake, if he was not thinking of more painful and imaginative ways of killing him. How could the Maguire put him through this? Cathal looked over to the left, and the knave scurried behind his master. There was a heap of cloth on the floor. Fiona never left the house like this, Cathal thought. Where was she? Then he saw a foot poking out from beneath the cloth.

"Cathal ran over. The cloths were drenched in blood, and he could see the pale skin of a protruding arm and the top of Fiona's head. Cathal gently unwrapped the cloths, taking particular care around the bloodstains. He picked up her battered body, and she groaned, signalling she was still alive. Cathal pulled together the remains of her tattered clothes to cover up her private parts. She was bruised and battered all over from what parts of her body he could see through the blood. Cathal held her tightly in his arms and wept. She groaned in response, for everything hurt. The knave saw his chance and dashed to the door.

'You little beast!' cried Cathal, reaching for his hunting knife. He cornered the boy before he could make it to the door. 'I'm going to gut you like a rabbit for what you did!'

'Master, master!' cried the boy, but the beast snored on.

'Come here, boy! You're not going to get away!' screamed Cathal, and he lunged at the boy.

"Cathal missed. The boy took his water bottle off his belt and threw it at the head of his master. His aim was true. His master awoke with a grunt and was furious. He was a red-haired giant, a foot taller than Cathal and a veteran of many battles. He saw Cathal, knife drawn, and reached for his sword. His fingers met with thin air. He roared at his knave who saw his chance and ran out the door. The Galloglass arose and searched for his weapons. Fiona groaned in the background.

Cathal realised he was dead either way, for the knave would get help or the Galloglass would slice him in two and then watch his wife die as he stripped them bare of their last belongings. He was the representative of the Maguire. How could he die, murdered in this pit, by this beast, standing over the body of his raped wife?

"Cathal charged forward and swung at the Galloglass. He missed. The Galloglass punched him in the side of the head and Cathal fell into the fire. Cathal howled as he beat the flames from his sleeve. The Galloglass continued to look for his weapon. Cathal could hear a commotion outside. He could only assume that the knave had gone to fetch help. He could die at the hands of this beast or fight back throw himself at the feet of the Maguire. He lunged towards the Galloglass, who easily evaded him. The Galloglass found his sword on the floor beneath his axe and dagger. He unsheathed it and advanced towards Cathal. Cathal swung his blade but he had nowhere near the reach of the Galloglass. The Galloglass raised his sword above his head to slice Cathal in two. Cathal raised his arm to protect his head.

'Lord, save me!'

'No lord will save you now!' bellowed the Galloglass and the sword was extended fully behind his back and started its descent.

"Cathal life dangled beneath the point of a sword. He heard a groan and saw his wife move. She plunged the Galloglass' own dagger through his calf until the tip showed through his shin. The Galloglass cried in agony and collapsed onto one knee. He dropped the sword. Cathal saw his chance. He ran and leapt upon the Galloglass and plunged his dagger into the Galloglass' heart. The Galloglass fell back, but was not dead. He writhed around on the floor and grabbed Fiona's leg as she tried to drag herself away. Fiona screamed. Cathal picked up the sword.

'May this be the end of you, devil!' he cried. The Galloglass raised his head, and Cathal lopped it straight off.

"The front door came crashing down. The knave and the constable of the Galloglass came rushing in to see the Galloglass' head hit the floor. The knave raised his javelin to avenge his master, but it was knocked out of the way before it could connect.

'No,' said the constable. 'I've got a better way. Take him.'

"Several other Galloglass entered the house and picked Cathal up by the arms and dragged him out. By now, everyone had heard the commotion. They came out of their houses to see Cathal being dragged through the streets. The Galloglass threw Cathal to the ground in the centre of the village. The fire torches of his neighbours and the Galloglass surrounded him. The constable stood beside the kneeling Cathal and put his sword to Cathal's throat. The constable was Seamus.

'Your chieftain killed one of my men. Therefore, he must pay. However, he is the man in the village who represents our paymaster, the Maguire. Therefore, the village must pay. Along with the coin and keep owed to us for defending you from the English, the MacMahons and whatever cattle raiders may come along, we want twenty cattle in compensation for the death of my man.'

'We don't have twenty cattle to spare!' cried a lone voice from the crowd.

'Cathal O'Keenan Maguire, the representative of the Maguire, will ensure we receive them, or we will take it out on the village. What this man didn't release is that he killed my brother. Not my brother in arms, but my flesh and blood brother. Therefore, I will live with him instead, and he will supply me with the coin and keep owed to my brother as well as the coin and keep due to a Gallowglass constable!'

"Cathal almost fainted onto the tip of the sword.

"So Seamus moved into Cathal's house. Cathal became no better than an indentured servant to the whims of the constable. He became hated by his other villagers because the other Galloglass became more vicious in extracting their coin and keep, to avenge their fallen comrade.

"As time passed, it became apparent that Fiona was with child, and from her reaction, it was probably not her husband's. Seamus showed his paternal feelings with the tip of his sword. He ensured that Cathal fetch and carry for his wife while he shared his rations with her to protect the child. The villagers did not see what went on in the house and became jealous, for they saw his wife with child and how she prospered more than them.

"Nine months elapsed and the child was born. Only Seamus wished to remember the birth of the child but nobody celebrated, not even him. Still, Seamus cared enough to ensure that the child was nurtured and did not die after childbirth.

"At last, war came to the country, and the Galloglass were called upon to fight. Even though war could mean famine, death and destruction, the villagers were inwardly delighted, for it meant that the Galloglass would be leaving. However, Seamus delayed their departure until he knew the baby would survive.

"Seamus packed his things and stood before a silent Fiona, Cathal and Eunan, the baby.

'I will return. I expect to see that baby alive and well and if I do not, I will slice the both of you in two.'

"Cathal did not react; he had become accustomed to ignoring threats and avoiding punishment the past couple of years. Seamus instructed his knave to pick up his bags.

'Remember my words,' and with that he was gone.

"Fiona turned to her husband and cried on his shoulder. That evening they stared at the crib of the child of the dead Galloglass. They looked at each other and discussed how they could raise such a child; surely a boy born of such circumstances could only bring bad luck to them and the village in general. They remembered an old Irish folk tale of fairies taking away children and bringing them to a better place, swapping them for a fairy child instead. The fairy child surely could be no worse than the Galloglass child? Or even better, no child at all. They decided it was worth the risk.

"They took the baby from the crib and wrapped him up warm, for they did not want the child to die before the fairies took him. Cathal then left the house first and signalled to his wife to follow when he knew it was safe. They set out for the wood beside the lake, thinking the moonlight reflecting on the water would attract the fairies. They followed the winding path until they found an old tree, shaped a little like a cradle. Fiona placed the child there and wept. The baby joined in with his mother. Cathal and Fiona turned to leave.

'Sorry, no changeling for you!'

"Before them stood Seamus and his men, the knave grinning from behind him. He must have tipped them off.

'Fiona, pick up the baby and bring him back to the village. Men, grab him!' The Galloglass took hold of Cathal.

"Cathal was dragged in front of a circle of his neighbours yet again. The tip of Seamus' sword touched his forehead while he knelt before the villagers.

'Not only has this wretch killed one of my men, but he also tried to kill his own baby!' roared Seamus.

"The crowd made its anger known.

'Should I kill this man, who has the protection of the Maguire and risk the wrath of the county coming down upon us all? Or should I show mercy?'

"The crowd was silent.

'Since you cannot decide, I declare myself the protector of the child! Once war is over, I will return for him. If I return and the child is dead, my Galloglass will level the village, no matter the wrath of the Maguire. And if I find that this man and his wife have looked after the child and he is fit and well, I will absolve you all, he included, of your debt. So decide what you wish to do. For this man to openly declare the child as naturally his, or for me to exact revenge for his heinous crimes?'

"The crowd was again silent but not for long; cries of 'save the child!' soon rang out around the circle.

'I take it you have made your decision. Cathal O'Keenan Maguire, do you swear that this child is your flesh and blood and you will look after him always, and upon my return, he will be fit and healthy?'

"Cathal looked to his wife, who nodded back to him.

'I will take the child as my son.'

'And?'

'And look after it if it were my own. Until he comes of age.'

'Then get off your knees, feed and bed the child and let us never speak of this again.'

"Cathal got up and went to his wife and put his arm around her shoulders. They walked to their house. The crowd disbursed.

"Later, Seamus knocked on Cathal's door.

'I meant what I said.' With that, Seamus turned and departed for the war."

38

Finn

Father Patrick paused to take another drink. Eunan had turned white and silent. He stared into the fire. Father Patrick dared not go on until he could assess Eunan's state of mind. He looked to the heavens once more for inspiration.

"Is your story finished?" asked Eunan finally.

"Sadly not. We must bring it up to the present day," and father Patrick paused once more for water.

"The story then moves to the time of your youth, and when I first became aware of you and your story.

"Seamus and his band of renegade Galloglass had hidden out in the woods. They had been in the pay of the MacMahons but had abandoned them when the money ran out. Seamus said he had planted a seed in Fermanagh, and that it should be ripe for the picking now. He promised them riches as long as his special child was still alive. Seamus sent some of his men as traders with the last of his cattle to seek out Cathal O'Keenan Maguire and to see what had happened to his child. One of the men was Finn, the horse boy of Seamus' brother, because he would recognise Cathal O'Keenan Maguire, but Cathal would not recognise him since Finn was no longer a boy. When they arrived in the village, they saw no child, only you.

"Seamus was ecstatic. He sent a man to the English sheriff in Monaghan to tell him that the cattle raiders who had ransacked Monaghan were from the village of Cathal O'Keenan Maguire. The English sheriff sent his Captain to retrieve his goods. The Captain, who was Captain Willis I believe, killed Cathal O'Keenan Maguire for resisting him and then searched the village to retrieve the supposed stolen cattle and also for valuables to compensate them for the inconvenience. They heard that Maguire warriors were on their way, so they fled. They killed your uncle and anyone else they could find. But some of the villagers managed to escape to the islands.

"The villagers returned, and your mother had survived hidden in her house. Seamus and his men had been hiding in the woods, watching all of this happen. They saw you leave the village. The men could not contain their greed and Seamus wanted revenge on your parents. They ransacked the village and stole what they could. They found your mother on the floor of your house, as she had fallen out of her chair. Seamus dragged her to the well and cast her down in revenge for his brother's murder. Then they followed you until you reached the woods, where they ambushed you."

"How do you know all this?" asked Eunan.

"I was their priest."

The English had been busy while Eunan searched for a quiet spot to hear the tale. They had dug trenches and laid siege to the town. The English cannonballs struck the walls just as the priest finished telling the story. Eunan sat there in total silence. He finally spoke.

"Why are you telling me this, priest, when my heart is so low, and my axe is a tool of my rage?"

"I thought you needed to know."

"So who is Finn? Is he the horse boy of the Galloglass that raped my mother?"

"Thou should not kill in anger," pleaded the priest.

"Answer me straight, priest. Is he the horse boy, the knave?"

"That he is. I hope my words don't condemn him to die!"

Eunan stood up and grasped the shaft of his axe.

"What I need to know is how you let this happen? You're a priest. Surely you should have stopped this."

"How? I am but one old man against twenty and one Galloglass. I can only tell them of their sins and hope to steer them towards the virtuous path!"

Eunan's face went red, and he started to gesticulate as if anger had taken possession.

"Excommunicate them, curse them, banish them, I don't know! What would God have you to do? How could you let this happen to me? How could God have let this happen to me? I am a good man, yet bad blood burns through my insides. How could you let this happen!?" Eunan gripped the axe handle with both hands.

The priest got up and started to back away.

"Now look here Eunan, I was only trying to help…"

"Help! How much worse could you have made this?"

"We both may die when the English attack. You wouldn't want the blood of a dead priest on your soul when you try to get onto heaven, would you?"

"Some priest you are! God might be grateful if I got rid of you!"

Eunan had him cornered against the wall. Dust fell from the ceiling as the English cannonballs pounded.

"Answer me one thing and remember you are a priest. How do you know so much about my mother's death? Where were you at the time?"

"I know I'm a weak man, I should've done better and stood up to Seamus, but I was afraid. He would not care about a priest's blood on his conscience, but I know you are better than him."

"The bad blood that courses through my veins is from him, and therefore I am no better than him! Now, where were you when Seamus killed my mother?"

"Please have mercy on me! I am weak! I failed you. I failed your mother. I failed your village. But I can pray for them. I can! I can pray that their souls get to heaven!" The priest fell to his knees.

"Don't be a coward all your life! Tell me the truth. Where were you when my mother died?"

"I was there! I was there! Forgive me! I pleaded with Seamus to have mercy, but he would not listen, and I was powerless to do anything! Have mercy on me!" The priest began to weep and clawed at the bottom of Eunan's chain mail shirt.

The bad blood seared in his veins.

"It's God that deals in mercy, I deal in death!"

Eunan lifted his axe to sweep the priest's head clean off. He closed his eyes to pray for the departing soul. But to his surprise came a vision of his mother. She could walk, and she smiled sweetly at him, like she never smiled at him before. There were no comments, no judgment – just a sweet smile.

"Please!" the priest croaked, and the image was gone.

Eunan swung the axe. But it was not like any axe swing he had experienced before. He swung, and an English cannonball disintegrated the wall and flying stone and fragments knocked him off his feet, and he fell and bashed his head on the ground.

* * *

Meanwhile, Connor O'Cassidy rowed silently along the river on a dark and cloudy night. It was several hours before he would reach Devenish Island but he had to row with the greatest of stealth, such was the importance of his mission. But the clouds abandoned him and the moon betrayed him. He found himself alone on the moon illuminated waves of the River Erne. He heard shouts. He rowed faster. The noise of men grew louder. The moon hid the shame of its betrayal behind a cloud. Connor O'Cassidy heard the cacophony of oars lapping up the water coming towards him. Once more, he could barely see into the night. He must dispose of the letter and quick. He put his hand in his shirt to retrieve it. A boat crashed into his and knocked him off his seat. He tried to pull himself up only to find a dagger in front of his face. A heavy object to the back of his head knocked him out.

* * *

Eunan woke with water spilling on his face. He spat out the water, liquefied dust and fragments of rock that had gathered in his mouth and sat up to brush himself down.

"Are you alright?" asked the voice.

"The priest, the priest!" Eunan started to panic and clawed through the rubble. "There was a priest here too. I don't see any blood. Is he buried under the rubble?"

"There was nobody in this room but you. Maybe you were about to die, and a priest came before you got to heaven to take you back? You are here now, and we need all the soldiers we can get to fight off the English assault. Clean yourself up and get out on the ramparts. Come on, we need everyone fit to fight!"

Eunan stood up and made sure he was alright. He could feel blood on his face, but he could stand. He splashed some water from the bucket on his face and ran out to fight.

* * *

A bucket of water ensured that Connor O'Cassidy had a rude awakening. He was surrounded by sneering faces, bad breath and broken teeth.

"I am so glad you are awake now," came the sound of a distant educated voice. "Thanks for the letter by the way."

The faces moved to either side and Connor saw an English officer sat behind a small field operations table. Connor realised he was in the English camp. Captain Dowdall had the letter to the Maguire in his hand.

"I really don't want to execute you for being a rebel, but you need to prove to me your loyalty to Queen and country."

"Kill me now! I'll never talk!"

"Please! Don't be so dramatic. How about if you help us take the castle, we'll make you a knight of the realm and we'll grant you some of this land you seem to love so much?"

"Kill me now! I'll never turn on the Maguire! Never!"

"I'm a great believer in redemption and by the time my boys finish with you, you'll love the Queen, gladly become a knight and relish in delivering Enniskillen Castle to us. Gentlemen, roast his feet on the fire and do whatever it takes for him to be pliant and co-operative. There's no rush. I'll be in my tent when you are ready."

The sneers, bad breath and broken teeth overwhelmed Connor O'Cassidy Maguire.

39

1594 - The End

The bombardment of the castle continued for eight days. Every soldier was needed to man the ramparts, and every corner of the castle was taken by either civilians seeking shelter or wounded soldiers seeking solace. The castle was small, and Eunan soon saw the priest, but the priest saw him first and ran and hid. Eunan saw Finn on the ramparts, and the way Finn looked at him told him that Finn knew he knew. The priest must have escaped and warned both Finn and Seamus that Eunan knew. Eunan saw Seamus, but Seamus was far too involved in the defence of the castle to have time for Eunan's issues. The defenders were a rapidly diminishing force as the English bombarded the castle from both the main island and across the River Erne. The cannons battered the walls it seemed without pause. Musket fire swept the ramparts. Surely it was only a matter of time until the castle fell.

On the ninth day at dawn, a shout came from the top of the main building in the castle.

"Ships are coming! Ships are coming from the south!"

Eunan was in the main building and scrambled up the stairs to the roof to see for himself. To the south were three large riverboats.

"Who are they?" he said to the watchman.

"They are the ships of the Lisnaskea Maguires," he replied.

"Are they here to relieve us?" said Eunan.

"I don't know. Wait!"

"Ships to the north!" cried the north-facing watchman.

"Whose side are they on? Are they the Maguire ships from the lakes?"

"They certainly bear the same design!"

Hope rose in the castle. However, Eunan observed the musketeers and artillery of the besieging army ready themselves.

"What are the ships going to do? Are they going to land above the English, and we sally forth and join them?" asked Eunan.

"It's too early to say."

The ships drew ever nearer. More and more of the defenders lined the walls facing the River Erne to look out and see what they would do. The English guns remained silent.

"Come on, Connor Roe Maguire, come through for your clan," said Eunan through gritted teeth as the ships came within five hundred yards. "I'll forgive you for everything if you don't let us down now!"

The castle had no cannon, for only the Spanish survivors of the Great Armada knew how to use them and no northern lord had any. What few muskets they had were all with Hugh Maguire and the main army. So the defenders could only wait.

Four hundred yards, three hundred yards…

"Do we fire on them?" shouted Eunan at the castle commander who had joined them on the roof.

"No! They may be friendly. Wait until they make their declaration!"

Two hundred yards…

* * *

On the largest of the northern ships, Captain Dowdall readied his men for the assault. Connor O'Cassidy was reduced to using crutches for both feet were heavily bandaged to help them heal from the burns. He had taken much persuasion but that was of little solace to him now. He dared not look at the castle but set his gaze on the empty shore on the opposite side of the river. Captain Dowdall approached him.

"It's a beautiful countryside, isn't it? You can have your pick if the walls prove as vulnerable, where we are going, as you claim they are. Or else you will be the entertainment for the men back in the camp tonight as they contemplate their defeat."

"I am true to my word Captain," Connor replied.

"I hope, for your sake, you are. Or at least truer to me than you were to your former comrades"

* * *

The men in the castle watched as the boats to the south lifted massive wall-scaling ladders from the decks of the boats.

"It's the English! It's the English! Fire on the boats, fire on the..."

The besieging English land army opened with a volley of fire from their cannons, and the musketeers tried to pick off individual men from the ramparts. The boats from the north raised ladders from their decks. A hail of arrows came from the ships as they closed to a hundred yards. Men fell from the wall and the tower to their deaths in the river. The boats crashed their sides into the walls of the castle. The men threw hooks that settled on the edge on the other side of the walls. They rested their ladders on the top of the walls, and came pouring in. Captain Dowdall's ship moored beside a weakened, undefended wall. He looked back to Connor and grinned.

"Arise Sir Connor O'Cassidy!" he saluted and he joined his men in scaling the walls.

Connor O'Cassidy could only stare down over the side and into the river on the other side of the boat.

* * *

In the main building Dathai MacCabe realised this was the final assault.

"Everyone, man the walls," he screamed as he ran down the stairs to lead the defence.

Eunan heard the call and rushed down the stairs only to run into Finn heading the other way. Finn froze and then tried to back away. Eunan felt for his throwing axes.

"I know what you did! Defend yourself! I'm sure you don't want to die with an axe in the back of your head, but I'm not bothered either way," growled Eunan.

"Th-the priest told me you knew! I w-w-as young! If I hadn't of told Seamus he would have killed me. He doesn't protect me as he does you, because you're related to him and with him not having a son..."

"I am no son of a Galloglass! I want to eradicate this cursed blood from my veins. But the first thing I will do is avenge my father!"

"He wasn't your father!"

"You are only making it worse for yourself." Eunan grabbed Finn and threw him into the room beside the stairs.

The floor of the room was covered with the dead and dying, with a couple of women attending them. The building shuddered as the cannonballs struck.

"They're in the yard!" came a voice from above them.

"Why don't you kill me now?" said Finn. "We're both going to be dead in the hour anyway!"

"I wouldn't give you the pleasure of dying from an anonymous bullet after what you did to my parents. Death, for you, is from my blade."

"You wouldn't strike me down when I am unarmed, would you?"

Eunan looked around and saw a Galloglass axe beside a man who was recently deceased.

"Pick that up and defend yourself!"

Finn stepped over a few bodies and took hold of the axe. Someone grabbed Eunan from behind and twirled him around, throwing him towards the stairs.

A familiar voice said, "get out there and fight and don't die like a coward trying to get revenge for a past that never happened!"

* * *

Eunan found himself on the stairs and the entrance door below him being battered down. The axes of the English smashed through the door, and the men kicked away the remaining splinters and door frame and charged through. Eunan stood in the hall with two other Galloglass. He swung his axe hard and true, and the air filled with blood, bones, chain mail, flesh and splinters. The bodies fell and clogged up the doorway. The next group of soldiers tried to kick the bodies away and charge through. But Eunan swung his axe again, and the bodies fell before him. The pile of bodies formed a wall, and Eunan could pause for breath. Seamus appeared at the top of the stairs.

"Well done Eunan, you can hold them off for now and then we can think of how to escape."

Eunan turned in a fury and ran up the stairs after Seamus.

"Don't abandon your post!" shouted Seamus, but when he saw the look in Eunan's eye, he turned and fled up the stairs toward the roof. Finn came out of a room and onto the stairs. Seamus grabbed him by the shoulders and flung him down the stairs.

"Defend the door!"

Finn got up, and Eunan was behind him. Eunan shouldered him into the wall.

"Defend the door unless you want to die here!"

Finn picked up an axe from the ground. He went down to the door and waited for the inevitable attack.

Seamus ran up onto the roof. Dathai MacCabe was nowhere to be seen, so Seamus was the highest-ranking officer left.

"Clear the roof and defend the stairs!" he roared at the last of the defenders who sought sanctuary on the roof.

Not all of them obeyed him, and he strode over to several who crouched beneath the ramparts.

"Get up you cowards! Better you die fighting than cowering in a corner. You are going to die today, if not by the hand of your enemy, then by mine for cowardice!"

He reached down and dragged them up, pushing them towards the stairs. Eunan came up the stairs and pushed them aside so he could confront Seamus.

Seamus saw the anger boil in Eunan's eyes.

"Can we not resolve this later? I would rather die at the hands of my enemies than the axe blade of my relative."

"The vengeance of my parents comes before any petty fight over who controls a field of cows."

"So which parents are these? The ones who got medicine to kill you before you were born and tried to leave you in the woods to get eaten by wild dogs? What would be a suitable vengeance for them?"

"Feeding you to the fishes!" Eunan raised his axe and charged at Seamus. Seamus parried the blow with relative ease.

"Why would I want to kill my brother's child when I have expended so much of my time and energy to keep you alive? Are you not a chieftain? Have you not come from nothing to being a friend of the O'Donnells and possibly the next Maguire, and now you want to kill me for two people who resented and hated you?"

Eunan turned and charged, and Seamus parried again.

"You're far too angry to fight. I could kill you so easily, but I don't want to. Let us try and escape!"

Eunan plunged his axe downwards, but Seamus blocked it.

"You killed my mother. You threw her down a well! How could you be so heartless?"

Seamus threw him back.

"How can you be such a sentimental fool for someone who tried to kill you as a baby? I'm the only reason she brought you up. When your father died, who was going to become chieftain? You? You're a bastard. Who was going to cry from the roofs that you're a bastard? Your mother. Then you would never become a chieftain."

"I never wanted my mother to die! I never wanted to become chieftain!"

"Then you are a fool!"

Seamus swung his axe at Eunan and forced him on the defensive.

* * *

The English waited at the door of the keep until they could fetch some musketeers. When they arrived, they lined up before the door and released several volleys into the doorway and the corridor beyond. They waited for the smoke to clear and removed the bodies from the doorway. The hallway was empty. They charged in and started to kill everyone they came across.

* * *

Seamus began to fight. Eunan struggled to defend himself.

"Why do I have to waste my time on you? The castle is about to fall.

311

If I have to kill you to survive, I will!"

* * *

The English reached the second floor. Finn and the only surviving Galloglass stood at the top of the stairs to defend the wounded. Fire raged in the building, and smoke climbed the stairs. The English spotted Finn at the top of the stairs and waited.

* * *

Seamus swung his axe and drew blood as he shaved Eunan's cheek.

"Give up while you still live!"

"Not while you breathe!" Eunan swung his axe and grazed Seamus' arm.

"Be careful, Eunan. You may be blood…"

"Bad blood!"

"But you are not a chieftain anymore."

"I am still the O'Keenan Maguire!"

"A chieftain with no lands or no people."

Eunan landed a blow. Seamus stood back and felt the breach in his chain mail. He sucked the blood off his fingers.

* * *

The English musketeers sent several volleys up the stairs. Their Irish kern charged up into the smoke and started to search the rooms. Finn had made the most of the cover and fled. He stood with his axe over his wounded comrades lying moaning on the floor. The kern found and circled him.

"Come on then!" he shouted as he swung his axe around his head.

But the kern just circled him. Some of the wounded men tried to grab the legs of the kern, only to meet death at the end of a sharp sword.

The kern thrust their swords in Finn's direction like a pack of hyenas looking for weakness. Finn swung his axe and fended off the blows while his energy sapped away. The kern parted. Two musketeers aimed and hit Finn mid-chest. He reeled back but did not fall. The kern descended upon him to finish him off.

* * *

Seamus heard the commotion downstairs. He knew he did not have long.

"This is your last chance. Do you want to die by my hand or make one last stand against the real enemy?"

Eunan charged at him again, and Seamus parried the blow.

"I'll take that as a no!"

Seamus swung his axe down on Eunan, which he managed to block. Seamus forced his axe downwards and Eunan's energy slowly crumbled. They were locked together, axe to axe, with their faces almost pressed against one another. Seamus could feel Eunan weakening.

"You were always like a son to me!" With that, Seamus gave a last heave to force Eunan's axe shaft down. Seamus thrust his forehead over the axe shafts and crashed it down on the bridge of Eunan's nose. His nose disintegrated into a mass of blood and bone. Seamus could feel Eunan's axe fall. Seamus butted him again, as hard as he could on the forehead. Eunan collapsed, out cold.

"Sorry!"

Seamus heard the sound of fighting getting nearer. He lifted Eunan up and stripped him of his chain mail. He picked up Eunan' unconscious body and walked to the ramparts. Once he had a clear shot, he lifted Eunan's body as high as he could and cast him towards the river. Eunan crashed into the water near one of the assault boats.

Seamus collapsed, for his energy was spent. The sound of footsteps on the stairs made Seamus reach for his axe. Seamus stood up to meet his end like a Galloglass. The men reached the top of the stairs and stopped.

"Hello, Seamus!" came a familiar voice.

Seamus raised his axe.

Bad Blood timeline

While 'Bad Blood' is a fictional novel it is based around historical events. Below is a summary of the main historical events in Ireland over the time period covered in Bad Blood. It is compiled from several sources and some of the exact timing of events are unknown. Therefore, some events are not dated and are placed where they logically or probably appear in the timeline.

1569

The Queen's county of Fermanagh formed

1570

Enterprise of Ulster. This was an attempt by the crown to counter resistance in Ulster by granting land to English entrepreneurs and settlers.

1584

East Breifne (County Cavan) indentured (traditional home of the O'Reilly clan).
    October – three lieutenants were created for Ulster: Sir Henry Bagenal (Tyrone), Hugh O'Neill (Fermanagh), and Turlough O'Neil (Coleraine)

Sir John Perrot made Lord Deputy of Ireland

1585

Oriel (County Monaghan) shired.

May - Connor Roe Maguire knighted

Composition of Connacht. This was a form of surrender and regrant where the Gaelic lords of Connacht agreed to set tax payments to the crown in exchange for hereditary English titles.

Summer - the parliament of 1585 gave Hugh O'Neill title of Earl of Tyrone

Mac Shanes gathering power. Hugh O'Neill took control of central Tyrone which was indentured from Turlough O'Neill for seven years.

Turlough O'Neill retained overlordship of Maguire and MacCann

Harsh winter. Many cattle died. This made baring the soldiers all the harder.

Hugh O'Neill bargains down the number of troops in Ulster to 550

Maguire, O'Donnell and O'Cahan eject troops

Composition of Connacht collapses

1586

Maguire surrenders to the crown and pays 500 cows - 200 stolen by Lord Deputy John Perrott

O'Donnell agrees to high rent of 700 cattle (plus 700 cattle fine) to be free of troops

1587

Red Hugh O'Donnell engaged to Rosie O'Neill, Hugh O'Neill's daughter

Hugh O'Neill secures Tyrone

O'Neill settlement - Maguire remains under Turlough

Sir Ross MacMahon (subservient to Hugh O'Neill) accepted surrender and regrant without O'Neill's permission, so does Sir Oghy O'Hanlon. They are invaded by Sir Henry Bagenal and forced to take a sheriff.

September - Hugh Roe O'Donnell imprisoned in Dublin castle. Tirconnell breaks down into several warring factions

Hugh Maguire joined up with Art O'Neill (Turlough O Neill's son) to attack Scots invading County Down. Maguire then turned on O'Neill on their way back towards Fermanagh

1588

January - MacMahon back in control of Hugh O'Neill. Maguire under pressure from MacMahon and Donnell O'Donnell

April - Hugh O'Neill defeated by Turlough and Hugh O'Gallagher (leading an O'Donnell faction) at Carricklea

April - Maguire lost to Hugh O'Neill and then regained by Turlough O'Neill

Sir John Perrot removed as Lord Deputy of Ireland to be replaced by William FitzWilliam

July/August - Spanish Armada off the coast of Ireland

Maguire in league with the O'Rourkes and Burkes to retrieve and hide Spanish survivors from the Armada

Hugh O'Neill massacres Spanish prisoners at Inishowen

October - Turlough O'Neill hires English mercenaries. Captain Mostian's company reasserted Turlough O'Neill's control over Maguire

Late 1588 early 1589 - Maguire goes back to Hugh O'Neill

1589

Hugh Maguire Inaugurated by Donnell O'Donnell in Sciath Garbha and receives military aid from him

Turlough O'Neill enters an alliance with the MacShanes

Red Hugh O'Donnell kidnapped

Sir Ross MacMahon dies - the succession of the MacMahons begins. Brian MacHugh Og MacMahon made himself chieftain. Lord Deputy Fitzwilliam and Hugh O'Neill tried to impose Hugh Roe MacMahon but were defeated by Brian Og. Brian Og potentially bribed Fitzwilliam. Hugh Roe MacMahon imprisoned, put on trial and executed.

1590

Spring – West Breifne (county Leitrim) led by Sir Brian O'Rourke invaded

Hugh Gavelach MacShane captured by the Maguires and ransomed to Hugh O'Neill and then executed. Hugh O'Neill held under house arrest for most of 1590 and put on trial for the murder

3rd September - Donnell O'Donnell defeated and killed by Ineen Dubh at Doire Leathan. Tirconnell falls into chaos

Sir Henry Bagenal made chief commissioner for Ulster and Marshall of the Irish army

September - Captain Willis arrives in Tirconnell

1591

Minor wars of succession continue for both the O'Neills and O'Don-nells

February – Brian O'Rourke arrived in Scotland

April - Brian O'Rourke handed over to the English by the Scottish King

October - Brian O'Rourke hung as a traitor in London

1592

January - Red Hugh O'Donnell escaped from Dublin prison

February – Red Hugh O'Donnell drives Captain Humphrey Willis out of Donegal

April - Inauguration of Red Hugh O'Donnell in Kilmacrenan. Hugh McManus O'Donnell stands aside

May/June - Red Hugh O'Donnell attacks Turlough O'Neill

June - Red Hugh O'Donnell supports Lower MacWilliam Burkes revolt in Mayo

July - Red Hugh O'Donnell submits to Lord Deputy in Dublin, brought by Hugh O'Neill

August - Red Hugh O'Donnell takes care of his rivals - ambushed Hugh McHugh Dubh's men in Belleek castle and executed 16 gentlemen - Niall Garbh also surrendered (then married off to Red Hugh's sister Nuala), Sean Og O'Doherty captured at a parley and thrown in prison until he surrendered, got rid of the bandits in central Tirconnell mountains

December – the Bishops plot. Edmund Magauran sent to King of Spain - returns with the promise of Spanish troops

1593

January - Red Hugh O'Donnell attacks Turlough Luineach O'Neill in support of Hugh O'Neill. The O'Donnells burn Strabane and make an agreement with Turlough O'Neill who retires

Spring - Captain Humphrey Willis appointed as sheriff of Fermanagh in spring. Captain Willis has command of 100 men and tried to turn disaffected Maguires against Hugh Maguire

April - Hugh Maguire besieges sheriff and party in a church. Hugh O'Neill intervened on behalf of the sheriff and saves him.

8th May emissaries sent to Spain to seek help

May – Maguires raid Sligo

June - the marriage of Red Hugh O'Donnell and Rosie O'Neill

June/July- large cattle raid into Connaught which reaches Tulsk

11 Sept - Bagenal starts campaign in Fermanagh

24 Sept - reaches Enniskillen but does not have the equipment to lay siege

October - Hugh O'Neill raids Connor Roe Maguire

10 October - Battle of Erne ford / Belleek

1594

Jan 24 - Feb 02 - siege of Enniskillen

Clans and military formations

Clan structure

Irish clan structure came from ancient times. Clans were kinship groups that would have various septs beneath them. Therefore, there were usually various branches of the family, each with different strengths of claim to be the clan leader. The leader of the clan is usually referred to as being 'the' and then the clan name (e.g. 'the Maguire'). Within this system, you could have septs with a different surname that would still be part of the clan (e.g. Keenan Maguire).

They used a system called tanistry to elect their leader, so to be elected leader you had to galvanise support amongst the men eligible to vote. This inadvertently created a number of different power bases, and therefore rivals, within the clan. After being elected, and during the normal course of events, it was usual for the clan leader to demand the eldest male children of his rivals to be handed over for lengths of time as guarantees of loyalty.

These clans usually had subservient clans, outside their internal sept structure, that paid tribute to them. The example in the story is that the Maguires switch between paying tribute to whoever was the dominant O'Neill at the time and also paid tribute to the O'Donnells for a period.

Gallic military formations

At the time of the outbreak of the Nine Years War, with the exception of the O'Neills, the fighting formations of the Irish were at best outdated, but in truth obsolete. The main European fighting formations were pikemen and shot. The main Irish battle tactics were the ambush, to which their soldiers were suited. They were not capable of facing the English in a pitched battle. Hence the urgency of O'Neill and other leaders to train their men in the use of firearms, import weapons from the continent and Scotland, and get as many Spanish trainers as they could.

Below are the main troop types of the Irish clans at the time of the outbreak of the Nine Years War:

Galloglass – mercenary soldiers usually Scottish or from Scottish descent. These were heavily armed mercenaries who used long axes with curved blades. The main Irish houses usually had clans of Galloglass that worked for them on a permanent basis. A Galloglass leader was called a constable, a formation of Galloglass a battle and a Galloglass usually had the support of a horseboy or Kern and this was referred to as a spar. Galloglass got paid around three cattle per quarter.

'Coin and livery' (referred to in the book as 'coin and keep' for simplicity sake) – the leader of the clan would hire Galloglass and in order to share the burden of paying for them, he would assign them to different areas. The population of that are assigned would be responsible for the payment and upkeep of the Galloglass for a time period at the discretion of the clan leader.

Redshanks – these are 'new Scots' or Scottish mercenaries hired directly from Scotland, usually on a seasonal basis. They were called Redshanks because they went barelegged. They were usually armed with swords and bows. They normally got paid the same as Galloglass, around three cows per quarter.

Kern – traditional Irish light infantry. They were usually not armoured and supplied their own weapons. The weapon of choice was the dart. They also used javelins, swords and bows. Their main uses were to support the heavier armed Galloglass, capture and herd cattle away from enemy territory, and against the English, they were used for lighting attacks and harassment. They usually got paid around one cow per quarter.

Horseboys – Galloglass usually had horse boys to support them. When they fought they normally functioned as light infantry armed with javelins.

Horsemen – these were usually the nobility of the clan. They rode without stirrups, which potentially made them unstable when facing heavier English cavalry, and were usually armed with javelins.

Shot – these were armed with muskets. The Irish lords tried to retrain their Galloglass and other experienced soldiers to become either shot or pike as fast as circumstances would allow. The amount of shot the Irish armies could field would depend on the clan. The O'Neill formations were mainly armed with shot while the smaller clans were not.

Pike – there is little evidence that the pike was widely available to the Irish rebels. These formations also did not suit the Irish style of ambush warfare. Agin, mainly the larger clans such as the O'Neills would have had the most pikemen.

The Irish formations were supported by experienced Irish mercenaries who had fought mainly with the Spanish army in the Dutch Revolt. These men would have been skilled in modern European warfare and made a vital backbone to the Irish military formations.

English military formations

The English forces in Ireland usually came from four sources: Irish conscripts (mainly from the Pale), Irish allies, raw recruits from England and veterans who had served in France, the Scottish borders or the Netherlands. There was much changing of sides between the Irish on both sides.

Shot – the English were mainly armed with calivers but also had a small number of muskets. The men armed with calivers, the lighter of the two guns, were mainly used for skirmishing. The muskets were used to support the pike as the muskets were heavier and less manoeuvrable.

Pike – Pikemen were the core of the army. They had a ten to fifteen-foot spear, a helmet and breastplate armour and were mainly used for defence. They could also make a very effective charge.

Horsemen – these were comprised mainly of Irish cavalry. They were more heavily armoured than the Irish cavalry and were armed with a lance, sword and occasionally a pistol. They were the most feared element of the English armies. They were mainly used for skirmishing.

English system of government in Ireland

Lord Deputy – the representative if the Queen and the head of the Irish executive under English rule Irish Council – the executive branch of English rule in Ireland

Lord President (Governors) – these were the English military leaders for the various provinces of Ireland with wide-ranging powers

London Privy Council – the body of advisors to the Queen

Glossary of terms

Brehon law – ancient legal system of Ireland

Composition - a formal arrangement for the payment of taxation for a particular geographical area to pay taxation to the crown. These arrangements normally meant the formal abandonment of tanistry and the adoption of hereditary English titles and the passing of land to your direct relatives.

Crannog – usually an ancient partially or entirely artificial island in a lake or estuary. They were normally repurposed as forts or storehouses

Lordship – the territory ruled by a Galic lord

Sept – a branch of an Irish family

Surrender and regrant – the surrender of a Galic lordship and the regrant of the land with English hereditary titles, the abandonment of tanistry

Tanistry - was the Irish system of passing on titles and land. Candidates were elected by all the males of the clan. The candidates were usually from a specific branch (sept) of the family who could trace their ancestry back to a particularly notable figure in their family history.

The Pale - the strip of land on the eastern coast of Ireland that comprised the most Anglicised part of the country. This area would have covered Dublin and the coastal parts of Louth, Meath and North Wicklow.

Further reading

There are a number of excellent books available that I used for research that are history books rather than works of historical fiction. They are listed below, and if you enjoyed the subject matter of this book, you should thoroughly enjoy these. There are other books available on the subject matter that I have not read. I am sure some of these books are excellent too, but unfortunately, there comes a stage where I have to stop doing research and actually write the book!

Tyrone's Rebellion - Hiram Morgan

The Nine Years War 1593 -1603 - James O'Neill

Red Hugh O'Donnell and the Nine Years War - Darren McGettigan

Galloglass 1250 - 1600 - Galic Mercenary Warrior - Fergus Cannan

The Irish Wars 1485 - 1603 - Ian Heath

About the Author

C R Dempsey is the author of 'How to be a saint' and 'Bad Blood'. CR has always had a deep interest in history and this has heavily influenced his fiction writing, but he likes to have a sense of humour about it. C R spends lots of time working on his books, mainly in the twilight hours of the morning.

C R lives in London with his wife and cat. He was born in Dublin but has lived most of his adult life in London.

There is a mailing list link below where you can keep up with all C R Dempsey news.

I would be grateful if you would leave a review of the book at the vendor where you purchased it.
    Please click here: https://amzn.to/2ThNONl

You can connect with me on:
- https://www.crdempseybooks.com
- https://twitter.com/dempsey_cr
- https://www.facebook.com/crdempsey
- https://www.instagram.com/crdempsey

Subscribe to my newsletter:

✉ https://www.subscribepage.com/c4m9k5_copy

Also by C R Dempsey

How to be a saint
Newsflash! – Weekly sin count smashes three trillion for the first time!
Who let the snake out? Not me!

The shepherd's hook yanked the Guardian down to earth. No more cushy life in heaven, it was straight to the front line in the War Against Sin.

The Guardian awoke and wondered if he had made a wrong turn and arrived in hell. Up to his ears in sin, the last thing he needed was a pair of Sin Detectives, but that's what he got. Detect sin? It was everywhere! It was his job to get rid of it! Feckin didn't have long as the game had already begun, the salvation game.

With only the advice of a reluctant mentor and a pair of Sin Detectives, he must stop the boy from going to hell. Otherwise, he could be next....

A satire about heaven, hell, and all in between. With a hell of a lot of sin.

Printed in Great Britain
by Amazon

79662692R00193